A Step Ahead of

Scott McPherson

A Step Ahead of Death

First printing

Book cover design
by Colin L. Kernes

ISBN: 978-1-936695-00-3
Published by Comfort Publishing, LLC
www.comfortpublishing.com

Printed in the United States of America

devotional book, never expecting that I might write fiction. Many were totally unaware that it is possible for an "ordinary" person to write a book and have it published. It has given hope to some, too who have aspired to write their own books.

I greatly appreciate all the hard working, skillful people at Comfort Publishing who have given me this opportunity. I offer many thanks to my wonderful photographer, Rebecca Tredway. The following people helped me through educating me about their own specialties or by providing editorial advice. Some just kept me focused and cheered me on as encouragers. To these people I give my heartiest thanks: Gale Engels, Mary Beckman, John Dietrich, Robert McPherson, Jim Powell, Jeff Frey, Gary Plank, John Grubb, Dennis Nun, Elisabeth Eberspacher, Gary Potraz, Kim Robb, Chris Kent, Matthias Okoye, Warren Wiersbe, Craig Workman, Bruce Toney, Doc and Christi Chaves.

Dedication

A Step Ahead of Death began as a kernel of thought and grew into a full length novel. I honestly can't say that I alway aspired to write a novel, but the desire grew in me as I found myself writing various articles and newsletters. I was encouraged as some of the things I wrote actually drew praise from friends and family, sometimes our greatest critics. Had I received criticism I may never have attempted to put pen to paper and start this project.

Many of the characters in the book are loosely based upon people I have known at some time in my life, though no direct correlations should be drawn. No disrespect is intended toward any person or organization depicted in the story. The book is fiction and the characters are fictional as well.

As a Christian I have written the book hoping that it will also honor the Lord. While it is not intended as an evangelistic instrument, the reader will see that some people take their relationship with God seriously. God interacts with His people and real people trust in Him. I am thankful to God for the joy He has given me in writing this and sharing it with others.

I thank my patient wife for putting up with a tired husband. Waking up extra early for a year to write a few pages each day meant going to bed before most people are tired. My brilliant, insightful daughters, who read my manuscripts and offered editorial advice, have been a great encouragement to me as well. I consider them to all be superior to me in their manipulation of the English language and expect to see their writings in the public eye soon.

I have friends who helped me as readers and editors. Some of my own patients helped me by giving me examples and ideas from their lives. One of the most enjoyable aspects of writing this book has been to see the surprise on faces of people when telling them that I had written a book. Invariably they asked me what I had written about, suspecting a medical topic or

1

A Thursday in October

Out for his daily exercise, Jack walked briskly along the crushed gravel path. He had no way of knowing to just how dark a mystery the path would lead today. In every other way the path and the day seemed normal. The fine white rock of the bike path had replaced a busy rail line through the heart of Lincoln. He liked coming here. Leaving the office for the pleasure of a walk on the path was not just exercise but relaxation. It was a place to unwind and erase from his mind whatever was happening in his day. On this beautiful fall day the leaves, like huge golden rain drops, were beginning to cascade down from the surrounding cottonwood trees.

Removing his attention from his work today was necessary, because he was thinking of a family whose mother, he believed, might have a condition like Alzheimer's disease. She had been full of disbelief, almost indignant, when he had broached the subject with her the previous week. This patient had been resistant to him talking about her with the rest of her family and he knew it would be a violation of her privacy to go against her wishes. Nevertheless, she was having significant problems with forgetfulness. In addition, she had gotten lost twice in the past month when just driving to the store from her acreage, a few miles outside of town. What made it harder was that she had called him to help her. This patient, Kathy, had known Jack for many years and at one time he had thought that he was in love with her. Now their friendship made his choices even more difficult. At fifty, Kathy was still very attractive. A widow for about five years, most of her seven children, some married with children of their own, had stayed in the area. They were a close family, but she had not mentioned any of her memory problems to them. Jack did have one great concern. Eleven-year-old Esther, Kathy's youngest daughter, was still living at home.

Pointing out that her memory issues could affect Esther, Jack had gotten Kathy's permission to schedule a consultation with the whole family for later this very afternoon. She had been reluctant, so he still wasn't certain she would let him discuss her condition openly with her children. His plan was to meet with her first. Jack hoped to convince Kathy that she needed her children's support and that they needed to know her condition. He knew, though, that he would have to tread with care. It was his desire to maintain his friendship with Kathy, yet try to remain objective.

His reverie was broken by a rustling sound as a squirrel leaped from the fallen leaves to the trunk of a hackberry tree. It disappeared almost instantly as it expertly hid on the opposite side of the trunk. The momentary distraction helped him to return to the world around him. He put Kathy and her troubles at the back of his thoughts and began to enjoy his walk.

Jack never wore earphones or listened to music or radio when he walked. He noticed that many other people on the trail had mp3 players or radios on their ears tuning out the world that he was there to enjoy. Jack wanted only the sights and sounds of the natural environment in his head. Now all he heard was the crunching sound of his feet on the gravel and the little breeze as it whistled through the branches. He glanced down at his watch unhappily. Soon he would have to turn around and return to the world of work and the difficult decisions that lay ahead. This respite was a welcome relief for him, even though it always had to come to an end.

Jack loved being a doctor, but knew there was other work he could do that could add meaning to his life. As a Christian he had a strong interest in missions and he had been in the mission field earlier in his life. As years had gone by, he had taken advantage of short trips sponsored by the Christian Doctors Association. These lasted one or two weeks and were usually to needy areas of the world. They had kept medical missions alive in his mind. Unfortunately, on the short trips the team could see many patients but no on-going management was possible. He had learned that, to fit in and understand a culture took time, usually years. He had not become a career missionary and this bothered his conscience from time to time intruding upon him with feelings of guilt. His life was comfortable now, but he felt the burden that people in many nations lived without even basic comforts.

Being single, Jack also sometimes felt "hollow." Why he had never settled down had been a constant mystery to his parents and friends, but Jack knew why he had never gotten married. It was because he had never quite gotten over his relationship with a young woman he had met in Africa. He was aware, too, that he must have passed up some other wonderful relationships in his life. Singleness wasn't all bad, though. He liked his independence, but realized that now, he might be too set in his ways for any woman to be able to cope in a relationship with him.

Jack looked at the surrounding fields. The local farmers planted right up to the city limits until developers bought them out for new construction. Here and there were tall dried corn stalks ready for harvest and a gully crossed the path at this point. It was his usual turn-around point, though if he walked more quickly he could go a little farther.

Jack was about to reverse direction on the path when a flash of color caught his eye. He stopped and looked back in the direction from which he had come. He now could see nothing out of the ordinary. Yet he was sure he had seen a flicker of bright blue at the bottom of the gully just north of the path. Perhaps it was a blue bird or a blue plastic bottle. He often picked up trash along the trail, although today, he had forgotten to bring a trash bag.

The wild plum thickets still had most of their leaves and some over-ripe fruit hanging on their branches. He backed up a little and, leaning down, peered through the undergrowth. The tangled branches and leaves were dense so he had to strain to see anything. The blue color was clear in his memory and he knew that there should not be anything but earth-tone colors out here. Curiosity overrode his good sense as he left the trail and, without another thought, he began descending into the gully.

Jack realized his error almost at once since he still wore his business slacks and sweater. Thistles and burrs pulled at his clothing. Half-way down the embankment he nearly turned back. He could see that this would lead to a mess he would have to clean up before starting his afternoon clinic.

Jack you're being stupid. What do you think you are going to find? Then he said aloud to no one in particular, "It's probably some antifreeze jug or surveyor's flag."

Jack hesitated, but now he saw that he was committed. The more he thought about it the more he realized how ridiculous the enterprise was, but once at the bottom of the slope there was no advantage to retreat.

The weeds ahead of him were deeper than he had anticipated. His ankles chafed now and were covered with cockle burrs. His sweater would need repair, as several threads of yarn had caught on overhanging locust thorns. He was getting dusty and now with less wind, he noticed that he had begun to perspire. The flickering sunlight down here was less intense and the colors less pronounced. Reaching forward to move a plum branch out of the way, he pulled away in pain as he encountered a wild rose bush.

He yelled "ouch!" and sucked at his hand. He tried to see the nearly invisible thorns stuck to the side of his palm. Peering over the rim of his glasses as he looked down at his hand, Jack had another shock.

Only a few inches from his own shoes was a white stocking-covered foot. It was clearly human and unmoving. Following the contours of the protruding leg he saw the item which must have caught his attention earlier. Nearly covered by leaves was the body of a young woman. Jack caught his breath. He had seen death before, but it was usually in the context of a hospital emergency room or ICU.

This woman still wore a blue skirt with what appeared to have been a cream colored blouse. Part of the skirt had torn off and was stuck higher up on a branch of the rose bush. It was wafting lazily in what little breeze there was, and must have become visible just at the moment his eye had surveyed the area. He looked up, able only to barely see the edge of the path from where he stood. He marveled that he had even seen this little piece of fabric.

Seeing this stricken body made him want to get away, even more than the thorns and burrs. However, reacting quickly, he

4

knew from his experience that there were several things he must do. He knew enough not to touch the body, but Jack's eyes took in the entire scene so he could report everything to the authorities.

The woman's features were still quite apparent, though her skin wore the pallor and waxy consistency of death. There did not appear to be significant decomposition to her body and her clothes while soiled and bloodied, were not faded. Though he knew little of forensic science he could tell that she had not lain here long. There were flies buzzing around but he could see no signs of deterioration of her skin. The young woman's milky eyes were open in a fixed stare. Her expression was one of surprise but not horror. He hadn't realized that one could actually see expression on a deceased person's face. Usually he had seen death after multiple attempts at resuscitation. These bodies had a more clinical appearance.

Death by violence clearly created an altered visage.

Since he was not on call today, Jack had chosen not to carry his cell phone. He liked to have some time when he was not available. Anything urgent would go to his partner, Don Miller, who was taking call that day. So now Jack would have to go all the way back to his office to get help and report finding this body. Now, too, came the realization that his afternoon was going to be much different than he had planned. His patients and his office staff would not be pleased. All those people would probably have to be rescheduled while he dealt with this new crisis. For a fleeting moment he entertained the idea of acting ignorant and letting someone else find the body, but immediately dismissed this as unprofessional and downright cowardly. It was necessary to drop everything and take care of this situation first.

Oh, but what about Kathy? This will not help.

Jack had no police training, but wanted to ascertain any clues that might be found. He mentally catalogued the scene. The body lay flat and parallel to the path as if it had been placed rather than dumped. Had someone pushed or thrown her from the path, she would not have made it all the way to the bottom and most likely would have been in a more crumpled up position.

Though the skirt was torn and the body dirty, she was not terribly unkempt and there did not appear to be blood on the ground or surrounding vegetation. The blood stains were centered in the chest and he saw several small vertical linear tears in the blouse. He guessed that these were knife wounds. She had a watch on her right wrist, a bracelet around the left wrist, a necklace and an ankle bracelet. The necklace had a round pendant, but he could not tell if it was a locket or solid metal. She wore an antique ring on her left middle finger and her nails were perfect. She appeared to have had a recent manicure with an Asian theme. He saw no purse or wallet. He desperately wanted to see whether she had any identification but knew that it would be considered tampering with the crime scene and that he would leave fingerprints if he touched anything. The last thing he wanted was to invite suspicion. Her blouse was partially unbuttoned revealing evidence of a tattoo on the inside of her left breast. It was not faded but he could not tell what it represented. All this took moments as he turned 360 degrees to memorize the surroundings.

Jack then gingerly retraced his steps away from the body to find a less arduous way up the slope. As he was about to ascend he froze. He saw a very clear footprint in a small open area of dirt just ahead of him. He didn't want to disturb this so he began to look for yet another path. Just then he heard the familiar crunching sound of a jogger coming back down the trail from the east. Should he show himself and get the jogger to help or hide himself to avoid suspicion? He decided that if he hid and was still seen it would look even more incriminating so he skirted the footprint and began waving his hands in hopes of attracting attention.

Jack moved quickly along the plum thicket until he found a way to the bike path. By then the jogger had slowed looking puzzled. He was tan and solid looking and wore a plain white t-shirt and shorts. The young man was definitely a body builder with large biceps and his t-shirt strained against his large pectoralis muscles. He looked perturbed at having his run interrupted but pulled the earphones from his head and asked,

"Hey what's up? You all right?"

"Yes," Jack said a little out of breath himself from the adrenaline and from hurrying up from the gully. "I'm fine, but there's a woman down there and she's not. In fact she's dead. I just found her body." Jack stood hands on hips getting his bearings and his breath. "Do you have a cell?"

"Wow! You sure she's dead?" the runner said incredulously.

"I'm certain. I'm a doctor and there is no doubt." Jack hung his head at this and shook it. "It looks like murder too."

"Man! I don't know!" the runner began to look scared. He took in Jack's somewhat unkempt appearance and started to put his earphones back on, moving away from Jack.

"What? Can you help with a cell phone?" Jack asked.

"I don't know if I want to get involved," said the runner.

Jack tried to calm him. He got in front of him and put out his hands. As they came into contact with the young man's shirt he noticed that he was in such good shape he was hardly sweating. He didn't want to anger him or get in any conflict here,

"All you need to do is call 911. You don't have to go look or anything. You are hardly 'involved' Okay?"

"Well . Yeah I guess." The runner seemed somewhat mollified. "My cell phone is back in my car." He nodded up the path, the way Jack had come originally. "You want to come and make the call yourself?"

Jack thought a second. "No. You go ahead and call I'll wait here for the police. All right? My name is Jack Sharp. I'm a family doctor here in town. You just need to tell them your name. If they want to talk with you they will let you know, I think. I'll just sit here by the path until they arrive."

Finally the runner put out his hand. "I'm Greg Connolly. I work at that company over there," he said pointing to the large modern red brick building about a quarter of mile away. "Sorry. I kind of freaked. Sure, I'll make the call and wait in the parking lot for the cops. You going to be all right out here?"

The jogger was now all business and seemed to have completely recovered his composure.

Jack gave a wry smile and chuckled lightly, "Yes. There's nothing to be afraid of now. She was the victim, not me. Could you call my office too and let them know I was unexpectedly delayed? I'll try to call them as soon as I can."

He fished out a scrap piece of paper from his pocket and wrote the number down handing it to the young man.

With that, the jogger took off for the parking lot about a half mile to the west. Jack was relieved to have found someone else to help out. He was a little curious about the jogger's initial reaction but figured he would have been reluctant too if their roles had been reversed.

As Jack sat by the path no one else passed him by. This was not unusual on a week day when most people tried to get their exercise done during the lunch hour or after work. It was now past one o'clock when his normal afternoon clinic hours were supposed to begin. He wondered what the motive for murdering the unfortunate young woman had been. Who would want her dead? She wasn't bad looking even in death. He didn't think she had been sexually assaulted but from his limited examination could not know for sure. He still marveled at her facial expression. With such a look of surprise, death must have been very sudden. The multiple wounds made him think that it may have been personal. Why was her body here? This puzzled him as much or more than any other question. Did the killer think her body would go undiscovered? If so then why not bury her too. Jack would never have found the body had it been even in a shallow grave. Then again he realized that the body could not easily be seen from the path until the leaves had all fallen to the earth in a few weeks.

By then, even the few clues available would be long gone.

2

After waiting twenty minutes with no sign or sound of police, Jack became first worried, then angry. *Why had Greg Connolly been taking so long?* The runner must have decided not to get involved after all. He made up his mind that he would have to leave the area and walk back to the parking lot himself. Getting up, he brushed off his slacks and headed back down the path. When he came within 100 yards of the parking lot he heard the sound of sirens wailing. They were fast approaching and sounded like many cars.

"Finally," he said, "that guy decided to call. Maybe his phone was dead or something."

Jack stood still, awaiting the police. He could tell by the racket their sirens made that it wouldn't take long for them to arrive. The parking lot was not in view but in the distance he heard car doors slam. After a few minutes several uniformed policemen appeared on the path. They were hurrying toward him but not running. Walking behind was a woman in plain clothes who matched their pace.

The first policeman approached very deliberately and Jack noted the movement as he unsnapped the trigger guard on his weapon. It remained holstered, but the act was disconcerting to Jack.

Why did they appear so nervous? What did the jogger tell them?

The young policeman stepped up to Jack and asked, "Are you the one who called about finding a body?" His words were clipped and precise. No emotion could be discerned.

Jack answered just as matter-of-factly, "Yes I found the body of a dead woman back up the path a ways. I didn't make the call. I told this other guy, a jogger, to call you. Didn't the jogger tell you?"

"The jogger?" shot back the policeman. "Sir, maybe you should give me your name and tell me where this body is."

Jack said, "I am Jack Sharp. I am a family physician here in town. My office is just down the road." He pointed back up the path, "If you follow me I will show you where I found the body."

9

This first policeman had short, dark, hair and a thick neck which made Jack think he had once been a marine. Even his body armor didn't hide the fact that this young man was a serious weight lifter. He was even more muscular than the jogger whom he had recently met. Two other uniformed officers stood back quietly appraising the situation. The woman was still walking up about 20 yards behind.

The bullnecked policeman stared first at Jack then past him along the path. Then over his shoulder he told the other two. "Mike and Arvillo, go with this guy. I'll talk with the detective and call it in." He wordlessly scowled at Jack and retreated up the path toward the woman in plain clothes.

Jack now had the distinct impression that he was being escorted. While not actually in custody he had no doubt that he could not do anything other than what the officer was instructing him to do. This was not how he had expected to be treated.

Jack quickly led the police officers to the place on the path with the plum thicket where he had found the body. He pointed, "If you go down there you will find her lying on her back."

The officer called "Mike" stared into the tangle of branches and leaves looking from side to side. "Sir, how did you know to look down there?" His tone was not pleasant, but Jack had anticipated the possibility of doubt about his merely finding the body. He explained seeing the blue fabric first and finding the body while searching for the elusive object. The second police officer seemed slightly less doubtful, but he didn't warm up much and said "Hmm. You went down there because of a blue cloth?"

"Well, I didn't know what it was. I only thought it was odd to see something that color in the brush," Jack explained trying to keep the irritation out of his own voice, realizing how lame it sounded.

At this point the woman in plain clothes stepped forward. "Officers Jackson and Ruiz, why don't you carefully see what you can find. We'll stay here while you go look." The young muscular policeman was no longer with them. He apparently had returned to his vehicle.

The officer named Ruiz took out a notebook and the two of them carefully worked their way down to the body. They were cautious, taking in every detail, as they did so. Upon reaching the bottom of the slope Officer Jackson, -"Mike,"- checked the body for signs of life and Officer Ruiz, - "Arvillo," - began the crime scene log. Jack knew that this was used to document who had been, and would be, in and out of the crime scene.

Up on the bike path the woman detective looked at Jack with a hint of a smile. "Do you come out here often, doctor?"

"Who is asking?" Jack smiled back with his hand outstretched hoping to ease the tension.

"I'm Detective Rebecca Sweate. Spelled like sweat with an 'e' at the end." She took his hand firmly and shook it. "Please understand that we have to establish exactly what happened here."

"I believe I understand, but I feel like I am under suspicion."

"Well, sir, you need to know that we are not sure what is going on yet," detective Sweate said with her eyes slightly narrowed.

"What do you mean? Didn't the jogger tell you what happened?" Jack asked.

"That is a curious thing. I don't know anything about a jogger. We received an anonymous tip our tip line about a body being dumped somewhere along the bike path east of town. We arrived here to find you ready and willing to help us. Wouldn't that sound suspicious to you?" Rebecca Sweate opened her hands in question and Jack saw immediately that things were not going the way he had expected. "Sir, why didn't you call it in yourself?"

He sighed, "I can't believe it. I thought that guy was going to help." He hung his head. Apparently his faith in the jogger was unfounded. "I didn't bring my cell with me. I like to leave it in my office when I come on these walks. I'll tell you what I can." She made notes while he proceeded to explain his presence and how he had come upon the body. He didn't give her a full description of the scene but admitted to having been in the gully. He mentioned the footprint he had found and pointed out where it was. He also told her about Greg Connolly, the jogger, and asked that she check on why he had failed to call them. Perhaps he had been the anonymous caller on the tip line instead of calling 911.

"Do you have a phone I can use to call my office? They are probably getting upset and a little frantic by now. If the jogger didn't call you he probably didn't let them know either." Jack wiped his forehead and breathed out heavily. "I don't think they'll quite understand." He made the call to his nurse. She told him not to worry, though a few patients had left in a huff already. He checked his watch and asked her to keep his last patient on the schedule. "I may still be late, but it is very important that I see Kathy Sanders and her family."

By now about a dozen other people had arrived at the scene. Photographers, crime scene specialists, and those who would collect the body were making their way along the path. Mike, who had climbed back out of the gully, motioned to Detective Sweate and they walked back along the path, out of ear shot, to talk. They left Jack alone standing in the middle of the path. He was feeling hot and dirty. The scrapes and thorns were beginning to sting and he was getting quite thirsty. Every so often Detective Sweate looked up at Jack eyeing him carefully. At last she shook her head, said "No" firmly, then turned back to Jack. Mike joined Arvillo as they stood "guard" over the scene and Rebecca approached Jack once again.

"Gus will drive you," she ordered.

"Where are we going?" Jack replied. He wondered who Gus was.

"He can take you back to your office, but I will need an official statement." She shook her head slightly to swing her medium length brown hair out of her eyes.

Jack noticed that she was not a bad looking woman. Her slightly bronze colored skin was smooth and her features angular. She appeared to be in her mid forties, but considering the stresses of her profession might actually be younger. Her voice had a harshness that probably reflected her life on the police force.

"I think I need to clean up at home and then I have one very important appointment I don't want to put off. After that I can come to the police station. Is that all right?" Jack wanted to be able to get the dead woman out of his mind before meeting with Kathy and her family. He couldn't believe how the day had changed. One minute he was talking to a squirrel then everything twisted and now he was talking with the police.

"So much for a pleasant walk," he muttered.

"I'll tell Gus to take you home. But I want him to stay with you today. We'll need your clothes anyway."

"Why does he have to stay with me? Do I have a choice? I only live about fifteen minutes from here." Unwanted anger was beginning to well up in him. Jack didn't want to lose his cool, but sometimes he couldn't help it.

"Put it this way," she said with a voice like steel, "He will provide you with transportation at the city's expense. And, no you don't have a choice."

Jack saw the determination in her face and backed down. More quietly he said, "I want him to stay outside while I meet with patients, though." Rebecca Sweate made no verbal response to this but nodded and dismissed them with a wave of her hand.

As they were about to leave she turned once again to him and said, "Did you touch anything or pick anything up at the scene?"

"No. I knew that the police–I mean you- wouldn't want me to do that. I looked around, but I was careful not to touch anything."

"Good. That was smart." With that final word she spun and began to instruct the rest of the crew in their respective tasks.

Jack was now resigned to the fact that the police weren't sure if they believed his story. He tried to console himself that they were supposed to be skeptical, but he couldn't help thinking about all those real crime dramas he had watched on TV. In some of them the police arrested the first likely suspect who later turned out to be innocent. These hapless "victims" weren't themselves exonerated until their lives were a shambles.

To himself he just said, "Tell the truth. That's all you can do."

3

Rebecca Sweate had grown up in a tough family with older brothers who always seemed to be getting into trouble. Her name was a constant problem for her as well. Other kids, even teachers who heard it, made fun of her being "sweet." Far from knocking down her self esteem, though, she grew up with a tough outer shell. Insults didn't bother her as much as they did her girl friends. She decided early in life on a career with the police wanting to "set the world right." Going to college and then to the police academy had been in her plans for years. Her parents were supportive, although they could not help her financially.

Rebecca had made it to Lincoln early in her career, hoping to get away from her family influences. Her rowdy brothers had matured with time and were settled with familiesof their own. Rebecca's father had died suddenly, of a heart attack, two years earlier. She knew that he always had high cholesterol and that he had a pack-a-day habit. It should not have been a surprise, but the shock of his death had caused her mother to go through a serious mental collapse.

Reaching the rank of detective in a small mid-western city had been no easy task. She had not found the progressive atmosphere promised in her school. Enduring the months of being a "meter maid" had caused Rebecca to realize that discrimination including women was alive and well in the heartland.

Detective Sweate had caught the eye of the police chief when she discovered fraudulent dealings in the meter money collections. The corruption shot right up to through the mayor's office, though, supposedly, the mayor herself was not involved. Rebecca was given the opportunity to be in on the bust and after that assignment, she had moved up quickly. While this had made enemies for her in the department, most of her coworkers respected her capabilities. Her intelligence and persistence won her accolades from the entire community and no one made fun of her name any more. In her mind, she clearly had the chief position in her future sites. Nevertheless, she was realistic enough to know that just being a good cop wasn't always enough. These things often were controlled by politics.

Being a shining star in the police department took a toll elsewhere in her life. She had little social life and aside from a few brief relationships had never been seriously involved with a man. The rumor mill on sexuality had done nothing to help her in this regard, either. She learned to bury herself deeper into her work and ignore the innuendos around her.

This new case had grasped Rebecca's attention. Homicide was always a major challenge for her. There were only a few such cases each year in their family-oriented college town and these were usually assigned to the more senior male detectives. This time she had been fortunate enough to be the only detective around when the call had come in. She had snagged it, not giving the chief much choice.

There was still a great deal of information lacking in the case. The victim had yet to be identified, so no motives nor actual suspects could be discerned. Also, still very curious was the issue of timing. Contrary to what she had told Dr. Sharp, the anonymous caller had actually made his call before the doctor claimed to have found the body. They had yet to determine if the caller was a man or woman because their voice had been disguised. The caller had not been specific about on which bike path the body was to have been found. The call had come in from a cell phone with its caller ID blocked and their community did not have cell phone GPS tracking as yet. Rebecca would probably be able to find out whose phone it was eventually, but she had a feeling it would be a dead end. That would take time and calls to the local phone company. They had not mentioned the details of the anonymous call to the doctor in order to keep from contaminating his story.

How did this doctor fit into the picture? She had walked up and down the path and could not see any sign of the body from there. Was it possible that he had actually seen the blue cloth in a flash of light as he claimed? She had tried hard to duplicate the feat but had been unsuccessful. The sun was now clouded over so, perhaps, lighting was the key. For some reason she had a hard time doubting this physician. He seemed sincere. She had dealt with smart people before, though, and had found them to be some of the most devious criminals and the hardest to catch. She would have to reserve judgment for now. Jack Sharp would remain a suspect (for lack of any other) as the police always work out from the last person to see the victim.

Rebecca bent down under the crime scene tape already in place. It was time to see the body for herself and she followed the route marked out to avoid disturbing the scene. At the bottom of the gully lay the body of a still pretty, young woman staring into space. Her mouth was fixed in a silent yell and her hands were outstretched, as if to ward off- or plea- with an attacker. There were seven or eight overlapping stab wounds to her chest and upper abdomen. Any one of them could have been a fatal blow. There were no blood stains in the surrounding underbrush and no pool of blood beneath the body. This meant she had not been killed in this location.

No purse nor identification was found in the area, so they would have to check with missing persons to see if any women had recently been reported missing. Of course, she may have come from a totally different city or state. Their city was situated on a major interstate highway exchange, making it an easy target for such a dump. However, considering this particular location, far from the interstate, such a scenario seemed doubtful.

Rebecca saw that the medical examiner had just finished with a liver temperature. "Joseph, what is approximate time of death?"

"Rebecca in a rush as always. Good to see you too!" He smiled up at her. His charming smile usually got at least a nod from most women but Rebecca showed only irritation. Resignedly he said, "18 to 24 hours. That is as close as I can come at this time. That should give you someplace to start."

"Joseph, a six hour window is huge, but I know better than to badger you at this juncture. Any initial, preliminary comments?" she added.

"Well they would only be preliminary wouldn't they?" He smiled sarcastically. "I'll keep you in the loop, you know that."

Rebecca frowned but shrugged her shoulders, "It can't hurt to ask." She went on with her own observations. Her gaze took in the clothing and like Jack, found no wallet or identification. Unlike Jack, though, she had no compunction about touching the body, because she wore vinyl gloves. There was nothing else in the pocket, though, and Rebecca let out a sigh.

"Not much to go on. We have no identification yet at all. I hope the crime lab folks can work it out if they ever get to the case. We need to check this for finger prints as soon as possible. Maybe we'll get a hit." As if to ward off criticism she added, "I know there's plenty to process but identity is very important." Rebecca would think it through later. The woman's jewelry was removed and catalogued. No initials were found, no locket or name anywhere on her body. Her teeth were startlingly white, perhaps too perfect. That could help. Not even a filling, though. The thought came to her mind, "Are people really born with such perfect teeth?" It spoke of affluence as did the quality of her clothing. This could aid in establishing her identity. "Upper Middle Class White Woman Missing." There had not been such a headline lately so she may not have yet been missed. It may only take a day or so. Rebecca noticed the woman's perfect finger nails on the outstretched hands

"No evidence of putting up a defense," she said to no one in particular. She bent down over the body and noticed a tattoo for the first time. Rebecca was still wearing her gloves so she gently lifted the woman's blouse to peer at the entire tattoo. It was relatively new, a red broken heart with an arrow plunging through it.

She looked up at the medical examiner. This is in kind of a prominent place, wouldn't you say?"

Joseph saw where she was going. "Sure, and it looks fairly new. Maybe a recent breakup? You might be able to find out who did the tat."

"It's a place to start if we can figure out where she came from. Thanks, Joseph. Let me know COD as soon as you can." Rebecca stood and found her way back up the slope. She was still curious about how the doctor fit into all this.

"Is he a suspect or can I believe his story?" she said to herself as she began walking back toward her car. She stopped, remembering the footprint. She found one of the crime scene technicians. "Did we get an impression of that footprint down there?" she asked.

"The young woman whom she had approached looked up and said, "We found several partial footprints near the body. We will probably need to check shoes to be sure they don't belong to any of our guys."

Rebecca fired back, "What about the one Dr. Sharp told us about over here?"

"I didn't know about that. Let me look." She worked her way down the slope and found the spot where the detective was pointing and grinned. "This one *is* almost perfect. Thank you ma'am. I'll have a great impression of this in no time."

"One more thing, I want a good photo of the woman distributed to the officers right away. I have a place for them to start with their questions too." Rebecca Sweate hoped there weren't any significant screw ups today. She knew better than to try to tell crime scene people how to do their job, but sometimes she worried more about the evidence than the suspects. If she hadn't checked they might have forgotten about the footprint until it was too late. Shaking her head she walked silently away.

Rebecca began thinking about the whole scene. Why here? Why not bury the body? When did all this take place? Where was she killed? The answers weren't coming now. Perhaps she would gain insight from Dr. Sharp. At this point he seemed to be telling the truth, but she had learned to always be vigilant. Sharp criminals always had a plausible story. It took time to find the holes in them, but they were always there. That thought reminded her of something and she took out her cell phone.

"Gus," she said when Officer Wilson answered, "please stay with the doctor when he goes into his home and collect all his clothes, shoes etcetera. And keep your eyes open while you're in the house. If you see anything questionable we'll want to get a warrant to search it thoroughly. I'll have Mike and Arvillo start questioning his office staff today."

Gus's answer revealed his surprise, "Won't he get a little defensive if you start there?" He spoke knowing that the doctor could hear what he was saying on his phone. Gus knew he shouldn't question the detective, but he had hoped to personally disrupt this physician's life a little to see what he could shake out of it.

"Don't tell me how to investigate. You'll get plenty of credit and plenty to do." Rebecca fired back. Sometimes the men had good ideas, but her instincts told her not to dawdle. She liked Gus and wanted his help, but time was passing quickly and with a twelve to eighteen hour head start their killer's trail was getting cold.

The good doctor seemed too sure of himself and too observant. His description of the crime scene was very accurate. So far her crime scene technicians had mentioned little else of importance at the scene. There wasn't much trace evidence on or near the body. Doctor Sharp hadn't mentioned the tattoo or the woman's jewelry, but he wasn't a trained policeman either. Nevertheless, he had seen a great deal. Why would he have been so careful to remember these details? She realized then that he had said nothing about the condition of the decedent's body at all.

"Wouldn't that be a doctor's focus?" She made a mental note to ask specific questions about this when they met downtown later. Why had he been so insistent about an important appointment? Why not just call it a day and go to the police station? And the story about a jogger whom he had sent to make a call seemed fishy. She would find out about that too.

According to her uniformed officers, so far there was no one in the whole town called Greg Connolly.

4

Jack did not appreciate being driven home in a police vehicle. He could just imagine what the neighbors must already be thinking. At least they weren't handcuffing him and pushing him into the back seat.

"Watch your head," he could almost hear the comment. He rode up front with the officer named Gus. This was the short haircut guy. Jack tried to make small talk, but the officer just looked at him unsmiling and answered "yes" and "no." "No," he had not been a marine. "Yes," he had been with the local department since he finished at the academy. "No," he wasn't from Nebraska originally. After that Jack stopped trying and rode in silence. He felt like he was getting the silent treatment, perhaps to make him more willing to talk later. How had he gotten into this mess? He had only wanted to go for his usual noon walk and now instead of the freedom he usually enjoyed he was beginning to feel like a prisoner.

Once home he quickly showered and changed clothes. He was about to toss his soiled clothing into the washing machine when Gus appeared with several paper bags.

"Sir, please put all your clothes and shoes into these bags." There was a separate bag for each item of clothing. Jack asked, "wouldn't it be easier to use a big garbage bag?"

The officer blandly answered, "Some evidence deteriorates in plastic sir."

Jack was taken aback that they had to remove all his clothing but did as he was told and then wondered why they had let him shower. If they had suspected him, wouldn't they have wanted to test everything? While the Officer Gus carted his belongings to the police car Jack dressed in a new set of clothes.

He felt weary even though it was only mid-afternoon.

Gus became a little more talkative on the way to the office, surprising Jack . "Where are you from, Dr. Sharp?"

Jack looked over and after a moment's hesitation said, "I grew up out west in Hartville. I came here for college and medical school in Omaha. My parents are gone now so I have no reason to go back to my home town very often."

"How long have you practiced here?" He continued now, a positively verbose person compared with his earlier reluctance to speak.

Jack went through his history of medical practice briefly touching on all the places he had been in his life, his military and missionary work, and how he had finally settled here. By then they had reached his office and Jack asked, "Do you have to come up to my office?"

"Sir, I will remain in your waiting room, but please don't leave the office without me. When you are finished we will go 'visit' with the detective."

Gus thought gravely, "This guy doesn't realize how good he has it. They could have just taken him downtown and questioned him immediately. For some reason, Detective Sweate has consented to let this overpaid jerk finish his work day." He knew his own job was not to question his superiors, but they often made little sense to him.

In the waiting room Gus found several magazines, actually current issues, and he sat down to read. He kept one eye on the door lest Dr. Sharp should decide to make an exit. Glancing around he saw that there was a group of people sitting near a corner. They appeared to be together, probably a whole family, and were chatting amiably. When a nurse appeared at the reception door she called out, "Kathy? You and your family may come back now. We'll go to the small conference room since there are so many together."

****

Kathy Sanders and her family were led through the reception hallway and on to the small conference room. Usually this room was used for lunches and office meetings, but it served well for consultation when there were more than 2 or 3 people in a discussion group. Its broad windows looked out over a beautiful park and with the leaves starting to change color today was a perfect day to sit and just gaze over the wooded area.

Today, however, Kathy didn't feel like looking out the windows at all. She knew why she and her family were here and wasn't happy about it. She had not let on to her children, but she was aware that Jack, as she called Dr. Sharp, wanted to discuss some of her recent problems with them. She had mixed feelings about it. On the one hand she knew she was having trouble remembering some things. Cynthia, her best friend, had told her about her getting lost last week. She apparently had driven unnecessarily all the way to the next state, filled up the gas tank and then returned to her house when she got back to town, she had had to stop and call Cynthia for directions to get to her own house. Cynthia, in a panic, had met her at the convenience store where she had stopped. Cynthia had found the gas receipt as it drifted to the pavement. As she had moved to return it to Kathy she saw that it was for the purchase of gas at a station in Lawrence, Kansas over two hundred miles away. Cynthia had insisted on taking her to the doctor and Dr. Sharp had seen her that same day.

Kathy could not understand what had happened, having no memory of the event.

She now knew, too, that this was not the only episode. Another friend had come to her acreage for a visit and had found her picking dandelions in the front lawn like a bouquet. She had told the friend that they were roses for her son's wedding. However, her oldest son had been married five years already and her younger boy didn't even have a steady girlfriend. It was enough to make Kathy doubt her own sanity, but she didn't want her children to worry about her.

Dr. Sharp poked his head in the door and looked smilingly at Kathy.

"Kathy, may I speak to you for a minute?" She pleasantly nodded and rose to join him in the hall. Jack led her to a small examination room where he offered her a seat.

"Hi," he gave her hand a gentle squeeze and motioned for her to sit in the chair. He had tried to put his other problem out of his mind as much as possible. He wanted to focus on Kathy and her needs.

"Hello, Jack. I know what you want," she said with determination still standing.

"Kathy. It isn't just about what I want but what I think you need to do. I'm worried about what has happened with you lately and I want you to have a thorough evaluation. It is best if your family is involved to help you get the answers."

"So you don't just think I'm crazy?" she asked genuinely curious finally taking her seat.

"Crazy?! Of course not. I'm concerned that you have a memory problem not a mental problem. You have experienced several total lapses of memory of which you have no recollection. This is important and may be serious. I want you to have some tests." He reached out and took her hand again gently. "Kathy, I honestly don't know what this is, but it could be some kind of dementia or amnesia. If it is Alzheimer's, there are medications available to treat it, but your family will need to be involved in helping you more and more."

Now Kathy was surprised. "You think I have Alzheimer's? I thought you were going to put me in an institution." She didn't know whether to be relieved or more worried. Unwanted tears began to come and Jack reached for a tissue and handed it to her. Now she could see what he meant. "How could I have that horrible disease without being aware of it?"

"Unfortunately, real dementia is often this way. Others are aware of it before you. I want to ask your kids if they have noticed lapses or memory problems. Have they said anything to you?" Jack was somewhat pleading, hoping that she would finally consent.

"No. They haven't said anything to me about that," Kathy answered, puzzled. "I guess you can talk to them. Now you really have me worried. I don't feel sick or anything. I have had a few headaches lately, but that isn't too unusual."

Kathy was almost always cheerful and Jack had never seen her cry not even at the graveside when her husband was buried. She had a strong faith and had seemed to always find the good in everything. Now he was seeing a side of her he had not known. Her face was drawn and she had a pallor he had never noticed before.

Jack's association with Kathy had begun many years earlier when they were both young and in school. They had been close once but that had ended a long time ago. Jack looked at Kathy with compassion and said,"Tell me more about the headaches."

"Oh they're nothing really. I wake up with a twinge and by noon I have to take an aspirin or something. It doesn't keep me awake or interfere with anything." Kathy seemed to have calmed a little. "Let's go back to my family and see what they have to say. I'll let you talk to them. Maybe it will help." She stood and gave Jack another pleasant hug. "Thanks Jack for being such a good friend. I'm sorry I was upset with you. I honestly thought you were going to tell the kids that I'm crazy." She tried a little laugh. "I guess I worried unnecessarily. I should have known to trust you." Her voice shook a little and she looked him directly in the face, "Okay."

Jack followed her to the conference room and stepped in ready now to diplomatically present what he knew to Kathy's family. He greeted them warmly shaking hands and giving hugs. All of her children, except her youngest daughter, were there.

He opened by saying, "I imagine you are wondering why I wanted you all here today." He went over the memory loss episodes and asked if any of them had seen unusual behavior.

Kathy's oldest son, Frank, looked hesitantly at Jack then said,

"Esther is the only one still at home with Mom. She has told me a few things."

Jack looked mildly at Frank, but Kathy looked shocked.

"What things?" Jack asked.

Frank looked first at his mother then back at Jack. "One day, Esther said that Mom put a cake she was about to bake into the dishwasher instead of the oven."

Kathy's hand flew to her mouth and she gasped. "No! I don't remember her saying anything about that. I don't remember doing anything like that."

Frank looked sheepishly at his mother. "She made me promise

not to mention it. Esther put it in the oven and set the temperature according to the recipe."

"Have any of the rest of you noticed any problems with your mother?"

Sarah, her second daughter, cleared her throat. "Mom. You called me five times in one day last week. It would have been all right but you told me the exact same thing with each call."

"Sarah. Why didn't you mention it to me?"

"I did, Mom." There were tears in her eyes.

Jack looked over at Kathy. He had previously done a thorough physical and neurological examination on Kathy which had revealed no deficits or abnormalities. Yet today he noticed that her right hand seemed to be shaking noticeably. This had not been apparent at her physical examination. Her voice also didn't seem as strong as usual.

"Kathy, do you mind if I examine you again? It won't take long."

Kathy, still uncertain, "You saw me just a few days ago."

"I know but I want to see if there are other findings today."

Reluctantly she nodded and Jack led her back to the exam room.

"Where do your headaches occur?"

Kathy pointed and Jack began by tapping the part of her head where she said she had pain. He took both of her hands in his and looked at them again. He thought back to her other exam. He had performed it in the morning when she was fresh. Now, later in the day and somewhat stressed he could easily see her right hand shaking while her left hand was perfectly still.

Jack proceeded to repeat his neurologic exam going through the cranial nerves and muscles, balance and reflexes. He noted a few new things. She was shakier than he had remembered and when she walked her right leg seemed more sluggish than the left.

"Well, doctor, what is the verdict?" Kathy bantered.

Jack looked directly into her eyes. As he began to answer he was struck by how beautiful a woman she was. Since becoming his patient he had tried to keep a "clinical" distance, yet he couldn't deny that he still had an attraction toward her. Setting these unwanted thoughts aside he answered, "I am a little curious about that shakiness in your right hand. Have you noticed it?" he asked in reply. "And have you been having tripping or having any trouble walking?"

Her eyebrows went up. "No I can't say that I have noticed shaking." She thought for a second. "I did fall carrying the laundry up the steps last week. Oh such a bruise." She pointed to her knee.

Jack took her hand helping her down from the table. "I hope it's nothing, but something different is going on. Your memory lapses cannot be ignored."

Kathy reached for Jack's hand and held it firmly, "Is all this really necessary? I feel fine."

Jack said as evenly as possible, "Kathy, I really want the best for you." They stood looking directly at each other until Kathy turned to go.

They went back to her family and Jack stopped at the nursing station. He made arrangements for blood-work and an MRI of the brain to be done in the morning. He set up an appointment with a local neurologist, another friend of his, to be done in about a week. Jack had to call and set this up personally or it would have taken six weeks to get in.

He encouraged the children to plan on phone contact with their mother daily until more information was received. Frank was enlisted to talk to Esther about watching out for her mom too. Kathy promised to let her children know when she was going to drive somewhere and would talk things over with Esther. That was the best he could do. Kathy staunchly refused to relinquish her car keys and Jack could not find any way to dissuade her.

It had all gone very well and Kathy had been more cooperative than Jack had expected. She was last to leave and waited for her children to depart. She looked up at Jack and said,

"The boys have always liked you Jack. I'm surprised none of them went into medicine because they have held you in high esteem for years. Please let me know as soon as you are sure what is going on."

She reached out and this time pulled him close again for several moments.

He hugged her back and spoke softly in her ear, "I'll do my very best for you Kathy. You know that." He felt the emotion of the moment rise in his throat too. He knew that, whatever was wrong, it would not be an easy road ahead.

To him Kathy was a special patient and friend, perhaps because he had known her so long. While her husband, Steve, had been alive he had been a close friend to Jack. But even when he had died, Jack had made a point of keeping his relationship with Kathy friendly and professional. He had avoided any possible romantic involvement. Legal and conventional wisdom dictated that he could not date nor have too close a relationship with a patient. Violating this could actually lead to the loss of his medical license, and he had no desire to demonstrate even an appearance of unethical behavior.

He poked his head out into the waiting room and noticed that his "shadow" was still there. "I have a few charts to finish then I can leave," he said, thankful that there were now no patients in the waiting room. However, as he spoke two more officers entered through the office door.

"What do you guys need? Isn't one enough? I promise to go quietly." He said this half jokingly though he felt more nervous inside.

"Sir we are here to just ask your office people some questions." It was Mike Jackson who spoke. They were both carrying photos. Mike handed one to Gus. "Gus, you can help us and it would go quicker."

Officer Wilson jumped at the opportunity to do something. He was beginning to think he had been sidelined for some reason. Dr. Sharp took this in, shook his head, and stepped back through the door. He decided he had better warn Doug Katzberg, his office manager. There hadn't been time to go into details before.

He reached Doug's office as the three policemen stepped up to the reception desk. "Doug, these three officers need to ask questions about what happened this noon. I'm sorry to disrupt the office like this."

Doug was very sharp and had already anticipated something

like this, though he didn't expect the questioning to start so soon.

"That's fine Jack, I'll show them around." He walked over to June Levin, the receptionist. "June, could you show these officers into the back-office and let the MA's and nurses know not to leave yet?"

She looked from Doug to the officers. She wasn't intimidated by them but had no previous experience like this.

"Gentlemen please go through that door and I will meet you." They turned and followed her pointed finger. From there they fanned out through the office asking general questions, but they were mainly checking on the character of Dr. Jack Sharp and ascertaining his actions for the previous few days. They looked at his appointment schedules and had copies made. They showed everyone the photograph of the dead girl to see if any of them recognized her. According to the medical assistants she was not a patient of this practice. One officer spoke with Amy, Jack's nurse ,while another looked into his office.

"No offense, Officer, but I thought you were questioning people not going through my things. Don't you need a warrant for that?" Jack was becoming irritated at the boldness of these policemen.

"Sir, is there something you don't want us to see?" The police-man was brusque but not offensive.

"I have nothing to hide but I know you have your limits. If you want, I can confirm this with the detective." He reached for his phone and pulled out the card Rebecca had given him.

"Well, we may have to come back if we need more," said the officer, a little less sure of himself.

"I expect you will. Please finish up your questions so these people can get home." Jack was gaining confidence with the situation. He knew he had done nothing wrong and was feeling bolder. He found Gus Wilson and said, "I've done all I can do here tonight. Can we get going to meet the detective?"

"Yes sir, I think the other men are about done with their questions too." So far, everything the doctor had told them had been true. His office staff had no concerns about his character, though they would have to ask questions again when he wasn't around. Maybe a few patients should be asked too. The lady he had seen last might make a good choice. He jotted that down in his notes and followed Dr. Sharp out the door.

In the car again Gus felt less edgy. "You have a nice office, Dr. Sharp. I see Dr. McMahon over on the west side of town. He is in an older building and it smells like antiseptic when you walk in."

"We try to have a 'family friendly' atmosphere." Jack noticed the change in his companion's attitude and wondered about it. "Where are you from, Officer Wilson?"

"You can call me 'Officer Gus' if you want. It feels more normal for me. I'm from Iowa. I grew up in Red Oak and moved to Council Bluffs in high school. I was a cop in Omaha for a while, but moved here four years ago." Gus was downright chatty now but he didn't care. The real questioning was still to come and would be handled by the detective.

5

They reached the city-county building at about five o'clock. Jack felt that his day had been much longer than usual. Now he had to endure more questions at the police station. He was not looking forward to it, but if being interviewed could bring this to a conclusion, so be it. Nevertheless, he was beginning to regret that he had ever gotten involved.

He was shown down the hall and upstairs to the third floor. He wasn't taken to an interrogation room as he expected. Instead, they went to a corner windowed office with a sign that read, "Lt. Rebecca Sweate" on it. The desk was much neater than his own and there were several photos were on the bookcase, giving some personality to the workspace. Chargers for pagers and phones were lined up along the side of the desk and a digital recording machine sat to the side of the desk blotter. There was an electronic lapel microphone resting on the edge of the desk which he presumed was for him to wear while she asked questions.

He turned toward the door as Detective Sweate walked through the door. She was all smiles and seemed much more pleasant than she had been on the bike path. Reaching for his hand, she said, "Hello again Dr. Sharp."

"Hello Detective. Nice office and 'high tech' if I may say." He was genuinely impressed. "Do you have helpers who keep your office so neat? You should see mine."

"I have to keep it cleaned up or the chief gets on my case. It gets messy at times, but I try to be a tidy person. As for high tech, I'm afraid cell phones and tape recorders push my limits. I use a computer too but I still hunt and peck." Rebecca didn't know why she was being so talkative, but she was actually pleased to see Dr. Sharp again. So far he was squeaky clean, but she knew she needed to keep an open mind on that point.

"Please sit down, Dr. Sharp." She motioned to the comfortable office chair and he took the proffered chair gladly. The atmosphere had changed and he hoped that they were finding nothing wrong with his version of the story. Their initial meeting still bothered him, though. Why had they been so suspicious?

"Dr. Sharp, first of all, I must inform you that you are entitled to have a lawyer present."

Jack hadn't even considered this. "Do I need one? Am I a suspect?"

Rebecca didn't have to tell him anything. She warned him again, "We are not arresting you, but everything you say will be recorded, so please be sure to tell the truth. You don't have to answer anything if you want to speak to a lawyer first."

Jack thought for a second. He didn't have anything to hide. "I guess I can talk to you without my lawyer." Yet he wasn't altogether sure it was the best idea.

"All right sir. Could you go over everything you did and saw for me again?" The detective was now all business but not unpleasant.

He sighed, "I had a feeling I would be repeating myself again. First, would you mind telling me what you have found out about the woman?" He was genuinely interested and now concerned for the young woman's family. This would be someone's nightmare come true.

"Doctor, I can't really go into detail about the case at this time. I will say that we still don't know the identity of the woman. Let me start. Why were you on the bike path today?"

"I try to walk there every day if I can. It is usually relaxing and refreshing and it is a healthy thing to do. I can honestly tell my patients, 'do as I do.'" He smiled, "Do you get enough exercise?"

She flushed, "I'll ask the questions if you please." She wasn't angry but it was as sore point with her. She had to practically starve herself because there didn't seem to be enough time to do much exercise and she didn't want to gain weight. "Do you usually make it that far out on the path?"

"Today I had a little more time so I walked a little farther. Most days I make it to that large cedar tree about a quarter mile farther back."

"I see you know the path well. Do you often go into the gully along the path or walk off the path?" She decided to pursue a new angle just in case.

He saw where that was leading, "Detective, I walk the *path,* I don't usually explore the weeds. I don't have time for that. Besides you saw how dirty I got. I couldn't go back to the office looking like that."

"Just being thorough, Doctor. Please try not to take offense at every question." She let her annoyance show.

Jack proceeded to recount his noon walk for the detective. He re-stated seeing the flash of blue color. He described the scene of the dead woman and was more complete this time. He decided to mention everything that he had noticed. "She had a small tattoo on her chest, but I couldn't see what it was and I didn't touch her clothes or her body. There was no visible purse, though I didn't reach into her pocket. I know it would have left fingerprints and that could cause problems for me."

Rebecca Sweate's eyebrows went up. This was not the description he had given her before. "Why didn't you mention these things before? What else did you notice?" She was taking notes even though the session was being recorded.

"Well, she had a necklace, a wristwatch on her right wrist, a bracelet on her left wrist and an ankle bracelet. There was an antique-appearing ring on her left middle finger. I thought the wounds on her chest looked like knife wounds because of their shape and there wasn't any blood around her body so I figured she had been put there not killed there."

"Crime TV really does make an impression," she said somewhat astounded. "I need to compare my notes." She shook her head slowly from side to side. "Have you ever considered forensics as a profession?" she asked.

He laughed, "I much prefer dealing with the living, Detective. I made a real effort to memorize the scene because I knew someone, like you, would want my description and I didn't have my camera. Is that a problem?" He was starting to feel a little cocky, but didn't want to antagonize the questioner. He hoped this would be his first and last interrogation.

"Being thorough isn't a problem. It is refreshing. I wish all our witnesses were so observant." She actually smiled as he took the picture.

The uniformed policemen who waited outside the office, overhearing this, looked at each other. Without speaking they both shook their heads slowly and simultaneously.

"Now what can you tell me about this jogger?" Rebecca asked as she referred to her notes. "You said he called himself Greg Connolly?"

"Yes, he approached as I was coming out of the brush. I actually thought about hiding, but realized it would look suspicious to anyone coming down the path. I was a little surprised there weren't more people on the path today. It is usually busier on nice days." He gave her the full description of the muscular young man.

"Was there blood on his clothing or did he act suspicious, to you?" Rebecca figured that if the doctor was such a good observer he would be able to remember these details too.

"I saw nothing like that. I did notice he wasn't sweating much. It was nice weather, but if I had jogged a mile or so I would have been pitted out. He could just be in superb shape, but most people sweat anyway." Now the questions she was asking were raising alarms in his own head.

"Oh, no! You are beginning to suspect the jogger! Did you check to see if he called you?"

Jack was now aware things were not well. *What if the jogger had been there all along.* "I didn't stop to think he could have been involved." He thought about his encounter with 'Greg Connolly.' "I can't see anything in my memory of him that would make it obvious that he had been near the body."

"We don't necessarily suspect this jogger." She seemed to dismiss this issue. "You let us worry about that. He may just not want to get involved. We will keep trying to track this guy down and see what he has to say." She was lying. If the doctor was telling the truth and there really was a jogger, his behavior was very suspicious. Rebecca asked a few more questions then stood and Jack followed suit. "Thank you, Dr. Sharp for your candid interview. We may have additional questions." Rebecca opened a card case on her desk and handed Jack her business card. Jack, in turn, reached into his wallet and drew out one of his homemade cards.

"Please, let me know. I am also aware that you don't usually keep us civilians apprised of your investigations. Still, I wouldn't mind knowing what you find out about the jogger or the young woman. You never know, I may know her family."

They shook hands officiously and Jack moved toward the door.

Before he stepped into the hallway Detective Sweate asked one last question, a technique used to try to catch people off guard.

"Dr. Sharp, what was your relationship to the deceased?"

Now he got angry, though he tried to curb it. "I told you," he said tersely. "I had no relationship to that woman."

"I see. Thank you again, Dr. Sharp."

He turned and was out the door.

The policeman, Gus, had moved down the hall. When he saw Dr. Sharp emerge he approached. "All finished?"

Jack answered curtly, "Yes, Officer. Let's get out of here."

Officer Wilson nodded, "Sure Doc. I'll get you back in no time."

Jack and the officer rode back to his office in relative silence. He was still fuming over the final question. Then he began thinking about the possibilities that were posed by considering the jogger to be a suspect. His office parking lot was nearly empty so he had the policeman drop him off at his own car. He then took out his keys, his mind wholly absorbed with thoughts of the murder. He knew he would have a long night ahead without much sleep.

He slipped the key in the door lock and unlocked the car. Jack liked larger cars. Smaller sporty cars could be fun to drive and he appreciated the reliability of some of the foreign made vehicles, but he currently had a three- year- old Buick that ran great and was very comfortable. The engine turned over and he started to leave. As he pulled out of his parking lot he felt a nagging sensation in the back of his head. He wasn't sure if he was forgetting some-thing in his office or if he was just being nervous. He glanced around, but nothing jumped into his mind so he resolutely faced forward and drove home. He usually listened to books on tape or

CD, but he reached over and punched the eject button on the stereo. The radio came on automatically to his favorite station.

When the music finished there was a news break. He picked this station because it had good music and some local news and weather. "Today, in an East Lincoln neighborhood a local physician reportedly found the body of an unidentified woman. Jack Sharp, M.D., was questioned by police who say they currently have no leads. So far, no one matching her description has been reported missing in the local area and police are looking for another man whom they want to question as a "person of interest" in the death. They are considering the death to be a homicide at this time. Detective Rebecca Sweate has asked that if anyone knows of a young woman who is missing or has information relating to this death, please call the Crime Hotline 800 55C RIME. That's 800 551 7463. In sports..."

Jack turned off the radio. "That was fast," he said out loud. "My name is already in the news. I wonder if I'll be dealing with reporters tomorrow. The report didn't exactly make me out to be a mere witness either. '*Questioned by police-*'"

When he arrived in his neighborhood he turned up his street and was chagrined to see two television trucks parked on his block. "Good grief," he said under his breath. He stopped, deciding what to do. He didn't want another interview right now, especially one that would go on television. Besides he didn't know if he was allowed say anything to reporters. He might say something stupid which would increase the police suspicions about him. His next thought was that he really should speak to his lawyer just to be sure he hadn't already messed up. Tentatively he pulled forward, pressed his garage door opener and drove up to his home. As he emerged from his car was besieged by the local news people.

His first impulse was to close the garage door and retreat to his house, but he had worked with these reporters on medical shows before. They were just regular people trying to do their jobs and he wanted to remain on their good sides. Chris Porter from Channel 6 was first to stick a microphone in his face as he stepped out onto the driveway. "Dr. Sharp," he began, "what can you tell us about the murdered woman?"

With camera lights glaring in his eyes he put on his most professional look, though he knew his appearance was somewhat disheveled. He was tired and his brain was sluggish. "Chris, members of the media, I know you have a lot of questions. Frankly, so do I. I am merely a witness and my observations are for the police. I'm sure they would prefer that you get your details from them. All I will say is that a young woman lies dead today. It is a great tragedy. In my profession we look to save lives and care for the sick. I am sorry I could not accomplish that for her." He waved, shook hands with Chris and shook his head to the other reporters who were trying to get him to answer their loudly shouted questions. "That's really all I have to say. Good night." With that he turned into his garage and, pushing the garage door button, stepped into his home glad for the solitude.

Unfortunately he was greeted by the sound of the phone ringing.

"Jack," the caller began, "What have you gotten yourself into?" Samuel H. Boniface III J.D. was on the phone. Despite his twenty years in the heartland he spoke with a distinct Boston accent and often enhanced it during media interviews, thinking it made him sound more distinguished. Sam was Jack's lawyer and, in his practice, usually only dealt with family wills and minor disputes. "Am I going to have to defend your..."

"Sam, I was just about to call you," Jack interrupted before Sam could lay into him. "It looks like I'm mixed up more in this thing than I want to be. Tomorrow's normally a busy day for me, but I suppose we should talk about it." Jack genuinely liked Sam. He was the one person Jack often felt he could open up to. They had a true friendship, not just a business relationship. Sam, however, was very married with six busy children. He was a good father and loved spending time with them so the friends' get-togethers had languished somewhat lately.

"I was thinking right now, buddy. This is the kind of thing that can blind-side you. I'll bring the beer."

Though he was tired and wanted some respite Jack didn't even try to dissuade him. Sam was the right person to have here now. Before Jack could get too worried Sam would help him get perspective.

"Sure Sam. Like usual, you bring it and you drink most of it. Doesn't your wife let you have it at home?" he joked.

"As a matter of fact, dear boy, I have a bottle of 18 year old Glenlivet in the cupboard she lets me have for 'medicinal purposes.' But you're right. I have to drink it when the kids are in bed. She won't touch anything. All right I'll be there soon. I need to read 'The Cat in the Hat' one more time." Jack could hear a child's giggle in the background as Sam hung up the phone.

Jack smiled as Sam had said he would be there in an hour. He cradled the phone and wondered if there was anyone else he should call. Kathy? Would she have seen the news and wonder about their meeting today too? He decided against calling her. If she had seen the news, it wouldn't help and if she had not he would only cause her grief.

He looked out his window. The media vans, mercifully, had left. He was alone now with his thoughts. He couldn't remember having had a more stressful day. He had never been mixed up with anything involving the police, outside of his practice. In his medical experience there had been patients who had attempted or succeeded at suicide, as well as child custody and suspected abuse cases. Jack, however, had always been the advocate not a witness or a suspect.

An old desire was beginning to surface. Despite what he had said, Jack really wanted that drink Sam was about to provide. He knew alcohol could be a problem for him, but it was something he had never told anyone. There was a time, nearly twenty years ago, that was all but a blur to him today. He had just returned from Africa where he had witnessed terrible poverty and illness. He had witnessed some of the worst cruelty man can commit, a scene he did not like to relive.

Had Jack gone right to work at a clinic upon returning to the U.S., he probably would have lost his license. Instead, he spent three months wandering around the country sometimes in a drunken haze. Few people knew of his debacle. He had gradually pulled himself out of his alcoholic stupor and eventually sobered up. Nevertheless, he had never admitted his problem to anyone and had not attended an 'AA' meeting. While he didn't consider himself to be proud, it was his pride that had kept him from confronting his weakness.

The way he now felt was the first time in years that he "wanted" a drink. He was glad Sam was coming over because he was sure, left to himself, he would have made the trip to the local liquor store.

Instead, he made the decision to write out a record of what had happened that day. This, he reasoned, would keep him from forgetting the details and allow him to look back if he ever wanted to do so. He got out his laptop computer and opened the word-processing program. The words flowed and he became absorbed in the description of the scene.

Just as he had put the last few words down and saved his work he heard someone try the front door. Then the doorbell rang several times. He realized he hadn't even turned the light on for the front porch. Hurrying over, he unlocked the door, and greeted a slightly annoyed Sam. "What you don't leave the door open for your friend?"

"Sorry, I was worried about snoops. I've been writing out all my thoughts for the day since I called you."

Sam's eyebrows rose as he walked in carrying a sack making clinking sounds of glass on glass. "That was a good idea. Can you make a copy for me? I still want you to verbally tell me everything. It's always better than reading it." Sam came in and took out two cold bottles of Heineken beer. "I hope you don't mind imports. The American stuff just doesn't match up."

Jack said, "I don't mind, but that one gives me headaches. I won't drink much. All right let's go into the living room and I'll fill you in." Jack and Sam sat on two overstuffed chairs in his comfortable living room. There was a baby grand piano in the corner and a few original paintings on the walls. Jack loved music but was not very good at playing the piano. It usually sat un-played for months at a time.

"Jack, when are you going to get a wife who can play that thing?" Sam asked, only half joking.

"Get serious, Sam. You know how that usually goes. I tell them I have a baby grand and they fall in love with the piano, not me." They both laughed.

"Okay here's the story. Today I went for my usual noon walk on the bike path behind my office. I left the office about 11:45 and headed east." He proceeded to go over the entire episode. For Sam, he didn't leave out the meeting with Kathy, though he did not reveal her medical information. Kathy, and his mixed feelings about his relationship with her, were subjects Jack had never brought up with anyone. Not even his best friend. When he had finished the story, including his interview with the police, Sam sighed. Jack had also finished his bottle of beer and opened a second one causing Sam to look surprised, but he said nothing.

"Jack, why didn't you call me right away? You may have already gotten yourself into something you don't want." Sam was mildly irritated and seemed to be doing mental calculations. With an ironic smile he said, "Rebecca Sweate is anything but 'sweet.'"

"She seemed decent to me. Anyway I don't see how they could have any suspicions about me. I don't know the young woman and have no reason to want to kill anyone. I thought if I called you right away it would look like I had something to hide." Jack was truly puzzled. He knew he was innocent of any wrong doing yet he felt like he had to be defensive.

"You're probably right, this time," with a wry look Sam pointed at Jack's chest. "Next time, at least give me a call."

"Next time! There ain't going to be a next time partner." Jack tried his best John Wayne impression. "If I find a dead body I'm going to just walk on by."

"How is your lovely wife, Sam?" Jack enjoyed Sam and his whole family. They had the kind of family life he had wanted, but had somehow missed. Sam's wife was pretty and patient. She was a good mother and their children were still pretty young. They had only been married ten years. Sam had married her, a younger woman, years after a messy divorce had nearly cost him his legal practice. Now, in his late forties he had two young children to distract him and he was wise enough to know he needed to spend time with them. He had become successful enough to be able to set his own schedule too. He had started going to church and even talked about early retirement from time to time.

"Jack, you wouldn't believe me if I told you. There isn't a better woman on the planet. I can't believe how blessed I am. Gorgeous- and she loves me. I think I enjoy life more now than I ever have. Jack, you should come with me to church. There are lots of nice women there. Some are divorcee's and there are a few who haven't even been married." They had had this conversation many times before.

"Sam, you know I'm a Christian. I already go to church, but I don't want to be a hypocrite and come to your church just to look for a wife. I don't know why the ladies in my church aren't interested in me." He changed the subject. "Do you see any problems for me being involved in this murder, Sam?" He finished his second and began a third beer, a fact that caused Sam to raise his eyebrows again.

Getting serious again Sam answered, "Hey, slow down on that stuff. You're a light-weight, remember?"

"Sure, Sam. But you brought it."

Ignoring that, Sam answered his question. "I don't really see any trouble for you. You have no motive, you don't know the woman, and you reported her body. Well you tried. I'll talk to the detective in the morning to see what I can glean from her. Don't talk to them again without me, though. Okay?"

Jack nodded. "You had better get home to your family. Sorry for keeping you up late."

Rising he made for the door, "Well it just means the kids will be in bed and it will be just Sue and me." He gave Jack a sly, knowing smile.

He got in his royal blue BMW and cruised down the block out of sight as Jack waved.

Jack looked back. Sam had left the beer. He shook his head already feeling a little buzz. His resistance down he reached in the sack, only mildly grateful that there was only one bottle left. He took it out, throwing the bag and the cardboard case in the trash. The clock on the fireplace mantle struck eleven PM. Its mournful tolling sent a shiver up his spine. He had actually thought it was later, but the tiredness was becoming evident. Suddenly he was jarred by the sound of the phone ringing. Instinctively he looked at the calendar to see if he was on-call, but remembered that this week he was off every day.

On the third ring he picked up the phone and tentatively said, "Hello?"

"Jack? I'm so sorry to bother you so late but I was worried." The voice belonged to Kathy, but he was confused that she would be calling him. He didn't remember having given her his home phone number.

"Hi Kathy." He tried to sound normal but thought his words sounded thick. "Are you all right? What's worrying you?"

"Oh, Jack I saw the news tonight. Are you in trouble? They made it sound like you could be mixed up in a murder." Her plaintive voice was trembling. "I decided to call you now rather than wait, I hope you don't mind. Jeff gave me your number." Jeff Hollenbeck was one of Jack's partners. Unlike most physicians he had a phone number listed in the phone book. "I hope you don't mind," she repeated.

"No, it's all right. Kathy, I'm glad you called." He shook his head to stay focused, "I don't mind, in fact I can't think of anyone I would rather have call me," he said with obvious relief in his voice. "You don't need to worry for me. I didn't do anything wrong. I just found the body. You know how reporters are; they like to blow things out of proportion."

There was silence on the other end of the line for a moment. Then, "I'm glad you are not in trouble." More silence, "Jack, can we talk? I mean privately and not on the phone."

"Sure, but there isn't much I can tell you about this..."

"No, not about the murder, but ... I want to talk to you ... about me." Jack wasn't sure exactly what she meant, though he could tell it was important.

"Do you want to meet somewhere? Now?" Jack yawned in spite of himself.

"Not now. I think it's too late. Looks like we've both had long days." Now she was trying to sound more upbeat. "But I want to see you soon. How about breakfast in the morning?"

Jack laughed out loud, "You are curious. You name the place. I have to be at the office by eight-thirty."

"You're sure tomorrow's okay? How about Greenfields Restaurant at six-thirty? They have good breakfast and it won't be too crowded on a Friday morning," she said matter-of-factly.

Hearing her voice on the phone had actually given Jack a lump in his throat. He realized that he had feelings for her he had been actively suppressing. He had good reason for this, he felt, but now his resolve was waning. "I'm happy you called. I would love to have breakfast with you. I didn't know you were such an early bird."

Her answer startled him. "Jack there's still a lot about me you don't know, yet. I'll see you in the morning. Bye."

What had started as a timid conversation had ended with much more confidence, even forcefulness. Jack was mystified but anxious. He had dreaded their meeting at the office, but was genuinely anticipating their breakfast together with pleasure. He wondered what was so important that she needed to talk again, so soon. He looked at the still unopened bottle in his hand and said, "Not tonight."

He set it in the refrigerator and walked away, heading for bed.

6

Friday

Jack slept fitfully and strange people filled his dreams. Violence and anger seemed to permeate periods of semi-wakefulness. Faces drifted in and out of his awareness and when he awoke he found himself sweating despite the cool temperature. He had inadvertently left his window ajar and there was a definite chill around him. The sheets and blankets were wadded up at the foot of the bed denoting a restless struggle of which he had no recollection. The one thing that remained in his conscious memory of the night was the face of the jogger, Greg Connolly. His memory of this man, now tainted by phantoms flitting about his mind, was not a picture of a benign passer-by. For some reason the thought of him caused a twinge of fear to pass through Jack.

He asked himself, "Why does he bother me? He seemed so normal yesterday." Yet Jack had questions which remained unanswered. Why had he not noticed him further down the path when he had descended into the gully? This had not occurred to him yesterday, but the more he thought about it the more it bothered him. He couldn't have been down there that long and one could see nearly a mile down the bike path from that spot. And the jogger had not been even a little sweaty. It had been a warm enough day that he should have been drenched. Detective Sweate had been somewhat evasive when he asked if they were suspicious of the jogger.

Jack determined to take his concerns to Detective Sweate and let her know of the inconsistencies he had worked out. He looked at his watch and saw that he had little time to get ready to meet Kathy for breakfast. Thoughts of Kathy animated him and he headed for the shower.

*****

Rebecca Sweate had tried to go to bed early, but she had felt nervous and tense. A new case always led to some sleeplessness. The myriad possibilities of criminal intent were difficult to grasp at the outset. It was like beginning a chess match. The first moves are scripted and deliberate, but seeing past the next move to the third or fourth permutation becomes increasingly complex. She had investigated few murders and this one appeared to be difficult already. They still had no identity for the victim, which left motive open to speculation. So far, only two names were associated with the crime: the doctor who had reportedly found the body and the mystery man, Greg Connolly. Yet she also remembered that her mentor, Detective Arnie Leavy, had once told her that even the most complex crime had basic elements. The primary element in murder was that one person just didn't like another one enough to want them dead.

"All you gotta do is find out who didn't like the victim the most and there you go, crime solved." He had made it sound easy, but it still took hard work. The basic police work was critical. No detail could be overlooked. She believed that they had started well, but they needed to keep it up.

She had tried to imagine what motive the doctor could have had. Every idea was fanciful because the victim was still a Jane Doe. She could have been a daughter from a previous relationship or perhaps she had been the object of a fling the doctor was having with a much younger woman. Yet she had not been reported missing. If the doctor had been seeing her, then she would most likely have been a local woman. No one at his office was aware of any current significant female relationships.

She didn't want to do it, but Rebecca knew they would have to continue asking these kinds of questions. It could be damaging to the doctor, yet she had her job to do. Nevertheless, she would wait a little while. She found Dr. Sharp to be an interesting, intelligent man. He was not intimidated by her and had treated her with respect. She had to admit he was also attractive, despite his age. She reminded herself that she was not that much younger.

What about the jogger? He seemed to be the fishiest player.

Despite her previous musings she was beginning to think that he had to be tied to this murder in some way. She found it easy to want him to be involved and not the doctor. Besides, she knew that doctors often used more subtle means when it came to murder and she doubted that he would have been the one to report the body. Jack Sharp really didn't fit as the murderer in her mind, but she had to try to keep her thoughts open. The mystery man Greg Connolly had vanished, *if he existed at all*. So far they only had the doctor's word about that.

She made a mental note to get Dr. Sharp to work with a sketch artist today so they would have a better description of the jogger. They should have done it right away. She hoped his memory was still good. Her overnight staff had been combing missing-persons reports for multiple states and would have checked all fifty by noon. She would have to see the medical examiner today to get an update on the cause of death.

As she readied herself for the day Rebecca peered at her image in the mirror. Leaning on the bathroom sink she noticed the gray hair streaking past her ears. There were small crow's feet by her eyes and her lips were no longer quite as full. Tiny lines extended from the edges of her nose and lips but her skin was clear. She still didn't need to use much make-up, but she hated the thought of getting old. She, once more, thought about what life would have been like with a husband and children. The loss of such a past sometimes gave her an ache in some deep place, yet she knew that it was now too late to reclaim that past. Perhaps she should think about settling down. She didn't need this stress forever. There were more administrative positions open to her, and she knew she could do them well.

Rebecca didn't know, though, if she could ever be "domesticated." She loved the hunt and was now on the cusp of a new challenge. The anticipation of it pushed aside her more mundane and wistful ideas and she turned and strode from her room.

Rebecca's coffee maker was beeping at her and she automatically reached to the cupboard for a fresh cup to fill. It was still dark outside, and as she peered out her back door she could see a huge orange moon just about to slip below the roof of the house behind her. The stars were piercingly white and the air seemed extra clean. She could tell that summer-like days were fleeting past and soon there would even be more of a chill in the morning air.

"God," she thought to herself, "when was the last time I just looked at the stars or went for a walk?"

Her "faith" had faded as a teenager. She had grown up in a Catholic home and attended Mass until her parents no longer forced her to go. She hadn't been to confession for years and rarely thought about the church. However, thoughts of religion had recently entered her mind unbidden. She had begun to think about heaven and hell because of those she knew who had already died. Would she ever see them in heaven? The God she thought of was judicial and stern. He would be severe with someone who had pulled away from their faith. Rebecca had almost gone to Mass a few weeks earlier. She had found an old Bible and gotten ready, but a call had come that had forced her to go in to work. She had vowed that she would go again soon.

Setting her cup on the countertop she picked up her notebook and started reviewing her notes from the previous day. The harvest moon and thoughts of God pushed aside, she delved into another work day and the painful ugly facts she had to digest.

****

The medical examiner began his day in much the same way he always did. Dr. Joseph French stopped at McDonald's for an Egg McMuffin and coffee. Driving a 1975 Black Mercedes 450 convertible, he wore a classic country gentleman's cap to cover his bald pate. Wisps of gray hair floated over his ears in the cool morning wind as Dr. French traveled through town to the little brick building across from the city/county structure. He liked to hold his old pipe in his teeth, though he hadn't lit it for years. It just felt comfortable there. He had the largest morgue in the state, and that held only four bodies. Although it was also true that there were few homicides in Nebraska and he had filled all four only once. He knew that someday there would be a disaster or crime spree that would stretch his meager resources beyond their limit. Using his own money, Joseph had refurbished the facility just to keep it up to standards. He had tried to arrange the use of hospital facilities, but the private hospitals wanted nothing to do with county politics. Dr. Joseph French was an internationally acclaimed forensic pathologist having literally written the book on forensic medicine a dozen years earlier. He was often asked by his colleagues from much larger cities why he put up with such dismal conditions and his answer was always the same.

"I wanted a great place to raise a family." This he and his wife had done well.

Dr. French's assistant, whom he had carefully trained, had started the preparation of the body and had obtained all the appropriate swabs and cultures. She had checked the finger nails and carefully photographed all of the young woman's features. There had been small traces of cloth and bits of vegetation, but no apparent skin under her nails. No suspicious bruises had been revealed under various lighting techniques.

Now, as he gazed upon this pretty, young woman whose body was marred by so many wounds, he shook his head. She appeared to be about the same age as his daughter Kristin. He was always struck by the brutality of his fellow human beings. What could drive a person to such an extreme? It disgusted and saddened him. Sometimes he lay awake at night laden with fear as well. What if this had been his daughter or son? Could they be in danger where they lived? At these moments he was glad that his wife was a music teacher and not a physician.

Nearly ready to begin, he picked up his office phone and dialed Detective Sweate. "Rebecca. Would you like to come down?"

"Thank you—I'll be right there."

After a reasonable wait Detective Sweate arrived with a camera slung around her neck. She carried a pen and notebook to keep her own record of the proceedings. She had already tanked up with coffee as Dr. French's autopsies could be very long, drawn-out affairs and he allotted few breaks. "Okay Doc, let's go."

Dr. French smiled broadly at Rebecca and took her hand, "So

good to see you again. Welcome to my lab-*or*-atory." He drew out the last word with an accent that could have won him a part in a Dracula movie.

Rebecca laughed, in an unusually good mood. She noticed that there were already opened paper sacks ready to receive the victim's clothing as Dr. French inspected them piece by piece. He was always careful to examine them thoroughly for evidence before sending them to the crime lab.

Dr. French methodically photographed the body with his own special Nikon camera with a lens-mounted ring flash. This type of flash left no shadows and the expensive camera allowed for extremely fine detailed examination later on computer. He rechecked the areas already documented by his assistant. She could not be present today, meaning he would have to do all the work himself.

He used a headset microphone to record his thoughts as he performed the autopsy. This was used with a high-end wireless system allowing digital recording. It used a sophisticated software program to convert his spoken words to text and he had personally modified the program and "trained" it to recognize the unusual words associated with autopsy and anatomy. The system saved his budget from the cost of paying a transcriptionist for performing the same task. The added benefit was the rapidity with which he could provide a printed report to the police.

With a glance at Rebecca, he began, "This is Dr. Joseph French beginning the autopsy on Jane Doe 346 on October..." dictating his usual introduction. He began by inspecting every centimeter of the woman's body. At one point he asked Rebecca to assist him in rolling the body and providing support for the head and neck. He always did x-rays, but CT scans and MRIs were being used more and more in pathology cases. He found these high-tech methods could help in some cases, but they were much more highly useful in the living than the dead most of the time and much more expensive.

He was thorough and methodical and this autopsy consumed hours of time to complete. He didn't intentionally ignore Rebecca, but he always became so engrossed in his work that other stimuli went unnoticed, even with her occasional photograph. Once performed, he knew nearly everything about this woman that can be discerned from examination of the body. Toxicology screens, cultures, trace exams, and microscopic examination of tissue would require days and weeks more to complete, but by late morning Dr. Joseph French had found out something surprising. He had dictated it, but he suspected that Rebecca had not noticed.

At last he looked up.

Detective Sweate was one investigator to whom he felt he could talk plainly. She was good at her job and didn't come in ready to throw her authority around. He, likewise, was respectful of her position and was less abrupt with her than with her male counterparts. He found it humorous to see the looks on their faces when they encountered death in this bleak cold room. A few of the younger ones had turned unusual shades of green, necessitating a bucket for their own stomach contents. Detective Sweate had never been put off by the sight of a dead body, no matter how mangled or malodorous. However, she was relieved when he finally spoke to her.

"I think I can even surprise you today. Given the appearance of her body what can you tell me?" He liked to play teacher with the detectives. Most of them got flustered and angry demanding his results and not his questions. Rebecca played along even though today she was in somewhat of a hurry.

"Well, to me it is rather straight forward, ," she began. "All cleaned up like she was initially I could see no bruises or defensive wounds. Her skin is generally in good condition except for about a dozen holes in her chest."

He reached down to close the "Y" incision on the chest. "Look more closely at her chest Detective." His voice carried a hint of mystery now and he was beginning to enjoy himself. It was not often he could surprise Rebecca Sweate.

"All right I count eleven wounds. But some are horizontal and some are vertical. That's unusual. It's almost like the killer intentionally changed the angle of their hand. Not something you usually do in a rage. So many wounds made me think it was pretty personal."

"Very good, my young apprentice."

She scowled, "Give me a minute." She bent closer and the doctor applied extra lighting. She then moved away from the chest and examined other areas.

"You're getting colder," smiled Dr. French.

"I don't see anything under the nails now. Did you find anything?" she asked.

"There was very little there. Some dirt, some vegetation, but no obvious skin or blood." He picked up the hand and said, "Lovely fingers and a well done manicure. It is so sad to see this. She obviously tried to remain in good health and cared for her appearance."

She murmured, "Yes, she is young."

"So much like my own daughter. It is on days like today that I begin to fear for my own family." Rebecca knew that Joseph and his wife had had seven children. All but one were now in college or on their own. He was not an ostentatious physician, though he was unsurpassed in his own field. And once he crossed the threshold of his little morgue he was one hundred percent business. In this case, he had known there was some urgency, but he had decided to start fresh on this day instead of working through the night.

"One of my sons had a birthday yesterday, and his sisters and brother are still in town. We enjoyed a special dinner out." Some things took greater priority for him than the job. He seemed startled with himself and changed the subject. "Well, back to business. What else do you see? Let's go back to the chest."

She looked at him, puzzled, but began to re-inspect the chest and the wounds. "Okay," she said at length, "this cut seems more ragged than the other ones. It looks like a little 'divot' has been taken out of the edge." She pointed to one of the more central knife wounds.

"Bingo! Congratulations you win a gold star," he said happily. "You should go to medical school and come back to work with me."

He really was pleased.

"Note that the divot has a fairly sharp contour. If that had come from the knife it should be in all the cuts, but it is only on the one near the horizontal cuts. I'll speed this up by telling you that the answer was not discovered in inspection, but in x-ray." They moved over to wall to the bank of fluorescent light boxes where he had arranged x-rays of the girl's body to be viewed from left to right. Pointing toward a middle x-ray he began, "notice that she has many metallic objects along her spine. There are surgical scars on her back to go along with these. She must have had scoliosis and an extensive repair. I would say they did a remarkable job. Her spine appears straight and no one could tell without an x-ray that she had any problem before. Now look these over a minute while I start some coffee. Do you want any?"

"No thank you Dr. French," she muttered as she delved into the stark white on black images that seemed to violate the very body they had just inspected. Except for her spine, the young woman's body seemed well proportioned and the bones were in good shape. She looked at all the films, not just the one Dr. French had pointed out. Her teeth were nearly perfect. The long bones of her arms and legs were not as slender as she expected and she saw no evidence of old fractures. Then she peered more closely at the spine where the surgical appliances were seen. She traced them down each side. There were slender rods coursing along the edges of the spinal column on both sides. Then she saw it. Almost like a smudge or artifact, near a screw, was a ragged metallic object.

Dr. French approached, steaming cup in hand. "I see you found it." In my opinion the knife wounds would have killed her. I have explored deeply enough to see that she would have bled to death from the wounds eventually, but the 'coup de gras' was a bullet. I don't know if the killer knew there was all this hardware in her spine or not, but maybe he thought he could get away with shooting her by covering up the bullet hole with stab wounds. She was still alive when he stabbed her too. A tough girl."

"Why go to the trouble to cover up a bullet hole? That is strange. I suppose once you have the bullet we will be able to find the creep who did it. Can you tell what kind of gun was used?" She was still staring at the x-ray boxes when she turned he stood grinning next to her. He had a little baggie in hand.

"I'm not sure, but it looks like a .38 to me. It is pretty smashed up so who knows if you'll get any hits. It is possible that the gun was used in a previous shooting." He was genuinely pleased with himself and knew that Detective Sweate would appreciate the skill necessary to have gotten to this point. "I may be able to find out something if I remove some of the spinal hardware but the bullet is the biggest help I can offer. The hardware may have a serial number on it. It would most likely have been done when she was a teenager. If she is from around here that would limit the field, but she could be from literally anywhere."

Rebecca stepped out to make a call. When she returned she shook her head, "We've checked NCIC and so far there have been no reports of missing persons matching her description."

The National Crime Information Center was an FBI database accessed by local law enforcement to try to find just such information.

"We will enter this information into the Violent Crime Apprehension Program, ViCAP, to see if there are any similar murders."

Doctor French smiled.

"I know the acronyms and I know you'll do your best Rebecca. Here."

She took the proffered bag containing the bullet as a cloud seemed to come across her face. "I can't believe that someone hasn't noticed that she is missing yet. She wasn't a hermit camped out in the park. We could use a little more luck finding out who she is." She tossed the bag up and down. "At least we know how she was killed. A gun may give us the murderer.

"Don't rule out the personal angle. 'Shooting is too good for you.' You know, the stabbing was done deliberately in a rage. The extra horizontal wounds an afterthought to cover up the bullet. You know it's just a guess. There may be powder burns on the clothing to indicate how close the killer was too, though I didn't see them." He saw that she was prepared to leave, "Rebecca I have enjoyed your company as always." He put out his hand to shake hers.

"Compared to your usual 'company' I don't know whether to take that for a compliment. They don't talk to you." She grinned and instead of shaking Dr. French's hand she gave him a gentle hug.

"You make my day, Dr. French! When I come to see you I

know I am in the presence of a professional. Let me hear from you if you have any other earth-shattering news."

She smiled warmly, turned and strode from the bleak cold room. The remaining evidence would have to be dried and sent to the crime lab for closer examination, but she hoped to get the bullet looked at right away.

Dr. French sighed inwardly as Rebecca left his room. He had yet to test the young woman's organs and provide tissue samples for pathological examination. Getting the spinal rods out would be difficult and he would have to have his assistant to give him a hand.

****

Rebecca stepped out into a windy, fall day that was almost as bleak as the morgue from which she had just come. The weather had changed and there was such a contrast that she marveled at how different one day could be from another. The sun was obscured by scudding gray clouds and the leaves swept by in waves that looked like flocks of colorful birds. She knew that winter was still weeks away, but this weather made it seem that snow could come any time. In all her years in Nebraska, one thing she never got used to was the rapid change in the weather. In her native North Carolina, the Atlantic Ocean to the east or the Appalachian mountain range to the west affected the temperatures statewide There were bad days and winter wasn't always pleasant or mild, but the temperature didn't usually vary so widely–it just depended if one was on the coast, in the mountains, or in the Piedmont, the middle of the state. Here, though, it didn't much matter where one was in Nebraska. The day could start well below freezing and by midday, the thermometer might read in the sixties. On the other hand, she had once awakened to a sunny fall day with bright, warm sunshine and by bedtime there were four inches of snow on the ground. People here took it in stride, but she still felt surprised by it whenever there was such a severe alteration. However, she supposed that it was one of the things she liked about living "out west."

Her family had never understood what the draw had been and

at first, neither could she. She thought it was the job, but gradually she noticed how she thought more like a Nebraskan. She had even begun to follow football, a sport she had never liked growing up. Her father had been a rabid baseball fanatic and daily had pored over the sports pages to see how his teams were doing. In Nebraska, though, where there were no major professional teams, the University of Nebraska football team dominated the news during the fall. No other sport received as much attention. The spring scrimmage attracted more people than other teams could get to a season opener. Rebecca had learned football terminology just to keep up with the conversation in the office.

Facing the wind, Rebecca pulled her hair back and expertly slipped a band around her locks to make a single ponytail. The movement caused her to think of the young woman lying in the morgue who would never again comb her beautiful hair. The thought further saddened her as she stepped out to cross the street to the city/county building where the criminal laboratory was housed.

On the third floor she stopped to register the item she carried with its case number and date. Signing the evidence book she looked up at the uniformed policeman/clerk who entered the information into his computer.

"Good morning Detective Sweate," he said pleasantly glancing up from his computer display. "Nasty little piece of evidence you have there. I hope it didn't come from a person."

"George, it's a sad business. I'm going to take this directly to the lab." The dark cloud had not yet lifted from her countenance. The policeman, George Sternberg, was near retirement, but still liked to feel like he was 'in the game.'

"Of course," he countered. Seeing her downcast eyes he took her hand in his. "Rebecca, it's the job. It'll be okay." He smiled right at her, "Hey, when you going to get married?"

A little startled she looked up. "George, I keep waiting for you to ask."

His smile was infectious and she almost laughed despite herself. He had been a fun-loving, jovial cop until his partner was killed five years ago. It was the first time she had seen him happy and she didn't want to break the mood. They squeezed each others' hands, hidden meaning passing unspoken between them. She felt that she understood the pain that still haunted him. Rebecca gave him her sweetest smile and moved down the hallway to the lab. Then with a second thought, she turned back to the evidence room.

George was surprised to see her once again. "Hi, again," she said. "I just had an idea. May I look at the evidence log sheet for my victim?"

"Sure. She's your victim. The sheet is all yours," said George pleasantly. He sat at the computer again and typed in a series of letters and numbers identifying this most recent case.

Rebecca noticed he had typed in the dozen or so characters from memory. "George, how do you do that?"

"Do what?" he asked mystified.

"Remember all those letters and numbers," she answered back.

"Well I've been told it's 'photographic memory.' It helps with this job, but I didn't even know I had it until I started doing this." George said this humbly but Rebecca was impressed.

"Do you remember everything on every case?"

"Oh, I can remember everything, but I have to have something to get me started," he said in a cautious way. "Take this one for instance. Now that you have me thinking about it, I can list everything in that box. But that's why we have computers. I can do it, but I don't need to."

"But you could also tell if anyone ever changed the logs couldn't you?" Rebecca asked.

He straightened. "No one ever does that." He was serious now. "You got reason to think someone is doin' that?"

"No, no," she backed off, "I was just making an observation." As he handed her the list he had a little more of a suspicious look to his face.

"Thanks George. If I had a memory like yours I wouldn't have had to ask for this."

Once again she headed to the lab. Inside the door of the crime laboratory was a cabinet with multiple, locked doors. To preserve the integrity of the evidence, she had to place her labeled item in the cabinet, lock the door and give the key to one of the lab technicians. This system worked extremely well unless there were too many cases for the number of cabinets or if the evidence was too large to fit. Rebecca hoped that by bringing it in herself she would get quicker service. She deposited the bullet in cabinet number ten and went to hand the key to Cindy. Barely looking up, the tech said it would be a day before she could look at it. That was the best she could offer. Cindy was new but had come with impressive credentials from a 'big city' lab. She wore a lab coat and her hair was pinned tightly up on her head. She wore no-nonsense glasses with an eye-shield over them. Her overall appearance made Rebecca think of a hospital nurse from a generation or two ago.

Rebecca decided to exert some authority. "Do you know this is the only murder case we have right now?" she asked, feeling irritated. "What takes priority over that?"

Cindy was definitely uncomfortable. She had her own orders and priorities and she did not appreciate being pushed nor having her schedule challenged.

"Detective, you know that I am not in charge. If you want something changed please see the head of this department. I'll see what I can do, but expect it to be *a day or two*." She put intentional emphasis on the last phrase and then pointedly turned back to her work.

Rebecca's anger boiled to the surface. She had several pointed even graphic things she desperately wanted to say to this young woman, and but she tried to stay professional. She stood seething for a second but knew she had no authority over her.

Rebecca slammed the key into a box on the counter next to Cindy and said, "The girl that bullet came from was about your age, only she is dead!" She let that statement hang in the air and stormed out of the lab.

7

Friday

Kathy woke with the same dull headache which she had experienced now for several weeks. She didn't know if the headache was the reason for her waking, but she had not slept well last night. The pain in her head seemed to have blown her thoughts around like a tornado. She had seen what seemed like hundreds or thousands of faces flashing in and out of her vision. Her late husband had been there and each of her children, in turn, as youngsters in this dream. Jack was also there, floating in and out with his characteristic grin. The only verbal thing she could remember from the nightmare, for that was really what it had been, was Jack saying, "I'm sorry, there's nothing I can do." He had looked so sad it made her tearful even now.

She wrapped her arms around herself as she sat in her bed. The room felt cool and she was unusually aware of being alone. She still missed waking up beside her husband, even though it had been years, now. Steve had been a kind, happy man who had loved their children and until the latter part of their marriage, herself exclusively. Their union had been good for many years, but what no one else knew was that he had had an affair for the last three years of their lives together. She didn't know much about it or who "the other woman" had been. But this much younger woman had been at the graveside and the funeral, crying as much as Kathy. He had never spoken of her and Kathy had never found out what had gone so wrong that Steve had needed another woman to love. He had died driving back home from *her* place late at night. He had either suffered a heart attack or fallen asleep at the wheel, but he had crossed the center lane and hit a median. The car had flipped into a ditch and it wasn't found until the next morning. She had told the police that he had needed to work late. Thus, she had protected the woman she disliked as well as her own family and reputation.

Yet, even today the secret still weighed heavily upon her.

Kathy was lonely and wanted to speak to Jack about her personal feelings. Her mind shifted to that time in high school when they had been on the school bus. Somehow they had ended up in the same row. Though Jack was on the inside seat another girl had switched places with him so she could sit with her boyfriend. Kathy had been going steady with Tom Havers, but Tom, a jock, not a musician, wasn't on that bus. Kathy played the flute and Jack the saxophone. It must have been a marching band trip, but Kathy couldn't remember for sure where they had gone. Somehow by the end of the trip they were holding hands and had even stolen a few kisses. Kathy now smiled to herself. She had strung him along for a few weeks, but Tom had been too jealous and overbearing so she had dropped her fling with Jack, partly to protect him. She hadn't thought Jack could stand up to Tom in a fight.

Jack had seemed interested, but as long as she remained Tom's girl he had kept his distance. Nevertheless, they had occasionally chatted in the halls and they had remained friends. In college they had seen little of each other until Jack's last year of pre-med. They bumped into each other in the library and he had asked her out on a date. They had hit it off right away. She smiled to herself. She had really liked him in those days. Then Jack went away to medical school and it was harder. She had stayed in touch for another year, but that had meant expensive long distance calls. She remembered days of not hearing from Jack because he was so busy. Then she had met Steve and Jack seemed not to have noticed. Steve swept her off her feet and they were married after only a few months of dating.

Jack had been totally oblivious to the relationship and was stunned, when he had called one night, just before the wedding, to find out that she was even engaged.

It had been almost by accident that she had become Jack's patient. Her husband had changed his medical insurance and without her knowledge, he switched medical offices to the one in which Jack practiced. The first time she had seen Jack there she had nearly fallen off her chair in surprise. He had stayed in decent shape and, besides the gray hair, still had the boyish face and good looks she remembered. He had been almost as surprised as she since he had not known Kathy's married name. He had seemed genuinely glad to see her, but they had not spent time catching up.

Even after Steve died she saw Jack infrequently as she usually had the female physician assistant take care of her annual check ups. Jack had showed up one afternoon, though, at her home when she had been in the midst of depression and self doubt. He had talked with her and had shown real caring. He and Esther had hit it off right away and Jack occasionally dropped by to take her out for ice cream or to help her practice her volleyball. Though she had not seen him often as her personal doctor, at her last visit the PA had suggested that she see Dr. Sharp because of some "concerns" that Kathy had brought forward.

And now Jack was telling her that she had a memory problem.

Kathy had called Jack last night because she had seen how hard this task was on him. She genuinely liked him and had decided to make it easier for him. She would go to another doctor. She thought she had planned out carefully what she wanted to say. Kathy didn't want Jack to think badly of her, though, so she planned to tell him at breakfast today. Now it was hard to think clearly because of the little sleep she had gotten and because of her irritating headache. For some reason it was worse today than it had ever been.

She thought, "It's probably the lack of sleep." She rubbed her eyes and as her sleepiness lessened she felt a little better. She swung out of bed and upon standing felt that the headache had let up significantly. Relieved, she made her way to the bathroom and began to ready herself for her breakfast with Jack.

****

Jack was adding just a drop of cream to his coffee when he saw Kathy at the door of the restaurant. He had to admit she looked great. She had always been very pretty and age had not diminished that quality. He chuckled as he noticed several other men eyeing her appreciatively over their breakfasts. It made him wish this were a date and not a physician-patient meeting. Then again, what was it exactly? He had seen Kathy as a patient yesterday.

He rose as she caught his eye. *What a smile she had this morning.* Kathy was genuinely glad to see him. Maybe there was hope for him yet. The hostess, being very observant, showed Kathy to his table without even being instructed. She gave him a little conspiratorial wink which he doubted anyone else would have noticed.

Kathy greeted him with her hand outstretched. Not the hug of yesterday. However, instead of just shaking his she kept moving forward and gave him a light kiss on his cheek. Stepping back, while still holding his hand, she appraised him.

"Have you started running?" she asked. "You look trimmer than I remember."

They sat opposite each other at the booth while he thought about her question.

"No, I still just walk. I think I'm too old to take up running. It's hard on the knees."

"I run several times a week and you are no older than I," she stated matter-of-factly.

"Yes, but you have been a runner all your life. I think some people are just better suited to running than others." Jack was now clinical. This conversation wasn't what he had expected, but at this moment he didn't really care. He was enjoying himself.

"Is that a medical fact, or do you just think that way?"

"That is a big can of worms. I think I'll dodge the question and just say it's great to see you again Kathy." Jack smiled again and offered her coffee.

She accepted the coffee without cream or sugar and for a moment they sat looking at each other. Just then the waitress appeared from nowhere.

"Do you want to order this morning? Our special is two eggs, hash browns, and toast." Her hair was tightly held by clips and she was wearing a red and white checked apron. Her uniform made her appear to have come from a restaurant decades earlier carrying an order pad in her hands poised to take their order. Her voice was brusque, however, and she appeared a little rushed.

"Kathy, what do you want?" Jack asked.

"Oh I think oatmeal with raisins and brown sugar sounds good. Breakfast is my treat, you know. I asked you here."

Chagrined by not knowing whether to challenge that statement or go ahead and order he looked quickly at his menu. He knew everything on it since he had eaten there at least once a week, but wasn't quite sure what to say.

Looking back to the waitress he answered, "Okay, I'll have the two by two by two please."

When the waitress had picked up their menus and walked away Jack looked back at Kathy. "Kathy, I don't mind paying. You just paid me at my office yesterday to talk to you." It was the wrong thing to say. Jack sometimes didn't have the right tact or skills with women.

Kathy's face darkened a little, "Jack, I don't mind and I'm paying."

Seeing the futility of argument with that terse statement he took a deep breath and sighed. "I'm sorry. Sure, its fine. Do you want to talk about yesterday?"

Kathy couldn't help herself she made a short laugh and said, "Jack you shouldn't jump to conclusions. I guess what I want to talk about involves yesterday, but it affects other things too." Her planned speech was getting fuzzy, but she tried to keep her face unemotional. "I just can't believe that I have a condition as bad as what you think. Jack it scares me. I've known people with Alzheimer's and their lives were terrible. I don't want my children to go through that ... and ... I don't want you to go through it either." The latter part slipped out but she realized that she meant it.

That statement struck Jack hard, "What does that mean?" Jack was getting truly worried. "Kathy, it's what I do. I'll go through it with you as your doctor, whether it is Alzheimer's or something else, whatever you have. It's not just because it is my job, but because we are friends. Besides, I'm not ready to commit myself to a diagnosis. It's still early."

She reached for Jack's hand across the table and looked directly into his face, "Jack, I know you are my friend. Do you realize you are the only person I can think of who has known me so long? Since my parents died, I haven't even seen any one else from home."

"So what do you mean?" Jack was clearly not following where Kathy was going. She wasn't upset with him.

"Jack, you have been my doctor for several years now. I want you to be with me and help me, but as a friend. For my medical problems I'm beginning to think I should see a different doctor." Her words were like a blow to his gut and Jack was genuinely surprised. "Jack, don't take it wrong. I trust you like no one else, but I just think I should consider having a doctor who isn't so close... personally." Tears were beginning to form in her eyes. It wasn't coming out the way she had hoped. Her feelings were getting mixed up with her thinking.

He let go of her hand his head shaking. "If you were going to fire me why did you want to eat breakfast with me?" He was beginning to feel anger well up inside. "I don't expect to be the only doctor you see. Remember I am sending you to Mark Braken-horst, the neurologist."

Kathy now realized her blunder and quickly tried to clarify her position. She stood and walked around to his side of the table and sat next to him. This maneuver effectively blocked his escape until she could soothe his ego. She touched his shoulder. "Jack, you are taking my meaning all wrong. That's just the point. I want you to be there as a friend and being a doctor you can give me great advice. But you will see me as a friend and you won't have to deal with my medical stuff. I still ... care deeply for you, don't you understand?" She took his arm in both hands.

Now Jack was truly surprised. He had tried to be careful to keep his feelings and thoughts private. He had been "clinical" whenever they had talked. He had never taken Kathy to dinner or a movie, yet he knew that he would have liked to do these things. He half turned in his booth to lessen the awkwardness of her hold on him and slipped his arm around her shoulder. The waitress brought their breakfast just then and, seeing them, hesitated. Jack nodded and said, "It's all right- just some bad news."

Kathy burst out laughing, "Is that what you call it?" She beamed at the waitress who was readjusting the place settings.

"I've got a little more private spot if y'all want," she said with an impish smile.

Jack and Kathy looked at each other and Jack led, "No, I think this is okay. We won't make a scene."

Kathy made a "tsch" sound with her tongue and smiled. "A scene? No I guess we won't."

"Well let me know if y'all need anything more." She placed their food before them. "I'll get you some more coffee." She moved away anxious to relate what was going on in her booth to the other staff in the kitchen.

Jack and Kathy sat for a moment in silence taking in the emotions and processing what was happening. At last Jack said, "Kathy I've ... always liked you." He still felt awkward, "I still remember how things were in college. What happened to us?"

Kathy leaned into him, "I don't really know now. You got busy. I got impatient. Then Steve ..."

"Then there was Steve." Jack had a hard time keeping the irritation from his voice.

"Jack, Steve was there. You weren't."

She kissed his cheek again lingering slightly longer. "But now you are and you've been wonderful."

Jack was still puzzled. "Wonderful? I've had to give you bad news and you say 'wonderful'? Now I am even more confused." Jack said still uncomfortable. "Do you want to see another one of my partners or do you think you want to change practices?"

"Well, if I see your partner you might still have to take care of me from time to time, isn't that right?" Kathy asked.

"Yes, but not too often. You've seen the PA's before." He hesitated then started again. "If I'm not your doctor how will I see you?"

She grinned back, "How about taking me on a date? I like movies and dinners et cetera."

It had been a while since he had dated a woman. He had thought, at his age, it might continue that way.

Jack was still confused. "So does that mean you're asking me out? Or just asking me to ask you out?" His eyes glinted and he gave Kathy's hand a little squeeze.

"You can take it however you want," she retorted with an indiscernible, though alluring, look on her face.

"Kathy, I care for you too. I have for a long time." He made a decision to open up to her about things he had never said to anyone. "I know that I thought I was in love with you in high school and even college, but I got ... busy. When I saw you again at the office you were married and had a great life. At that point it just wasn't right to have feelings for you and I've tried to keep our relationship professional." He hesitated, "But I confess that I have thought about you often. I know it's wrong to want another man's wife and against everything I believe."

Now it was Kathy's turn to feel awkward. She tried changing the subject a little, "Jack, why didn't you ever get married?"

He hesitated, "I really don't know. After I finished medical school I had a lot of relationships, but residency was hectic. I eventually just stopped looking. There are a fair number of single and divorced women at church, but my life just stayed busy and I guess I just quit trying. There was one woman, in Africa..." Jack just stopped, staring into space. He didn't want to talk about Sharon. The memory of her was too painful to mention.

Kathy looked at him sympathetically but didn't ask any questions.

Jack shook off his reverie and turned to Kathy. "I can spend a quiet evening alone, now and not feel too lonely." That wasn't completely true. He still ached for companionship. He had a few friends, but they were usually busy with their families. The guys he knew who were single, most were divorced, often wanted to hang around the bars or seemed to feel sorry for themselves. With his call schedule he couldn't take off and go fishing or hunting whenever he wanted. He was involved with a men's group at church and that was good. He said, "God has given me a full life and it has been enough for me."

Kathy read a little pain in his eyes as she looked up from her breakfast. "Jack, I've been lonely too."

Jack realized he had been thinking only of himself. Of course she was lonely. "I'm sorry. It must have been hard."

She didn't weep. She set her face sternly, "It wasn't just his death. I lost him before that."

Jack had known about Steve's affair but had been unable to divulge the information to anyone. He nodded comprehensively. "I think I understand."

"You knew?" Kathy wore a slightly shocked expression. "But ... you couldn't tell me could you?"

Jack looked down at his plate. He didn't want to acknowledge his awareness of her struggle. He also noticed Kathy's hand shaking more than the night before.

"Wow, this day is starting out in an interesting way," he said trying to shift the subject. He then grew more serious. "Kathy I need to say something else... medical, I mean."

"What?"

"I told you I was not certain of your diagnosis. After my exam yesterday I think there could be something else going on besides just a memory problem. That is why I ordered the MRI. Look you can barely hold your coffee cup." He pointed to her right hand which was tremulous. She had even spilled some coffee trying to raise it to her lips.

"What do you mean? I'm just a little upset, thinking about my late husband and all." But she continued to stare at her hand as if it belonged to someone else. Her coffee was spilling over the edge and she set the cup down with a rattle. A little worried she said,

"What else could it be, Jack? Please don't keep me guessing."

"Are you still having the headaches?" he asked and he could see the answer in the startled look on her face.

"It was worse this morning when I woke up, but I feel all right now," Kathy observed. That wasn't exactly true, however. She had noticed that now her stomach was upset. She had thought it was merely the stress of their conversation and her anxiety about bringing up such emotional issues but now she wasn't sure. "I think they scheduled the MRI for Monday. Is that all right?"

"Sure, just let me... I mean let your doctor know if anything changes. Okay?"

"I will. Jack, I didn't bring this up to hurt your feelings."

They continued eating and at length Kathy changed the subject and asked, "What was that about you finding a body yesterday? It was in the news last night."

"Oh, that," he didn't know what he could say. He had failed to ask how much of what he knew could be revealed to others. "It was pretty awful. I don't know if I can talk about it. I had to go down to the police station to give a statement yesterday"

This surprised Kathy, "Why? Couldn't they just talk to you at your office?" Then she grinned and said conspiratorially, "Or do they suspect the good doctor?"

Jack half smiled in reply, "No, I don't think that they may actually harbor suspicions toward me. I had nothing to do with it so I should have nothing to be afraid of. The problem at the moment is that they need a viable suspect. I don't even know if they have identified the victim."

"That sounds terrible," she said. "I was only kidding about them suspecting you. That would be ridiculous." Now Kathy felt a shiver of fear, but also true nausea. She started to say something and was interrupted by an even worse wave of nausea. Without even excusing herself she suddenly rose from the table and rushed into the restroom. Her retching was audible even in the dining area, though no one else seemed to take notice. Jack now felt the doctor side of him take over, but he resisted the impulse to go to the restroom and waited as patiently as possible. In a few minutes she unsteadily returned to the booth with a pasty white appearance on her face.

Jack rose from his seat to help her. "Kathy, maybe we should go right now to the hospital."

She wanted to argue, but felt too empty to put up a defense. She put her head in her hands and said, "I can't believe I got sick so quickly. Oh, my headache."

She reached for her head with both hands trying to sit. In a few seconds she lightly shook her head, as if to clear her vision. Looking up at Jack she said, "All right we can go, but please just get my purse. There's money in the wallet for you to pay them."

Shaking his head with a smile, "Ever the practical one." He motioned to their waitress and she approached cautiously.

"Are you all right ma'am?" she asked tentatively. "I hope it wasn't something you ate."

Jack spoke for her has he began to escort her to the door. "I think she was already coming down with something." He left the payment at the plate along with a generous tip and carefully walked out with Kathy. He spoke to her quietly, "What was that about not being your doctor?"

All Kathy could do was lean against his arm. She felt dizzy and disoriented, "What is wrong? Why do I feel so sick all of a sudden?"

"Maybe you shouldn't have let me know how you feel about me. It's making you sick," he said trying to lighten the situation. "We'll just get to the hospital to check it out. Have you had the nausea before?"

"Oh, I can't think. I don't think so."

Jack helped her into his car. Once seated, she closed her eyes as if the morning light was bothering them.

"Do you want to call one of your kids?" he asked.

"Yes," she said gaining composure. Her head wasn't spinning quite so much now. She reached for her purse to dig for her phone. "Frank won't be at work yet and he is doing well enough that he can probably get off for a while." Before dialing, though, she leaned across the seat and kissed Jack on the cheek. "Thank you, Jack, for being there when I need you."

Jack could only look ahead, fearful of letting his emotions show. He was deeply concerned and genuinely cared about her. Without voicing it he shot a quick prayer to heaven for Kathy.

Kathy speed dialed her oldest son who picked up on the second ring. She explained the situation to him as well as possible without alarming him.

"Just a second, honey. Jack, where should he meet us?"

"Just have him go to the main admissions desk. If you aren't there they will know where you are and they'll have him wait."

She passed this on to Frank who said he would call the rest of family. "Oh, Frank, maybe not yet. Why don't you come alone. We can call them when we know more." She folded her phone closed, once more feeling very ill. "Jack, please stop a second." He pulled to the curb on a side street .

She opened the door and became violently ill once again.

8

In her own office, Detective Rebecca Sweate saw the three pages of evidence which George had given her the day before. She then began to rummage through the other piles on her desk. The tidiness of yesterday was waning. She knew where everything was, but couldn't decide where she wanted to start. She had several cases that required her attention, but her mind was fixed upon the murder case at hand. Their chances of tracking down a murderer grew slimmer for every hour that they fumbled around looking for direction and she would need help. That meant going to the chief, hat in hand, to ask for another plain clothes detective to give her assistance. They did not have that many murder cases in their small city and she hoped he would agree.

Piecing together the file of what she had accumulated thus far, Rebecca gathered up her notes and tried to organize her thoughts. Then she stood and walked across the busy room to the large corner office occupied by Chief of Police Max Barber. Her knock on the door frame caused heads to turn in the office, but his head remained bowed over his own paperwork.

"Good morning Rebecca," he said, at length, without even looking up from his desk. She took a tentative step into his office.

"Good morning sir. I..."

"Where are we on this murder case? Any suspects? Do you know who the victim is yet?" He looked up with a half-smile, his pock-marked face unreadable. His habit was to try to unnerve the recipient of his comments, as he clearly liked being in charge.

"Sir, the investigation is just getting started. We know of only two people with any connection to this case so far and we do not know the identity of the victim. We have questioned the doctor who found the body and he seems legit. We have not been able to find or positively identify the other man, the so-called 'jogger.' He strikes me, in some ways, as more suspicious than the doctor." Rebecca made her report, giving the details with a near monotone voice to avoid the trap of appearing intimidated.

The Chief sat back, considering the information. "Hm. How do you know that there is a jogger? Maybe the murderous doctor made him up."

"Sir, I have considered that option. The doctor has a good reputation. He did not come across as if he were lying or avoiding questions. I met him shortly after we took the call." The chief sat, mute, staring into space. "I could use help on this. I will need to do canvassing and probably a great deal of phone calling. Can you give me Samuelson to help me out?"

"Samuelson? He's barely dry behind the ears. He's been working on the Williams case with Kobacek and Stilley. They might be miffed if I pull him off their case." Barber leaned back and chuckled. He knew that the older detectives were using Samuelson as their gopher for coffee and snacks. He fiddled with his pen as he looked straight at Rebecca. Now he was frowning, but she could see him working things out in his head. Rebecca knew, too, that now was not the time to say anything. He liked to ponder things. "I guess three detectives on a robbery are more than necessary. I'll talk with Kobacek, but I will expect results. Keep me up-dated daily, okay?"

"Thank you, sir. If Samuelson is going to help I'll need him as soon as possible. Can you have him start with me this morning?" she asked evenly. She couldn't believe he had been so easy today.

At first he glared, then softened, "It might be this afternoon." As Rebecca turned to go he said, "How's your mother?"

"My mother, sir?" Rebecca was a little unsure of the question and the abrupt change of direction.

"Yes, I know your father's death was hard on your family. How's she doing?" He seemed genuinely interested and sympathetic. He was leaning on his desk still looking directly at her. This was a side of him she had never seen. He had a tendency to be a lone wolf, keeping to himself. He was big into working out and lifting weights and could run faster than many of the younger officers in his own department. His marriage had created no children and he fell into the habit of working late at the department. His wife had eventually grown weary of waiting at home playing second fiddle to his career and had left him for an insurance executive.

"Well, I haven't talked with her for a while, but she seems to be doing all right. She moved to a townhouse in Omaha a year ago so she doesn't have so much work to do."

"Do you think she would mind a call from an old friend of your father's?" he asked.

That question really shocked her. She hadn't known that her father and the chief had been friends and she had a hard time picturing her mother being interested in chatting about old times with him. "Sir I really don't know. I didn't know you knew my father."

He smiled, "It was really a long time ago, but we were pretty good friends. I used to live in North Carolina too. Isn't that a coincidence? We both just got too busy to stay in touch after I moved here. I had considered talking with her earlier. I thought your mom might be interested just to talk to someone who knew him back then."

She was pleased to hear this from him, "Chief, I think she would be very interested in that. She hasn't made a lot of friends in Omaha yet." She grabbed a sticky note. "Here's her number, but let me call her today just to be sure." She jotted down the phone number, but not the address. She really thought her mother could use some company, but wasn't sure how she felt about that company being her boss.

"Good idea. It might be awkward if I just called her without preamble." He slid the slip of paper across the desk and picked it up. "I'll talk to Kobacek this morning, Rebecca. Have a safe day." He actually winked at her before returning his attention to his paperwork.

As Rebecca returned to her own desk she smiled inwardly at how interestingly the day had begun. Barber had a soft side and no one else had any idea. As she approached her desk she saw that she had visitors. The two uniformed officers with whom she had gone to the crime scene were loitering by her door looking pleased with themselves.

"Hello boys. You look like the cats that got the canary."

Gus's expression changed, "Huh? Oh sure. We have a little interesting info about the doctor."

"Okay, come into my office and let's see what you have." She slid around to her seat and pulled out her own note pad to add their information to what she already had.

"Well, as for yesterday, it looks like he's telling the truth about the time and everything. But uh ... we also found he has military training and has spent some time overseas. He was a doc in the Special Forces. You know that all the Special Forces members get the same training in killing." The officer smiled jauntily at his partner, Mike who nodded in return.

"That's interesting, Gus. Does any of the evidence point to a "Special Forces type" of killing? She said quietly. "It's good to know he has that training, but it doesn't increase the likelihood of his guilt, does it?" She began to stand. "Okay. Keep an eye on him, but I don't think he is going anywhere soon. He has a medical practice to keep him close by. Let's keep him at arms length, but get me the ID on the jogger or find out who the girl is. I think we've spent enough time for now on the doctor. Remember that even though he was trained in the Special Forces, he is still a doctor who cares for the sick." She had tried to stay pleasant, but her patience was wearing a bit thin. Her voice rose with a little more edge than she had intended and the two policemen slunk back a bit.

"Yes ma'am," Gus said. "We really don't have much to go on about the jogger, but the crime scene folks found some other interesting things. As they expanded the ground search they found some tire tracks that could be related and drag marks nearby. Maybe whomever dumped the body drove along the brush first. Otherwise it would have been a long way to carry a body."

"Tire tracks? Hmm that is good, but unless they can find tracks connecting the vehicle to our vic it isn't conclusive. As for the jogger, have you physically gone to the insurance company or tried to find out if anyone else saw this guy? Did you think about a security camera at the parking lot entrance to the bike path? We need results and some hard thinking on this point."

Rebecca was standing now, her body language aggressive.

She said, "I hope to have another detective on this soon. Until then, see what else you can find out. I'll work on trying to identify the victim."

Gus and Mike were just outside her office when she thought of something else. "Why don't you send Josie over to Dr. Sharp's office to see if he can provide enough description for a sketch?" She hesitated, thinking of what the Chief had said about the possibility of the doctor lying. "No, on second thought, I'll take care of it. Maybe we should ask the doctor to come down here again. It will keep him a little off balance. He may still be able to help us with more than just a description."

"You sure? I could call his office. Sorry if we got off track." Gus said quietly.

"No, it was right to check him out. I think I'll put the new detective on him, though, once he is involved. I guess we can't rule out any potential suspects just yet. Especially not until we find out more about our victim."

Somewhat mollified, Gus and the silent Mike ambled out of the large squad room. As they reached the hallway Mike looked over at Gus and said,

"Maybe she kind of likes the doc." Gus looked back raised his eyebrows.

He answered back," Maybe, but I don't think she likes men as a general principle."

9

Jack pulled up to the emergency entrance of St. Francis Medical Center and jumped out. Having called ahead on his cell, there was an attendant waiting with a wheel chair. He went around to Kathy's side of the car where she sat groaning about her headache and the nausea. He was amazed at how quickly her condition had changed. She had gotten very ill so suddenly he knew something major was wrong. Helping her into the wheelchair, he then pushed it along and the attendant followed them through the automatic door. As Jack was wheeling Kathy past the admissions desk, a young woman called out to him,

"Sir, you can't just go in there..."

He flashed his physician's ID at her and tried a wan smile. "Please buzz me in. You can get the information you need in the room."

As he had turned, she recognized him from the frequent times he had been in to admit patients of his own. "No problem, Dr. Sharp, Sorry." She was a little puzzled because she had not thought he was married, but it looked like he must be escorting his ill wife. Her friend Connie from the out-patient department would know what was up. She sometimes worked with Dr. Sharp in their weekly disability clinic.

Jack moved on through the swinging doors and asked the nurses to which room he should go. Jackie Nun began to make her way around the nurses' station and pointed,

"Room One, Dr. Sharp." Clipboard in hand, she took charge of the situation.

"Bruce, will you please help this woman into the bed?"

"I got her," he said and smiled at Dr. Sharp as he expertly guided Kathy into the treatment room.

Kathy saw only that it was a stark room filled with mysterious instruments, lights, cabinets, and an ominous gurney in the center of the room. The fluorescents were blinding and because of her headache she covered her eyes and moaned loudly. Bruce flipped a switch and the bright white was replaced by a warm incandescent side light which still providing adequate brightness for working in the room.

"Oh, thank you," she managed to say as she began to sob. "Jack, I feel so awful. What is wrong with me?"

Jack had stepped back in preparation to fill the nurse in, but at this question he reached out and helped Kathy out of the wheel-chair. "I'm not sure yet, but we'll have an ER doctor in here very soon to start looking at you."

Bruce produced a cloth hospital gown with blue lettering in a pattern over the material. "Ma'am, we'll need you to take off your clothes so the doctor can examine you. Do you need any help?"

Sounds in the room seemed harsh and amplified to her ears. She looked at him and despite her feeling of profound nausea and now dizziness answered,

"Young man, I think I had better do this myself."

He pulled a curtain around her, "We'll be right out here if you need anything and the doctor will be in soon."

Jack spoke to the nurse, Jackie, giving her the details of his meeting with Kathy the previous day and the events of the morning. The records clerk walked up.

"May I go in to get her information?"

Jack was about to say something, but the nurse gave him a "look" and he thought better of it. She then motioned that the records clerk could go on into the room.

"Dr. Sharp, I know you want to help, but please let us do our jobs." Jackie was a no-nonsense ER nurse with many years of experience. She was not intimidated by even the toughest doctor and the emergency department ran smoothly under her tutelage.

"I'll do her vitals and then get Dr. Shamborg. She's in with a fractured hip at the moment."

Jack relented and paced outside the room. He realized that the nurse was right. His emotions were on edge at the moment and he needed to change roles. Nevertheless, he fidgeted, needing something to do while he waited for the more mundane things to be accomplished. He poked his head into the room and said, "I'm going to step out for a few minutes, but I'll be right back."

He looked at his watch and saw that it was still early. He didn't have to worry about his office just yet. He went out and moved his car to a parking spot. Frank, Kathy's son, pulled into the lot just then.

Jack met him with his hand out, "Frank, I'm glad you're here."

"Doctor Jack, is Mom all right?" Frank had a very worried look on his face and his hair was disheveled. Kathy must have caught him just getting ready for the day.

"We don't know yet what is going on. I have my suspicions, but, at your mother's request, I have stepped back from my "doctor" role for now. The ER doctor will see her and make her own assessment. Do you want some coffee?" Intimately familiar with the department Jack knew where the coffee maker was.

"Sure. Why did Mom ask you to 'step back?' I want you here."

"Maybe you should talk to her about it. Okay? Anyway, I want another set of eyes to check her out."

"Yeah, I'm sorry. Can I see Mom?" He looked expectantly at Jack and somewhat nervously looked around the waiting room.

"In a few minutes the nurse and admissions people will be finished. I'll get you some coffee and they might be done by then." He clasped the younger man's shoulder and patted him on the back. "We are doing the best things we can at the moment." Jack did not go into his current suspicions, opting to wait for tests to be completed. He ushered Frank to a seat. They would all know the truth soon anyway.

Jack reached the coffee maker and filled two cups. He picked up a plastic cup of cream in case Frank might use that, too. As he was approaching the waiting area nurse Nun walked out of Kathy's room. "We're done with the basics now doctor if you want to go in."

"Thanks Jackie. Her son is here too, so I'll get him and be right back." He smiled at her, trying to ease the tension a little, and walked down the hallway. Pushing open the door he called out to Frank, "Here's your coffee. We can go back now."

Frank stood and moved quickly toward Dr. Sharp. He grasped the coffee cup as if his life depended upon it and they went together to room one. On entering, they noted that the curtain had been pulled back. Kathy now lay on the gurney with the head portion raised up and she looked somewhat better.

"Hi, Mom. How are you feeling?" Tears stung his eyes and he had trouble keeping his own emotions under control. He wrapped his mother in his big arms and said. "Mom, I hope everything is okay. I love you."

Kathy remained calm, but was taken aback by the emotions of her son. "Frank, it's okay. I'm just sick and nauseated this morning. I don't know why. I feel a little better now but my head still hurts."

Just then Dr. Aneta Shamborg stepped into the room. She was not a tall woman, but proportionate to size. She was in her early thirties and wore her dark black hair cut evenly just above her shoulders and for work, held back from her face by twin clasps. She wore a white smock with her name embroidered in cursive on the left pocket below the emblem of the hospital. Pens festooned the pocket and a stethoscope hung from her neck. She wore light blue hospital scrubs and white athletic shoes with socks.

"Hi, folks. Dr. Sharp, it's good to see you again." She gave him a pleasant nod. They had had many late night conversations in the emergency room while he admitted patients. Dr. Shamborg had been at St. Francis for about four years and was well liked by the staff and other physicians.

Glancing down at the computer printout Dr. Shamborg said, "Mrs. Sanders?" she began, "I have the nurse's notes here, but what can you tell me about how you have been feeling?"

"How far back do you want me to go?" she asked uncertainly.

"When did you begin to feel ill? I mean, when do you think your health began to change?" Dr. Shamborg was beginning her ritual ingrained from thousands of patient encounters. 'Let the patient tell you what is wrong with them.' It was sage advice she had received from some medicine professor years earlier. With no prior knowledge of the patient she had the luxury of having a fresh perspective on her condition untainted by prior relationship.

Kathy began with the past few days. She didn't mention the memory problem because it had not seemed like "an issue" to her.

She spoke of her headache and very recent nausea. Kathy also mentioned feeling light headed at times as well as a little unsteady. Jack was surprised. He thought he had asked that question and she had said 'no'. This underscored the value of Aneta re-asking some important basic questions, he thought. Remaining in the background he kept his peace and listened to the interview.

Jack noticed as Kathy spoke her face began to relax and there was a quiet strength that had returned. She appeared more confident and, he had to admit, even more beautiful than he had previously thought. Her make-up was a little smudged and her hair awry, but her eyes were bright and cheerful despite the gravity of the situation.

Once Kathy had filled Dr. Shamborg in, it was his turn to render his observations. Jack said, "Well the only other thing she didn't mention was that she has had some memory issues lately. We were considering getting an MRI scan of the brain for completeness sake. Her lab-work has been unremarkable and she has been basically healthy until now. I didn't find anything localizing on her exam except a mild right handed tremor."

Dr. Shamborg asked some questions of Frank and then launched into her physical exam. She was thorough, and Jack noticed that she seemed unhurried. Perhaps that was for his benefit, though she had no office appointment schedule to meet. When she was finished she turned to Jack,

"Jack, and Mrs. Sanders, I agree that an MRI is in order. I also found a tremor on the right side. It is fairly pronounced and there is objective weakness in the right arm and leg. I think there is something in the central nervous system going on so we will set up the test ASAP." She left quickly giving verbal orders to the nurse. Jack overheard the words "mannitol and dexamethasone" mentioned. These were drugs used to reduce intracranial pressure.

Grasping the chair with one hand he slid it close to the bedside and without a word took hold of Kathy's hand. Her eyelids trembled but remained closed. She gave him a light squeeze as she returned his grip holding onto his hand. Frank sat and turned away, emotionally spent.

"Kathy," Jack began, "Before we do anything else, I really want to pray with you. I know that God knows all that is going on even when we don't."

"Do you really think it's that bad?" She looked worried.

This brought a warm smile to Jack. "I pray when I know we need guidance not when we are out of choices. I know it helps. Is it okay?" He looked straight into her eyes as he said this.

"Yes, of course, I'm sorry I thought you meant..."

"Its okay," he said as he clasped both her hands. The nurse was just entering the room as they bowed their heads. Not sure what else would be appropriate, she bowed her head, too.

"Dear Lord. We need your strength and guidance. I pray that whatever is going on will be made clear with the tests we do today. Lord we don't know what to think, but You know what is going on. We ask for Your comfort and place this burden on You. In Jesus name. Amen."

"Thank you, Jack. That was about the best thing anyone has done for me for quite a while." She pulled his hand to her cheek as tears slipped down her cheeks.

Jack said, "I am going to call a good friend of mine. Mark Brackenhorst is a very good neurologist. Once we have the MRI back I'm going to go over it with him and ask him to come take a look at you. Is that all right?"

Jack wanted to comfort her, but he also felt a need to be acting. He had never been good at just sitting at the bedside. A physician's presence alone often gave patients comfort. Jack often prayed with them and held their hands, but he rarely sat for lengthy sessions. Rising, he nodded at Frank and the nurse who was about to take another blood pressure. She smiled up at Jack, too.

Rounding the nurse's station Jack asked the unit secretary to contact Dr. Brackenhorst. He gave her his own cell number for the neurologist to call back. Just then his cell phone rang. He jokingly said, "Wow that was quick!" He flipped it open, "Hello."

"Dr. Sharp? This is Officer Wilson from yesterday."

"Oh, hello, Officer. Yes, I remember you. You drove me to the station."

"Yes sir. I'm calling because Detective Sweate would like you to visit with her again. We were also hoping you could work with a sketch artist to make a likeness of the guy who was jogging."

Jack frowned and thought for a few seconds. "Officer, I'm in the middle of a crisis with a patient. Is it possible to come at the noon hour?"

"Sure Doc. If that is more convenient. The sooner we have his description the better. I know you've got a lot to do. I'll let the detective know. Thanks Doc."

"That's all right Officer. It's just turning into a horrendous day."

"Yeah, I hear ya. It's kind of like that for us too. Have a great day." The irony of the officer's last comment struck him as he hung up and Jack was left thinking about his own messed up schedule.

"Well at least it's Friday," he said to no one in particular. He glanced at his watch. "Great. Now I'm late for clinic this morning too." Feeling like he needed to "act" like a doctor, he looked over at the room Kathy was in. He wasn't part of her family and had no reason to hang around. She was in capable hands at the moment and he had other patients whom he needed to see.

"Nurse," he said to one of the nurses sitting at the nurse's station. "Would you please have Jackie call me as soon as we have any results?"

"Sure Dr. Sharp. Shall I call your office?" the young woman said pleasantly.

"No. Use my cell number. The unit secretary has it." He stepped over to Kathy's room and in a more professional manner stood near the bedside.

"Kathy," he began, "I have to get to the office. I'm sorry I can't stay here right now. As soon as they have any reports I'll talk to you. Okay?"

Kathy smiled up at him. "I know you need to go. You have already been so helpful. Did you talk to the neurologist?"

"No, he hasn't called me back yet. I'll try him again if he doesn't call soon." He shook hands again with Frank. At the door on his way out he turned once more and winked at Kathy, who waved goodbye.

10

Rebecca couldn't sit still. Her desk just wasn't inviting. The three separate piles of paperwork needing attention were acting like opposing magnets, pushing her away. She had few facts to go on in her murder investigation and those were not getting her very far. She needed much more. Then the three pages of evidence came into her field of vision. She hesitated for a moment and then picked up the pages. She thumbed through the paperwork and then reached for the notes she had taken in her interview with Doctor Sharp. Reading down her own list, Rebecca then looked back at the list of evidence. Dr. Sharp had told her what he had seen. It hadn't meant anything to her at the time but something didn't quite match up. It was what the doctor had seen on the body.

She pored over George's list several times.

Dr. Sharp had mentioned a necklace. There was jewelry, but no necklace on the properties list. She picked up her phone and called the evidence room.

George was still there.

Rebecca breathed a sigh of relief.

"Hello," he said in his low voiced slow drawl. "This is George in evidence."

"George..." Rebecca started.

"Rebecca! You come see me and now you're callin' me. Did you want to set up that date with me?" He chuckled in his deep and quiet, pleased voice.

Rebecca smiled in spite of herself. "Not this time, George. I wonder if you could use that wonderful memory and help me out?"

Cautiously he said, "Yes, I can try. What do you need?"

"On the case we were just accessing do you remember any necklace being entered as evidence?"

"A necklace? Give me a second. I have to get the gray matter working," he said calmly. "A necklace," he repeated. "No, there was no necklace in the evidence. There were two bracelets, a watch, and a ring. I'm sure of it, Rebecca."

She didn't ask again if he was sure. "Thank you so much George. I'll think about that date."

"Okay. Just don't tell my wife," he laughed knowing it was all in jest.

Slowly hanging up the phone Rebecca sat staring at the paper. *A necklace missing. When did it go missing and where did it go? Who could have taken it? If the doctor had picked it up, why would he have mentioned it to me?* This was a mystery she could not fit to the facts as she knew them. Unconsciously she shook her head as she wrote down her questions.

As her hand had just about laid the papers in a drawer the phone at her desk rang. At first she stared at it like it was a foreign object. Then, blinking, she picked it up on the third ring. "Hello. Detective Sweate."

"Detective, we have a call from a Bonnie Ogilvie about your body. Can I put her through?" The officious voice of the operator, whose cubby in the basement of the building was no bigger than a prison cell, sounded tinny and distant.

Coming instantly out of her reverie she stammered, "Yes, put her through."

"Hello?" came a strained aged female voice on the other end of the line, "Is this the detective working on the ... murder case?" The voice was tremulous and Rebecca recognized fear in the other party.

"Yes, ma'am. My name is Detective Rebecca Sweate. I must tell you that our conversation is being recorded. How can I help you?"

"Oh. I see. Well, that's all right. Um, I saw the TV news this morning that you found a body of a young woman?" She said this all as more of a question pleading for an answer.

"Yes ma'am. May I have your name please?"

"Oh, yes. I'm Bonnie Ogilvie. My niece has been working in Chicago and the day before yesterday she called. Well, she said she and a friend were going to come by and would need a place to stay for a night. It was nice of her to call. It has been some time since she visited us. They came by to drop of some things then went out again. She said she would be late, but she never showed up later."

She burst into tears at this point and it took a few minutes of consolation for Rebecca to get her to continue.

"Ms. Ogilvie..."

"It's Mrs. My husband is Fred."

"Mrs. Ogilvie, what is your niece's name and how old is she?"

"Her name is Alicia Winters. She's my late sister's daughter and she is twenty eight."

"Mrs. Ogilvie, could she just have decided to stay somewhere else?"

"I thought of that, but she hasn't answered her cellular phone. She doesn't have a phone in her apartment she just uses the cellular one. Oh, I hope she's all right." Again Mrs. Ogilvie quietly began weeping.

"Mrs. Ogilivie, the young woman we have my not be your niece. I'm going to send an officer to your house. We will want your statement and a little later we will need you to come down to the morgue. Do you want your husband to come?"

"No, he's at work, but I'll be here all day." Rebecca made her arrangements and they hung up. She then dialed Gus's cell phone and relayed this new information to him. Maybe now they would get somewhere. She left a message for Dr. French, the medical examiner, that he would be getting a visitor later. She sat back in her chair. Those piles were no more inviting, but now she had energy to work on them. She started with the top form and she began to fill in the blanks.

****

Half an hour into her paperwork, Rebecca was interrupted by a form moving in front of her. She looked up and saw a tall young man wearing a wrinkled white shirt, unpressed navy suit and a narrow dark tie. His dark suit appeared to hang from his slender shoulders. His lanky appearance aside, though, she knew that he was no weakling. He had been a finalist in three local marathons in the past two years. Justin Samuelson was a young detective as she had once been, anxious to earn his "stripes."

"Good morning Detective Sweate." His face was smooth and she almost wondered if he was shaving yet.

83

"Today, Justin, you may call me Rebecca." Her half smile was intended to let him know that this was a privilege. "As of now we will be working together. Were you able to tie up loose ends on your other case?"

"Lieutenant Kobacek said he would finish the paperwork. Of course I know that means my name probably won't even be on the report." His look of chagrin was obvious.

"I'm sorry I interrupted your big case Justin."

"No, don't get me wrong. I'm glad I can work with you. Those guys just use me as their grunt. Besides I haven't worked on a homicide before."

Now he seemed like a puppy sidling up to his master, thankful for a tender morsel.

"What have you heard about this case?" she asked.

"I know it's a homicide and I heard that the ID on the victim is still unknown and it was all over the news about the local doctor being involved somehow." He seemed pleased with himself for what he had gleaned from office scuttlebutt and the news.

"Well, that's basically true, but there is much more to it so far. And now we may have a lead on the vic. There's a lot to do in a homicide investigation and we don't have much to go on yet. Pull up a chair. You may find you're not as happy to be here as you think."

Justin slid a chair from the squad room into her office and sat down across the desk from her. Rebecca took her notepad from her desk and looked up. "First of all don't let the media sway your thinking. They will put spin on everything they report. They want headlines. We want results. We now know the cause of death and we are actually classifying this as a 'murder.' You know the difference?"

Justin nodded. Homicide could be an accidental death but murder was intentional.

"As for the doctor, he can help us, but at the moment I currently think less of him as a suspect and more as witness." She went down the items in her notes while Justin listened and took notes of his own. She noticed he was using some kind of electronic device for note-taking. "Justin what is that?"

"This is my PDA," he replied proudly. "I find it much easier to organize my notes if I do them electronically."

"Justin you have to keep hand-written notes. They are admissible in court and they have to be in your own hand writing." She was puzzled because he had been here long enough to know the law and the rule of detective work.

"Ah, Rebecca, I see you haven't been kept up to date on the latest technology. You see I write them on the face of the PDA in my own hand and it stores them that way. I can print them off just like that. But I also have a little program that turns them into a word processor document, then I can do this." He reached over to Rebecca's computer printer and unplugged the USB cable. He took out a small object from his pocket, inserted the USB plug in one side and set it on the desk. He performed a few maneuvers on the PDA and suddenly the printer sprang to life.

When the page was finished, Justin proudly presented it to his new "partner." "Here is a perfectly legible copy of my notes."

Rebecca looked at the sheet with great surprise. Before her was half a page of printed material in outline order, and as Justin had said, perfectly legible. Stunned for a moment she just stared at Justin.

"As long as I have the original this is admissible as evidence in court. The good thing about this is that I can organize it on my computer. You should get one." His smile was genuine, but his comments only made her feel old.

She sat back and thought a second. She was pleased to have such an intelligent young man working with her, but she wanted to get the initiative back.

"All right boy genius you can teach me about your toys later. Let me get back to my notes." She disliked computers except when they found things she couldn't find on her own. She couldn't see herself changing to one of those PDA things, but it was intriguing.

"I would like you to take charge of picking up the doctor, Dr. Jack Sharp. He said he could come in to work with a sketch artist at noon. Gus Wilson has talked with him, but I want you to finalize his statement. Maybe we can let him get back to his life a little sooner that way." Rebecca jotted down Dr. Sharp's phone number and office address. "Take it easy on him for now. We want his cooperation. He is a busy man. He doesn't really fit as a suspect but we can't totally rule him out yet."

"Okay, Rebecca. I'll check in with him and talk with you later this afternoon." He slipped his PDA into its case and clipped it to his belt.

"Justin, where's your weapon?" Rebecca asked as she looked once again at him.

His Cheshire grin made him look even younger. He opened his jacket to reveal a shoulder harness. "Dick Tracy was one of my favorite comics. I bought this when I became a detective." He slipped a snub-nosed .38 revolver from his shoulder holster.

"That isn't department issue. You have to have special permission to carry anything other than a nine millimeter." She said somewhat, irritated.

"Sure. I have it. Anyway, when was the last time you needed yours?" If I need more than six shots I have reloads."

Rebecca shook her head her face growing dark. "I'll discuss it more with you later, but I'll let you know now that I would prefer that you had an automatic with a full magazine." She waved him out of her office dismissively and returned to her own work.

Justin realized that whatever goodwill he had engendered with his PDA demonstration was just wiped out. He owned a standard issue nine millimeter semi-automatic pistol, though he had never even fired his weapon in the line of duty. He loved his little thirty eight! Why would he ever need more bullets than his .38 allowed?

11

Once back at his building, Jack climbed the stairs to his office. As he walked through the waiting room, he felt that all eyes instantly were on him. Even his staff members were staring. He tried to brush it off, but began to wonder what the news had actually said about him. At his desk he found piles of charts. This was typical at the start of the day, but for some reason these were at least thirty percent higher than usual. His first patient was scheduled in just fifteen minutes; he sat down and began to deal with the multitudes of reports, phone messages, and lab results before him.

After a few minutes, he noticed his nurse manager standing at the doorway of his office. She was smiling, but he could see strain on her face. "Amy. Hi, how are you today?"

"Oh I'm fine Doctor Sharp. Um can I talk to you for a minute?" She was hesitant and quiet, not like her usual gregarious self.

"Sure, Amy come on in. What's up?" He was beginning to be concerned that she had some trouble or family problem. "Go ahead have a seat and close the door."

"No that's okay. Your first three patients called already. The phones weren't on so they left messages with the answering service."

"What did they call about?" Jack was now a little annoyed and beginning to wonder where this was headed.

"They cancelled their appointments. Dr. Jack, did you see the news this morning?" Amy was now showing concern and it looked like she was concerned about *him.*

"No, I had to meet with a patient and then I went to the hospital. What did they have to say? I told the reporters just what I witnessed and that the police had questioned me about this."

"Oh Dr. Jack !" Now her calm façade began to break. "They showed you turning away from the cameras and shielding your face. They didn't air anything that you said. It looked like you were trying to hide from them and the police called you a 'person of interest.' I'm so worried. It made you look like some kind of criminal when they did that."

"Great!" He shook his head. He had kept his cool until now, but he was starting to realize that this was having a bigger impact in his life than he could have expected. He ran his hand through his hair. "Are the phones on now?"

"Yes. I think more of your patients will cancel."

"Amy, listen. I was just out for my walk. I had nothing to do with this. How can they expect people to get involved if they get raked over the coals like this?"

"I don't know. People in town know you, so I suppose the news media knows they can make it a bigger story."

Jack sat bewildered for a few moments. "Can you call all the staff together in the nursing station for me please?" He had made up his mind. He would have to play hard ball now and get through this situation. While Amy went to round up the staff he walked down the hall to Doug Katzberg's office. Around Doug's desk he saw miscellaneous parts of office machinery strewn on a table in the corner. Doug was clinic office manager, and he was also chief trouble-shooter and repairman.

"Doug, I guess I have a problem." He started in earnest.

"Yes, Boss I think so. Let me ask the question and get it out of the way. Did you do it or was it Colonel Mustard with a wrench?" His grin was inviting and Jack knew instantly that he did not have to worry about his long-time friend.

"No, the butler did it." Their combined laugh lightened the atmosphere. "All joking aside, I guess my patients are more on the fence than you, thanks to the news media. Doug, I think I should take some time off and try to get this behind me. What do you think?" He really wanted Doug's opinion. He had never faced this kind of thing before.

"Jack, I don't know. If you keep going 'business as usual' people may be more inclined not to worry."

"Did you know that my first three patients have already cancelled?"

"No, I wasn't aware of that." He furrowed his forehead and drummed his desk. "Well if the patients don't come I guess you haven't helped yourself if you keep working. What will you do?"

"I don't intend to leave town. That *would* look suspicious. I think I need some time for ... other things." Jack hadn't thought he meant Kathy, but her face flashed in his mind as he said this.

"Jack, stick out the day and then see where it goes."

"Doug, you're probably right, but I think I need to get this over quickly. I want to talk to the reporters. But before I can do that I need to talk to that detective again. I asked Amy to get the staff together. I've made up my mind. As of now I'm on vacation. Okay?"

Doug could see that argument would be futile and gave a small shrug.

"What about your being on call?" he asked.

"I'll talk to the other three about that. Maybe I can take phone calls and leave the admissions to them."

"Okay, Boss. It's not like you use up all your vacation. I'll mark you down and we'll start calling patients."

"Somehow, I don't think it will be difficult to cancel most of the appointments. Give me two weeks off and we'll go from there." He reached for Doug's hand. Jack's expression was ominous.

"Just two weeks. Don't go thinking you're on too long a leash."

Jack walked out of Doug's office and into the back of the office suite. Most of the staff members were there. They looked a bit anxious having discussed the already circulating rumors.

Jack began, "Hi, everyone. I know you have all seen the news and you know the police were here in force yesterday. They might be back too. Right now you know almost as much as I do. I don't want what is going on to disrupt the office any more than it has already, so I'm going to take some time off. I am not guilty or in trouble so you don't have to worry about that. However, I don't think the police want me to give out details about what happened. Here is what should have been reported..." He went on to give a brief sketch of what had happened the previous day. "If the police come back asking questions just tell them what you know and give them honesty. I hope things will quiet down very soon. I could use some time to myself anyway." He answered some general questions and sent everyone back to work.

Then Jack called, "Amy, could you come to my office please?"

Amy glanced around with a worried expression. Someone said "uh-oh" and everyone laughed. Sometimes "come to my office" meant you were in trouble.

Once in his office, Jack said, "Do you think that will help?"

Amy was pleased that Dr. Sharp would ask her opinion. "Doc, we trust you. No one here seriously thinks 'you done her in'. I still don't know what the patients will do."

Jack grinned at her expression and leaned back in his chair. "If people leave the practice because of rumor or press coverage maybe we can't help that. I hope most reasonable people will give me the benefit of the doubt." He added, "I hope the police do too." He thought a second debating whether to mention Kathy. "Kathy Sanders is worse today. I had to take her to the ER."

"You? Were you ... at her place?" Her eyebrows were raised in question.

"Huh? No! We were having breakfast at Greenfields."

That generated another smile. "I see."

Jack, now slightly embarrassed said, "It was just breakfast." He went on to explain her general condition. "Would you ask the ladies to pray for her at your prayer meeting? Don't give any medical details. Just ask them to pray."

"Of course, Dr. Jack. We meet at noon on Fridays. And ... we'll pray for you." She stood to leave, "I hope everything goes okay. Have a great couple of weeks. You need some time off anyway." Then with a wink and a sly grin on her way out she said, "And say 'hi' to Kathy."

Jack waved her away. Once Amy had gone, he glanced around his office. It was rather messy so he decided to at least straighten things up before leaving later. He checked once more with his front office to see if any patients had arrived. The answer was negative. Jack then cleaned and filed for about half an hour. He dictated a few letters and signed some previous dictation.

Then he tucked a few things he wanted to take home under his arm, flipped off the light and closed his door.

12

Once again in Dr. French's domain, Rebecca steeled herself for the nauseating odor that permeated every nook and cranny of the facility. No matter what cleansers were used, the smell could not be completely expunged. Vanilla candles or piney window hangers merely ratcheted up the complexity of scents without improving the atmosphere. Soon the officer and Mrs. Ogilvie would arrive and she wanted to be present when the body was viewed. It wasn't that she was, in any way, suspicious of this woman, but the initial shock of seeing a deceased loved one sometimes opened people up and made them more talkative.

She poked her head into the sterile interior of the morgue area. It was small with just enough space for the four refrigerator drawers and the autopsy table with its accoutrements. Sarah, Dr. French's assistant, was there quietly waiting for the family member she knew would be coming to see the body of the deceased woman. Rebecca had met her before and knew her to be a sober, heavy young woman. Her long dark hair was now rolled up and tucked beneath a surgical cap.

"Hi ,Sarah. Mrs. Ogilvie will be down in a few minutes. How are you doing these days?"

"I'm fine, Detective Sweate. I got accepted to medical school," she put forth proudly. "I got an early acceptance so I won't actually start until next year, but I'm in."

"That's great! Sarah I'm impressed, said Rebecca.

"I know. Dr. French really encouraged me to go this direction, but my options are wide open. Not many people get accepted this early." Her expression changed suddenly as her eyes widened and focused behind Rebecca.

Rebecca turned and saw that a female officer was escorting a "50-something" year old woman down the stairs. She gave another quick smile to Sarah and moved to the door of the autopsy suite. The door closed behind her as she met Mrs. Ogilvie.

"Hello ma'am. I'm detective Rebecca Sweate; we spoke on the phone."

"Bonnie Ogilvie," was all the woman could get out. Mrs. Ogilvie's face was filled with dread and Rebecca could tell that this was an extremely foreign experience for this poor woman.

"We'll be with you, but if you want some time alone please let us know. Are you ready?"

"Honey, is anyone ever ready for this?" Rebecca let the question hang. They pushed through the doors and approached Sarah.

Sarah quietly turned and opened the latch on the drawer. The body was draped and laid on a metal table which slid soundlessly from the wall. She pulled the drawer so that about two thirds of the body was in the room, facilitating viewing. Glancing up at Mrs. Ogilvie Sarah reached on either side of the body's head to grasp the thin sheet. Rebecca watched Bonnie's face, rather than the corpse, as the sheet was drawn back. Her expression which had initially shown fear and anxiety now softened to a much sadder countenance.

"Oh dear," she began as she moved toward the drawer. "Oh dear, it's not my niece." Tears were streaming down her cheeks. "It's not my poor Alicia, but I know who this is." She was sobbing now, whether from relief of not finding her niece or sadness at the loss of an acquaintance, Rebecca was not sure. "This girl is Alicia's friend who came here with her from Chicago." And that was all they got from Bonnie for a while as she began crying in earnest with a mixture of relief and remorse.

The police officer showed Mrs. Ogilvie back through the doors toward the street. Rebecca asked that she be taken to one of the interview rooms at the police station and she thanked Sarah. She told her to let Dr. French know that they had a possible identity and would have more details soon.

*****

Jack was puzzled that he had not yet heard anything from the hospital, either from the neurologist or the emergency room. Once out of the office he decided to return to the hospital rather than go straight home. He felt obliged to see this situation through. He was sure now that they were not dealing with a "simple" case of dementia. Something more sinister and dangerous going on with Kathy. The severe nausea and headache were pointing a different direction. He was fairly certain they would receive an answer from the MRI.

His office was only a few minutes from the hospital. Having driven this way many times in the past he felt like he was on autopilot heading toward the hospital. The physician's parking lot was, thankfully, nearly empty. Most physicians would have finished their rounds by now and only surgeons and hospital-based physicians would be parking there now.

He pulled into a space and looked around. He was always amazed at the luxury vehicles casually parked here. Even if one didn't know where the physician's lot was located, merely seeing the Lexus, Audi, Jaguar, and Mercedes hood ornaments would be tell-tale signs. Jack had never longed for such cars, but couldn't help feeling a little envy at the level of income it must take to own one. He did not regret becoming a family physician though the financial prospects were not stellar. He wondered at how two medical students with equal abilities who chose slightly different fields could end up having such vastly different levels of income. Several of his physician friends took home four to five times his annual income. They worked no harder than he, but reimbursement was vastly different for certain specialties.

"You have to quit thinking like that," he told himself. "You'll just get jealous." He knew he had had a good life. He was not suffering and never had to worry about losing his job.

He entered the hospital and made his way to the reception desk.

"Hi, Shirley!" He said with enthusiasm. "How are things here today?"

"Hello, Dr. Sharp. I'm just fine and you look like you're having a good day. Shouldn't you be in your office? I know I didn't call you." Shirley smiled sweetly at Jack and held up a finger while she answered a call on her headset.

When she was off the call Jack answered her, "You know how it is. I just work when I want to. Could you page Dr. Brackenhorst for me? I think he is still in the hospital. He should be doing consults today."

She did as he asked and then her eyes got big. "I saw you on the news, didn't I? Are you mixed up in some murder? Maybe I shouldn't talk to you." She said this in a mocking tone with a smile indicating that she didn't mean it.

He said and winked at her. "I'm just a witness, but it has caused some ... hmm... let's say 'disruption' of my schedule."

"Well I hope everything works out all right. Oh, here is Dr. Brackenhorst. You can take it on that phone over there." She turned and pointed to a dictation station where he could see a telephone.

Jack picked up the receiver. "Mark, how are you?"

"Hi Jack. I'm fine. Say I was just about to call you. Are you in the hospital?" Mark seemed rushed as usual. He often had several dozen consults to see in a day and little time to himself.

"I'm at reception," Jack answered.

"Meet me in radiology. I have some things to show you." With that short message he was off the line and Jack looked at the receiver a second before putting it down on the cradle.

"Bye, Shirley." Jack waved and headed down the hall. He realized it must be important or his friend would have told him more details over the phone.

A few minutes later Jack and Mark were shaking hands in greeting. "Jack, you need to come over for dinner some evening. Betty is dying to cook for someone other than me."

"Okay, when are you off call?" Jack smiled as he remembered the last gourmet meal Mark's pretty wife had prepared. "Why don't you just leave me a voice mail or email me with a date and we'll see. What are you being so secretive about?"

Mark's professional face came up and he put on his reading glasses as he turned toward the computer monitor. "Your patient, Jack, has a large tumor right here." Jack thought he was prepared for bad news, but the suddenness of it took him off guard. "I'm afraid I don't think it is a meningioma either. It looks like a glioma or it may be an astrocytoma. See where it seems to invade here and here?" Mark looked back at Jack and could tell Jack's face was ashen even in the low lighting. "Jack, what's the matter?"

Jack exhaled, "I guess I just know this patient too well. I thought all she had was memory loss until today. She got very ill when we were having breakfast together."

"I see," said Mark looking back at the screen. He was silent for several seconds. "Jack this is not without hope. It is in a relatively accessible area of the brain. Mack Clark is top-notch in this type of surgery. She'll probably need radiation too, but she might still do all right." He was trying to soften the blow because any brain tumor was bad news. Even non-malignant tumors can keep coming back and even kill the patient if they can't be completely removed.

"Have you examined her yet Mark?" Jack was a little dazed. He was not looking forward to giving this news to Kathy.

"I did see her. Kathy, right?" Seeing Jack nod he went on, "She has already had dexamethasone and, other than the tremor, I didn't find much. If it is any consolation I would not have been able to diagnose this without an MRI."

Jack looked at the floor, "Thanks, Mark. I appreciate that, but it doesn't make the news any better. Is there any chance that this is a metastasis from someplace else?" He stared at the images on the monitor memorizing the location and size of the offending tumor. To him it appeared to be the very essence of evil.

"Well, I can't be one hundred percent sure, but the location and shape of the lesion makes me think it arose at that spot and is solitary. The pathology will tell and a PET scan might be a good idea." Mark's professional demeanor was comforting to Jack.

"I had better go talk to her and her family. Can you give Maximillian a call for me, let him know what you have and see when he can come by. I'll get her admitted. Anything else I should give her?"

"I'll call Mack right away, and no you don't need to add any-thing else. The nausea means the pressure is significant or the tumor is causing localized irritation. The sooner it is out the better." Mark looked straight at Jack, "This woman must be a good friend of yours." Mark put his hand on his friend's arm. "You're close to this patient, I can tell. Do you want to have one of your partners take over for you?" He was subtly pointing out that a physician who is too close to his patients may not be the best one to manage their care.

"I've actually known her longer than I have you. We were in high school together so, yes, she is a close friend, but I think I can remain objective. You don't need to worry about my judgment, besides I am not going to be managing much. You'll be there won't you?"

"Sure," he said with a grin. "If I didn't know you better, though, I would think maybe you are 'interested' in this woman." He chuckled, "But you've been a confirmed bachelor too long. You had better go and talk with her. Her life is about to really change."

"Thanks again, Mark. You may not realize it, but I think of you as my longest and best friend, and not a bad neurologist." He smiled.

Mark punched his shoulder but was grinning. "See ya. I hope you have a better day."

They shook hands again and Jack slipped out into the hallway headed for the ER. He was trying hard to think how best to give Kathy the news.

13

"This is Detective Rebecca Sweate interviewing ..." Rebecca began the tape recorder for her session with Mrs. Ogilvie. The woman had regained her composure and told Rebecca that she would help in any way if it would safely bring back her niece.

"The young woman who came with Alicia, the ... body, was Connie ... I can't remember her last name. It was Johnson or Thompson, I can't be sure. They arrived together on Wednesday evening. I remember because almost as soon as they got to our house they said they were going out again. Alicia had invited her to stay with us, without asking me, of course. I wondered why they left again so soon, but Connie said she had someone to see. I assumed it was a boyfriend. They were giggly and talkative like they had some kind of secret. Alicia seemed so happy and excited."

"Mrs. Ogilvie, how close have you been to your niece? Was it common for her to come and stay with you?" Rebecca asked.

"I was very close to her mother, my sister Betsy. Betsy died of breast cancer two years ago. No, it isn't usual. I've seen Alicia at reunions and when my sister was alive they would visit, but Alicia has never come alone. I was so surprised when she called and said they were already on their way, but I looked forward to seeing her again. I've been hoping she would come and stay so I could get to know her better. I thought maybe we could go shopping or do something special while she was here, but when she arrived she told me she would have to leave the next morning."

"Was your husband okay with the visit?" Rebecca needed to know if he could somehow be involved in the disappearance.

"Fred?" she made a small laughing sound, "He hardly paid attention. He works at the gas company, comes home and then sits in front of the TV most of the evening. He didn't care one way or the other. He was home when Alicia got there, but he didn't get up. And he left, the next morning, without checking to see if she had come back in. I doubt he said two words to her before she went missing." Tears welled up in her eyes and she looked in her purse for a handkerchief. Rebecca pushed a box of Kleenex across the desk. "Thank you," she said as she wiped her eyes and blew her nose.

"Did you see either of them again after they left later in the evening?" Rebecca was honing in on information to try to establish an identity for the young victim.

"No, not really. Well, I thought I saw her car the next morning, but when it kept going I decided I was wrong. I didn't realize that she had not gotten in at all. When I found her bed empty I was at first surprised and as the day went on I became more worried. When she got in, Wednesday, I thought she looked a little thin and told her so, but she just laughed and told me it was "the new look.""

Mrs. Ogilvie had a good memory for details so Rebecca pushed a little harder. "What kind of car were they driving Mrs. Ogilvie?"

"Let's see. It was a compact and white. It had that little letter "H" on the front of the hood. I think that's a Honda, but I don't know the model. The windows were pretty darkly tinted so I couldn't see the driver from the house."

"Where does Alicia work?"

"She told me when she called that she has been working as a secretary to some big wig in Chicago. I don't think she said who or which company. It might be in Naperville, I think."

"Did she say anything about her friend, Connie or where they were going the next day?" Rebecca pressed.

"I didn't really ask. She mentioned meeting her recently so they aren't old friends. And, no, she didn't say where they were headed." Mrs. Ogilvie was trying to be helpful, but there was still not much to go on.

Rebecca continued asking questions and learned a little more about Alicia, but nothing more about the dead girl. Mrs. Ogilvie continued, 'Yesterday when I found that they hadn't gotten home I didn't know what to do. I tried her cell phone, but there was no answer. I haven't gotten any answer on it since then. It just goes to voicemail."

"Mrs. Ogilvie we'll need that cell number. Did you get a number for Connie?"

"No, but Alicia's things are at home maybe she left something there."

"What things did she leave?"

"Well there was a small overnight case that she brought in when they first arrived. There weren't any big bags. I did think that was odd, but they might have still had them in the car."

Rebecca sat back searching her mind. "Thank you Mrs. Ogilvie you have been a great help. Is it okay if the officers who picked you up go with you and get Alicia's things?"

"I suppose, but what if she comes home?" Mrs. Ogilvie was clearly concerned.

"If she comes back home all her things will be returned right away." Rebecca was reassuring and stood to end the interview. She led Mrs. Ogilvie out to the hallway and then spoke to Gus who had been at his desk.

"Gus, Mrs. Ogilivie's niece's stuff is at her house. Can you pick it up?"

"Sure, Detective. We'll have a look around her room there too. You never know. Francine went with me to pick her up. I thought it would be less stressful for her if a woman officer came along." Gus was already moving to get Officer Francine O'Connor.

"That was thoughtful, Gus," Rebecca said almost to his back. "Gus, we need to try to establish this 'Connie's' last name and find next of kin too."

"I'll get right on that too." He half turned, touched his forehead with one finger in a pleasant mock salute and moved across the room.

"Oh, Mrs. Ogilvie?"

"Yes, dear?"

"One more thing. Do you know if your niece owned a gun?" Rebecca had held onto this last question until the very last moment.

"Oh my goodness no! Oh you couldn't think... No Detective. Alicia could not be mixed up in this." She turned and strode from the hall without another word.

Rebecca had known she would touch a nerve with that last question but she had to consider every angle. She stepped to her desk and reached down to rewind the tape. She labeled it and inserted it into a plastic case. A transcriptionist would print out the contents of the interview.

Sitting down she stared at her legal pad. She had to get perspective and make plans. "What should we do next," she thought to herself. She began to write, "Establish ID on vic – Gus will get belongings. Doctor – sketch. BOLO for white Honda probably Accord or Civic." She picked up the phone and set the ball rolling on that "All Points Bulletin."

****

Jack was nearing the ER when he felt the vibration of his cell phone. The sensation evoked an immediate visceral response. Since residency, when he first began wearing a pager, he knew that anytime it went off it could mean bad news. All too often in those first years as a young resident he remembered that the message was "Code Blue in Room ..." He then had to run to a dimly lit room full of tension as nurses and technicians battled to "resurrect" the dead. They would see the arriving physician and breathe more easily. As a young physician he felt the weight of responsibility each time he drew up on such a scene and had learned to put on a façade of armor and a toughness he did not actually feel inside. Thankfully his calls were rarely so urgent these days.

He unclipped the phone from its holder and opened it. He did not recognize the number on the screen and it wasn't a hospital extension. "Hello," he cautiously said, "this is Dr. Sharp."

"Hello Dr. Sharp. This is Justin Samuelson, Detective Justin Samuelson. How are you sir?" Justin's voice showed his hesitancy.

"I'm fine Detective Samuelson. What can I do for you?" Jack noted the hesitancy of the young detective.

"Sir, we, Detective Sweate and I, are now working on this murder investigation together. I would like to speak to you if I may and get you together with our sketch artist as soon as possible. When can I, or we, do this, sir?"

Jack let out a sigh, "I am about to speak to a patient about a critical issue. I expect to be about half an hour. Do you want to meet me at the hospital?"

"All right, sir. I'll pick you up at eleven-thirty. Where shall we meet?"

"I can find you at the emergency room entrance."

"Very good sir. I'll have the artist meet us here at the station. I also have a few questions if that's okay." Justin was pleased that the doctor was being cooperative. He had worried that he would have to cajole him to take time away from his practice.

"All right, Detective. I'll see you then." Jack neatly folded his phone and smiled. He thought to himself, "I must no longer be a suspect if they are sending the junior detective after me."

As he arrived in the emergency department, he waved casually at the receptionist and she opened the door with the press of a button behind her desk. As it swung open he saw Frank and his sister, Amber, outside their mother's room. Approaching them, with an attempt at a smile, he gently took their hands in greeting. "Any results Dr. Jack?" Frank inquired.

"Yes, Frank." He smiled his most sympathetic smile and steeled himself for the conversation to come. "Let's go in and talk." They entered the exam room together and he saw Kathy lying, eyes closed, on the bed. She was now in a sterile-looking hospital gown, with her hair fanning out on her pillow and framing her tired face. She displayed a peace, though, that he wished he could feel. When her eyes opened the look of pleasure in them when she saw him almost took his breath away. He did not want to be there giving such news to this woman. What more irony could there be? He had begun to feel something for a woman who now would be in a desperate fight for her life..

"Hello Jack." She spoke first and it was as if they were just meeting for breakfast all over again. "I can read your face. You have something important to tell me don't you?"

Surprised at his own transparency Jack replied, "Do you want me to talk with you alone or with your children here?" He said this matter-of-factly, but it carried significant weight. This statement made it clear that there was definite gravity in what he needed to discuss.

"Oh let's just save time and have Frank and Amber stay." She smiled again reaching out a hand to Frank. Jack motioned to them to find seats near their mother's bed.

He sat on the edge of Kathy's bed. He wanted to be close and provide what comfort he could as his news rocked Kathy's world. He looked directly into her eyes and said,

"Kathy, I don't believe in sugar coating or beating around the bush. You already know I don't have good news. The MRI shows that you have a tumor in your brain." He stopped, letting this information work its way into his listeners' awareness. He could feel and hear the exhalation as Frank and Amber understood. Kathy's eyes never wavered, however. She looked directly at Jack waiting for more. "The tumor is close to the outer portion of the brain, but the pressure and swelling from it have been causing the symptoms you have noticed. It is the most likely cause for the tremor I noticed and for the nausea you suffered this morning and the headaches that have been getting worse."

Kathy spoke softly, "Is it cancer?"

Frank broke in, "Can it be removed?"

Amber began to cry quietly, burying her face in her hands.

Kathy spoke again, "What do we do now?"

Jack picked up Kathy's other hand and gently squeezed it. He felt her grip on his hand and he let both hands hold hers. "Mark says it is most likely a glioma. This can be cancerous, but in the brain any tumor is dangerous. Thankfully it doesn't appear to be near the part of the brain that makes surgery quite so complicated, but any brain surgery is risky. You will probably also need radiation and maybe chemotherapy if it does turn out to be malignant." That term 'malignant' summed up the total effect of cancer. It implies evil and danger and casts a pall over the heart when one thinks about their disease.

With the mention of radiation and chemotherapy Kathy's face paled, but she merely took a deep breath and, otherwise, kept her composure. She looked at Frank whose head was bowed and Amber who was wiping her eyes. "How soon can we do this?"

Jack smiled seeing the strength in this beautiful woman. She had steel in her backbone. "Maximillian Clark is one of the best neurosurgeons around. He trained at MD Anderson and the Mayo Clinic. Mark is going to speak to him about you and let me know what's next. I think it is necessary to do this sooner, not later."

Now Frank spoke up. "What about the new Gamma Knife? You know, the 'non-invasive surgery'?"

Jack replied, "Frank I don't know, but suspect that it is important for the surgeon to get every bit of the tumor out. If it is accessible I think it will be better to actually have surgery, but this is not my specialty. You should ask that question of Dr. Clark." He looked back at Kathy. "Any surgery in the brain could be dangerous. You could have an outcome much like a stroke. But if you don't have the tumor removed the pressure on the brain will increase. It may already be at a dangerous level."

Kathy looked puzzled, "Why did this all happen so suddenly? Is it growing that fast?"

"No, it probably has been there a while, months at least. However, once the tumor reaches a certain size there is no more room for it to expand. It starts to put pressure on the brain tissue and can literally push it out of the cavity in the skull. We can lessen the pressure for a while with medications, but eventually it will take your life if it isn't removed."

Kathy looked from Frank to Amber then back to Jack. "I guess we wait for Dr. Brackenhorst and Dr. Clark. Smiling at Jack she said kindly, "Jack, thank you for being so honest," she hesitated then continued as she squeezed his hand even tighter, "I think I need to spend some time with my kids. I want to call them all if I may."

Jack knew she needed this time alone, but felt a desire to stay at her side holding her hand, but he honored her request. "You can call out with the phone there on the table."

"Mom, I'll call them," Frank said quickly. "You just rest for a minute." Amber started speaking quietly to Kathy and Jack knew it was time for his exit. He had delivered the blow, and now could not expect them to be happy about his role in it.

He rose from the bed and quietly slipped out into the hallway of the ER feeling no better for having delivered his message. He worked his way over to the desk and pulled out a progress note sheet and orders and began the process of admitting his patient.

14

Friday Morning

Slumped on the edge of the Motel 6 bed with his head in his hands Dan wondered, *How had he gotten so off track?*

He was in big trouble and knew it. He wasn't certain what he should do. He was sure that, by now, there would be a description of him all over town.

Why hadn't he taken off earlier? He would have to chance it, but he still needed to stay around and get what he had come for. He was dead if he didn't, but he knew he risked jail or more if he stayed too long. What had started out as a simple, "snatch and grab" had gotten horribly messed up. Now the girl was dead and he didn't know where to find it.

As a kid, Dan Randizzio had played with all the other Italian boys in his tight-knit neighborhood in Chicago. His older brothers were all in prison, but he had kept his nose clean and had never been arrested for any significant crime. He had no adult arrests and his juvenile file was sealed so it wouldn't be easy to track him down even if the cops found finger prints. He liked being anonymous. Even though his physical appearance was notable he had always been able to keep out of the lime light and melt into the background. This time he had screwed up.

Dan had been sent to clean up the mess he had started. He couldn't help his feelings, but he had been stupid. He had really liked Connie too. It had been extremely hard for him to see her lifeless body. Even worse was that it was his fault that she had had to die.

He figured the cops would eventually put two and two together and think he could be the killer. He hadn't wanted to go there during the day, but was afraid he wouldn't find what he was looking for in the dark and he couldn't risk the locket. What if she *had* put a picture of them in it? The main item of his search wasn't there, though, and now he was doubly in trouble. He couldn't go back without it or he would be toast. Now he was possibly wanted for murder too.

How could he have been so stupid as to stumble onto that guy on the bike path?

He should have laid low until he was sure there weren't any walkers or joggers on that trail.

The television news had confirmed that the man he had seen was a doctor here in town. Maybe this guy was the key to getting himself out of trouble. Besides he might have picked the object up for himself and kept it. Dan needed to find out where this doctor lived and search his place. In addition, if he could, somehow, make the doctor appear guilty it would ease up the pressure and buy himself some time. Unfortunately, he was aware that the other girl could have taken it, too. That would be bad because he had no idea where she was, and even though that wasn't his fault he would still get blamed.

He had to hatch a new plan to extricate himself. Sitting in the worn upholstered chair, he took a few sips of beer and stared at the window with its drawn curtains. In his mind was the beginning of a plan that could get him back on the road and back in the good graces of his uncle. It was chancy. The risk of being caught now were higher, but his future and freedom depended on the success of this plan.

While everyone was still trying to figure things out he continued to have an advantage. He doubted they knew his identity yet. He wasn't a great thinker, but he liked chess. In that game one needed know the moves and anticipate the opponent's moves several steps ahead. He still had the edge and needed to capitalize on it while everyone else was spinning their wheels.

Summoning up the nerve he dialed his uncle.

"Hello?" came the voice.

"Hi, Uncle Jim." He tried to sound upbeat.

"It didn't go so well, did it?" queried his uncle. "What are you going to do about it? Not the details, just generalities."

"What? Oh yeah. I have a plan," and he filled James in on the basic idea without mentioning names or specific events.

"Sounds like you have little choice. Ditch your phone and buy a new one. Dan if you mess up again I won't be able to protect you." James sounded annoyed but not angry.

"Sure, I get it." There was a click and James was off the line.

Standing up from his double bed he set down his phone and walked to the tiny bathroom in his "honeymoon suite." He picked up one of the plastic glasses and tore off the wrapping. Filling it with tap water he downed it in a gulp. Needing a clear head he poured out the beer and tossed the bottle. He ran his hand through his hair, short-cropped though it was. The face that looked back at him was hard and unfriendly. Killing had never been part of his deals and he was not looking forward to it, but he knew that there might be one more dead body tonight if he didn't get what he needed.

****

"No, his hair was fairly short and light colored, almost blonde." Dr. Sharp looked at the drawing and added, "More cheekbone, I think and I don't think he smiles much."

It was amazing to watch the artist at work. He spoke his description and saw it develop before him on the paper. The likeness was nearly perfect as far as he could remember.

"His features are distinctive so if he is still around we may get lucky," said Justin, as he also peered at the drawing. I'll get this copied and scanned and out on the 'wire.' You know — it's not really a wire anymore; we just call it that. We send it email." Justin stood with his thumb and forefinger cradling his chin. "I wish we had one of those electronic billboards where we could display this picture. There are now several cities where they have caught criminals and found abducted children because they could get their pictures on the big digital billboard almost within the hour of the crimes."

Jack looked up, "I didn't know about that. There are a few of those in town, though."

"Oh, well you have to have a special arrangement and it isn't cheap."

"I suppose you are right, but I think it would be worth a call. It could be considered a 'public service,'" Jack said.

Justin's finger was posed to dial, then, he realized Rebecca had slipped in behind him as they were finished the sketches.

"Now," she said, "I agree, Dr. Sharp. Most companies like good will and public service. 'Is that a good likeness?"

"I am amazed. It is just as I remembered him," Jack said.

"He isn't average by any means. Someone will have remembered him." She walked over to the artist and lifted the drawing.

"Josie, you do marvelous work. Thank you for coming in. Josie teaches at the local college, but we have found her to be invaluable in this area. I wish we could bring her on full time, but thankfully we don't have that much requirement for her services. She's been pretty good about working us into her busy schedule when we need her, though." She smiled pleasantly at the young woman whose long auburn hair was plaited into a single thick braid.

Josie spoke in a low, husky voice,

"I'm happy to help. Faces are my passion. Rebecca, I still would love to paint a portrait of you. Let me know if you ever want to come down to the school." She gave Rebecca a light hug and began assembling her pencils and drawing supplies. She had a beautifully tooled leather case which held several sizes of drawing pencils and leads. There were places for brushes and a pocket for a small artist's palette.

"Dr. Sharp, you have a very good eye and a memory for detail. You should consider photography or art. We have classes for adults who want to start a hobby." She gave him a business card and smiled. "You never know what talents may be hidden within."

She neatly tore off the page with the jogger's likeness laying it carefully on the table which was covered with newspaper. She then reached into her substantial handbag producing a spray can. Gingerly she sprayed several layers over the surface of the drawing.

"This will 'fix' the carbon to the paper so it won't smudge." She spoke directly to Justin, "You should be able to copy or scan this now without risk of damaging the drawing."

She thanked him and lifting her case and handbag strode from the room without a backward glance.

Rebecca stepped in front of Dr. Sharp. "Thank you for coming down again. We appreciate your cooperation. I'm afraid we aren't too much farther along, though I guess I can tell you, we have identified the body. If I tell you who she is will you promise not to let it out to the press?"

"Detective, I'm hurt. I would never go behind your back. I don't know the woman so her identity won't enlighten me, but I must confess that I have been curious." He leaned against the wall, "Man I'm bushed. I took the rest of the day off so I don't have to go back to my clinic."

"Certainly, I understand." After a moment of standing quietly she continued. "I saw the way the news reporters portrayed you last night. Unfortunately reporters can affect appearances by what they do show."

Jack replied, "Yes, it has created some issues for me. Several of my patients decided they didn't need to see a doctor all that badly."

"Hm. I see. We believe the young woman was named 'Connie' and she was from Chicago."

"Really? Why was she here?" replied the doctor.

"We don't have the details but there may be another woman involved who is now missing." Rebecca surprised herself at her willingness to reveal this information. At this point the best thing we can do is find out who did kill this young woman and put to rest any rumors."

"I would appreciate that," Jack smiled and shook Rebecca's hand. Her touch lingered just a moment longer than necessary and Jack glanced at her curiously. However, the detective's face was a mask and the moment passed without comment.

As Dr. Sharp began to leave, Rebecca motioned to Justin to come over to her. "Justin," she said, "would you mind going to the crime scene with Dr. Sharp?" Then quickly looking back at Jack, "That is if you have the time?" Jack nodded and Justin began to reply.

"Yes, ma'am. I would be happy to go there. Dr. Sharp we want you to walk us through what happened again." Justin was a little irritated that Rebecca had 'sent' him on an 'assignment.' He was perfectly capable of planning his own line of inquiry.

"Well, Justin and Rebecca, I have taken some vacation because I can't concentrate very well with the police knocking on my door and reporters standing on my lawn." It was meant as a mild rebuke, but it was not offensive in its delivery.

"Dr. Sharp," came Rebecca's reply, "I wish all of our suspects were so cooperative."

His eyebrows went up in alarm and concern, "Suspect?" he questioned. "Do you think I could have killed that young woman?"

Rebecca realized her error and with chagrin answered,

"I'm sorry I can't totally rule out anyone at this time." She had a tight smile, "But note we aren't slapping on the cuffs."

"I see." He looked at Justin reproachfully, "I don't believe I have said anything incriminating, but in light of this little revelation maybe I shouldn't be quite so cooperative. I will accompany you, Detective Samuelson, to the crime scene, but I will ask my lawyer to come with us, if you don't mind."

Now Justin could not prevent the look of disdain he felt. "Of course, Dr. Sharp." His eyes flashed at Rebecca. "Could you just meet us in the bike path parking lot in, say, thirty minutes?" They both rose.

Jack countered, "Maybe forty-five. I haven't had lunch yet." He only glanced at Rebecca as he quickly found his way out of the room and off the floor.

Justin moved to the door and angrily closed it. "Rebecca,, what's the deal? You ask for help in this investigation then you come in here and mess things up for me? I thought you wanted me to deal with the doctor?" He was clearly upset and his attitude toward Rebecca had changed drastically. "Besides I thought he was a 'person of interest-' not a suspect."

Rebecca sat quietly, knowing that she had made a error. "Justin, I'm sorry. I don't say that often but I mean it." She looked down and ran her fingers through her hair, a gesture of frustration. "I must be a little tired or something." She stood and put a hand on Justin's shoulder. She could feel him tense up so she quickly removed it. "I do want you to deal with him. I'm not sure that he isn't a suspect, but I'll stay out of your way. I'm sorry that I put him on his guard."

"Now I have to deal with a lawyer." Justin fidgeted with the button on his shirt cuff then reached for a small brief case on the floor.

"All right, apology accepted," he hesitated, "Do we know of *any* connection between the doctor and the murder victim at this point?" Justin had changed tack again knowing that brow-beating his superior was not productive.

Rebecca, glad to see the discussion going a different direction, answered, "Nothing yet. There is no family connection. Gus is checking his office records for any professional relationship to the family."

"Won't you need a warrant for that?" Justin observed.

"We can see how cooperative the good doctor is now willing to be. Can you call the business manager before the doctor meets you? Maybe he will give you information."

Justin was somewhat mollified as Rebecca was now merely suggesting a course. "I doubt he'll be so forthcoming but okay, and I like the electronic billboard idea. I think I'll follow up on the 'public service' angle. I can't think of anything else."

Justin paused, then, turning said, "You really don't mind making enemies do you? I thought maybe you kind of liked this guy."

Rebecca grew serious, scowling, "I don't let personal feelings get in the way of any investigation. Please don't forget that. As for 'liking' the doctor, I have known him only for one day and, as a suspect in a murder investigation, at that. What do you think?" Justin thought she protested a bit "too much," but he caught the warning look on her face.

"Sure. Right. I'll call his office and get back with you later today." Justin quickly opened the door and strode to his own cubicle to call the clinic. He powered up his laptop and synchronized his PDA to keep his notes current.

He made a call to Dr. Sharp's office. The office manager came on the line.

"Hello. This is Doug Katzberg."

"Yes this is Detective Justin Samuelson with the Police Department. We have been speaking with Dr. Sharp and are inquiring about a murder that occurred yesterday," he began.

"Yes I am aware of that. What can I do for you?" The office manager's voice was even, with little emotion.

"We need to find out if patients named Alicia Winters, Fred or Bonnie Ogilvie have ever been seen in your clinic."

"I'm sorry. You know that patient information is protected. I am not allowed to give that out to you." Doug was firm, but his reply remained pleasant.

"Mr. Katzberg this is very important. You did hear me say 'murder' didn't you?" Justin was becoming frustrated, yet he was not surprised by the resistance.

"Detective, you may say what you like, but it is still protected by HIPPA laws and I cannot divulge such information. Is there anything else?"

"No, thank you. We can get a warrant to compel you to provide the information."

With that they ended their conversation. It was a stretch because they had too little to go on yet for a warrant, but building a case always took time.

15

Randizzio was surprised at the lack of police presence in the doctor's neighborhood. It seemed too easy. Dan hadn't seen the doctor leave his house, but knew from the time of day that he was unlikely to be at home. He drove his non-descript white van around the cul-de-sac and nearby streets. The doctor's yard was fenced, but he doubted that the gate was locked. The garage door was actually his favorite source of entry, though. He had a small instrument specially made for finding the frequency of a garage door, matching it, and then opening it. By gaining entry to a garage, he would have plenty of time to get in and out of the house unobserved. Dressed in typical maintenance workers' overalls he had added the label "Open Doors Computers" to the back and had the logo of a computer network on the front. It was a close copy of a regional company that provided internet and computer service. He had done the design on his computer with a simple program. An inkjet printer made an iron-on transfer which he had steamed onto the overalls.

Parking in front of the house just as if he were scheduled to work there, he calmly got out and opened the back door of the van. There was miscellaneous computer equipment inside, in case some busybody bothered to look. Grasping a plastic toolbox he dutifully strode up the drive. He wore sunglasses and a ball cap pulled low over his eyes. He couldn't do anything to hide his build, but no one would get a good look at his face. This was the trickiest part because he could encounter someone coming up the sidewalk. Nevertheless, he glanced up the street and then without hesitation made a beeline for Dr. Sharp's garage door.

There was a keypad along the garage door lintel, and he made an appearance of actually punching in a security code in the case that a neighbor was watching. At the same time, his other hand activated the illegal garage door device which was hidden in his pocket. The door went up with little hesitation. Once in the garage, he quickly walked to the inner door and pressed the button to lower the garage door.

As Dan had exited his van, he didn't go unnoticed. A neighbor across the street was observing his movements. Randy Johnson was a stay-at-home dad who was cleaning his living room carpet when he saw a man step out of a white van across the street. What seemed odd was that the man's van had no markings on its side. Most service companies had their company name on the side as advertisement. Randy had even seen a green and white computer repair van at the doctor's house in the past. Now he saw the overall-clad worker walk up to the doctor's garage door and open the keypad.

Randy started back to his work, but he felt that it was irregular that the man did not go to the front door, as well as the fact that the van was not marked correctly. Nevertheless, though, the guy looked like a computer network person, just like Randy had seen many times before in the area.

"Dr. Jack must have given him the code for the door," he rationalized to himself. When Randy saw the garage door go down, he scowled slightly, but returned to his cleaning.

Dan found the inner door to the house unlocked. Most people believed that their garage doors were secure and did not lock the house entry door. It was typical human nature believing it was safe, until a break-in violated their security.

He smiled at how easy it had been, but at the same time, he was careful to look for any sign of an alarm system. The house was fairly large, but not ostentatious. Dan noticed that there wasn't a lot of expensive electronic gear and he found no famous paintings on the wall. He doubted that the doctor left money lying around, either. Any thief would have a hard time making much of a haul here!

However, Dan was not there to steal any of the doctor's possessions. He hoped to steal back property that didn't belong to either of them. His plan also involved a more strategic play. Once he found what he was looking for he had another little surprise for the doctor. His hands were gloved and he had been careful not to walk on wet pavement on his way in. He had to be thorough, and he did not want to leave any evidence that he had been there. Dan was not new to this type of work. He had lifted many stereos and televisions in his time and he was familiar with favorite places to hide things.

Dan started by looking in the most likely places for a safe and was relieved not to find one. His skill sets did not include safe-cracking. Next he searched the bedrooms and bathrooms. He looked under the mattresses and in the dresser drawers, careful not to displace too many things. Books and shelves were a common place to hide things. He noticed the quantity of books and knew that he could not possibly go through all of Jack's library. If he tried, he would be there all day. He noted the titles. There were several Bibles and books on religious subjects. He saw a few novels and books on history. History would be good. He pulled all of them one by one from the shelf and opened them. A few note pages fluttered to the floor. He found one book hollowed out inside in which he found a bag with several silvery looking coins. These might be valuable, but the coins were not the subject of his search. Dan put those back.

He looked through as many books as possible, but did not find what he needed.

Finally, the kitchen. He had left it to last even though it was a very likely area to hide treasure. He checked the freezer first followed by the oven and then the drawers. After about an hour he felt defeated. *Maybe the doctor hadn't found it either*. He was beginning to think the other girl must have it.

Frustrated, but satisfied that he had checked everything, he now had a present for Dr. Sharp. In the kitchen he found a zipper-lock bag and crumpled it up to make it look like it had spent time in a pocket. Next he produced a small chain from his own pocket. There was a small distinctive pendant attached to the chain and this fit neatly in the bag. He had given that locket to Connie, but he found that she hadn't even kept his photo inside. Instead there was a picture of some old man and woman. If he had known this, he never would have gone back to the body nor met the doctor and he would still be unencumbered .

He closed the necklace in the bag and looked around. Dan

pondered the layout for a moment then went over to the silverware drawer. He reached in and placed the bag behind the tableware stowed in a plastic tray. He found a sharp kitchen knife and looked it over. It seemed right for what he wanted. He took it out of the knife holder and wet it down. He reached under the sink and picked up a bottle of bleach. After running a little water into the sink he added the acrid liquid and dipped the knife in. Anyone looking at the knife could think it had been cleaned with bleach to remove blood. He then thrust the knife into the back of the same drawer containing the necklace.

What he had done was little enough, but should be quite effective. He knew the doctor was innocent, but the police would not be likely to overlook both items. Either one could increase their suspicions of the doctor. Dan had a plan to get the police to search the doctor's house.

He adjusted the items on the counter to make them look a little out of place. It never hurt to give the police a little help. This time, for his exit, he didn't need to worry about the garage door. He merely walked out the front door locking it behind him. He had been careful not to leave any other signs of his having been inside.

Across the street, Randy watched the man leave. The worker had been in the doctor's house about an hour and a half. Randy knew the drill. The worker would claim he had been there at least two hours and charge for it. Randy was just curious enough, though, that he decided to let the doctor know about the visitor when he saw him again. He checked his watch and realized he had several errands to run before picking the kids up from school. Dr. Sharp wouldn't be home until evening. It could wait until then.

As Dan reached his van he felt that he was home free. He drove out of the neighborhood before setting the next part of his plan into motion. When he was far enough away he pulled out his cell phone. He was hoping to defer suspicion long enough that he could finish what he had come to do. The doctor should never have gotten involved. Dan didn't feel any remorse. This was the risk of playing the game with him. In his mind the words came to him unbidden, "Check! Your move."

16

Jack's cell phone vibrated again. He was standing in the parking lot next to the bike path where this whole mystery started. He had wanted to go home and change clothes, but he had been "encouraged" by this new detective to meet him right away at this place. He didn't know what could be accomplished by coming back here, but he had to admit he was naturally curious about the circumstances that had led to the death of the young woman.

He was disconcerted by the knowledge that the police could still think he had anything to do with her murder. He hadn't known her and as far as he knew he had no connection to her. How could he be a suspect? Rebecca Sweate had seemed reasonable at first, but he was beginning to see that she had a hard side and he would have to remain careful around her.

Sam, his lawyer, had agreed to meet him here. Maybe he was calling back with some excuse. Jack glanced at his watch. Three fifty. A car was pulling into the parking lot as he unclipped his phone.

"Hello, this is Dr. Sharp."

"Dr. Sharp. Hello. This is Greg Connolly." The caller's voice was quiet and calm.

That name made Jack straighten and nervously look around. He wanted Sam here now. The car which had entered the lot had been driven by the young detective.

"Great," Jack thought. Jack began walking toward the car as it pulled into a parking space. "Yes," he paused trying to delay the caller, "Greg Connolly, the jogger from yesterday." Jack was growing increasingly alarmed. He waved to the detective to hurry and come up to him. "How did you know me?" Jack realized this was a foolish question since he had seen himself plastered on the television news since yesterday.

"You are popular doctor. A regular media celebrity. Your office was kind enough to give me your cell number."

Jack doubted this because it was a private number.

"I just wanted to chat a little. Are you alone?"

"Yes, I'm alone." He continued talking, but as the detective approached he put his finger to his lips signaling for him not to speak. Justin's eyes grew large and he became excited. Jack pressed the 'speaker' button on his phone and increased the volume so the detective could listen to the conversation.

"Good. I decided to give you a little heads-up. Things are about to get hot for you. I just let the police know that you took something yesterday. It wouldn't surprise me if they were getting a search warrant as we speak."

Justin was close to Jack now and heard this last part of the call. "What do you mean, I 'took something'? It isn't true!" Jack was worried about this last warning. "Why are you saying that and why would you tell the police that?"

"Doc, it's like a chess game only I'm telling you the next move. Let's just say it is convenient for the police to think that you killed the girl. I didn't do it, by the way. It's just too bad the police will be looking more closely at you. It might turn out to be a short game."

"Look Connolly, can we at least talk about this? If you didn't kill that girl who did? Why are you setting me up?" Jack hoped to get him to give up something helpful.

"I think that's all the advantage I want to give you now. You had better brush up on your chess. Bye." The signal went dead.

Jack stood there looking at his phone. Then he turned to Detective Samuelson. "Did you hear all that? What's that?" He pointed to the phone-sized object in the detective's hand.

"That my friend just saved your hide." Justin was grinning. "Sometimes technology can be our salvation. It is my PDA."

"Okay, I have one too, but it doesn't look like that. What were you doing?" Dr. Sharp asked, still in mild shock from the jogger's words and more than a little surprised to see a detective so young.

"It has a small microphone and I was able to record some of the phone call." Justin checked and played back the recording. It didn't pick up extremely well in this outdoor environment, but the voice from the call was discernible. "I'd say this is one time you were happy to see the cops." Justin was now enjoying himself. He had valuable information and could expand their knowledge of the jogger. "We need to do several things. First let me call Detective Sweate."

At that moment two things happened at the same time. A car, which had been parked in the lot began to move. Jack's attention shifted to the car and noted that the driver's window was rolling down revealing a gun barrel. Jack's instant recognition and reflexes came into play. Without delay he dived toward Detective Samuelson. The glass of the detective's car rear window shattered, though he heard no report from a weapon.

Justin was disoriented at first, but his own training also began to kick in. He hadn't seen the weapon but recognized that he and the doctor were in danger. Laying on his side he drew his revolver. His car was between them and the gun but all the attacker would have to do was drive around his parked car and open fire again and they would be sitting ducks. Justin anticipated this and when he heard the engine roar to life he turned to meet the threat.

As the car sprang into view he opened fire. Stars of broken glass appeared on the attacker's windshield. Justin aimed for the driver but found it hard to hit the moving target. The would-be killer, though, also had trouble aiming, and only got off a few more shots. The shooter was, no doubt, surprised by the return fire.

Justin tried to be economical with his ammo since he only had six bullets in his revolver. The act of reloading would expose them to potentially deadly fire. He belatedly realized the value of the department issue nine millimeter weapon that held thirteen bullets in its magazine.

The attacker did not know he only had six bullets, though, and gave up the chase as Justin fired his final bullet. The car reversed direction and sped off out of the parking lot. By the time Justin had reloaded his weapon, the car was gone.

Jack, unarmed, had remained flat against the pavement. He was unscathed, aside from a scrape on his palm from the landing as they had fallen to the ground. When he was sure it was safe he stood and brushed off his slacks. He looked over at Justin who had broken cover trying to see which way the car had gone.

Shaking his head he turned back to the doctor. "You all right?" he asked.

"Yeah, but it has been a long time since anyone tried to shoot me. If they hadn't been moving I doubt they would have missed. They came too close." He glanced at his hands which were shaking. He didn't feel calm but tried to control his voice.

Justin picked up his PDA and switched to its phone function. It still worked. He was connected to Rebecca shortly. "Detective Sweate, this is Justin."

"Hello, Justin. Where are you?"

"I'm with Dr. Sharp at the bike path parking lot." He spoke quickly and somewhat breathlessly.

"We have a new development. I need you to keep him there. I'm getting a warrant to search his house and car. Can you do that?" Rebecca was back to giving orders.

"Rebecca, I have an even newer development." He explained what had just happened and the phone conversation he had heard upon arriving at the parking lot.

Rebecca was now the one to be stunned. She thought she had legitimate grounds for searching the doctor's house but now her reasons were disappearing. "Are you both all right? Were either of you hit?"

He glanced back at the doctor, "It looks like the only casualty is my car. It will need a new window and a few holes filled in."

"Thank God!" she exclaimed. "Do you have a description of the vehicle?"

Justin told her what he could. "The license plates were gone. I don't know if he headed north or south. I was reloading."

"Did you hit the suspect?"

"I don't know. I doubt it." With chagrin he added, "It was the first time I've fired my weapon outside the range."

"I'm glad you're okay. You'll need to meet a shooting review, you know."

"Sure. Let me know when that is. I suppose there are a lot of forms to fill out too."

He could now here the laughter in her voice. "You bet there are."

"As for that mysterious phone call, are you sure it was the jogger?"

Justin thought a second. "As far as I could tell it was legitimate."

"All right Justin. But if that is the case, who shot at you?"

"I have no idea, Rebecca."

"Could you put the doctor on the phone, please?"

Justin handed the phone/PDA to Jack. He put the speaker to his ear. "Hello Detective Sweate."

"Hello Dr. Sharp. Are you all right?"

"Yes. I think so. Your young detective saved my bacon."

"I'm glad he was there. We need to search your home."

"Why would you need to do that? Didn't you hear what Detective Samuelson said?"

"If this jogger went to the trouble to let us know you may have taken something maybe he planted it at your house. He tells us so we get a warrant and find the item at your house. That would have confirmed you as a suspect."

She had quickly diagnosed what appeared to be a deception aimed at the doctor. But for the overheard phone call to Dr. Sharp it would have been a good plan. Greg Connolly had made a mistake and didn't know it.

"Who do you think was shooting at us? It wouldn't make sense for him to call then immediately attack," Dr. Sharp asked resignedly.

"I really don't know. But here's what we need to do. I still need to search your house. I can get a warrant, but with your permission we won't need that. I will come to where you are and bring the list of items found on the body. Maybe you will be able to help us figure out what we are looking for. You go ahead and review the crime scene with Justin and I'll meet you there in thirty minutes." Her plan was quickly forming and she could see some lights beginning to come on.

"I'll do what you say, but I want to be there when you search my home. I don't want to get arrested after being helpful to the police and getting shot at." Dr. Sharp was wary seeing now that there was evil at work here.

Justin was back on the phone with Rebecca, "Can you get the IT folks to try to find the number used to call the doc's phone?"

"That'll take a warrant for the cell company, but I'll see what I can do. Time is not on our side. Oh, and Justin, just so you know, we still have no identity on our victim. Missing Persons in Chicago hasn't had reports of any look-alikes, but Gus is following up on that. We were able to get one of those electronic bill board companies to let us flash the drawing made from the doctor's description, though. Good idea." She hung up and immediately called the judge whom she had petitioned for a warrant to see about changing it from the house to the phone records.

Justin shook his head. "I wish we could at least find out who the girl is." He handed the doctor back his phone and retrieved a roll of crime scene tape from his trunk. With the doctor's help, he cordoned off the parking lot entrance. Crime scene technicians would have to check out the area for shell casings. His own car was now evidence until they could find the smashed bullets fired at him and the doctor. If they were lucky they might be able to compare one of them to the bullet used to kill the girl.

Once the black and whites were on the scene they walked down the bike path toward the first crime scene. "You still haven't found out her name?" Jack asked.

"No sir, we're still looking, though." Justin was somber.

"How long have you been a detective? You seem pretty young," said Jack.

"About six months. I'm older than I look," he countered. "But I am young compared to most of the uniformed police. Some of them are resentful about it." Justin liked Dr. Sharp and was surprised at himself for being so open to him. Their recent shared experience could have ended in tragedy had the doctor not pushed him down. Likewise, if he hadn't been armed they would have been easy targets. Having heard the jogger on the phone Justin now was convinced that the doctor was innocent as he had stated. He was confused, though, about who had shot at them. It made no sense for the caller to tip him off then come after them. It was beginning to look to Justin like there had to be two people involved.

A little farther down the path Jack began again, "I only wish I could have done something to help." This statement sobered them both. Jack stopped, looked around and said, "This is where I turned around yesterday and saw the blue material."

"And the jogger came from that direction?" Justin asked.

"Yes, I heard his footfalls before I came up from below."

"Let's just walk farther on then and see what we can see." They did so and around the next bend came to a road crossing the path. "They found some tire tracks along the other side of the trees there. If the jogger was coming from a car here he wouldn't have had to run past you at all."

They worked their way back along the path looking carefully into the underbrush beside the trail. Despite the reason for their visit Jack found himself enjoying the time. The leaves hadn't changed, the sun still beamed over the tops of the stately cotton wood trees. The sun felt warm on his face, but there was a coldness inside that had crept in since yesterday. Death had marred the landscape. He also thought of Kathy and the struggle she was going through. He realized he had not given any consideration to her problem for several hours. What was happening at the hospital? He needed check as soon as he and Detective Samuelson were finished.

There were more leaves scattered on the ground from the overnight breeze, but even so Justin spotted something out of place about half-way back. "Look! There's something down there." He pointed to a pale object whose corner was just visible under the far side of a plum thicket. The foliage was less dense here than where Jack had seen the body so there was less concealment.

Justin said, "You should stay up there. I'll get whatever it is." He donned vinyl gloves and gingerly wove his way down. He stopped, looking back up at the doctor. "There are broken twigs and branches here. Someone must have walked through here before me." He bent and retrieved the item, holding it carefully, and retraced his steps to the bike path. Once back he held it out for the doctor to see as well. It was a men's casual shirt with light-colored green stripes. It had been neatly folded and tucked under the brush, not carelessly thrown into the bushes. It had been nearly obscured by fallen leaves.

They glanced up together as they heard the crunching sound of footsteps on the gravel. Coming toward them was Rebecca Sweate, unaccompanied today. This time the greeting was much friendlier and, of course, Jack was now acquainted with Detective Sweate who advanced with her hand out to him.

"Hello again Dr. Sharp." She was actually smiling and it was an attractive smile. She spoke to Detective Samuelson, "What have you got for me Justin? A shirt? It's a funny place to leave your laundry."

Justin smiled, "Yes. It appears to be a size seventeen and a half. I haven't unfolded it yet. We need to be careful because we may be able to lift fingerprints and trace from the surface."

"You can get fingerprints from cloth?" Dr. Sharp was incredulous.

"Sometimes, if the conditions have been just right, it can be done. It's worth a try," said Justin. He spoke to Rebecca, "We walked all the way to the road. It doesn't make sense that the jogger would drive in behind these trees and then have to leave the opposite direction. If he had a car back there he would never have had to encounter the doctor. He could have just gotten in his car and driven away."

"How, then, do you explain the tire tracks and drag marks?" Rebecca countered.

"I'm not sure yet, but a theory is forming. Let me get back to you when I've thought it through." Justin characteristically stroked his chin as he pondered the evidence.

"Dr. Sharp, are you sure you're all right? Not many people are used to being shot at."

"Yeah. A little shaken but I'll be fine. Your young detective scared away the bad guy with his little revolver."

Rebecca looked at Justin raising her eyebrows and a slight scowl.

Justin understood the silent reproach.

"Bag the shirt, Justin." Rebecca turned her attention now to Jack. "May we go to your house now?"

Hesitantly Jack said, "Yes, but I would like to make a quick stop at the hospital if I may. I have a sick patient who may need attention."

She looked at him with irritation. "I thought you took the rest of the day off?"

"I don't have to go to the office, but that doesn't alleviate me of my obligations to all of my patients."

The truth was that he wanted to see Kathy and see how she was adjusting to the idea of having a brain tumor. He needed to know what Mack Clark, the neurosurgeon, had told her. He would try to call him later to get his opinion verbally too, rather than just reading his consult. He called Sam to let him know of the change in plans. Sam agreed to stand by and would come if asked.

Detective Sweate consented to a brief stop at the hospital. She wanted to go with him, mainly out of curiosity, but was not sure she should ask. Nonetheless, it had nothing to do with her investigation. She had decided not to ask to come along when he said, "Detective, would you like to follow me in? I assure you this is not some conspiracy. I mentioned you to Kathy so she probably would like to meet you. She is a real 'people' person."

Rebecca noticed that he now called the patient 'Kathy' her first name. She was also interested that he had spoken about her to this patient. "Why would you have mentioned me?"

"It's a long story. It is hard to believe, but we were having breakfast together just this morning. So much has happened. Will this day never end?" Jack realized just how tired he had become. He went over the day's events quickly in his mind and was appalled that all this had happened in a mere twenty four hours.

"My days seem to all be like this," Rebecca replied.

Jack looked at her with renewed respect. He slowly shook his head and said, "That must be terribly stressful. How do you relieve the stress?" He was becoming curious about this woman as well. She was not a 'beauty,' but she had good looks which obscured her age. She was in good physical shape without an extra ounce of fat. He could not guess accurately just how old she was, but he put her between thirty five and forty five, leaning more toward the forty five.

Jack's mind climbed back into the conversation with the detective. "How do you relieve your stress and tension?" he asked

124

again this time with genuine interest.

"Oh I run and go to the gym to work out fairly often. It loosens the kinks and helps to clear the mind."

Justin was somewhat amused by the conversation and had stayed on the sideline not saying anything. Now as he spoke Dr. Sharp and Rebecca seemed to startle as if they had forgotten he was there. "I have to get these things back to the crime lab. Did you bring that list of items we catalogued from the deceased?"

"Yes, thank you, Justin. I almost forgot." She pulled a folded paper from her purse and glanced at it. Dr. Sharp, please take a look here and try to remember if there is anything you notice about the items we found yesterday."

"I didn't search her body or pockets. I was careful not to touch anything." He said this with a slight furrowing of the brow.

"I know. You mentioned that. But you were also very descriptive and observant. Please see what you can do." She added a plaintive smile as she passed the page to the doctor.

He looked at the list. "Hm, there's one item I don't see here." He kept scanning the list running his finger down each column. "I don't see the necklace."

"She wasn't wearing a necklace, Dr. Sharp. We found a wrist bracelet, a watch and an ankle bracelet, but no necklace." Rebecca realized that wearing two bracelets without a necklace might not be typical. Unfortunately, though, it was impossible to guess what styles women followed these days. She could have had any combination of jewelry items.

"When I saw her body, I noticed part of a tattoo on her left breast and she was definitely wearing a necklace." They stared at each other for a long moment.

"Do you realize what you're saying and what that means?" Rebecca finally replied.

Dr. Sharp thought a second. "If the necklace was there when I looked at the body, but gone when your people arrived, someone had to have removed it while I was waiting on this path!" The realization hit him like a fist. Someone, possibly the murderer, had been down with the body while he was just yards away. "If they were there, how could I not have heard them?" he muttered.

"They must have been very careful and the necklace must have seemed important for them to take such a risk." Rebecca was thinking hard. "I think it must have been your friend Greg Connolly, or whatever his name is."

"He's not my friend. I only met him on the bike path yesterday," Jack said pointedly.

"I'm sorry. I wasn't implying an acquaintance. Anyway, he was the only person you saw. He must have doubled back once he was out of your sight." Rebecca tried to be soothing. She had been getting Dr. Sharp's cooperation and didn't want to blow it again.

"He could have waited until I started walking toward the parking lot. He would have had plenty of time and wouldn't have to stay as quiet," Jack observed.

"You're right and I'll keep an open mind, but I want this Greg Connolly. I want to get him wrapped up with ribbons, so we can find out what is going on. We need to catch whoever shot at you too but we have little to go on there."

Rebecca had grown serious and was frowning. She decided not to mention that the young woman had been shot as well as stabbed. "A necklace," she repeated almost to herself. "Was there a pendant or locket attached to the necklace?"

Jack could see that she was frustrated.

"I'm not sure. There was something on it, but it was also partially covered up by her blouse."

"All right, let's get you to the hospital to check on your patient. Justin, will you call Gus and Mike or Arvillo and have them pick you up and meet us at the doctor's house in ..." she looked up questioningly at Dr. Sharp, "thirty minutes?" Jack nodded his acknowledgement that they could complete what he wanted to do in that time. "I'll also check on the progress of finding our shooter's car."

They moved off together. Rebecca looked back briefly. "We may need to come back with a team again and check through this entire area to be sure we haven't missed anything else." She reached into her purse and took out her keys. "Justin, I guess you could just take my car and meet us all at the doctor's house. We can take his car since it was on the other side of the parking lot." She tossed the keys to Justin.

"Hey, thanks Rebecca," Justin said as he caught them and strode away looking forward to driving his new partner's car.

17

Jack walked into room 553 at the hospital to find Kathy sitting up in bed, glasses on, reading a book. The television was turned off and the room was quiet. Her youngest daughter, Esther, was sitting in the arm chair knitting what appeared to be a scarf. The late afternoon sun, shining into the room, reflected on Kathy's lovely hair and he could see that she had put on a little make-up. It was apparent that she was not going to let this hospital experience change her routine any more than it had to.

"Good afternoon. You look ... radiant," he commented, letting his guard down a little. He smiled at Kathy and she looked up from her book.

Kathy had been reading a book about the Bible figure Ruth, a woman who was devoted to her mother-in-law and was faithful to God. Laying it aside, she slipped off her reading glasses and crinkled her nose saying, "These things make me look like a little old grandma." Then she laughed, "Well I guess I am a grandma, I just don't feel old."

"You're not old and I don't think the glasses add to your age." Changing the subject Jack asked, "Did you meet Dr. Clark yet?"

Kathy was about to answer him when her face grew a puzzled look. She noticed the Jack was not alone and with him was a rather attractive younger woman. She had not thought much about her feelings toward Jack today since her sudden change of well being. However, suddenly a slight pang of rivalry came from within as she was not sure who this woman might be. She remembered that she had told Jack how she felt, but now she realized that he had not actually said that he felt the same way about her. What if he already had a girlfriend? The thought came unbidden and she began to feel foolish in how she had acted earlier in the morning. The woman stepped back into the hallway and Kathy decided not to say anything.

"Kathy. Did you hear me?" Jack was speaking to her and she

realized she had not answered.

"What? Oh, yes, Dr. Clark was in earlier this afternoon." She looked directly at Jack now and tried to pay closer attention. She set her concerns for the other woman aside. "He said that he thinks he can successfully remove the tumor, but wants to wait a few days until the swelling is better controlled by the steroids. He said, though, that if the pressure continues to rise he will have to start sooner."

"I see," said Jack noncommittally. "I wasn't sure if he would need to do something immediately or not. I suppose you will have to stay here, though, so we can keep giving you the IV fluids and steroids."

"No. Dr. Clark said he would set up home health to give the meds to me at home and he has me on the schedule for Tuesday morning. I'll spend the night and leave in the morning," Kathy answered.

Jack had noticed the lack of emotion in her voice and interpreted it as tiredness. He was unaware of the conflict going on in her mind or the angst brought on by Rebecca Sweate's presence.

"All right. It looks like they have you taken care of for now. I'll stop by in the morning to see how you're doing." He leaned over to give her a hug, but found two cold shoulders and no reciprocal movement. He stood back up and smiled weakly. He was taken aback by her lack of response until he recalled Detective Sweate. He had intended to introduce her to Kathy.

"Just a second," he said quickly. He quickly stepped to the door and called, "Detective Sweate?" and motioned for her to come.

Rebecca entered, feeling a little awkward. She stepped up to the bed, hand out but before she could say anything Jack put in, "Kathy, this is the detective I mentioned. Rebecca Sweate."

Kathy's comprehension was immediate. She grinned at Rebecca, "Nice to meet you. I hope you don't have to lock Jack up in one of your cells." She meant this jokingly.

Rebecca, with a strained smile said, "It isn't looking that way. Nice to meet you Kathy."

As Rebecca backed out of the room Jack waved goodbye. Esther, who had remained silent until now, put down her knitting and jumped up. Running over to Jack and giving him a hug she said tearfully, "Come back soon Dr. Jack."

"You know I will, sweetie. I'll pray for you both every moment I can. I'll see you soon."

Kathy smiled and waved, tears also beginning to run down her cheeks.

Once in the hallway Rebecca said, "I see that she is on the oncology floor. Does she have cancer?"

He glanced up, "Well, we don't know for sure." He decided he could say a little about Kathy's condition without damaging her confidentiality. "She has a newly diagnosed brain tumor and we don't know yet what kind it is."

Rebecca looked grave, "I see. That doesn't sound too good."

"You're right. When it comes to brain tumors it doesn't always matter if it is a cancerous tumor. Even a benign mass can kill the patient. She needs surgery and I'm a little surprised they are going to wait." He was not alarmed, but he had seen significant changes in just twenty-four hours. He hoped the steroids would do the job of reducing her cerebral edema, the swelling of the brain.

****

Jack and Rebecca said little to each other on the way to his house, and as they turned up the street he saw two cars parked in front of it. One was a police car and the other was Rebecca Sweate's sporty Honda Accord. Two officers were standing on the sidewalk and Detective Samuelson was near them now glancing in their direction. Justin was grinning as he stroked the all black Honda. It had tinted windows, stick shift, and special wheels. It was a powerful car and Jack was sure it could move quite fast.

Across the street from Jack's house, Randy was working in his front garden. He had turned and was staring at the police presence debating within himself whether to say anything about the visitor whom he had seen earlier. He made up his mind, took off his work gloves ambled his way down the driveway where he was noticed by the others now gathered around Dr. Sharp.

"Hey Jack, may I talk to you?"

Jack, who had watched him come down the driveway, was already making his way over to him. He half-turned to motion for the police to wait. "Sure Randy. What's up?"

Just out of earshot Randy stood with Dr. Sharp. With his face turned away from them he said quietly, "Were you expecting a computer repair guy today?"

"No. Why?" Jack asked openly.

"I thought you should know. I saw a guy with a computer shop shirt go into your house. He seemed to know the garage door code so I didn't think about it too much, but I've never seen anyone go into your house when you weren't around."

"Randy, thank you. You may have just helped me out a ton." Jack vigorously shook Randy's hand. "You need to tell the police what you saw."

Randy looked doubtful, "Jack what are they doing here? Is this something to do with that murder yesterday?"

"Randy, they are just checking out the house. The guy you saw may be mixed up in it, though. Come on let's talk to them." Jack led the way and Randy reluctantly followed him over to the group of police. Introducing him, Jack said to Rebecca, "Randy has seen something I think may be important."

Randy related to the detectives and uniformed police what he had seen and that the man hadn't driven his vehicle up to the driveway. They showed him a copy of the sketch made by Josie Reickmann. Randy looked at it for a while. "He had a hat and dark glasses, but he was big and had thick arms. It could have been him."

Rebecca answered, "About what time was that Mr. Johnson?"

"Oh, I'd say about ten-thirty."

She gave him a business card and said, "If you see that man again or if you think of anything else please call me at that number." She paused. Also, I need to get an official statement from you. May I send one of the officers over now?"

"I guess so. I have to start supper, but if it doesn't take too long it'll be all right." Randy returned to his house entering through his own garage door followed by Arvillo, one of the uniformed policemen who had come to Jack's home. As Randy moved away the group made their way to the front steps of Jack's house.

Rebecca led Jack to the door of his own house where he unlocked the door. She had instructed the policemen to look for anything out of the ordinary. She was also counting on Jack to notice anything out of place, although it would really be much easier if they could have done this without him. But the overheard phone call from Greg Connolly was a break they could not have expected.

Rebecca had made a brief call while Jack had talked to Randy. To Jack she said, "Oh, Dr. Sharp, I'm afraid there's no news about the person who shot at you and Justin. We found the car, abandoned. We're checking it out but it looks like it was wiped clean of prints.

"Whomever it was had to have followed one of us to the parking lot, but I don't remember anyone pulling in. It must have happened while I was on the phone after Detective Samuelson arrived."

"I'm glad I'm not the one who has to figure this out!" said Jack.

Rebecca changed the subject. "Your neighbor said the computer guy went in through the garage door. He was probably wearing gloves, but I'll have the forensic team come out here and dust for prints. We'll need yours for comparison. Has anyone else been in the house lately?"

"I have a cleaning lady who comes on Mondays and my lawyer was here last night. Wouldn't my prints already be in the system since I was in the military?" Jack asked with genuine interest.

"Yes," she said with a sly look on her face, "we found out about that. You are right, but the military system is separate and it would save time for visual and computer searches if we get our own current set. It is merely a formality to eliminate your prints from those we find in your own home," she said as she donned vinyl gloves herself looking around at the tastefully decorated interior of Dr. Sharp's home.

Rebecca noticed a painted landscape in the first room on her left and a baby grand piano in the corner. The room was not large, but big enough to accommodate this stately piece. It was a beautifully polished piano and its color was almost a golden brown with a shimmering finish. She could not help but comment, "What a beautiful piano. Do you play?"

"Thank you. I inherited that from my parents who bought it used, in the fifties. I have had it restored and I think they did a wonderful job. It is a Steinway and the wood is burl walnut, made in the 1920's. Notice the Queen Anne legs and detailed carving. It has a fabulous sound." He walked over to the piano and stroked it like a pet. "I don't play well, but occasionally I have small instrumental groups here for mini-concerts and jam sessions. My instrument is the saxophone."

He obviously loved talking about this subject.

Rebecca was tempted to sit at the keys and play, but knew that she must continue with her investigation. She rarely had the opportunity to play piano, as she did not own one. She sighed as she thought of all the years of lessons her mother had paid for and all the hours of practice she had put in. Now she closely inspected the sound board and interior structure. "Someday I would like to play on such a beautiful piano," she heard herself say. Then remembering her mission she opened the lid on the seat which held charts of jazz piano parts and some Chopin pieces. There was nothing, however, relating to a murdered young woman.

"So you are a pianist?" Jack observed.

"I have had my share of lessons and I played quite a bit once," she answered.

"I would be happy to have you play on this piano. I know this is not the time, but perhaps another time when this is all in the past you could join us." Jack was looking at her with interest. Until now he had merely thought of Rebecca Sweate as a detective, but realized that she was a person with interests and emotions too.

Gus, who had been waiting patiently by the front door, cleared his throat, "Dr. Sharp, why don't we go upstairs and you can check out the rooms up there?" Jack nodded, leaving Rebecca to finish the living room. He and Gus went through his bedroom and closets. Visually inspecting things, Jack saw nothing unusual. He peeked in drawers and found the usual clothing and miscellaneous things. Gus then went to work removing items from drawers and going through them systematically. Jack realized then that 'search' didn't mean just looking. He could see that he would have to spend a great deal of time picking things back up afterward.

Without touching anything else, he walked through each room checking on the sparse furnishings in the extra un-used rooms. He had chosen a four bedroom house plan mainly for the purpose of having an easily re-salable house. He rarely had overnight guests but occasionally his sister, from Oregon, had stayed there with her family. He really didn't need so much space for himself and, though he had a cleaning lady, he still did some of the regular clean-up. That and a little yard work were relaxing weekend duties.

Jack used one of the rooms as an office, but the others were typical bedrooms. As he descended the stairs he saw the officer, Arvillo, talking to Detective Sweate. If Officer Gus was muscular and powerful, Arvillo could be described as his opposite. Wiry and short in stature, Arvillo, nonetheless, appeared to be very self confident. His olive complexion belied a heritage from Mexico or a southern country and on the few occasions when he had spoken Jack had detected a faint accent. He and Rebecca looked up as Jack descended the stairs. Rebecca said, "Good. You are finished up there. Maybe you could help us as we go through the most used rooms."

Jack scanned the kitchen and noticed immediately that things were different than he had left them in the morning. He wasn't sure what, exactly, had changed, but knew it was so. He made note of this to himself then moved on into the great room where the books and entertainment equipment were kept. The books were lined up correctly but, again, something was different.

He said, "Something has changed in both rooms. I can't tell yet exactly what but I know it."

"All right," Rebecca said. She nodded at Arvillo let's take the great room and when Gus is done upstairs we'll all concentrate on the kitchen.

They began removing books from the shelves. Almost immediately Arvillo noticed something important. "Detective. Look at the tops of these books from the bottom shelf." He held them out for her. With the sunlight glancing through the panes of the great room windows she could see that the dust was disturbed along the top of the books. Someone had recently pulled these volumes from the shelf. Arvillo asked, "Doc, have you taken these books out lately?"

Jack answered, "No, I don't look through those too often." They were volumes of an old encyclopedia set he had purchased at a library sale. Despite the availability of online encyclopedias he sometimes liked to look over old articles and look at photos from the old editions. "And as you can tell we haven't dusted there for a while."

Rebecca said, "Let's see how many books have these marks on them." They found that most of the books on the shelf that had any dust on them showed signs of being examined. "Someone was looking for something in these books, but what?" There was little dust anywhere else in the room so no new answers were forthcoming. "Do you have a safe or something like a book-safe?"

"Not a book 'safe' but one book has some coins in it." He strategically chose not to mention his hidden wall safe. He would check that himself. "I don't have any valuable jewelry. I wouldn't normally need to hide anything I have. I use a safe deposit box at the bank for some things, though," Jack answered. He took down the hollowed out book and showed the coins to the officers.

Gus spoke from the steps, "Ma'am, I didn't find anything that looked important. Sorry for the mess, Doc. We take stuff out, but you'll get to put it away again." He had a cat-like smile and shrugged his shoulders as he spoke. Jack only nodded. With that the trio of police turned as one toward the kitchen. Left to last this was the most daunting room on this floor. Not knowing what to look for made the task maddeningly complex too.

Jack wanting to be helpful reluctantly reminded them, "Don't forget the basement." He hoped that by being cooperative now and allowing a thorough search this would be the only time the police invaded his privacy.

Rebecca scowled. She had actually overlooked the obvious. Most houses in their community had basements and the one in this home was, no doubt, extensive.

"Arvillo, you spotted the dust marks. Why don't you start looking at the basement. We'll join you if we ever finish with the kitchen," she gave out the order and found to her delight that Arvillo obeyed without a comment. He slipped down the door to the basement and she was left with Gus and the doctor. "Look once more around the kitchen and think hard, Dr. Sharp."

He walked back over and turned on all the lights. This reminded him of the CSI shows he had watched. On TV they seemed to like searching with flashlights in the darkness. To him it seemed much easier to search in well- illuminated room. He had cleaned up the few dishes last night and there hadn't been any more this morn- ing, since he had eaten with Kathy. He glanced from side to side taking in the room. The knife block caught his eye. He always had it turned exactly ninety degrees to the wall on the counter near the sink. Now it was at a forty-five degree angle, toward the sink. He kept looking that way but pointed.

"The knife block has been moved and there's a knife missing." A chill went down Jack's spine. He didn't like this. He recalled the woman who had been stabbed.

Gus stepped to the sink and looked carefully around. He pulled each knife out of its slot one by one. Looking at them carefully he held the blade in such a way that it reflected the light searching for fingerprints. He gingerly removed all the remaining knives and placed them in a bag for later fingerprint analysis.

"Do you do a lot of cooking doctor?" Rebecca asked benignly.

"About half the time I make my own dinner, but I eat out quite a bit," he responded. The officers were looking through cabinets and under the sink. He could tell they would still take a while to complete their task because of their thoroughness.

"The kitchen is a common place for people to try to hide things. There is so much to look through it is harder to spot contraband. But if you are careful most hiding places can be sniffed out." She crossed her arms then looked directly at Dr. Sharp. "Okay. I haven't changed my mind about you, but would you mind going outside while we finish? I think we can take it from here. The crime scene people should be here any time."

Jack didn't like these developments. After all, hadn't he invited them to look in his home? He also wondered what had become of Sam, his lawyer. Nevertheless, he did as he was told and left the house just as a dark blue van pulled into his driveway disgorging three dark-suited police crime scene specialists. They were a little surprised to see him exiting the home, but did not speak to him as they gathered their equipment and hurried in. Other neighbors were returning home from work and he noted the concerned looks on their faces as they drove past.

Jack breathed deeply hoping the crisp autumn air would bring clarity to his mind. The events of the past two days had filled his thoughts with horrific images. He had felt fear, anger, revulsion but also deep personal emotions toward Kathy and her family. He considered calling her to see how she was doing, but decided against it. He mulled over their breakfast conversation, so much had happened since that fateful meal. This woman had told him she didn't want him to be her doctor, but it was because they had strong feelings toward each other. It was hard for him to figure out. Was he falling in love with her or just feeling deeply sympathetic?

At first he sat on his porch in his wicker glider chair. Sitting here on warm mornings with his coffee and the paper was usually a pleasant pastime for him. Today, however, he was restless and sitting didn't suit his mood. He stood again and looked at his state-ly oak tree ahead of him. This tree, too, stood unwavering and silent. Its large leaves were among the last to change color and fall to the earth in the fall. His thoughts turned to God and closing his eyes, he sent silent prayers to Him.

The late afternoon light was beginning to fade as he wandered around the house past other smaller trees. He pulled a few stray weeds and inspected status of his waning flower beds. Planting trees and working in the garden were satisfying activities. As the plants grew they changed the character of the landscape. His plantings were beginning to mature and take on the, hoped for, appearance with bright spring flowers and colorful fall foliage.

As he rounded the corner at the back of the house he was met by the fiery glow of his Autumn Blaze maple as the last golden rays of the day struck its top. Each year this globe-shaped tree inspired him to take out his camera and photograph the brightly colored foliage.

Above him he heard the sliding door open. "Dr. Sharp, we are almost finished here for now." He looked up to see Rebecca standing at the edge of his deck. The light from the late afternoon sun seemed to be reflecting from the scarlet maple throwing auburn highlights into the waves of her hair. He wondered why he hadn't noticed her attractiveness before, then wondered why he was thinking about that at all. His life was getting complicated enough with one woman.

"We found something else. Her tone was flat and not challenging, but in a more matter-of-fact manner. "Come on up and I'll show you."

Jack ascended the deck stairs noticing a slight sway, indicating the need for some remediation to the decking. He was in no hurry and felt fatigue wash over him as he reached the open deck. Rebecca had not moved and now was smiling at him. "Detective Samuelson checked in with me a minute ago. He had no trouble getting the phone number of the caller, but he is not having much success in running down who used it. It may have been a throw away type cell phone. We're nearly done for the day, and will be out of your hair soon, I hope."

Rebecca's last comment was enough of a warning to snap Jack back to the present. He peered quickly over the railing sighing at his interrupted contemplation. Soon maybe his life would be back to normal. He asked as he turned back to the now pleasant detective, "What have you found, besides a missing knife?"

She held up a zippered bag whose spidery contents moved around as she lifted it. "This necklace was in your silverware drawer. Do you recognize it?"

He reached for the bag. "May I?"

Rebecca nodded as she handed the bag over, "Just don't open it. Oh, and we found your missing knife. It was in the drawer next to the necklace. It has been wiped down and is still damp as if someone had just cleaned it and smells like chlorine. We'll need to take it too, I'm afraid."

The coolness of her tone was obvious and he couldn't help wonder if she still thought of him as a potential suspect despite her assurances.

He held the necklace and bag up to the light. "I didn't get too close and the light was not strong when I was looking at her body, but this looks like the necklace she was wearing." Jack answered with as open and straight-forward a manner as he could muster.

He had, unfortunately, learned that just being honest didn't prevent suspicion so he waited for Rebecca's judgment.

"I had noticed a discrepancy in our property list with what you had told us about the scene yesterday. You mentioned the necklace, but when I went through the list of the young woman's belongings there was no necklace," Rebecca returned. "You have been open with us from the beginning. I don't usually apologize, but I am sorry for what we have put you through since yesterday."

"Well, I haven't even had much time to process it. I knew there was a risk just notifying the authorities, but I always thought a person would be believed and 'innocent until proven guilty.'" His mild reproach was not unnoticed, but Rebecca didn't say anything for a moment.

"Do you realize, though what this means?" she asked.

"What, what means?" Jack said scowling.

"You saw the necklace on her. By the time we arrived it was gone," Rebecca looked straight at the doctor. "Someone surely had to have visited the body between your finding it and our arrival."

"How could that be!" Jack exclaimed. "I wasn't that far away and it is hard to move quietly in the underbrush."

"Undoubtedly we were supposed to think that too. You know if Justin hadn't overheard that call you would be in handcuffs right now." Rebecca turned pacing the deck. She was chagrined that they could have been manipulated so easily by the jogger or who-ever had made the phone call.

Jack thought quickly. "All right I would be, but I'm not because I think you believe me now. So why did he take the risk of returning to the body? It had to be the jogger. He must have doubled back and slipped through the bushes from below. Maybe he had a car in the other direction. He wasn't out there for a jog at all." This small part of the puzzle was starting to reveal its picture. It didn't explain the murder, but placed suspicion squarely on the jogger.

"There must be some significance to the necklace. We'll find out," Rebecca declared. Jack looked more closely at the necklace. The pendant had lettering on it. He said, "I can't make out the lettering and this pendant is fairly heavy. Maybe it is more like a locket and he wanted what was inside it." Rebecca stepped over, reached out and lightly slipped the bag from Jack's hand smiling. She stood looking at him intently for just a moment.

Jack for his part noticed the look and considered his options. He had recently been a possible murder suspect in this woman's eyes. He had Kathy to consider, too, not knowing for sure exactly where he stood with her. He almost laughed. For a long time it seemed that no women had shown interest in him. Now he was confronted with attention from two women. One was his patient and one was his interrogator.

All these emotions passed in the literal blink of an eye. Rebecca broke the connection between them, stepped up to the sliding deck door and entered the house saying,

"The sooner we get this back to the lab the sooner we will know if it is significant." She left the door partly open as she coyly looked over her shoulder, "The crime scene folks shouldn't be much longer since they are mainly just dusting for prints."

"Okay, I'll stay here until they're gone and watch the rest of the sunset."

18

The police van pulled out of the driveway and Jack breathed a sigh of relief. Turning to his front door, however, he saw the mess his house had become. Not wanting to face the prospect of a microwave meal among all the ruins of the search, he decided to go out for dinner. He hoped that his status as a suspect had dropped a few notches due to his cooperation. Yet he hadn't been given any "all clear" indication from the detective. With so much happening he couldn't believe how long the day had gotten. He needed some "down" time to himself. Shaking his head once again at the chaos around him he shut the door and went to his car.

****

Dan was irritable. After the phone call he had expected the police to search the doctor's house and immediately arrest him. Yet there he was just standing in his own doorway. *Could they have missed the clues?*

Angry that the police had not taken the bait and arrested the doctor, he gripped his steering wheel tightly. Back in his car, Dan had watched them go to the doctor's house from a block away. Surely he hadn't hidden things too carefully. There had been nothing wrong with his plan so he couldn't understand why the doctor was not in custody. Dan wanted the doctor locked up so he could be free to pursue his next move then get out of town.

Dr. Sharp seemed to be a knot in the smooth cord of his plans. If this doctor hadn't seen the body, Dan would have been free to finish his search. Then of all things, this doctor had seen him and might yet connect him with the woman. Now he was boxed in. He decided that the only way he could extricate himself was for the doctor to disappear.

Dan followed the doctor to a local restaurant, but as they drove down one main street Dan saw something that nearly made him drive off the road. His own face stared down at him from a bright billboard sign. It was a drawing, but so much like his countenance that he was amazed. He was so dumbstruck that he almost failed to see the doctor's car turn into the parking lot. Slamming on his brakes and crossing two lanes he managed to turn in too. He saw the doctor park and get out of his car and enter a nearby restaurant. Dan parked in the back of the lot and tried to think. He was hungry too, but could not show his face here. He would really have to keep a low profile now. Pressing his head against the steering wheel he debated his next move

Should he just cut and run? The realization came to him, however, that he had no place to run. Either he completed his mission or he was dead.

Dan knew where the doctor lived so he really didn't have to watch him. Dan expected him to go home soon enough. Sitting, once more, in a parking lot could be risky too especially with his face lighting up the night. He decided to return to the doc's home and have another surprise waiting for him.

****

Jack was shown to a table where he sat and ordered an appetizer and iced tea. Looking over the menu his mind played tricks on him. He couldn't concentrate on what he should order. The problems of the day kept intruding in his thoughts. He laid the menu aside removed his glasses and rested his head in his hands. Silently he prayed, "Oh God, I am really needing you today. I feel pretty lost and don't know what to do next. I want to help Kathy, I want this murderer caught. Why did I get mixed up in this? What are you trying to teach me?"

As he sat in that pose, the server arrived with the tea and his appetizer. She was a little uncertain what to do. This man seemed to be sad and maybe was crying into his hands. She started to leave thinking she would watch and return in a few minutes when he raised his head.

"Sorry... Sharon," he read her name on her badge. "I have had a trying day. Go ahead and set things down."

She saw that his face was dry so she was relieved he had not been crying, but she hadn't seen too many people pray in a public place before.

"Hi," she said sweetly as if she hadn't noticed anything odd. "I'm ... oh you already know my name," she laughed nervously. "Can I bring you some dinner tonight?"

He realized that he hadn't chosen anything from the menu and quickly opened it again.

"I'll have the chicken fajitas. Okay?"

This satisfied her. He wasn't going to burst into tears or start moaning about his wife leaving him or something. She jotted down his order and nodded. "Okay. Be right back," she said automatically. Sharon decided to keep an eye on him. His behavior was a little odd and he probably wouldn't leave much of a tip either.

Jack ate his appetizer and sipped his tea as his eyes took in the restaurant. There was a bar with a few couples sitting and enjoying their tall glasses of beer. The televisions were tuned to a football game, but he was unable to see the names of the teams or the scores. He knew it wasn't college ball so he wasn't too interested. The Nebraska Cornhuskers had been *his* team for as long as he could remember. There had been some great years and he had been there, in Memorial Stadium, cheering on his team for many of the games. The football team was currently going through some difficult years, but the Nebraska fans remained faithful filling the stadium to capacity game after game for over thirty years.

The booths around him were empty and he glanced at his watch. It was later than he had thought, eight thirty.

His food arrived and the server seemed to hesitate.

Jack smiled. "Don't worry. I'm finished praying."

"Oh! You mean like grace?"

"Not just grace. I was praying about the day."

"You can do that? Right here in public?" she was incredulous but interested. Was he a priest? He didn't have a collar. "Are you a preacher or something?" she asked.

Jack smiled and laughed. "No, but I am a Christian. Do you go to church?" He knew that he might make her uncomfortable, but a little pang of guilt might be just what she needed.

She moved a little closer her head down, "I don't usually talk about religion. My dad told me it was a good way to start an argument."

Jack laughed again, "I assure you I don't want to do that. I just know how important a relationship with Jesus Christ is. Going to church can be a start for some folks."

"I go sometimes. I'm a Methodist. The new church out on 84th Street is really nice and I like the music there," she said not knowing why she was willing to talk to this man.

"I know the minister there. His name is Tom Litke. He is a good man and his wife is an excellent cook. Have you spoken to them at all?" Jack asked.

"I've only gone a couple of times," she said quietly.

"Sure. Do you like to sing too?" he said pleasantly.

Jill blushed, "I tried out for American Idol, but didn't make it past the first stage."

"God isn't as picky as those judges. Why don't you go this Sunday and after the service say hello to Pastor Tom? Tell him that you like to sing. I'll bet he would introduce you to the choir director." Jack saw her eyes get big. "Hey, if you can go before the judges at American Idol, you can sing in a church choir."

Jill marveled that she had gotten into this conversation. She did love singing, but had never considered church music. A far away look came into her eyes and she thanked her new customer. As she walked around picking up empty plates she continued to think about what he had said to her. *What could it hurt? Maybe I could go back to that church as he suggested.* She swept into the brightly lit kitchen, her mind on music and singing.

****

A plan had been forming in Dan's mind, but he faced a new challenge. He wanted to get back into the doctor's house to wait for the doctor, but this time could not use the garage opener. A lone walker entering the garage at night would definitely raise alarms. This time he would have to sneak around and actually break in.

At the back of the house he found sliding glass doors on both levels. These had locks that were difficult to "pick" because there was no key hole. He tried the windows then slipped around to the side. He debated with himself. He could try to break a window and get in that way, but the noise might arouse a dog or a neighbor and that would mess things up. He had to get in without leaving a trace. On the north side of the garage there was a regular door with a key lock in the door knob. These were inexpensive locks and easily picked. If he could open this one quickly without being seen he would, again, gain access to the unwatched garage. The garage front lights were on and he risked being seen, yet he knew he could do it quickly.

Dan crept forward keeping his face away from the glow of the garage lights. A few clicks of the pick and a twist and he was in. He entered the dark, garage but stumbled on the garbage can. He froze letting the noise die down hoping it had not been noticed. He heard nothing. Darkness was his friend and now he had all the time in the world. His nemesis, Dr. Sharp, would be home soon and his little problem would be behind him. This time he would make sure it took a lot longer to find the body. If Dr. Sharp disappeared while under suspicion everyone would think he had fled to avoid prosecution.

He looked around the house and saw that a thorough search had already been conducted. "Hm. It's messy around here. Good. When they see that he is gone and that the house is still messed up from the search they'll assume he took off in a hurry, like he had something to hide. I'll need to ditch the car too. One thing at a time," he said to himself. He gingerly opened the silverware drawer and peered in by flashlight. No necklace and no knife. They had found his clues! "I'll bet they are just waiting to make the arrest in a public place," he chuckled quietly. "This will work out just fine. They'll forget all about me while they search for the doc. Then I'll get my business taken care of and my uncle and the boss will be happy." The last thought made him shudder. He wasn't afraid of too many things, but his uncle's boss could scare the devil himself. If he didn't get this done soon he wouldn't have to worry about anything.

He'd be dead.

****

Jack could see the traffic light turn red on his last turn for home. He was tired and looking forward to a little peace and sleep. He stopped briefly then the green arrow gave him permission to turn. Just then his phone vibrated on his hip. He considered ignoring it, but decided to look at the number calling him. He pulled up along the side of the street and unclipped his phone. One look at the number brought surprise and a groan at the same instant. It was the hospital, but this time it was Labor and Delivery calling. He thought quickly. He didn't have any babies due for at least two to three weeks. He pressed the call-back button and listened.

"Labor and Delivery," came the pleasant voice of the secretary.

"Hello, this is Doctor Sharp. I was paged," he said automatically.

"Just a moment, Doctor. I'll get Sue she's right here."

Jack was a little annoyed. He had told Doug that he would be off for at least a week. He thought the call schedule and obstetrics coverage would be taken care of.

"Hello, Dr. Sharp," a much more stressed sounding voice came on the line. "Jevia Oaatu is here. She has been at home for a day with contractions and showed up eight centimeters dilated. She is contracting every minute or two. She's thirty seven weeks, but her last two delivered even earlier. Your last note said she was small for dates so you probably should come soon."

Jack groaned inwardly, but he knew his duty. Of all the things he did as a physician he enjoyed delivering babies the most and didn't usually ask others to take on that responsibility when he was in town. Even if he put this call off on his partner there was no guarantee that the nurses could reach Dr. Miller quickly enough.

"Okay," he said with a voice as pleasant as he could muster, "I'll be there in ten minutes. Tell her to hang on."

"Oh, we will. Thank you, Doctor Sharp."

He looked behind him and seeing no traffic did a U-turn heading back in the direction of the hospital. With energy he had not felt before, he hit the gas and smiled as he sped toward the hospital.

****

Jack arrived at the hospital in good time and pulled into the slot reserved for "OB Physicians." He still had a fair distance to walk to reach labor and delivery and he hoped he had time. He called the nurse while entering the building.

"Do I have time to change?" he asked.

"Yes," came the answer, "but not much more."

Jack hurried into the locker room and quickly doffed his clothes in favor of hospital scrubs. He threw his stuff into a locker and pulled on an old pair of tennis shoes left in the room for just this purpose. Trotting down the hall he paused briefly in front of the door of the labor room to put on hat, mask, and shoe covers. He could hear screaming from behind the door and he steeled himself for a wild ride.

Stepping into the room Jack found his patient lying on her back, hair damp and disheveled. She looked up at him and smiled. In deeply accented English she said, "I wondered if you would come. My last two were born in a village. We had no doctor..." then a look of anguish came over her as the pain from another contraction flooded through her. Her eyes rolled back and she began yelling, "I eeeeee, oh, oh, oh!"

The nurse was attempting to calm her, "Relax your arms. Don't push. Breathe with the contractions!" but little was getting through to her during the contraction. Jevia was in a trance-like state during the painful part of the contractions. Through all of this Jack was being gowned and gloved by an assistant and keeping an eye out for the crowning of the baby's head.

Once ready he approached just as a contraction was ending. Jack could hear the erratic beep of the fetal heart rhythm from the heart monitor. It was slowing, but not dangerously so. Once again Jevia's eyes opened and her gaze burned into him.

"Get it out!" she shouted then lay back breathing hard. He checked to find that everything was fine and she could begin pushing.

"It's okay to push with the next contraction, Jevia. You know what to do. I'm right here and soon you'll have a beautiful baby girl." Jack realized that he was not certain that she was to have a girl. It had slipped out. The nurse looked at him curiously.

"Jevia said she doesn't know if it's a girl," Lisa the labor nurse said to me. "Do you know something she doesn't know?"

Jack smiled beneath his mask and said calmly, "We'll just have to wait and see won't we?" Then the yell began again. This time he spoke, "Jevia, hold your breath and push, no noise." She closed her lips and the energy flowed through her. He could feel the pressure transmitted through the baby's scalp. This one would be out soon. In fact, one push was all it took. The baby's head began to slip out into the world. The baby's lips were already moving and as the arms came free they were reaching out trying to hold onto his hands. All at once Jack held a small but lively baby girl crying almost as loudly as her mother had done a few minutes earlier. Jack, with the help of the assistant, clamped and cut the cord and wrapped her in a blanket, handing her to her mother. Jevia was now saying, "Thank you God, thank you God. A girl, oh a girl, thank you God! Dr. Sharp, how did you know?"

She didn't expect an answer and anyway, Jack had none.

"What is her name?" Jack asked dodging her question.

"We haven't thought about girl names much ... I think she is Tavatea. In my language that means 'Blessing.'" She was rocking her baby and smiling even as tears of joy rolled down her cheeks.

The delivery had occurred with no complications and the mother was fine. She needed no suturing and was doing very well. The baby needed nothing either, but the nurses gently lifted her from her mother's abdomen.

"We'll just weigh and measure her and the doctor will need to check her over," said the nursery nurse. She had listened to the baby's heart and lungs as Jevia held her and knew that she was vigorous.

Jack stepped back and went through a quick exam of the baby girl judging that she had no problems that they could identify. She weighed five pounds four ounces.

"Just a little squirt. It's a good thing I got here when I did or the nurses and you would have had this party without me."

Jack walked over and Jevia reached up. She gave him a warm hug and whispered in his ear, "Thank you, this is such a blessing."

Jack returned the gentle embrace and prayed with her thanking God for His gift.

Next came the paperwork and Jack explained to the patient and nurses that his partner, Dr. Miller was on call for the weekend and he would inform him of the delivery. Dr. Miller would be around to see them both in the morning.

As Jack finished dressing back in the locker room his phone began to vibrate again. He was again tempted to ignore it, but looking at the number he saw that it was a hospital number. Jack didn't recognize it, but thought it could be a secondary nursery or obstetrics phone. He answered the call, "Hello. Dr. Sharp."

A somewhat frantic voice came on the line.

"Dr. Sharp, your patient is having a seizure. Can you come?"

19

Jack was shocked. "Who is having a seizure? Jevia Oaatu? The baby? Where are you calling from?" he asked, already starting to move.

"No Doctor, Kathy Sanders is seizing. She's in five fifty three," the nurse was composed but the urgency had not left her voice.

"I'm in-house and I'll be there in a minute. Have you called Drs. Clark or Brackenhorst?"

"We have a page out to Dr. Clark but he hasn't answered yet."

"Okay, give her five milligrams of valium, IV and I'll be right there." He closed the phone running through the hallway. Jack flashed past patients and nurses who looked surprised that he was running away from the delivery rooms. He burst through the door into the hallway adjoining the different parts of the hospital. He didn't wait for an elevator, but took the stairs two steps at a time. Through another door Jack was only a few steps away and he could see people standing outside the room. He slowed his pace and panting, addressed the family. Esther saw him first and hugging him said, "Dr. Jack! What's happening to Mom?"

Jack gently extracted himself and held her arms. "Esther, I'll go in and see. You just wait out here and I'll let you know in a few minutes. Okay?"

She nodded her tear streaked face. Jack glanced up at two of her brothers, Frank and Jonathan, and nodded to them. Then he went into Kathy's room. He could hear a rhythmical noise of movement on the bed and as he drew closer could see Kathy still having a seizure. Her neck was arched and elbows flexed. It wasn't as violent as some he had witnessed, but he knew this belied the violence taking place in her brain. She was at risk of running out of oxygen if the seizure was not stopped. Jack noticed that she had an IV line still in place. No other doctor had arrived yet, but the crash cart was there. One of the nurses was adjusting the IV flow. He noticed her name on her name tag and spoke to her.

150

"Arlie. How long has the seizure been continuous?"

"Almost ten minutes now, Doctor," she said holding the syringe in the air.

"Did you give the valium yet?"

"Yes doctor. Just before you arrived."

"Okay. Give five more milligrams." Jack knew she could think on her own, but her training was to act only if there was no "higher" authority available.

The nurse didn't hesitate. She repeated the order, "Five milligrams of valium IV, yes doctor." She attached the syringe with its needle-less connection to the IV and watched the barrel as she injected the prescribed amount into the line. She then opened the valve slightly to allow the IV fluid to flush the drug into Kathy's system.

This time the movement on the bed subsided. Kathy was relaxing and her arms fell to her sides. She had not become cyanotic, a purplish color of the skin that is a sign of the lack of oxygen, but there was blood on her lips and she was making a gurgling, groaning noise. She was still unconscious and another nurse picked up a suction catheter gently working it in her mouth to clear the secretions. A nurse's aide appeared with a moist wash cloth and wiped her face. Expertly, no one had tried to restrain Kathy, as they were aware of the risks of this. Their training and education had taught them that doing so can potentially cause more harm than good and could lead to injury of the patient or the helper. Someone had slipped an oral airway into her mouth which would allow her to breathe on her own. Once she was more alert she would cough it out. At the moment, though, she was totally unaware of it. The oxygen saturation monitor read "97%" meaning that she was getting enough oxygen without additional supplementation. "Please get an arterial blood gas stat."

The nurse acknowledged the order and reached for her phone.

Esther, who had heard the noises subside, appeared behind Dr. Sharp. He felt her grab his shirt and then heard her say, "Did Mommy die?"

Jack looked down again at Kathy and saw why Esther would

have asked the question. She lay disheveled on the bed head bent away. Her skin was pale and moist and she now lay totally unmoving.

Compassionately he said, "No, Esther, she's not dead. After a seizure people sleep very deeply. She'll wake up," he said with more confidence than he felt. He hoped he was right. The seizure may have occurred because of a stroke which could leave part of her body paralyzed. They wouldn't know until she did wake up. She was breathing evenly and her vital signs were returning to normal. "We will have to move her to a special room, but I think she'll be okay. She does have a problem though and more seizures could happen. We'll call the specialist and see what he thinks we should do."

Esther now buried her face in Jack's side and cried unhindered. This was getting to be too much for her. Jack had known Esther since birth, having delivered her in this very hospital eleven years earlier. Esther had always enjoyed coming in for check-ups and even talked about becoming a doctor. She had started calling him "Dr. Jack" and the name had stuck. Now missing her father and faced with the real prospect of losing her mother, she was overwhelmed with grief. Jack knelt and held her close until her sobs lessened. Then she let go and went into the bathroom to blow her nose.

Jack stepped over to the bed and bent down to listen to Kathy's lungs and heart with his stethoscope. He covered her arms and body with a sheet. She was still warm so he didn't add a blanket. Jack thanked the nurses and techs as people began to file out of the room. "We need to move her to ICU," he told the nurse who had injected the valium.

"I've already called them. Thank you for coming so quickly, Dr. Sharp. I'm glad you were in the hospital."

Just then Mack Clark appeared in the doorway. He stepped in and immediately took charge. Jack moved aside, glad to relinquish authority to him and hoped he could do even more to salvage the situation.

"How long was the seizure?" he asked of the nurse. "Did she require resuscitation?" His rapid fire questions were answered quickly and accurately by Arlie who had remained in the room.

With a glance at Esther, Mack ushered Jack out of the room. In hushed tones he said Jack, "I think we need to go to the OR tonight. She may be on the verge of herniation. An MRI could tell, but we need to go in sooner or later. I vote for sooner."

"You have a clear majority of the votes, Mack. I agree, though it would be nice to know what shape she is in now from the seizure." He meant that they could not know if there had been any brain damage otherwise.

"I know. It's a calculated risk. If she wakes up from surgery with brain damage, who knows if it was the seizure or surgery, but she could be out for hours or even days Jack." He looked back at Kathy she was breathing smoothly, but hadn't pushed the oral airway out of her mouth. "We've got a great anesthesia group. They'll take good care of her. Do you want me to tell the family?"

"No, that's all right. I know them pretty well. I'll take care of it." Esther had come out of the bathroom and was looking for Jack. Poking her head out of the room she heard the end of the conversation.

"Mom isn't going to die is she?" she whimpered.

"We'll do our best, honey. Let's go talk to your brothers and sisters." Several of her siblings were now present loitering in the hallway. Jack directed them to a small family conference room where they could speak together in privacy. He told them the situation and the need for the brain surgery. "Dr. Clark is an excellent brain surgeon. He has done operations like this many times. Your mother desperately needs surgery because the pressure is building in her brain. Do any of you have objections?"

Frank spoke up, "I don't have an objection, but couldn't we wait until Mom wakes up so we can speak to her again?"

Jack hung his head before answering. He had anticipated this question because he would want the same thing. "Dr. Clark pointed out that because of the seizure we don't know when she will be fully awake. If we decide to wait it could be too late for her." There were nods all around the room and Frank drew silent. "Why don't we put this all in God's hands?" he said.

Jack took hold of two of Kathy's children's hands and began then to pray and ask God's guidance and skill for the surgeon.

Each of them prayed for her safety and tears flowed freely. God would surely know of the love for her in that room.

They then filed out and the family went once more to Kathy's room. They were allowed to quickly stop in. Each kissed their mother on her cheek. She lay quietly unaware of their presence, though Jack noticed that her airway was no longer in her mouth and she was breathing easily. Jack looked up at the nurse who smiled and nodded.

She was optimistic too.

20

Saturday

Dan was becoming annoyed. *Where is that doctor? Why hadn't he come home?* He glanced out the window in the front of the house and noticed that the sky in the east was beginning to lighten. He looked at his watch; it read six o'clock. He must have dozed off and nothing had aroused him. Could the doctor have come home and gone up to bed without seeing him there. He cursed himself for being so stupid. He could have been caught right there.

He quietly pulled his revolver from his holster and looked quickly around the first floor. Gingerly opening the garage door he peered into the still-empty garage.

Sighing involuntarily he thought, "Where could he be?"

Dan knew that he had been defeated in his move to get the doctor. With his plan beginning to unravel, he was on the verge of panic. He was still tired and now running out of time. Desperate, angry at himself and the doctor, he tried to focus his thoughts. Had the doctor come home during the night he probably would have found him sleeping and called the police and it would have been over anyway. At least he was still free.

He re-holstered his weapon and took one more look out the front window. There was a car approaching on the cul-de-sac. *Could this be him at last?* However, it stopped half-way down the block. Someone got out of the car and began going house to house tossing out the morning paper.

Dan watched the woman delivering papers trot through the yards, dropping the rolls one by one. It didn't take her long and after a few minutes the car had, once again, departed. Now, however, the sky was definitely lighter, taking on a faintly yellow glow in the east. He could make out more details in the street. Now he was really worried about being seen, but waiting was not an option. Into the garage, he hurried and slipped out the side door to find

155

the air crisp in the frigid morning. The street was devoid of traffic and the houses were still quiet. If he could get to the sidewalk unnoticed, he could act like an exercise walker out for an early morning amble.

****

Randy Johnson, an early riser, stepped out onto his porch to get the paper. For some reason lately the "paper-person" had been leaving his by the garage instead of the front door. He made his way around and found his Saturday edition by the corner of the house. He started back when he noticed movement across the street. Randy quickly hid behind the corner of his garage and peered out. Someone was walking around outside Dr. Sharp's house. After the events of the previous day he knew this could be trouble so he froze in place.

Was that the doc going for a walk? He felt secure in his position and doubted that he could be seen as he was in the deep shadow cast by his own house. He observed the figure and noted that he seemed to be looking at the outside wall of the garage. The person crept forward then Randy saw the man quickly move down the drive just beneath the street lamp. He couldn't make out the features too well, but the body shape was familiar and it wasn't the doctor. He was almost sure it was the same man he had seen the previous day. This time he wore no cap or overalls and was dressed in very dark clothing. Briefly, just as he was moving away, the man looked around. At that moment Randy was certain that it was the same face he had seen in the police sketch. He had seen it too on the bright electronic billboard by the grocery store so he knew that he had seen the man wanted by the police.

Once the man was out of his line of sight, Randy sprinted to his back door, with his heart pounding. His wife was making coffee in the kitchen and was surprised by his urgency. She tried to question him about what was going on, but he was determined first to call about what he had seen. He grabbed up the phone from its cradle and dialed 911. He told the operator about the prowler and mentioned Detective Rebecca Sweate's name. He was instructed to hold on the line while the operator reached the police dispatcher. He moved to the front window in his darkened living room. Just catching sight of the man turning the corner at the bottom of the hill, he made note of his heading. When the police dispatcher answered, Randy told him all that had gone on. He was thanked and told to stay indoors. Police cruisers would be on the scene very soon.

****

Deep in thought as he walked down the street, Dan worried about his future. His plan would have been a good one if the doctor had cooperated. Now he had to walk several blocks to reach his van. He had not wanted to leave it in an obvious place nearby so he had parked near a home construction site. It probably would have been unnoticed for a few hours where he had left it, but it made his current situation precarious. He wanted to be on the road. It was quiet and he didn't know why he should worry, no one seemed to be outside and had done nothing all that wrong.

"Ease up a little," he told himself.

If he acted normally no one would pay any attention to him.

He approached the corner of his last turn and could see his van. *Only another block to go.* Trying to lessen his anxiety he said to himself, "This walk is actually kind of nice. I needed the exercise."

Just then he saw a police cruiser coming down the road. It stopped when it was near the van, as if checking it out. He reversed direction hoping his van would pass scrutiny. He was still looking back at the van. As his head turned he saw another cruiser coming toward him less than one hundred yards away.

The flashers on the top of the car came on suddenly and there was a single "whoop" from the siren. One policeman jumped out weapon drawn, "Hands in the air. Get down!" he demanded.

He was totally surprised. *How had they found him here?*

In confusion he began turning around in circles.

"Get down!" the policeman shouted again, "Now!"

Dan debated the wisdom of running. He was in great shape, but there were two cars and he didn't know the neighborhood.

Where would he go? He started backing away from the advancing policeman.

"Stop!" came the demanding voice. Now the policeman was closer. Dan, looking at the black hole of the officer's weapon, knew that at that distance this cop was not likely to miss. Disgusted and defeated, he raised his hands and bent down on his knees.

By this time neighbors had appeared at windows and a few had stepped out on their front porches. Some were just picking up the Saturday paper and others were sipping there coffee just looking on, but this drama had never been witnessed in this upscale neighborhood. A few began applauding and there were even a few congratulatory whistles, though no one really knew what had just happened. Trying to ignore the notoriety, the police officers, nevertheless, smiled at each other. This was a righteous bust.

The first policeman, Rod Axtell, who had drawn his weapon held his aim on the prostrate felon while his partner, Susanne Janda applied the handcuffs. She was not gentle and pinched the man's wrists while clicking them into place. Dan winced, but did not call out. Officer Janda applied pressure to his arms instructing him to rise to his feet. She then began to "read him his Miranda rights."

Dan's first words were, "I'm saying nuthin'. I want a lawyer." With that, he clammed up and the arresting officers heard nothing more from their prisoner. He was loaded into the back seat of the waiting cruiser, while the two pairs of police officers discussed the situation.

The officers who had checked out the van, Gus Wilson and Mike Jackson, had called in the plates on the vehicle. It turned out to be a rental, not stolen. They found it unlocked but nearly empty. A small bag on the front seat contained some electronic gadgets whose purposes were not immediately evident. There were no weapons in the van.

Rod and Susanne had found a small switchblade knife in the pocket of their quarry. There had also been a thirty eight caliber revolver in a belt holster behind his back. Thankfully, they had not had a shootout with this man. He had wisely kept his hands away from the weapon and now was playing things pretty coolly. They drove their cruiser to the matching car near the man's van.

"It looks like the van described yesterday," said Susanne. "It seems like we got really lucky today, Rod."

Rod smiled and said, "Yeah and we got the guy. All the big dudes got was his van." The credit for this arrest would be important for both of them. They were no longer rookies, but needed all the positive outcomes they could get to enhance their careers.

****

It was supposed to be a weekend off for Rebecca. Nevertheless, with a murder investigation hanging over her, she knew she couldn't take much of a break. They had a suspect to run down and he would have ample time to get even farther away if they didn't work the weekend. There was also the mysterious shooter who had fired on both the doctor and Justin. At least she did not have to be at her office particularly early. Justin had agreed to go over the details of their case at nine o'clock. Rebecca would go for a run and have a leisurely breakfast before going down town. The sun had sent its first brilliant red reflections through her windows when she opened her door to pick up the Saturday paper. The air was brisk, but not yet hinting at the bitter winter days ahead. The freshness of the air made her ache to be able just to go out and enjoy the day, not spend it working.

The crime lab people had looked at the necklace and the shirt from the trail. There were no recoverable prints on the shirt and she doubted trace analysis would help after it had sat outdoors for a day, nevertheless they would try find usable DNA. Unlike television shows, though, the DNA analysis would be several days away, due to their huge backlog. They had found a pair of vinyl gloves in the shirt pocket, apparently unworn. The necklace was somewhat helpful. It did bear the deceased girl's name, so it was conceivable that it had been taken from her body to delay identification. The engraving had been done by an amateur, but it was legible. The locket had been smashed, but once open, they had found a photo of an older couple, possibly the young woman's parents. Rebecca would have the registrar find out where they lived so they could be notified of her death. The best part was the perfect thumb print found on the back of the locket. It didn't match the girl so Rebecca had hopes that it would provide a link between the jogger and the body of the girl. This, of course, meant they had to assume he had been the one to plant the evidence in Dr. Sharp's home.

The coffee maker buzzed that her first pot was ready for consumption. Lazily walking through the house in her slippers, she perused the front page of the paper. There was a small paragraph about the murder, but no new details had emerged. She disliked seeing her name in print. It felt as if she wasn't doing her job well enough, if they had to write about what she was doing, though journalism wasn't supposed to be personal.

Her coffee pouring and paper reading were interrupted by the raucous alarm of her telephone. She groaned inwardly. A seven o'clock call couldn't be good. She tossed the paper on the kitchen table and walked over to the phone. Should she let it go to voice mail? "No," she decided. After the third ring she picked up the handset and answered, "Detective Sweate."

"Detective," came the slightly tinny female voice on the other end of the line. "We received a 911 call a few minutes ago from Dr. Sharp's neighbor. The caller thinks he spotted the man you are looking for. We had a cruiser in the area to check on the doctor's house and we sent another one when we got the call. The caller mentioned your name too so I wanted to inform you."

"Thanks!" she was suddenly awake and thinking fast. No time for a shower. She needed to dress rapidly and get over there. "Have you had a call yet from the police on the scene?"

"No, ma'am, but they are going in silent."

"Good. Call Detective Samuelson. Tell him to meet me at the station. If they get this guy I want to be there waiting for him," Rebecca instructed. The dispatcher agreed to make the call to Justin and Rebecca hung up gulping down her still-hot coffee. She raced down the hall to her bedroom and began her "rapid-mode" preparation for work.

****

Justin had been up working on a new website design for his personal web page. Already dressed, he was passing the time until the appointed meeting with Rebecca. His notes were organized and he was planning to drop a little bombshell on her lap. He had finally found the phone number and ID from the caller's phone from a friend he knew at the phone company.

"He should have just used a throw-away cell phone," thought Justin. This had been the guy's second mistake that they could possibly capitalize upon. Justin was feeling good having scored points for getting the artist's rendition of the jogger uploaded to the electronic billboard. The doctor's suggestion of appealing to sponsor's "civic responsibility" had done the trick. The local cell phone company who owned the sign had agreed to display the picture intermittently for three days at no charge to the city.

After the shoot-out, Justin had changed weapons and now carried his nine millimeter Glock semi-automatic in a standard belt sidearm holster. It was heavier than his revolver, but he had decided to wear the standard weapon. Had he been using his Glock on the previous day he would not have run out of ammunition before the car had fled. He might have brought their case to a more rapid conclusion.

Working on a new embellishment on the taskbar of his web-page he felt his cell-phone vibrating. He wore a Bluetooth earpiece so all he had to do was touch a tiny button on the side of it to talk. "Hello. Justin Samuelson here."

"Detective Samuelson, this is Sergeant Richardson. There have been some developments in your case. Detective Sweate would like you to meet her at the station in fifteen minutes." The business-like statement was devoid of emotion.

"What developments?" he asked.

"Sir. I believe they may have apprehended the man you have been looking for."

"Oh. Great. Thank you I'll be right in," he answered with as much pleasantness as he could manufacture. Justin was chagrined and feeling put out because he had hoped to present key information that would help in finding the jogger. Logging off his computer, he stood, grabbed his jacket and was out the door in a moment. As he reached his rental car parked in his apartment complex lot, he almost kicked himself.

"It's not about you, you idiot. Maybe they got the guy. That's the point! It really doesn't matter who gets the credit."

He desperately wanted to do well in his job, but he was beginning to realize that working together would be more productive than doing things his own way. He was supposed to be on the same "team" as the uniformed police and other detectives, not try to play the one-upsmanship game.

The new Mustang roared to life as he turned the key. He knew the others thought he was weird, but his knowledge and skills could continue to be useful. He would just have to present things carefully and they would see that he could fit in.

For now, though, he and Rebecca had a murder to solve.

PART TWO

21

Saturday afternoon

In Naperville, a fast growing suburb of Chicago, four people met in an emergency meeting. They sat at a boardroom table designed for twenty in a room spacious enough accommodate twice that many. Alone with the entire wall of windows covered with full-length blinds they could feel the room lights burning brightly, but the room echoed with the hushed voices of the occupants.

The leader spoke up, "I am quite sure that we cannot be heard. We have had this room guarded and swept repeatedly. The windows are triple pane with special anti-vibration technology to prevent laser listening devices from being used. As far as I know no one is even aware of our little group's existence or that this meeting is taking place except for you three. Am I wrong?"

The voice was clear and sharp and no answer was expected. Anyone answering incorrectly knew what their fate would be.

"You are all respected in your businesses, thanks to me. We have the right connections. We all stand to make a very large amount of money and this is on the line because of the foolishness that is going on in some little town in Nebraska! What is going on people? Do I need to spell it out? If this goes any further we could lose everything. Be very clear. I will not be alone to profit in this enterprise, but I will also not be alone if it fails."

The second person spoke.

"Chief, we had no idea it had gotten to this point or that it was this critical."

The leader laughed, "James how did you get to be the head of your company? You should have seen this coming a mile away. You played big-shot and look what happened. If this doesn't get taken care of quickly you won't even have to worry about being arrested. Am I clear?"

The man was clearly shaken by this last comment. He closed his mouth and sat mute with his head in his hands. He now realized his own life was in the balance. "How stupid could he be?" he thought. He should never have trusted his nephew, Dan. He had just been showing off to his girlfriend Connie.

The leader spoke again, "The rest of you may not have had anything to do with James' idiocy, but you have to figure out how to extract us from this before it is too late. And don't make it worse!"

The woman seated to the leader's left dared to speak.

She said, "Do we have to do anything? Are they really smart enough to track this back to us and put all the pieces together?"

The leader sat down and reached over to gently take her hand.

"Cindy, you have a point. If they find it and don't understand its significance maybe this will all go away." The grip on Cindy's hand then became vice-like. "Are you willing to risk your life on that? Are all police idiots? And what if they do figure out even a part of it?"

The leader let go of Cindy's hand and stood again. Now as he paced around the end of the table each member of the small group was listening intently. "I will put at your disposal an additional one million dollars. James, don't you already have another operative in place?

James nodded.

"I should do this myself, but I am the most visible one here and I have other things that must be done. I have no choice but to trust that you can take care of this." Turning around once again the leader said, "Malcomb. What is the status of that Bozo Randizzio?"

The fourth person of the group found his voice. A little tremulously he said, "He was arrested this morning and called our Des Moines number to get a lawyer. We had set up this number for emergencies. It is not traceable to any of us."

"Did he get his lawyer?" asked the leader.

"Yes, Chief. We sent a good attorney who knows nothing about us. She is out of Omaha, Nebraska."

"How is she being paid?" their leader queried.

"Direct deposit from an account in Randizzio's name. The

money is being deposited in four different branch banks in cash so there will be no tie to any of us.

"Someone is thinking. Good job, Malcomb." Then staring at James he said, "How much does this young man know?"

James spoke up once again. This time he was a little more confident."He only knows what he is looking for not 'why' and not 'for whom.' Of course Dan knows me, but he has no reason to know I have any connection to you. He is my sister's kid from her second marriage. He thinks I am his boss, but he also knows there is a steep price for failure."

The leader grew steely. "And how much did that girl know? You don't think she told him anything?" The leader's voice was tremulous. He was exquisitely angry.

"Now you say he is related to you and he knows you personally?" A few curses came forth. "I guess we can't let you get killed or it will open an even larger investigation. Will he crack in custody and give you away?"

At the word 'killed' James shrank back once again. "Randizzio is old school. Family is everything. He would let them chop off his finger before he would give out a family name."

"That's the first good thing you've had to tell me. Let's hope for your sake you are right. What about the missing girl? Did he find her? Do we know if she knows anything about this?"

"No one has seen her. We've checked and neither the police nor her family are aware of her whereabouts," James said.

"I don't suppose you have anyone we can count on in the department of that little town, do we?" asked the leader.

"We actually do have one contact in the DA's office there. We got him appointed, but I haven't wanted to reach out to him because it would be another avenue back to us. He still doesn't know that this has anything to do with our organization." This came from Malcomb who had once again found his voice.

"You're probably right, but we may need to pull out the stops if it starts to unravel. What is our next strategy, people? Let's get some ideas on the table."

Cindy, in an attempt to lighten things up said, "Maybe we should blow up the police station."

The leader stared at her for a long moment, not seeing the humor. "I don't think that is necessary. At least not yet!"

That left an impression on each of their minds.

How far would their leader go?

22

Jack had arrived home around eight o'clock in the morning after a long night without any rest. When he was younger he had been able to go forty-eight hours without sleep, but now that would render him useless. A few hours with his eyes closed would recharge his batteries and he needed some quiet. Just as he had been about to get into bed, however had come the call that the police had detained the "jogger." They wanted him to go to the police station to confirm that he had been the man Jack had seen on the trail. They had said afternoon would be all right and, grateful for the respite, he had gotten into bed and fallen asleep.

The alarm woke him at twelve noon. When he got up, his eyes felt like they had sand in them and he knew that his breath could kill almost anything. Jack's immediate sensation, though, was hunger. He got up and showered, putting on fresh clothes for what promised to be another unusual day. He then went downstairs and had a mixture of breakfast and lunch with cereal, coffee, carrots and soup. As he looked at his fare he chuckled to himself,

"What would Kathy think of this meal?"

He knew that preparations had been ongoing for Kathy's surgery. It was scheduled to start sometime in the afternoon. Mack had wanted to start as soon as possible but the setup for such an intricate procedure still took time. Jack hoped to be able to sit with the family for part of the time. He was aware that the procedure could take ten hours or more and hoped Mack was better rested than he.

Putting on his jacket, Jack looked longingly at the colorful trees in his neighborhood. He deeply desired to just go for a walk. It would help relax him, allowing him to forget all that had happened in the past three days. Yet, Jack knew the police needed his corroboration. Once again, off he went in the car. His first destination was the police station, then on to the hospital.

Before starting the engine he realized that he needed strength he didn't have that day. He bowed his head briefly and made his request to the Lord.

****

Dan Randizzio sat, mind racing, as he was becoming agitated. He had said nothing and planned to keep it that way. He had no desire to bring down the wrath of the organization he knew his uncle worked for. James Rizzo, "the big man" had let it slip at one of their family meals that he and some other big-shots had the world right where they wanted it. Dan could tell, too, that James wasn't the head. He had spoken in a hushed tone even showing fear as he had realized his slip. Dan didn't know what this organization did, but was pretty sure they would kill him if he even mentioned it. *Connie must have found out something more. She had taken off so suddenly she hadn't even called him.* He couldn't believe that she had been so bold and stupid as to steal from his uncle, and her boss.

He was worried about his predicament. How had the cops gotten onto him so quickly? He hadn't thought that the police were so smart. He was still unaware that they had overheard his little phone conversation with Dr. Sharp, but one idea that kept running through is head was that the organization had had a hand in his capture. He would make a perfect fall-guy if they suspected that he knew about them. He had been careful in everything he had done; yet, somehow, the police had caught him in the doctor's neighborhood. That would make his actions all the more suspicious to the police. *How much did they already know? Where was his lawyer?* So far they hadn't charged him, but he had refused to talk, so it was a stalemate. He knew that usually they could hold him for a full day and maybe two if they wanted to before charging him.

Would his own uncle let them give him up? What about family? They expected him to stay quiet. How could they let him get arrested anyway? Maybe it was just a coincidence. Maybe he should answer some questions just to see what they had on him.

****

Rebecca was a little worried and pacing. She and Justin had been talking about their prisoner. "... But what can we charge him with? Our evidence is very circumstantial. The necklace is about all we have. We can't even prove yet that the shirt belonged to him. The phone conversation was our best lead, but it wasn't recorded."

Justin countered, "I was able to record some of it."

"You were?"

"Yes. Didn't I tell you? How about starting with breaking and entering? We know he was in the doctor's house. If we can figure out the significance of the locket, that might help too."

"We'll have to check out the recording quality. Get a voice sample from the jogger. That could help. Do we *know* or just think we know that he 'broke and entered'? We don't have fingerprints yet. The evidence that we have was in the doctor's home and the techs said there were no fingerprints on the knife. We are waiting for a comparison on the necklace." She rubbed the back of her neck and arched her head back.

Justin saw the movement that was vaguely seductive. He was suddenly struck by the realization that his partner was very good looking, for an older woman. He was surprised at himself because he usually avoided contact with women and didn't think of them in that way. Nevertheless, now was definitely not the time to start having such thoughts.

Forcing his mind back into the present issue he said, "We have the neighbor who is certain he can ID the guy and that shirt we found along the bike path should fit him. We'll have to wait on the necklace, but I'll see what else I can figure out. He doesn't need to know we have so little."

"True. So we could charge him with breaking and entering if the DA agrees. We need to organize a line-up for Dr. Sharp before he gets here. What about the murder, though? We have squat for that. Even if the shirt fits, it could fit thousands of guys, maybe even the doctor. And was the guy who actually owns the shirt the one who shot at the two of you yesterday?"

"We will get ballistics on the bullets. We haven't found any other weapon but I don't think it was a revolver that was used yesterday. There were more than six shots at us and the uniforms said he was carrying a Smith and Wesson 6."

With this reminder Rebecca looked at Justin's holster. "I see you changed weapons."

"Uh, yeah. You were right. If I had had my service weapon yesterday..."

"Don't beat yourself up for that. You did okay. And you're alive. I'm glad you and the doctor weren't hurt."

Rebecca smiled weakly, glad to see that her younger partner had some sense.

"I'll set up a line – up for the neighbor, and the doc too. But we need our prisoner to say something incriminating." Justin looked out at their captive. He sat, hands cuffed in front and resting on the table, face down not looking around. They had him in an interview room with a one-way mirror. He probably knew they could see him, but he made no attempt to look their way. All he would be able to discern was a mirrored wall.

"Let me go in there. I want to see what I can get from him."

"He asked for his lawyer. He doesn't have to say anything, you know that. And it wouldn't be admissible in court." Rebecca now looked as frustrated as she felt.

"I know, but I can ask if he has changed his mind. Where is this lawyer from?" Justin asked.

"Some high priced former prosecutor from Omaha," Rebecca replied.

"She should have been here an hour ago. He is beginning to look irritable. Maybe if he thinks she will let him down he'll say something to us." Justin had been trained in interrogation but had not actually carried a real one out on his own. He decided now was also not the time to reveal that fact.

Just then they heard their prisoner call for the guard and a few minutes later the guard appeared at the observation door. "Detectives?"

"Yes?" answered Rebecca.

"Your prisoner says he wants one of you to come in."

"Are your sure?"

"Yes ma'am."

She looked at Justin and said, "Be my guest, Justin. Just don't make things worse."

Her look made him want to shiver.

Justin left the dark space where they had been having their discussion. He purposefully opened the interview room door and drew Dan Randizzio's attention immediately.

"Where's my lawyer?" he demanded.

"Are you sure your lawyer is coming?" Justin began baiting him.

"You can't keep her from coming in here!" Dan was angry.

"I assure you, sir, we haven't seen your lawyer either. Are you sure you want to have your lawyer here?" Again Justin was attempting to plant doubt. He hoped there was already some doubt in this man's mind. Dan did not answer. "We can have a local public defender here if you want."

At that moment Gus opened the door to the observation room. "I thought the guy wanted a lawyer."

Rebecca didn't want company right now, but also didn't want to let on that they were stymied. "He asked for us to come back so I sent Justin in to see if he is more willing to talk than earlier."

"Sure, I guess you can try. He seemed pretty tight-lipped when we picked him up." Gus turned and began watching as if it were a television drama.

"You picked him up? I heard it was the young cops, Rod and Susanne."

Gus' face reddened. "Yeah, well you know how it is."

"Sure," Detective Sweate smiled. They turned to the drama in the interview room. Dan was talking to Justin.

"I've got one of the best lawyers in the state coming and you want me to agree to a PD? Get real, Sherlock." These were the most words he had spoken since he had been caught near the doctor's home.

"Okay. You asked for me to come in. Do you still want to wait for your lawyer?" Justin had used the most congenial tone of voice he could muster. "We can wait or we can charge you and get you going through the system," Justin warned.

"Charge me? What with?" Randizzio sneered. He should have

stopped there, but he was getting worked up. "B and E? Big deal. You don't have anything." His glare was challenging. He crossed his arms and smirked at Justin.

Rebecca was impressed that Justin's show was getting somewhere, but the prisoner hadn't yet said the magic words.

"Sir I can't talk to you if you want your lawyer." Justin started to leave. Glancing back he said, "Are you sure we can't come up with something much more serious?" Justin avoided being explicit. He knew that they couldn't go farther, and if he got any answers now it would be inadmissible because Randizzio had still not said "I don't need a lawyer." He would also have to actually sign a waiver. By asking his question about "more serious crime," Justin hoped to put doubts in the mind of his prisoner. He chose that moment to open the door and leave.

As the door closed behind Justin, Randizzio was stunned. He had been sure that the grilling was going to begin, but now he was left with no one upon whom to vent his wrath. Dan stood and shook his fist at the door. "Come back here you little pip-squeak! I was talkin' to you." He knew he was being watched, but was beginning not to care.

"Where's my lawyer?"

****

It was one of those "blue bird" days in autumn. Not a cloud could be seen and the sun felt warm. But Riley Peters was not happy. Her 2008 Lexus Coupe gleamed in the fall sunlight, but it sat on the side of the interstate unmoving. Rumbling semis shook the earth as they passed. Riley opened her cell phone once more literally yelling to be heard over the traffic. "Where is my road-side assistance?" she shouted. Her two hundred dollar hair style had long since been defeated by the Nebraska wind. Her spike heels seemed to stick to the pavement and, while her five hundred dollar dress might be a distraction to the men speeding past at seventy-five miles per hour, she now wished she had a pair of jeans and running shoes to wear. She was a mile from the turn off to her destination, but she might as well have been one hundred miles away. Having waited over an hour no help had yet arrived, and she was not about to put her baby blue dress at risk by changing her own flat tire.

Kicking the tire and nearly breaking her toe she resigned herself to wait out the delay seated in her convertible.

Riley Peters was rarely on the losing side in court, but today she had to accept defeat.

****

Frank, Amber, Sarah, Jonathan, Philip, Mary, and Esther, all of Kathy's children, sat together hands held with their heads bowed. Their families were gathered in a larger waiting area. Together they dominated the relatively spacious room, yet even the little children present made almost no sound. Several had arrived by plane that morning. They had all realized the importance of getting home and had dropped whatever they had been doing to be with their mother in her crisis. Kathy's church family had opened their homes to her children so none had found it necessary to make hotel arrangements and a shuttle service had even been arranged by the retired men. All very musical, friendly and outgoing, Kathy and her family had always been a hub at the center of the church in activities and worship. When their senior pastor left his wife and children for the arms of another woman, Steve, Kathy's late husband, had stepped in and filled the empty pulpit without hesitation. He had helped lead the congregation through the healing process and had ultimately assisted the board in finding a new pastor. As a family they often led worship. Even now with several of them living far away they were included in the worship schedule anytime they had plans to come home. Now, in the hospital, they weren't singing, yet they praised God that they could be with their mother.

The nurse waited for the prayers to conclude then caught Frank's eye. All of the family members turned toward her. "A few of you may come in to the anesthesia prep room if you would like."

Frank said, "Can all seven of us come in?"

She looked at them and said, "Why don't you come in two

groups. There isn't much room for you there." So Frank motioned to his sisters that they should go in first. The brothers would follow as their mother was about to be taken into the surgical suite. The girls stood and walked after the nurse, Mary holding Esther's hand.

23

Jack was just approaching the parking lot at the city/county building when a small red flash of light flew past him on the right. The car cut him off causing him to have to swerve and jam on his brakes as it entered the small municipal lot at an unusually high speed. Jack, though he liked to feel the freedom of a powerful car, was appalled that anyone would find it necessary to play "chicken" just to park their vehicle. With his heart still racing he pulled ahead and as calmly as possible found a parking space. His parking space ended up being actually fairly close to his destination whereas the driver of the sporty little car had entered so quickly she had missed this easily accessible spot. Jack noticed the woman doing her best to hurry through the parking lot, though not being too successful at jogging and limping with her three inch spike heels.

He stepped out of his car and, trying not to be antagonistic said, "Where's the fire young lady? You almost ran into me getting into this lot."

Riley was furious with herself for running late. She realized she had driven dangerously coming into town, but did not want to stop and chat with this man. He had a point, but she was behind schedule. "Look, I'm late and I can't stop now. Is there any damage?"

"No but..." Jack started to say.

"Fine, then there's no harm done." She swept past him and left Jack staring after her.

He was amazed to the point of mirth, and watched her try to move quickly, nearly laughing at the sight. She carried a brief case and her gait with the high heels exaggerated her body's swaying motion with each step. Jack doubted that she would make it into the building without breaking off one of the heels. Smiling to himself, he closed his car door and walked the same direction wondering about what was causing her to be in such a hurry.

Once inside he asked at the reception desk for either of the detectives Sweate or Samuelson and was instructed to wait. A few minutes later he was greeted by a smiling Rebecca Sweate. She seemed more relaxed and rested than their last encounter. He suspected that the successful apprehension of their quarry had something to do with that.

"Good afternoon Dr. Sharp," she said taking his hand. Her grasp carried less steel than the first time they had met. He even noticed a hint of perfume in the air. "Thank you for coming in again. I hope we don't have to keep bothering you. I'm sure you are a busy man."

"I have told my office staff that I needed some time off so I've intended to take it easy. However, I have been extremely busy the last two days and could use a good night's sleep. This murder business has me pretty dazed." Jack said more than he had intended. "I'm sorry. My schedule isn't your problem."

"No Dr. Sharp. I know we have been the cause of some of your busy-ness. I hope we can leave you alone soon. All we need today is for you to try to identify the man we have arrested. Well, we haven't truly charged him yet, but we are holding him for questioning." Rebecca said.

Jack's eyebrows rose, "You haven't charged him? Isn't he a murder suspect? At least we know he broke into my home." Jack thought that the police would definitely arrest the man and that he would go to jail. "Does that mean that you could still release him?"

"Technically yes, but we don't want to let him go now that we have him. You must understand, though, that we still have little evidence that connects him to the murder. We have to build our case. That's why we need you. He isn't saying much and now his lawyer has arrived so we need you to identify him in a line-up." Rebecca hesitated. Did she need to tell him this much?

As they approached the interview room the woman Jack had seen in the parking lot came out of the rest room. She glanced over at Jack and Rebecca and gave a little start. She then hurried along the hall and was admitted to another door by a uniformed policeman.

Jack said, "Don't tell me. She is his lawyer?"

Rebecca stared at him, "Yes. She is. Why?"

Jack shook his head and chuckled. "No wonder she was in

such a hurry. She nearly ran into me as I was pulling into the parking lot."

"Oh," Rebecca said turning her face back down the hall. "So she is a little rattled. Well it can't hurt us."

Rebecca led the doctor to a different door and showed him in. Justin waited silently along one wall. Jack was also mute as they stood in a darkened room before a large window. The room beyond was well lighted but currently empty. After a brief wait a uniformed officer opened a door in the side of the lighted room and walked in ahead of six men all average height and muscular. Jack thought, "They must have scoured the fitness centers for this line-up." Nevertheless, he knew immediately which one was the jogger. There was no mistaking his features. Jack had seen him face to face.

Rebecca looked at him, "Doctor can you make a positive ID?"

He pointed at the third man from the left. His mouth was dry and he realized he had been nervous to confront this man, even behind a mirrored wall.

"Number three."

"All right," she said. "Now we will pull the blinds and have you listen to each man speak a few words that you heard on your phone. This will help us to confirm that the man you saw also called you."

Jack's eyebrows went up. "That could be hard. What if I pick the wrong one? Won't that hurt your case?"

Rebecca was pensive, "It is potentially a problem but it will strengthen yours. Don't pick one unless you are certain. Do you understand?"

"Yes. Okay."

He strained to listen as each man said into a microphone, "They're going to search your house." Jack desperately wanted to be certain and thought he could tell the difference but in the end he chose not to pick one. He just was not sure enough. Rebecca thanked him and signaled the policeman to remove the men from the room.

Rebecca smiled to herself, crossing her arms. She looked over at Justin and nodded. He then escorted Dr. Sharp once again into the hallway. "That's really all we needed, Dr. Sharp. I'm sorry you didn't recognize the voice but you seemed pretty quick to pick the man by appearance. Are you certain enough that you would be willing to testify to that in court if called upon to do so?"

Jack hadn't thought about the possibility of testifying or being in court. He worried a little about the implications, but was acutely aware of his responsibility. He, after all, had been considered a possible suspect very recently as well.

"Yes, I'm certain and I would do that if you need it."

Just then the young woman re-appeared in the hallway. She seemed to be searching for someone. When her eyes rested upon Jack she smiled sweetly and with a little wave asked, "Excuse me, are you Dr. Sharp?"

Jack looked over at Justin who seemed baffled. "Yes, I'm Jack Sharp. Who are you?"

With a new sweetness that did nothing to reassure him she said, "Dr. Sharp, my name is Riley Peters. I'm a defense attorney. Do you mind if I ask you a few questions before you take off?"

Gone was the gruff in-a-hurry attitude she had exhibited in the parking lot. She had apparently fixed her hair, but she had a noticeable run in her right stocking which she had been unable to repair. Her right shoe was also missing a chunk of leather from its toe. Confidently, though, she walked up to Jack as if they had just met and stretched out her hand in greeting.

"I don't know. As you see *I* don't have my lawyer present." Jack was sparring with her and being cautious.

"Just a few questions Dr. Sharp. Of course you needn't answer them if you are concerned." She didn't wait for his response. "Did you discover the body in the ditch as reported and did you see my client near there?"

Jack again looked for help from Justin. He shrugged and made a slight nod. "Ms. Peters, as reported, I was the person who found the body of the unfortunate young lady. As for your client, I politely decline any comment. I do have a lawyer and you may speak to him or to myself in his presence. I really don't think we have anything else to discuss." He found it interesting that she had made no apology or even reference to her poor driving.

Jack smiled slightly, said goodbye to Justin, and turned in the opposite direction. He walked down the hall and out the door without looking back.

Riley was surprised at the confidence of the doctor. She had hoped to get him to say something that would help her client, but she knew she was only fishing. He had apparently known as much, too. She scowled at Rebecca and said nothing to Justin returning to the interview room to await the return of her own client.

Feeling satisfied with himself, Jack believed that he was about to leave this episode behind and move on to a more important chapter in his life. He also felt good about getting the last word in with a lawyer. Doctors tended to have negative feelings about lawyers as a general principle. As he pulled out of his parking space he eyed the Lexus in which his 'would-be nemesis' lawyer had arrived. It was a beautiful car and he was sure it must have cost seventy-five or eighty thousand dollars. It was curious that this young man should be able to afford such high priced legal help. Maybe he was into drug dealing and had loads of cash from his illegal activities. Whatever it was, it had led to the unnecessary death of a beautiful young woman.

He drove quietly to the hospital where Kathy had already gone in to surgery. The operation was to start by one o'clock in order to finish by midnight. Jack intended to sit with the family through much of the ordeal, but had not been sure how long he would be at the police station. As he approached the hospital parking lot he didn't know what kind of reception he would meet from her family. *Had Kathy told her children about her feelings toward him?* Jack decided he would say nothing regardless of the outcome of surgery. She might not even remember their discussion after surgery. Such a major procedure could leave her with paralysis or loss of memory. Even her ability to speak could be impaired. For now, though, Kathy's family needed him to be an optimistic family doctor and do what he could to answer their questions.

Most of all they needed him to just be there.

24

Dr. French stared at the box. One hand on his chin and the other scratching his head, his appearance was comical. Cindy Shaw looked on with a smile. "Can I help you Dr. French?"

The Medical Examiner self-consciously stopped scratching his head and quickly glanced at the crime lab technician. "No. I don't think so. I'm just puzzled about one of my findings on this case." He made a decision and lifted the lid from the box. Rummaging through its contents he finally said,

"Ah hah! Here you are."

Cindy set down the item she had been inspecting for fingerprints and removed her gloves. "What did you find?" she was quite curious at what had brought the "famous" Dr. French into her lab. She peered over his shoulder and saw that he held only a small plastic bag with an indiscernible substance within.

"This, young lady, is a wad of gum," he said happily.

"I see that sir, but what is interesting about it to you?"

"The other day when I did the autopsy on that young woman I found this gum in her stomach," he explained.

"Yes, but a lot of girls chew gum," countered Cindy.

"True, but most do not swallow their gum. That is a trait more common to our male population I believe." Dr. French inspected the gray mass inside the bag then carried it over to a counter. He looked up at Cindy with a serious expression. "Notice too how big this wad is."

Cindy approached and stood at his side. "Yes it is. That has to be at least two pieces maybe three all wadded up."

"That has been gnawing at the back of my mind since I drew this wad out of her stomach. It just seemed out of place." He donned gloves and picked up the gum. He noticed it still had a faint minty smell, even with the addition of the odor of stomach contents. He found a small plastic disposable scalpel and began nipping bits of the gum from the wad.

"Doctor what are you doing? Don't you want to keep that intact?" Cindy said.

"Normally I would say yes. But I have a hunch that I want to follow. This girl was killed for some reason. No one has yet come up with an answer to the 'why.' If my hunch is correct, this evidence will shed light on the motive." He continued on, leaving slivers of gray sticky gum on the counter. It had grown hard from its natural preservative. "Gum does not break down easily in the stomach so a wad like this might have come out the other end nearly intact or possibly gotten stuck in transit," he said as he worked. Then suddenly he stopped in mid stroke. Setting the blade down he began wiping at the edge of the surface he had just been cutting. He and Cindy saw it at the same moment. As Dr. French wiped the surface with a moist cloth they saw a differently colored object emerging from beneath the gum. He worked more vigorously with the cloth; the gum was tackier here. Dr. French pared away a little bit of gum from each side. There was actually not that much gum, but the wad appeared to be covering something slightly irregular.

As he cleaned one side of the wad and more of the material was revealed Cindy had a puzzled expression on her face.

"What is that?" she asked. "Why would it be covered in gum?"

Silent for a second, Dr. French picked up a metal tray. He drew the gum-covered object across it, leaving a thin scratch. With the proud expression like that of a new father he said, "Cindy, I believe you are looking at a diamond and a fairly large one at that," he said.

The light seemed to come on in Cindy's face.

"Oh. It's not shiny because it's uncut! Do you think it is valuable?"

"A girl gave her life after trying to hide it with gum, and by its size I'd say it was very valuable. It certainly held a special value to our victim." He had a grim expression as he continued to clean the diamond. "Cindy can you finish cleaning this? I would like to speak to Detective Sweate right away." He laid down the instrument and the now partially exposed yellowish object. It did not have the appearance of a beautiful gem, but he knew that to determine the worth of a diamond was a complex process. They would need an expert.

Cindy broke into a grin as Dr. French handed her the diamond and started out of the room. "Dr. French, no one has ever given me a diamond before!" she bantered, fluttering her pretty eyelids.

"Just don't tell my wife," he said returning her smile.

****

Rebecca stared at Riley Peters. Riley stared back with a bit of a mocking grin. The icy silence was broken by Justin, who anxiously looked from his partner to their adversary.

"What has he got to lose by letting us know where the other girl is?"

Riley, fire in her eyes, shot back, "What makes you think he knows anything about some other girl? What is her name again?" She looked at her client slightly shaking her head as he seemed about to say something. Her warning went unheeded, however.

"Alicia Winters," Dan blurted out. Realizing his error in speaking out, he became flustered. "I heard it on the news. Look, I'm getting tired of this. And where have you been? They don't have anything on me. They're talking murder and I don't know anything about that."

A similarly mocking smile slowly crept onto Rebecca's face. Apparently young Dan did not have perfect confidence in his pretty, high-priced lawyer. Rebecca was vaguely aware of Riley's reputation and she believed he underestimated his lawyer's capabilities.

She said, "Dan, we haven't released her name to the press. Tell us what you know about Alicia Winters. She is still missing and with her friend dead, we are fearful for her as well." Rebecca decided to play this one as if he had nothing to do with her. He had opened the door and she wanted to push it open wider.

Riley quickly said, "Mr. Randizzio, I strongly urge you to say nothing more. So far they haven't even charged you. Like you said, they don't have any evidence. Don't give it to them."

Dan looked at his hands. He had been arrested only once as a juvenile. He feared the lock up, even though now he was grown. Dan knew that there were always people inside who were bigger and scarier than he. The anxiety he felt came from days spent in fear of the older boys who had abused him and belittled him. He had never talked about it with anyone, but he felt the icy pangs despite attempts to purge the thoughts from his mind.

"I had nothing to do with Alicia's disappearance. I swear."

"Mr. Randizzio! Dan- stop right now!" Ms. Peters was getting angry. *Why didn't this guy listen to her? Didn't he know how good she was?* "The more you say the more likely you will give them ammunition." She looked at Rebecca and Justin with a plastered on smile. "Will you please give me a few moments with my client?"

Rebecca looked at Justin who nodded. "Sure. We can leave you alone."

"No one watches through the glass." This was a command, not a request. Rebecca and Justin knew they would have to comply.

Rebecca said grudgingly, "Okay. No one in the observation is fine. I wouldn't want to violate your attorney-client privilege. Will five minutes be enough?"

"It had better be," Riley said looking at Dan.

Dan no longer appeared to Justin as the muscular hulk he had seemed. His countenance had shrunken. He and Rebecca silently stepped into the hallway where Justin spoke first. "What just happened? We haven't really done anything to 'break him.'"

"I don't know, but maybe he's cracking. You're right. He must be worried about something. I only hope his lawyer can't convince him to clam up again." Rebecca was practically rubbing her hands in anticipation. She pulled out her cell phone and quickly dialed.

"Pete, this is Rebecca Sweate. I think you might want to come down. Our suspect may be about to give us a statement. He isn't listening to his lawyer." She listened to the assistant district attorney for a moment. "It's Riley Peters from Omaha." There was a pause. "Oh you know her? Good. See you in a few minutes." A short laugh, followed. "Okay. Bye."

Justin was a little puzzled. "Do you really think he's ready to talk to the ADA?"

"Our suspect doesn't know his lawyer and doesn't know her reputation. That's good, because she is an excellent lawyer. I don't think he trusts women, so I am going to stay out and let you boys run with it for a while."

The admission that Rebecca's gender could be a disadvantage was surprising to Justin. He thought she would push hard to be involved at every moment.

Her willingness to step aside raised his level of respect for her another notch.

25

Alicia Winters shifted behind the wheel of her car feeling cold sweat slide down her back. It seemed to her that she had been looking over her shoulder for weeks instead of only a few days and that she had experienced the same nightmare every night. She hadn't slept well and was constantly hungry. She was almost out of money and would have run out much sooner had she not been carrying Connie's purse. She was afraid to use her credit or debit cards because she knew these could be tracked. She had never been so scared in her life and the fear never seemed to let up.

For Alicia, the worst part was that she really didn't know from whom she was running. She wanted desperately to trust someone, but she doubted that the police would believe her. Connie had told her that they couldn't trust anyone.

Alicia had hidden out in an unused barn for two days and now she was on the run. She had stayed on small highways and was working her way back to Chicago, though she was afraid to go there, too. She was certain that her job was history, and besides, she was suspicious that her employer was somehow mixed up in this whole business. The horrible scenes kept coming back to her even when she was awake. The sight of her friend being killed and all that blood was indelibly burned into her memory. She wondered if she would ever stop seeing it. She could even hear the deafening shot ringing in her ears.

Along the road she saw the sign of an all night truck stop ahead. She was hungry, but had only a few dollars. She had lived on sunflower seeds and beef jerky and was getting shaky. Needing some real food, she decided to risk using her debit card to get enough cash to get her back to Chicago. The police might figure out her location, but she would change direction to throw them off. She couldn't sleep. She would eat and leave immediately. Alicia knew she could easily be in Chicago by morning.

****

Jack had sat with Esther's head against his chest for hours. The operation had taken longer than he had expected, but, remaining in the waiting area, he had talked to the family and dozed off a few times. Jack knew that if he walked back to the OR he could probably find out a few details, but he chose to be a "civilian" and wait like everyone else. He had enjoyed conversations with Kathy's family. Her mother had come down from Minneapolis where she lived in a retirement facility. She was so much like Kathy that he had found it just as easy to talk to her as it was with Kathy. She was very physically capable, even at age eighty four. Like an increasing number of her contemporaries, she didn't even need a walker, though she did use a cane. She would have driven herself from Minnesota, but Frank had insisted upon her flying down.

Jack got along well with Frank, too. He found out that Frank enjoyed fly fishing and promised to go with him at the first opportunity. Jack loved the sport, but found little time to get to places where the clear water flowed. Nebraska was graced with few trout streams.

Esther had been very quiet, solemnly worried about her mother. Her hand had remained in Jack's for much of the afternoon, a fact that pulled at his heartstrings. He hoped Kathy would come through the operation with little trouble. The excessive length of the procedure, he believed, did not bode well.

Just as this last thought crossed his mind, a female dressed in surgical scrubs, still wearing her surgical cap and mask, appeared at the door. She pulled down the mask and her face was unreadable.

She said, "Who is here for Kathy Sanders?"

Both Frank and Jack spoke at once. Jack nodded to Frank sheepishly acknowledging that he wasn't actually part of the family. The woman was the nurse anesthetist assisting the anesthesiologist on the case. She approached Frank and spoke quietly to him. Frank looked at Jack with a serious face. He then disappeared with the woman through the door from which she had come.

Jack spoke to the rest of the family trying to be reassuring. "They probably want him to come in to explain what was done.

She probably will not be awake for some time so they can let her brain rest. I'm sure Frank won't stay in there long."

Esther woke then with a start, "Mommy!" she said fearfully in a loud voice. She looked around as if she expected to see her there.

"Its okay honey," Jack soothed stroking her head. He pulled her close. We'll know something soon.

"I saw her," Esther sobbed. "She was right here." There was a frightened look on her face. The family members looked at each other. Jack too began to wonder if the could be some kind of premonition, though he didn't believe in ESP or the paranormal. A few minutes later Frank appeared at the door.

His expression wasn't joyful, but he was smiling. As he approached he glanced around to be sure their family was all together. "She's doing fine. She'll be on her way to recovery soon. They had a little scare right at the end of the procedure. For some reason her heart stopped briefly and they had to give her a shock — but only one."

Jack looked at Esther with interest. *Had she seen her mother at the moment her heart had stopped?* He asked Frank, "Did you speak to the surgeon?"

"He spoke to me briefly over the intercom because he was still doing something in the room. They just wanted me to know the seriousness of the situation. We won't all be able to visit for a while, but they said she is through the worst now."

Jack decided it was time to be "doctor" again. He smiled at Esther and squeezed her hand. "I told you she would be okay."

He stood and shook Frank's hand. "You are truly a leader of this family. I think I'll peek in too." He winked at Frank who took up Jack's spot next to Esther.

Jack found Dr. Clark at the sink outside the operating room. "Hey, Mack. I'll bet you're tired."

Dr. Clark had removed his gloves and was washing his hands. He looked up with a funny expression. He then reached up and pulled his iPOD earphones from his ears. "Sorry. I like to be in my own little world sometimes." He paused, "Jack, it was tough. I couldn't quite get everything. The tumor had little fingers everywhere. I'm sorry. She'll need radiation and maybe chemo. We'll wait on the path report, but I think it is a glioma."

Jack stood mute for a moment. He knew that this meant that recurrence of the tumor was possible and it was probably a malignant, or cancerous, type. "Mack, thanks a lot. I don't know how you can spend twelve hours working constantly."

"Well, we do use assistants and take breaks throughout. Of course, I deal with the really tough areas. That way we stay as fresh as possible. You learn to take 'power naps.' Let's go out and talk with the whole family." Though his hair was plastered to his head, Mack looked like he had only done some minor procedure, not as if he had spent twelve grueling hours wrestling with a dangerous brain tumor.

Jack and Mack walked side by side out to the waiting area. They looked around and saw that there were no other groups in this room. Approaching the family, Mack said,

"Hi, folks. As you know, I've already spoken to Frank and to Dr. Sharp. Your mother is now in recovery. She will be asleep for several hours while we let everything rest. We'll know how she is when we wake her up, but the tumor was extensive. I don't think we did any major damage to the brain tissue around the tumor so she should be pretty close to the same wonderful woman she was before surgery. Do any of you have questions?" He purposely left out the details of the surgery having given that worse news to both Frank and Jack.

Most family members were smiling looking at each other, murmuring and nodding. Esther broke the silence with a tearful cry, "Is Mom going to live?"

The abruptness of the question took Dr. Clark by surprise. He wasn't sure what he should say and looked to Jack for a little help. Jack took up the mantle and said, "Honey, she is doing fine right now. She made it through the hard part so I think she'll do all right." This was all true to a point. He knew that eventually the full scope of their mother's disease would have to be clarified, but now was not the time. His answer seemed to mollify Esther and she sat back eyeing Jack a little suspiciously.

Jack turned to Dr. Clark. "Thanks, Mack you should get some rest."

Mack shot back a little quieter, "You should look in a mirror, man." He winked and gave a little wave to the family who each spoke their thanks as he walked away.

Jack walked around the room giving hugs to Kathy's children and reassuring them to the best of his ability. When he got to Frank he said quietly, "Mack told you about the surgery, didn't he?"

Frank responded just as quietly. "Yes. I'll talk to my brothers and sisters when the final pathology report is back. We really don't know everything until then anyway."

Jack was impressed by this young man. He shook his hand and firmly gripped his shoulder. "Frank, if I had any sons I would want them to be like you." He looked him in the eye for a long moment, "I think they'll let me into recovery so I'll stop in there before I go home. I'll talk with you again tomorrow," then looking at his watch he added, "I mean later today, okay?"

Frank merely nodded and vigorously shook Jack's hand. "You don't know how much it means to our family to have you here, Doc."

With that, Jack also exited and strode down the corridor to the recovery room. The bay where Kathy had been taken was a bee-hive of activity. Her head was bandaged and she was still intubated. Two nurses were adjusting instruments and injecting medications. The anesthesiologist was still monitoring her ventilator status. Jack was familiar with this, but sometimes family members became agitated and upset when they saw their loved one "on a machine."

He spoke to the anesthesiologist. "How is she doing?"

John Vanderval, another friend of Jack's, looked up. "She had a run of V-tach so we had to shock her heart once, but she seems stable now."

Jack was a little surprised. Cardioversion was a major step. She could well have died. Thankfully, it had successfully stopped the dangerous rhythm.

One of Kathy's hands was relatively free of tubes and he reached down and tenderly held her limp fingers. Jack leaned close to her ear and spoke gently, "Kathy you're doing all right. Dr. Clark did a great job. You are going to sleep a while, but I'll be here when you wake up." He hoped what he said was true.

Yes, he truly wanted to be there when she awoke, but he didn't know what lay ahead for her.

****

Justin and Assistant District Attorney Pete Sears loitered in the hallway as Riley Peters looked at them smugly. As she stepped out she closed the door of the interview room. Briefly acknowledging them, she said,

"Gentlemen," then looking directly at Pete added, "And I use the term loosely."

Pete scowled and shot back. "Can it Riley. Let's go talk to your client."

She smiled, "Oh, you can talk all you want he won't talk back much."

Justin joined in, "He seemed pretty interested earlier. Why don't you just let us see for ourselves?"

She stepped aside. Half turning to the door she held up her hand as if leading them in. "Come on in. He's all yours."

This time the two men entered and found a sullen, stone faced Dan Randizzio. Pete smiled slightly, "What did you do, threaten him?"

"How and why would I threaten my own client?" Riley asked with a feigned look of innocence. "I merely pointed out that you have nothing on him and that you will have to let him go if you don't charge him. Dan, this is the Assistant District Attorney, Pete Sears."

"Oh we'll charge him all right." Then to Dan, "Do you have anything you want to say to me Dan?" His approach was confrontational and Justin was surprised that he would start with such a high pressured method. Dan had seemed on the verge of 'spilling his guts' earlier.

Dan's expression changed from stoniness to mild surprise as his eyes met the ADA's stare. He began, "Go to ..."

He was interrupted by Justin who put a hand on Pete's arm and said, "Wait a minute." He glared at Pete. "You're not helping."

"I think I know how to interview a murder suspect," Pete shot back.

Justin could see that they had actually lost ground and that things were rapidly deteriorating. Without a word he lifted his hands away and backed up looking only at Pete.

Riley smiled sheepishly and said, "See. I told you Dan. They probably don't even have enough to hold you."

Dan's cold look returned and his lips remained closed.

"Charge him or spring him," Riley said.

The ADA said, "You know we can keep him on ice for forty-eight hours without formal charges."

Riley Peters had fire in her eyes. "You had better have reasonable evidence or I'll file a harassment petition."

Pete didn't answer and looked one more time at Randizzio. He ignored Justin. Dan didn't meet his gaze and the ADA left the room. Justin wanted to appeal to the ADA to keep trying, but finally turned to leave as Riley Peters began to chuckle at his dilemma. "We know you broke into the doctor's house, we have evidence and witnesses."

"I'll make bail," was all they got from Dan Randizzio after that.

Outside the interview room Justin raced after the ADA. "What was all that? We had him primed and you just gave in. Why did you badger him?"

"Shut up .You're out of line. Do you want me to let your chief know how you handled this?" Pete Sears spat at him. "I'll take this up with Rebecca."

Justin, mystified, could only stand and stare at the back of the Pete Sears as he opened the stairwell door and let it close behind himself.

26

Rebecca sat staring at her "done" pile. She had finally gotten her reports caught up and having worked on a summary for the current case, felt reasonably up to date. Nevertheless, she knew that by working through all the other case files she was only putting off her current dilemma. She had a suspect for murder in jail, but felt she had been led up a blind alley. The young man they had in custody had acted like a guilty party and she had thought he would lead to a solution to the case, but he remained silent, not giving her what she needed. The evidence they had against him was circumstantial at best. He had done too well at covering his tracks. She looked up as she detected the presence of someone at her door.

Dr. French stood at her door looking very anxious. He was smiling and bursting with news.

"Come on in Dr. French," offered Rebecca, "What's on your mind?"

"Rebecca we have come across some very interesting evidence. I think you will appreciate its importance." He proceeded to relate to her what had recently transpired in the crime lab.

"A diamond!" exclaimed Rebecca. "Now what have we stumbled into? How does a murder with a missing person involve a large uncut diamond?" She had been standing and now sat down hard. She looked at Dr. French with a blank stare.

"I just cut 'em open. You have to piece it together," returned Dr. French. "We need a diamond expert on this one, Rebecca."

Rebecca remained mute for a second longer. "Can you bring it in for me to see?"

"Cindy and I will need to finish cleaning it. We are trying to be careful."

She thought a minute. "I agree. And we also need an expert but I don't know any."

"What about a local jeweler?" asked Dr. French helpfully.

"Yes but are they really 'experts'?" She picked up the phone and dialed. "Justin? Can you come in? You're here? Okay come up to my office. We have some serious thinking to do ... I'll explain when you get here."

She took Dr. French's hand. "This could give us just what we need. We didn't have a motive, but now it looks like you have provided us a new direction. I was stuck, but now we have a new rabbit trail to follow. Let me know as soon as the stone is clean." Rebecca smiled genuinely with her mind racing as Dr. French made his exit.

Justin approached Rebecca's office hurriedly. He greeted Dr. French in passing with a curt nod and "hello."

"What's going on?" he asked as he burst into the office. He wanted to tell her about the failed interview, but was curious to hear her news too.

"We have another good development!"

"You caught the guy who shot at us?"

"No. Be patient." Rebecca began to share the news. Justin held his own tongue as she told him about Dr. French finding the diamond and Justin sat down with much the same stymied look Rebecca had displayed.

"Man! I've got to think about this. How does that fit?" Justin asked the air. Then he changed the subject. "Rebecca you need to know what went on earlier too. I'm confused about that."

Rebecca pulled out a note pad. "Okay, but can it wait, Justin? I want to brainstorm a little about this new evidence."

"Sure. I guess that sounds like a good approach," he responded. He was still feeling a little inferior after his encounter with the ADA, but setting aside his misgivings he entered into the discussion with Rebecca.

"What do we know?" Rebecca began, her pen poised.

"First there was a body. No- the girl actually went missing first, though we didn't know that at the time." Justin corrected himself.

"Right." Rebecca began a diagram with names. "Then Dr. Sharp found the body of one of the missing girls."

"Okay. Then this Dan Randizzio was at the scene of the dumped body. But this we don't know..." he began ticking points off on his fingers. "One, did Randizzio murder the girl? Two, why was he there in broad daylight? Three, what was he looking for? The necklace? That's the only thing he took." Here Rebecca interrupted him.

"Now I think that was the diamond," she countered.

"Oh yeah. Okay, he's looking for the diamond. You know he could have been there searching for quite a while. So if he had killed her why dump her body there and why look at in the middle of the day?" Justin asked.

"You have a point. He was looking for the diamond, but if he had killed her he could have searched her before dumping her there. Then we have yesterday's shooting. It isn't likely that he did that but we can't be sure. Still, it fits if there is a second person, the 'shooter,' in this." Rebecca stood pacing again, chin in hand. "I guess he could be off the hook for the actual murder, but he's still an accessory." Rebecca struck her fist. "Could you go back and work on him to find out who else is involved? It could make him feel like we would let him go. We still don't have a case against him for murder."

"Sure, I could try to talk to the guy, but he isn't talking now." He decided this was a good time to let Rebecca know about the interview. "Rebecca, I thought you said this assistant DA was pretty good."

"He is. Why?" she asked.

"Well when we went to talk to Randizzio he started out by jumping down his throat. Randizzio got mad and quit talking."

"Maybe his lawyer talked sense into him," Rebecca said in Sears' defense.

"I think she did talk to him, but he wasn't defiant until Sears started threatening murder charges before even asking a question. When I asked Sears why he was confrontational, he made it out to be my fault. I never said a word in there. Something's not right."

Rebecca thought a second. "Justin, Pete is a seasoned lawyer. He has done this many times before and is experienced. I think you're blowing this out of proportion."

Justin scowled, "All right, fine." After sulking briefly he

continued, "Okay, but Randizzio doesn't know we have the diamond. So if we don't have evidence to charge him with murder I don't think we should tell him or his lawyer about it."

"Well, if we do charge him we won't have a choice, but for now you're right." Changing tactics, she asked, "Does Dr. Sharp fit in here somewhere that we've missed?"

"I thought we had cleared him from any involvement," Justin mused. "But doctors do have money and it takes a lot of money to deal in diamonds." Justin made a few notes on his PDA thinking hard. Rebecca put Dr. Sharp's name to the side of her diagram with a question mark.

"Well, you never really clear someone until you have your case sewn up, but don't mention the diamond to him either if you speak to him. We need to know more about that diamond. And here's another point. There's still a missing girl, Alicia. Where is she? Is she running scared, did she murder her friend, or is her body lying in a ditch somewhere? Is she Randizzio's accomplice?"

"Whoa. It's getting too convoluted. If she is the accomplice she's acting like a professional hit-man. Is that likely? If not, it still doesn't make sense that anyone killed the first girl, Connie, before they got the diamond if that was the prize," Justin said.

"Unless they were convinced the other girl, Alicia, had it." she stated. "That makes the idea that Alicia killed Connie less likely, too. Listen, if Randizzio was out to get a diamond why is he hanging around the doctor's house? Does he think Dr. Sharp has it? Who would have thought she would swallow it?" Rebecca said making another note.

"If this girl, Alicia, is still alive she is an important witness and is in real danger. That is for certain," said Justin. "I think I should talk with her aunt to see if she knows how Alicia would be involved with diamonds or jewels."

"Great idea, Justin. First I'll need to update the chief. Then I need to find a diamond expert whom we can trust. I'm afraid I know only one way to do that." Rebecca looked directly at Justin when she said this.

"What way is that?" Justin queried. Then seeing the pained

expression on her face said, "You don't mean the FBI?"

"Justin, this case just changed from a local murder and disappearance, to some kind of diamond affair. We don't have any diamond mines in Nebraska."

Her matter-of-fact statement was contrary to her own feelings. She didn't like involving the federal agency because they would want to run everything their own way. There were too many loose ends unfulfilled. She and Justin were mute for a long moment.

Justin finally broke the silence. "Well, the more I get done the less the FBI can take away from us. I'll get Gus to look again on Dr. Sharp's background to see if diamonds show up and I'll go see the aunt. Do you want me to come with you to see the chief?"

"No I have it." She ripped the diagram she had been making from its pad. "I'll tell you what, though. You should work on Randizzio again. I'll take the aunt. He seems less interested in talking to me. Maybe without Pete you'll get somewhere."

"You're right. Okay. Check in with the chief and let me know when the FBI takes the case away," Justin said chagrined.

"Don't be so pessimistic. We can work jointly."

"We'll see. Do we have anything else to add to the diagram?" Justin asked.

Rebecca thought for a moment and glanced at her notes. "It seems that there's something outside all this. We don't know what or where it is coming from."

Justin said, "I think Chicago is a good bet. Maybe someplace one or both of the girls worked or frequented."

"There you go," Rebecca grinned at Justin. "giving the FBI another reason to step in and take it away from us."

Justin shook his head in disgust. "I guess we're done for now. I'll check back with you in the morning." He stepped out of her office, already dialing Officer Wilson's number.

Rebecca looked at her watch and realized it was getting late for a Saturday. She liked to avoid coming in on Sunday morning, but knew she wouldn't be able to sleep in this week.

27

Alicia was driving on fumes and she knew it. She needed to stop and get gas before the engine died. She hadn't seen an ATM or open gas station for twenty miles and now her plan was not working out like she had hoped. Driving north, hoping to make anyone tracking her think she was going to Minnesota, she had passed Mason City a while ago.

Why hadn't she gotten gas there? She had then turned east again planning to go to Chicago on smaller, less obvious roads. It was late and in the little towns the gas stations had all been closed. She almost kicked herself for not going on into the larger town of Mason City. She hoped that there was a reserve gallon or two once you got to "E" on the gas tank.

She felt it more than heard it, a slight miss in the engine. She started trying to encourage the car, "Just a little more. Please don't run out of gas, please." But her pleading had no effect. In less than another mile her engine coughed, sputtered and quit.

Alicia let the car roll onto the shoulder and put her head down on top of her hands. She was in the middle of nowhere, soon to be in pitch black night. She hadn't even seen a car for ten miles. Now, because of her stupidity or paranoia, the nearest town was at least ten miles away.

"This just goes to show you don't know how to plan any-thing," she said disgustedly. Angry at herself, she grabbed her keys and coat, thankful that she had at least thought to have it, along with gloves and a scarf. During the day the temperature was still pleasant, but it dipped below freezing at night, and now that she had driven farther north, it was downright cold.

Her Iowa map was on the seat beside her. She picked it up and locked the car door. On her feet she wore tennis shoes and Alicia knew that the only way to get anywhere was to walk. Tired and hungry, now she was going to be cold. *Did she dare try to hitch a ride?* She didn't even want to contemplate that and decided to stay out of sight of other cars for now if she saw any. In the failing light she squinted once more at her map. *How long would it take to walk ten miles? Three hours?* She knew she had no other choices for now and off she trudged.

Ahead of her the sky took on a deep lavender hue and she saw that the tops of the dry corn stalks, still standing in a few fields, were suddenly tipped with gold. Surprised at the sudden brightness Alicia stopped and looked to the west. While overhead was gray with low clouds, there was a break just above the horizon. It looked as if someone had painted the edge of the clouds with pure gold so brightly did it shine. The amber sun transformed before her eyes as it grew larger, yet redder in color. She felt as if she could actually see the sun moving lower, below the horizon. In all her life Alicia could not remember ever noticing a sunset like this one. Realizing that she had not taken a breath Alicia nearly gasped when the spectacle faded. She was not a connoisseur of art and, other than style magazines, felt unaffected by beauty. Yet this sunset moved her in a way unfamiliar to her.

The darkness brought a greater chill that seemed to invade her coat. She pulled up her collar and began trudging to the east.

After about an hour of walking she heard behind her the approach of a car. She was cold and had begun to shiver. Her cotton gloves weren't keeping her hands warm, her ears felt numb, and she could tell her legs were out of shape. Hitchhiking seemed like a more credible option now. The headlights approaching weren't encouraging. One was pointed slightly outward and was dimmer than the other. She stood facing the car with her thumb pointed in the direction she had been walking hoping the person behind the wheel was kind.

Miraculously, it seemed to her, the vehicle slowed when she came into its headlights. The driver pulled past her and stopped along side the road. As she came up to it she saw that the vehicle appeared to be an ancient pick-up truck. She didn't know what make it was, but could tell it had been around longer than she. The driver leaned over and rolled down the window. An older man, he also reached down and manually rolled the window down a few inches. "Do you belong to that car I saw back a ways?"

This man sounded more like her grandfather than anything. Surely he was safe. "Yes, sir. I ran out of gas."

"I see. Ya look cold. Ya need a lift?" he said reaching over to unlock the door.

"Oh, please! I just need to get to a gas station and fill a can or something." She opened the door, struggling with the stiff button on the door handle, and stepped up to the seat.

"Ain't no gas stations open now young lady." He had been nearly yelling when she had stood outside. He now spoke more quietly and with gentleness in his voice. "Where're you headed?" he asked.

She thought quickly. She doubted he cared where she was going, but decided to lie. "I'm headed to Chicago," she said matter-of-factly. Then realized it was a blunder. "I mean Minneapolis."

"Well which is it? Chicago or Minneapolis?"

"Minneapolis."

The older man eyed her carefully. "Is that so?" he replied without malice. "It's pretty late. Even if you were going the right direction you wouldn't get there till the wee hours." He thought a second and continued, "Ma name's Masters, Roy Masters. You should pro'bly come to my farm for some rest. I'll get you to a station in the morning."

Alarms sounded in her mind as she reached for the door handle, noting that it was missing on her side of the truck. Then, he had started to drive and was going too fast for her to jump out, but she began to fear that she had made another mistake.

What kind of ogre was this man? What would he do to her? Yet he had offered his name and accommodation without even asking hers.

"Yeah, Missy, my daughter, she's still up. I 'magine you'll like her. I'll bet she'll even make us some hot chocolate." He slowed again, "Ah wasn't thinkin'. Do you need to get some things out of your car? It'll pro'bly be okay sittin' there for the rest of the night." He glanced at her, "Hey you all right?" He had noticed the panicked look in her eyes.

At the mention of a daughter her paranoia began to wane. "No, I mean yes, I'm fine. Just a little tired and cold. I have a bag in the trunk if you don't mind." She managed to keep her voice calm and level despite the fear that still clutched her heart. She wondered if she would ever feel safe again.

The old man turned his truck around, then, and they returned to the car. It was only two miles back. Her hour of walking had not gotten her very far. "It's a good thing I came along. There ain't much traffic up here at night. If you were headin' for Minneapolis you turned the wrong way. You passed Mason City back a ways." He didn't mention the implied "stupid girl."

Alicia did not want to stay with this old man or his daughter, but didn't see any other way. He had shown kindness when she had expected savagery. He had gone out of his way to help her. Roy explained that he had been heading to his town apartment when he had come across her. His daughter lived in his farm house and kept it up herself. He now rented out most of his land, but loved to spend his days at the farm.

A few miles farther back the way she had driven the old man turned off onto a rutted gravel lane. She could make out the shadow of a homestead less than a quarter mile from the main road. There were lights still burning on the main floor. "Missy, she don't go to bed too early. Worries a lot," he stated, then grinned, "Mostly 'bout me." He pulled up in front of the large open porch his headlights illuminating a large white two story structure. Alicia couldn't make out many of the details, but what she could see appeared to be in good condition.

A woman materialized on the porch, hands on hips. Alicia remained in the car while the old man got out. She realized he still hadn't asked her name and she felt ashamed at her lack of manners.

"Hey, Missy. I ran across a stray up the road. You think you can make us some hot chocolate?"

"Dad! What do you think you're doing?" She peered at the truck trying to make out who was in the front seat. Missy could tell it was a young woman, but could not make out her features. At least it wasn't another homeless man. Her father seemed to find some of the strangest characters, but she had learned not to get too upset. He had a heart of gold and always wanted to take care of lonesome people. She was sure that his kindness grew from his own loneliness since her mom had died.

"Okay," she said after a few moments, "You'd best come inside." She beckoned to Alicia, whom she could barely see, to come in.

Alicia had not been able to see anything but the shape of the woman, silhouetted in the light of the doorway. She seemed tall and was a large woman. Her hair was either short or worn up on top of her head. She saw the wave signaling her to come in, and Alicia scooted across the seat and out the driver's door. "I would have opened the door for ya young lady," came the voice of the older man. He was carrying her bag coming around from the rear of the truck.

"It's all right. Here, let me carry my bag," she offered.

"No. It ain't right for the guest to carry her own bag," he grinned and she could see the reflection of the porch light from one silver or gold front tooth. Shivering again she turned and they ascended the front steps to the old farm house. The boards of the porch creaked under their weight, but Alicia could see that everything was well painted and in good condition, not old and worn out.

Once inside, she found a very comfortable living room and she could smell something wonderful cooking in the kitchen. Missy stood facing her, a tall, buxom woman with graying hair that had once been a dishwater blonde. Her full cheeks were slightly pink in the room light and she wore an apron. Alicia felt as if she had been transported back into the 1950's.

Missy, hands on hips, said, "Well, young lady, it looks like my dad brought in another lost soul. Where'd you come from?"

Alicia nearly slipped and let out her home town, but just said, "I'm from Kansas. I was headed north when I ran out of gas."

As if this was all the explanation she needed Missy patted her on the shoulder and said,

"I'm Missy. You look tired. Why don't you take the little room at the top of the stairs. I'm sorry, but there's no plumbing up there so you'll have to use the washroom down here." She pointed across the room to the small bathroom off the nearby hallway.

Alicia noted that the house appeared to have been professionally decorated with perfectly matching tones of cream and olive green. The furniture was in superb condition, and one glance into the kitchen told her that it had been recently remodeled. There were state of the art stainless steel appliances. *No upstairs plumbing?* Her curiosity got the best of her, "No plumbing? But this house is immaculate. Why wouldn't you add that when you remodeled?"

Missy's eyebrows went up. "You know a little about remodeling? That's what I do for a living. I have an architecture degree and my business is restoring farm houses." She saw the surprise on Alicia's face, "You thought what I did was keep house didn't you?" She added, "When we go into a house we leave much of the basic structure alone. Some people want the modern conveniences, but most want it to look new but remain old in style. Plumbing is variable. We do have telephone and data lines upstairs though."

Alicia was taken aback. Here she was in this fifties style home with an old farmer and his daughter talking about remodeling and 'data lines.' She sat down in a maroon overstuffed chair and looked around with admiration.

All she could say was, "Wow."

Missy smiled. "I'll go start the hot chocolate. How about a piece of apple pie?"

Alicia's mouth was watering already and she smiled back, "That sounds wonderful."

****

The phone line buzzed. There was a whirring noise as the encrypting device also turned on automatically. James Rizzo looked at the caller ID and picked it up. The slightly tinny voice on the other end said, "I've spoken to the Assistant DA. He will play ball. Your nephew will be out on Monday morning."

James hesitated, then said, "Has the other little solution been arranged?"

"Yes sir," came the reply.

"Don't call again. Understood?" James ordered.

"Understood." There was a click and the line went dead.

James slowly lowered his handset into the cradle. He put his head in his hands and tears began to flow. His toughness cracked and he began to realize how hateful this business was becoming.

He had just signed his own nephew's death sentence.

28

Sunday

Jack had finally gotten home, once again, for a few hours of sleep. Kathy's family kept a vigil in shifts through the night. He woke with only a little rest, but being Sunday he felt encouraged. Going to church always recharged him as he gained spiritual energy from the worship. His home church had up-beat music and a very good preacher. There was sound biblical teaching and a worshipful atmosphere. Even though going to church meant he couldn't sleep late, he rarely did anyway because mornings were too enjoyable to him.

Jack dressed and had some breakfast then he left for church with a light heart. He intended to stop at the hospital after first service today.

His phone vibrated on his belt just as he got in his car. "Hello?"

"Dr. Sharp, this is Frank," came the voice.

"Hi Frank did you get any rest?" Jack asked, recognizing the voice.

"Yes, a little, thank you," his voice was hurried. "Mom is awake and asking for you."

"She is?" He looked at his watch and said, "How is she?"

"Well, she wants to tell you herself," Frank answered somewhat mysteriously.

Jack smiled ruefully. "All right. I was heading to church, but I think I can swing it."

"Okay. See you soon, Doc." Frank hung up.

Jack was mystified. Had he heard a chuckle in Frank's voice? He hadn't thought he was in a hurry to go to the hospital again and surprised himself at how much he wanted to see Kathy again. He was also surprised that she was fully awake, and mystified at her reasons for wanting him there. He put his car into gear and slipped out of the garage heading to the hospital.

****

Dan Randizzio felt totally drained. Saturday had been a nightmare to him and he still didn't know where he stood with the cops. He at least had a cell to himself, though the toilet in the corner smelled as if it hadn't been cleaned in weeks. The noise, lack of privacy, and the brightness of the area made sleep almost impossible and he now ached all over. During the night there must have been a big drunken party with multiple arrests because there had been a steady stream of new arrivals into the early hours. They had been loud and abusive at first, then the sound of their retching had filled the hallways. Finally, they must have passed out and Dan had drifted into a fitful sleep.

His face was scratchy and his breath was really bad. Breakfast was on a tray in front of him and though the eggs were cold, it was actually pretty tasty. He had been hungrier than he had thought. There still had been no communication with him about what charges were being proffered against him, but he knew that he would have to be charged soon or released. The latter seemed unlikely since, according to the detectives, he was also a suspect in the murder case.

This whole thing had appeared to him like an easy way to make some big money. He would have saved face and squared himself with his uncle at the same time. He had thought he was running the show but it had gone totally wrong. Now he was facing a potentially long term inside and he could kick himself for getting involved. He had been doing pretty well in his job as an electrician and was supposed to have become a journeyman soon. A job like that actually paid pretty well and they would always need electricians. He decided that if he got out of jail he wouldn't do any more stuff like this. He wanted to have a life.

A noise at the entrance to his cell made him look up. His beautiful lawyer, Riley, stood there smiling at him. She was about the best looking woman he had ever met and regretted that he wasn't anywhere near her on the social scale. It was obvious to him that he was only a client to her and that she had no other interests in him.

"Hey," he said.

"Hey yourself," she said in a pleasant tone.

Dan took notice and set the tray aside. "What's up? Have they formally charged me?"

Riley turned and glared at the guard who obediently unlocked the cell door. "We have some things to discuss," then motioning toward the guard, said, "In private."

They went to an interview room where they could talk. Dan was even more acutely aware of his appearance. Riley was stunning in a colorful blouse that was low-cut and revealing. Her skirt was pastel and just above knee length. Today she had ditched the spike heels and was wearing more casual shoes.

Riley spoke first, "Did you talk to anyone last night?"

"You mean the cops?" Dan asked.

"No. I mean did you make any more calls or talk to your uncle?" Riley asked bluntly. She was no longer smiling as sweetly as before and Dan realized she had been putting on a show.

"What do you know about my uncle? I haven't been allowed to talk to anyone," Dan answered.

"Never mind, I just think someone pulled some strings. It looks like they aren't going to charge you. You're going to be released in the morning tomorrow unless they can find additional evidence to hold you. The ADA isn't happy, but he knows he has to have a better case. Right now all they have is circumstantial. If you can sit tight and keep your mouth shut you should be home free for now." She glanced around then looked straight at him. "That doesn't keep them from re-arresting you and charging you for murder whenever they want. Do you understand?"

"But I didn't have anything to do with that!" he insisted

"Keep it that way and don't say anything else. I'll be in here in the morning with your release papers by six. Be ready to scoot out of here. You should head home. Get out of this town. They'll need to know how to reach you in Chicago, though."

"How am I going to pay you?"

She laughed, "I'll get paid. Don't worry. You've been taken care of for now," she hesitated then said, "I don't know what to tell you if you need help later. You will probably have to talk to that rich uncle of yours. Stay out of trouble and get away from Nebraska."

"What kind of lawyer are you? You haven't even asked me about what I was doing," he said incredulous. "Don't you need to know my side of it?"

"I know that the prosecution has no case. If I have to defend you in court we'll get down to details. You just keep saying you didn't do it. They can't prove you did and for now that is all we need." It was unnerving to Riley because she knew she hadn't done anything, yet her client was going to get out of jail, no charges filed.

Who was that rich uncle?

She also knew how the game was played. The less she knew about the details the safer she would be. She stood up from the metal folding chair on which she had been sitting.

"I'll see you tomorrow bright and early."

He stared after her. It seemed too easy. "I can't believe it's over just like that."

"Just like that," she echoed with a wry smile. "Don't talk to anyone!"

Dan also stood as the guard approached. He was confused, his head in a daze. He started to reflect on the past few days. Seeing the dead body of his girlfriend had shaken him more than he cared to admit. He had been nervous the whole time he had searched her clothing fearing that he had missed something in the dark. If he hadn't gone back during daylight he wouldn't have gotten into such a mess in the first place. That doctor! He had been the only one who could connect him with the body.

Dan sat back on his cot shaking his head. He didn't like leaving things open and unfinished. He felt vulnerable, but what else could he do? Realizing he had to follow his lawyer's advice for his own sake he also knew that he still had to face his uncle. He hadn't found what he was looking for. One girl was dead and the other one was still missing and, as far as he knew, they were no closer to finding it. Would they make him keep trying? Maybe they would let him off the hook and he could just go back to work. He could keep his mouth shut. He just wanted out.

****

Jack approached the hospital doors with nervous anticipation. His mind had gone through the multiple scenarios of Kathy's potential recovery. He had visualized her with one entire side of her body paralyzed and in another permutation she was not able to speak. He considered the possibility that she wouldn't remember what she had said to him or possibly not know for sure who he was. Yet, this morning she had asked for him. This seemed like a good sign.

He was at the elevator about to head up when he spotted some of Kathy's children walking down the hall toward him. It was the three younger girls Sarah, Mary and Esther. They spotted him and Esther ran up to him and gave him a firm hug.

When she looked up at him her eyes were shining, "Morning, Dr. Jack." Then she surprisingly ran off to catch her sisters who were glancing back heads together and giggling.

"Morning!" he called after them, mystified. They had huddled together now as if they were having a conference. Esther turned to him and without saying anything, waved.

"Okay. I'm going up," he said. The huddle broke up and the girls headed down the steps toward the dining room. "I wonder what that was all about," he thought to himself and stood mute as the elevator door opened and then began to close again. He caught himself and quickly stuck his hand into the remaining space to catch the elevator before the door closed.

As Jack walked down the hallway he met nurses whom he had worked with before. They were unusually pleasant and everyone seemed to have a smile this day.

Karen, a nurse whom he had taken to dinner a few times in the past, said, "Good morning Dr. Sharp," and winked at him. A receptionist smiled and waved as she greeted him. He was puzzled by the apparent joviality of the workplace on a Sunday morning. As Jack approached the door of Kathy's room he saw that the nurse's desk was empty, but he could hear the sound of a quiet voice in the room.

"You just rest, sugar," came the voice. There was a rustling of sheets and as Jack glanced over the medical record the nurse arrived at the door. "Dr. Sharp, how nice to see you."

"Hello Inga," replied Jack. "How's our patient?"

"Oh she's much better this morning," she said with a grin. "She surprised us all. She woke up singing. It was like she hadn't ever been sick."

"Wow, that's great. Is she in pain?" he asked.

"She said there was a stinging sensation in her forehead and a throbbing in her neck. Everything works though, as far as we can tell. She's really tired and she just fell asleep again."

"Oh, that's too bad. Well maybe I shouldn't disturb her. I'm sure she needs her rest." Jack continued to thumb through the medical record checking vital signs and lab to hide his disappointment at not getting to speak to Kathy.

"Doctor," the nurse said.

"Yes?" Jack looked up.

"She woke up singing and talking about you. She said you saved her life and she wanted you here. She told her daughters she couldn't wait to see you. You got something going on with your patient?" she asked with a half smile and raised eyebrows. "We all thought you were a confirmed bachelor."

Jack put the record down and shuffled his feet uncomfortably. "She said all that? I guess I've made a good impression on her."

At this the nurse laughed reflexively and caught herself, putting a hand over her mouth. She glanced around to see that they were alone. Almost whispering she said, "I think, Dr. Jack, she might be in love with you." She returned to her charting chuckling under her breath. "Have a nice day and don't wake my patient."

Jack was dumbfounded. He knew Kathy had said she had feelings for him, but did that constitute love?' He quietly stepped into her room and looked over at her. She was sleeping peacefully. *Could this just be the effect of the steroids or the surgery?* Even if it was true, and she really loved him, did he love her? What kind of future would that love have? He couldn't help wondering how much time she really had left on this earth.

29

Justin usually bounded out of bed in the morning. But this day he felt sluggish and out of sorts. He desperately wanted to make a difference in this murder case, but so far whenever he had come up with anything useful, events had beaten him to the punch. With his technical skill, he had found out Randizzio's phone number. They would have been able to track him down with that, but the bumbler had managed to get himself arrested before Justin could even tell Rebecca about the phone. He had Officer Gus Wilson working on information about the doctor but he didn't personally believe Dr. Sharp could be the murderer. There just didn't seem to be any reason for him to be involved. He had merely been an innocent passer-by. For him at least one mystery was still evident, the whereabouts of Alicia Winters. Now he wanted to focus on Chicago. That seemed, to him, to be a likely direction for her to head. He knew there was a connection in Chicago because she worked there.

He checked the weather and headlines on his Apple laptop and went off for a leisurely shower. Then, dressed casually in jeans and a sweatshirt, he closed his computer and headed for the door. A new coffee shop had opened just a block away, within walking distance. Because there was wireless internet availablethere, he could begin his research while enjoying the energy boost of caffeine.

Justin found the air to be crisp and the sun was in his eyes as it rose from the eastern horizon. He had a long view of the countryside as he descended into the street toward his destination. In his mind, he reviewed what he had learned about this case.

On Saturday he had called the missing girl's aunt to find out if she knew where Alicia worked. She had not known the name of the business, but had given him Alicia's apartment address. He guesstimated that she lived within a thirty minute drive to work, from the download of a detailed map of Chicago which he hoped would narrow down his search. Before heading home the previous night, he was struck by another idea and had stopped by the forensic lab. There he had found a pretty young woman bent over the counter staring at a rather large wad of what appeared to be chewing gum. He recalled the encounter with a subconscious smile.

****

"Hello," Justin said as he approached the sandy haired woman from behind. Her head went up and she turned around swiftly. She wore dark-rimmed glasses and her hair was tightly pulled up into a bun, though strands had snaked they way around her face giving her a little unkempt, yet softer appearance.

"Hi," she said quickly. "What can I do for you?" She saw that he was not in uniform and thought he might be a visitor lost in the halls, though it was an odd time for anyone to be there.

She noted also that he wasn't bad looking tall and slender.

"I'm Detective Samuelson and I need to look at some evidence."

Without thinking Cindy burst out laughing, "That's good. No really. Are you lost? Can I help you find your way out?"

Justin's face fell. Once again he had not been taken seriously. He sighed and reached to his belt to get his badge case. It wasn't there. This technician clearly didn't believe him. It was embarrassing and now he wasn't sure how to convince her.

"Look," he said, "I really am a detective. My badge is at my desk and I need to look at some evidence. It's on the 'Connie Doe' case."

This did make her pause. How would a visitor know anything about a case? "If you really are a detective you know I can't just show you anything without some ID."

"Sure," he said and fished out his wallet. He had several forms of identification and one official license that cleared up the misunderstanding.

"Sorry," she still had a light voice, "you really don't look like a detective."

"Yeah, I get that a lot," he said chagrined. He noticed the lump of gum on the counter. "Is that the diamond?" he asked.

"You know about that?" she countered.

"Yes, Dr. French told us about it. I'm working with Detective

Sweate," he said.

"Oh, her!" she exclaimed.

He caught her sarcastic tone, "What? You don't like Detective Sweate?" Justin said with a half smile.

"I ... I had better not say since you are her partner." She frowned and stared at Justin for a moment. "So-what do you need?" she asked tersely.

"Hey, first you think I'm a visitor and you laugh at me, now you're mad at me and I haven't done anything." He pleaded his case with his hands out and shrugged his shoulders.

Cindy placed her hands on the work bench and took a deep breath. "I'm sorry. I'm just frustrated."

"Why?" Justin asked.

"I want to clean this diamond, but the gum is sticky and doesn't scrape off easily. It's small enough that I'm afraid I'll cut my finger trying to use this razor blade." She pointed to her tiny pile of shavings.

Justin stepped up to the bench and, staring at the gum covered diamond, thought a second. "Do you have a freezer? Or better yet some dry ice?" he asked Cindy.

Puzzled she said, "Yes, here." She pointed to a red plastic cooler with a white lid near the upright refrigerator.

Justin also asked for some gloves and tongs. He unclasped the lid and took out a small piece of dry ice with the tongs and carried it over to the bench. He laid the wad of gum on the flat surface of the dry ice.

Cindy looked alarmed. "What are you doing?"

Justin smiled back, "Don't worry. If this is a diamond you'll see in a second." As the dry ice touched the surface of the gum, a circle of frost formed and spread quickly. He moved the dry ice around a little and then sharply rapped the diamond on the hard surface of the counter top. Cindy, startled, jumped a little, but the process had the desired effect. A chunk of the gum shattered and fell away cleanly from the underlying diamond, which showed no harmful effects.

Justin looked up in triumph. Holding out the diamond he said,

"Now how about looking at the other evidence?"

Cindy had brought out the box containing evidence she had been working on. Justin had raked through the material, not knowing how it would help him. Cindy stood by offering bits of advice, but neither of them could see how the paltry bits of material and Connie's few possessions could help. It seemed strange to Justin that there had been no missing persons reports about any girls matching Connie's description in the entire region.

Justin smiled as he looked once again at the skirt Connie had been wearing. The label on this particular skirt indicated that it had not come from a large department store, but he recognized the name as a more exclusive women's clothing store. He took note of the name hoping it would prove useful.

"What would you call this style of skirt?" he asked Cindy, holding the dress up before her.

"It's kind of a pleated wrap around, I guess." She stared at the bloody skirt front and suddenly felt cold. "Oh, how awful."

Justin turned the skirt and saw the knife holes and blood stains.

"Murder is never pretty."

****

By figuring out where the deceased girl, Connie, lived and worked, Justin hoped to deduce the missing girl's work-place. It was a long shot and may not help a lot but he was filled with confidence. Any information was useful.

Having reached the coffee shop, Justin now stared at his note-book computer, with ideas flying through his head. He sipped the whipped cream from the top of his venti double shot mocha whip and let his mind wander. How could he track her down? He focused on the skirt label. It had to have come from one of six locations and only one of these was within his search area. He hoped this improved his chances.

With his search engine he quickly found phone numbers for the three stores in the Chicago area, then flipped open his cell and dialed. The first two attempts yielded only answering machines and he had left messages. On his third attempt the answering machine began its message and Justin almost hung up again. Instead the message was interrupted by a young woman's voice.

Justin had managed to catch the manager in her office doing some weekend paper work. He had made his case to her and appealed to her good nature to help him find an address for their victim.

The woman said, "Oh my, my. I don't know. This is frightening," she said with a notable tremor in her voice.

"I'm sorry. Please understand we are doing this as an official inquiry. I could have the Chicago police come to your store if you prefer. I know you have no reason to trust me. Let me give you my badge number and you can check on it tomorrow." He read off to her the number of his badge and gave her the police department phone number.

Cautiously she said, "I don't want a police car here," she said. "I'll try to help. I am the manager. Let me please move back into the office with the computer and then I'll see what can be done."

Justin waited on the line listening to some nice jazz in the background. A few moments later, the woman came back on the line. "Hello. Now what is it you want?" Her voice was still a little strained.

"What is your name?"

"I am Ramona Rivera. Don't you need a carté to get information?"

"A warrant? If you volunteer the information I won't need to get one, but this is important and I only need one name. Your help will save us time and may help someone else."

Ramona thought for a few seconds, "I guess I will help. I don't want trouble."

Justin gave her the information he already had, the skirt style, color, and size. He told Ramona to look for the name Connie or Constance in their sales records. Unfortunately, he had no idea when the dress had been purchased or if it had been purchased from this particular location. He suggested that she check records for the past year.

She sighed. "Connie is a common name. This will take some time. Can I call you back?"

Justin gave her is cell number and thanked her profusely. They hung up together. He was amazed at the cooperation he had received. He was used to doors being slammed in his face and people refusing to speak to him. Of course, she might never call him back either. In the meantime he had other ideas about how to proceed.

Justin went back for another mocha. He was somewhat underweight and, aided by youthful energy, could still eat almost anything he wanted without gaining weight. Biking was one of his favorite activities and tried to get in one hundred miles a week. It had been several days, however, since he had gotten his Cannondale Super Six out of his storage locker. He sat back and began checking his emails when his phone vibrated in his pocket.

"Hello?" he was curious about the number. He did not recognize it.

"Yes, Mr. Samuelson please?" Justin chuckled. He hadn't been called "Mr." before.

"This is Detective Samuelson," he said.

"Oh. So sorry, sir." He then realized it was the sweet voice of Ramona from the dress shop in Chicago.

"It's okay. I'm just not used be being called 'Mr.'" he replied.

Her laugh was genuine too and Justin regretted not being able to speak to her in person.

"I see," she said. "I think I have what you wanted."

"Wow! That was quick," Justin said delightedly.

"I started three months back. You said a year, but our designs are very up-to-date. Girls who buy clothes here don't wear old styles."

"I never would have thought of that," he said, mystified.

"I suspected so," she chuckled. "There have been ten Connies here in *tres meses*. I mean three months. Only one who bought the skirt you found."

Justin was now listening intently.

"Connie Ridgeway is the name I was able to come up with. Do you want her address?" Ramona inquired.

"Yes please," he said like a child asking for a cookie.

Ramona gave him the information she had. "I call' you from

my cell phone. So if you have other questions you may call me back. I'm going to go home now so I won't be able to answer the phone you called earlier."

Justin replied, "You don't know how much I appreciate this. You have been more than helpful."

"Well. I like your voice. Maybe you come buy a dress for your girl-friend sometime."

"Maybe so if I'm I Chicago." Justin had smiled thinking of Cindy, the crime lab tech. Perhaps if he had an opportunity he would ask her to dinner sometime. He was now doubly excited, possessing some useful information. He had broken this one himself! Entering the location on his map he found that Connie and Alicia, the missing girl, lived only one block apart. It was probable that they worked near each other as well. Armed with her name and address he decided to see what else he could find out before calling Rebecca. He knew that he would probably need the Chicago police to do the leg work, but nothing much would get done there today. He might as well see what else he could dig up.

He needed a business address. He now had the address of the shop where the skirt had been purchased. Next he looked at a map of corporation offices. He assumed that she worked in one of the major companies.

He stared for a minute at the maps and realized that there was a complex of offices in Naperville, Illinois near a small shopping mall where the specialty shop was located. It was not far from Connie's home address.

It was a guess- but also a place to start.

Next he entered Alicia's and Connie's names into several search engines. He found old addresses and found sites that would cost plenty to check them out. He was reluctant to spend his own money yet, but he had no luck with trying online white and yellow pages. His boldness grew along with his frustration. He didn't simply want to go, hat in hand, to the Chicago police and request their help. He was sure he could find out where they worked if he just used his brain. He examined the office building complex and focused on about two dozen different corporations housed there.

He had not been a true hacker, but had learned many of the techniques from various places. He decided to see what he could find out about the larger companies in the area he had designated. Now that he had both names he could narrow his search and he felt confident that he could do it without getting into too much trouble. He was, nevertheless, treading on dangerous ground here. He knew it was illegal to electronically break into the private information of the companies he was going to check out. Yet he believed the end justified his means and went forward despite his better judgment. Any information at this stage could help.

He looked at his business listings and went to the first one. He knew he should probably wait and just call these places on Monday, but fired up by his earlier success, he pressed forward.

Using the ideas he had learned and some tricks he had thought up he actually managed to hack into the main computer of the first company, "Jax Corp." He searched for the personnel file and found a long listing of employees. He then searched by name and by years of employment. He knew about Alicia and figured Connie had worked there less than two years. He had looked for "Connie" and "Constance Ridgeway," but had found none listed. Then he tried "Alicia Winters." Likewise, no luck. While he was in their system he looked at the basic business information and found that they produced small plastic connectors and parts for use in the manufacture of office furniture. There didn't appear to be any connections with diamonds.

He backed out feeling safe and that he hadn't "tripped" any alarms. If all the companies were this easy he should have his list of ten done in no time. He knew that if he got caught, police or not, he could get into some serious trouble so he worked as quickly as possible.

The second company, "Hammerton Smith," however, was not as easy to break into. He sipped some more mocha and settled down for a long session.

****

Alicia blinked. She was initially mildly disoriented as she opened her eyes to a bright filtered sunlight. The nightmare had come again. It was dark and Connie stood, about to say something to her. In the dream she could see her turn slowly and then another person appeared. They faced each other and the other one pulled a gun up and fired. She woke this morning before seeing her friend die, but she remembered seeing her fall.

In the beautiful morning sunlight, the ceiling above her was revealed as a cream-colored decorative pattern. She wondered if it was made with pressed metal. Despite the nightmare she felt rested and calm for the first time in days. She also felt safe and began to wonder what she should do. She knew she should probably get gas and leave immediately, but the comfort she felt made her want to curl up and sleep some more. Her stomach growled then and she remembered that it had been a long time since her last good meal.

Alicia got up, all in one movement. She padded over, barefoot to the window and peeked out, but was careful to conceal herself, mainly because she was dressed only in her panties and a nightie she had hurriedly pulled from her suitcase last night before falling fast asleep in the comfortable bed.

In the front yard she saw the drive they had come down last night from the main road. On either side were fields. The one to the east appeared to have already been harvested, but in the west field stood row upon row of tall, heavily laden corn stalks.

The main road was no more than a quarter of a mile away and most of the neighboring fields, likewise, had yet to be harvested. She had no idea when harvesting started or how it was done. She had seen the huge combines, but rarely paid much attention. Having already partaken the warm country hospitality of these special people, now she was beginning to awaken to the beauty of the countryside.

A hot shower was high on her list of things to do, but she remembered that there was no plumbing upstairs in this house. She found a robe laid over the footboard, put it on and opened her door. The wood floor creaked pleasantly as she approached the stair. She crept along quietly, not wanting to wake her benefactors. She needn't have worried. Half way down the curved staircase Missy called out to her, "Well good morning to you! Or is it good afternoon? We weren't sure you would wake up at all."

"What time is it?" she asked dumbly.

"It's about nine in the morning. We're getting ready for church. You're welcome to come along, but you'll have to hurry a bit," Missy answered. "We'll have a nice lunch and then you can get on your way if you want."

Reaching the bottom of the steps Alicia noticed the sound of something frying and a luscious smell wafting from the kitchen. "Oh, I don't usually go to church," she responded. She spotted the old man sitting at the kitchen table with a coffee cup in one hand.

Roy said, "Honey, you ought to come anyway. You're troubled about somethin' and it never hurts to get God involved." He set his coffee down. "Now you just get a quick shower. We can wait for you. It won't hurt us to be a little late. Missy, I'll bet she's still hungry. Do you have some of those sweet rolls she could work on while she gets ready?"

Alicia was mute. It wasn't only that she didn't want to disappoint these nice people, but there was something more. She hadn't been to church for years staying away since the death of her father. At first the pain had been so great that she had blamed God. Eventually God just didn't cross her mind. The severe pain of the loss of her father lessened over time, but she had not renewed her relationship with God nor gone to church anywhere.

Now the thought came to her that maybe Roy was right. It couldn't hurt. She was in trouble and needed all the help she could find.

Missy handed her a warm, frosted cinnamon roll and said, "You'll find a towel and washcloth for you on the rack. Please try to hurry we should be leaving in about twenty minutes." With that she herded Alicia into the bathroom and closed the door. Alicia had not gotten ready that quickly for a long time but felt obliged to do so. She thanked Missy and started the water. Looking in the mirror she was astonished to see just how haggard she appeared. The events of the past days had taken their toll.

Alicia showered quickly and dried off, glad her hair was fairly short so she wouldn't have to do much to it. She wrapped the robe snugly around her and then she concentrated on her face. In a few minutes, she had covered the worst of the lines that had recently developed. A little mascara and a touch of lip gloss from her purse made her feel much better. Stepping out onto the beautifully finished wood floor into the kitchen, she rushed to her room. There she found her outfit neatly pressed and hung up. She smiled realizing that she was actually enjoying herself for the first time in a while. Most important of all, she felt safe.

As she left her room brushing her hair she heard a loud "wolf" whistle. Roy was looking at her with a huge grin. "You sure clean up pretty!" he said.

Missy groaned. "Dirty old man," she chuckled. Then she said, "Looks like you're ready. I have to admit I didn't think a city girl could do it in less than an hour."

Alicia had a sudden fear, her car! What if the state patrol or sheriff had found it and reported it?

She barely dared to ask, "What about my car shouldn't we get it?"

Roy swatted his hand in the air, "Done taken care of. Missy drove me back out last night with a can of gas. I drove it home. It's in the barn out back."

Alicia breathed a silent sigh of relief. All she could think of to say then was,

"Shall we go?"

They didn't take the old pickup truck. It would have been a tight squeeze, but in the garage to the side of the house was a late model Buick. It had leather interior, a high end sound system and a screen for a GPS unit. Alicia was impressed and said, "GPS?"

Missy countered, "Listen. Out here its better than bein' told, 'My house is one mile from the Schmidt farm across from the power lines.' I just need their postal location and it works great. I've lived here all my life and it is still hard to find some folks' places."

They drove in silence toward Mason City. Alicia could see the town ahead when they turned off on another gravel road. About two miles farther they turned once again. She spotted the country church ahead nestled in a small grove of trees. There were cars parked in the close-cropped dry grass and people were making their way to the sanctuary, greeting each other. Some carried plates and some had children in tow. When they had found parking near the edge of the church lot, Missy reached in at the back door and pulled out a large covered bowl.

"What's that?" asked Alicia.

"Oh, I forgot to mention it. We have a potluck lunch every Sunday after services. I made potato salad," Missy answered.

Alicia thought she must have made enough for two dozen people considering the size of the bowl. She hadn't been to a potluck dinner in ages. As they stepped inside the church Missy and Roy were warmly greeted by other members. Everyone seemed to be enjoying themselves and Alicia was introduced as a "friend" who had stopped in for a visit. Nobody seemed surprised or nosy. They greeted her kindly and included her in their conversations.

She wondered when the service would start and was also curious about what kind of service would last until lunch time. It was only nine-thirty. She hadn't ever spent more than an hour in any church before. They had entered a large foyer with beautifully carved wooden doors leading into the main part of the church. The building had looked old from the outside, but it was definitely well restored inside. There was a kitchen to the right in an addition where coffee and pans of home-made cinnamon rolls gave off an inviting aroma. These were warm and too tasty to pass up. Missy moved over to her and touched her elbow. "We're going to Sunday School down the hall. You can come with us or go to the one for young adults. They have that right here in the sanctuary," she said pointing back to the main church area.

Alicia was again surprised. She had thought Sunday School was just for children. She debated being left alone, but decided it would be nice to see others her own age. "I'll go to that one, I guess. When is the main service?"

"I'm sorry honey. I guess I didn't fill you in. Sunday School lasts until ten-thirty and then we have a few minutes to socialize all over again before the service. Okay?" Missy smiled warmly.

Alicia nodded and thanked her. She saw others carrying their rolls and coffee into the sanctuary so she did likewise. She was determined to sit as far back as possible, but this idea was derailed as there was a circle of chairs set up in the front portion of the church. A man about her own age, wearing a suit stood there, smiling as other twenty-somethings arrived and sat down. She began to get uncomfortable not knowing what she would be expected to do.

"Hi," he said as she approached cautiously. I'm Jason Koch. You must be Missy and Roy's friend. Welcome." He offered her a chair as she awkwardly tried to hold her coffee and roll and shake his hand. Others who sat down were just as pleasant, but no one pressed her for details about herself. In actuality this was unusual, but upon their arrival, Missy had cornered Jason and asked him not to ask her many questions.

The subject for their study was a chapter in the Bible from the book of Luke. Alicia hadn't opened a Bible for years, but still remembered that Luke was in the New Testament. She hadn't brought a Bible, but another young man who must have been close to six-and-a-half feet tall picked one up from a nearby pew, opened it to Luke, and handed it to her. There were eight in the group, equally divided four men and four women, including Alicia.

Jason read the passage, a parable about a servant who had cheated his master and they all discussed what it meant. Jason had several commentaries and books about the passage. He had studied these carefully before the class and he seemed to understand the parable in depth. Alicia rarely joined in, but found herself listening and thinking about the points that were made. In the parable the servant was about to be fired. When he realized his precarious position he went to others who owed money to his master and told them to reduce the amounts. He hoped to improve his status with the local people. His master was so impressed by his shrewdness that he decided not to fire him. Alicia was surprised at the parable. She was even more intrigued to learn that God wants his people to be as intelligent and shrewd as the servant, though not with the same cheating mentality.

The time flew past and before long Jason said it was time to end. The little group then bowed their heads as a unit as Jason closed in prayer. Alicia felt uncomfortable again, not knowing how to pray, but she bent her head forward and listened as he earnestly asked God to help each of them that day. When she looked up again everyone seemed to be looking at her. They had finished and she had still kept her head bowed a moment longer. Embarrassed, she stood to go, but no one said anything unkind to her. One of the other girls tried to talk with her, but she extracted herself from the conversation.

Jason was less easily put off. He had stepped out and retrieved two cups of coffee. Holding one out to her, Alicia couldn't very well say "no".

"You haven't been in church for a while have you?"

"What makes you say that?" she said, trying to keep the chagrin out of her voice.

"Oh nothing really. I don't mean any offense. It is just an observation."

"No. You're right. But I am really enjoying this. Thank you for including me in your group. I was afraid I would feel out of place, but you made me feel welcome."

Jason grinned a toothy grin. "We try to be friendly. We don't get too many visitors, cuz we're out in the country here. But you won't find nicer folks in any big city church."

Alicia could tell he was working hard at making a good impression. "I don't expect to be around here long, but I'm glad I came." With that she smiled back at him and began looking for Missy.

The church service was well attended. The singing was vibrant and actually fun with a small band who accompanied some choruses and one hymn from the hymnal. Alicia saw that Jason played the electric guitar. She didn't sing much, but on some choruses they repeated the verses so many times she was able to learn their melodies. The sermon was interesting, but Alicia wasn't sure she agreed with everything the minister said. He was older, about fifty ,and seemed to her to be a little too dogmatic and sure of himself. How could he be so certain about what God wanted? He spoke as if he understood God. She wasn't that certain about much of anything anymore.

Near the end of the service the minister asked if anyone wanted to be forgiven of their sins. Hearing this Alicia was shaken. After what he had said and the discussion in Sunday School she had begun to feel inferior to the people around her. There was fear and shame in her heart at what had happened to her and her friend, but she was more fearful of admitting it to others. Her feet remained frozen as several others left their pews and walked forward. She heard the minister say,

"God loves you and wants to forgive you. Do you desire for your sins to be forgiven? Do you want to accept Jesus as your Savior?" To these questions the people, who knelt before him, responded, "yes."

Alicia felt a tug on her heart, but she closed her eyes and her mind.

30

Rebecca Sweate found herself once again at her office. Sunday had flown by and no new information had come to light. The stack of papers on her desk, however, had diminished significantly. She had gone over and over the information they had about their victim. They still knew very little background about her, not even her last name. Rebecca wondered what Justin was up to. She hadn't heard from him, though she knew he didn't have to report in today. She was also worried about their lack of evidence against Dan Randizzio. So far, except for the neighbor's eyewitness report, what they had was circumstantial. The thumb print from the necklace had been a match to him. It could place him in Dr. Sharp's house, however, Cindy had told Rebecca that it was fairly old. The print had been etched into the metal, like acid. It was not a fresh print. It really proved nothing about the either murder or the break-in. Noting that he had been near the body in broad daylight made her now doubt whether he was the actual killer. But she had still more questions than answers and she wanted answers. Who had shot the girl? Who had taken shots at Justin and Dr. Sharp? They were no closer to solving these mysteries and they had little more to go on at the moment. She wanted another crack at Randizzio but had decided to wait until morning. She gave up on her desk and went home, succumbing to the desire for some peace and quiet.

Her microwave zapped a low calorie frozen dinner and she found that she was craving some real food. As the years passed it was hard to keep her weight down. This made her decision about food difficult. Restaurant food tended to contribute to the unwanted pounds, so she exercised. But running three times a week was taking its toll on her knees. She had access to a fitness center and could use exercise bikes and elliptical equipment or run on a treadmill there, but she loved the outdoors.

Into a crystal wine glass she poured an Australian red wine, one indulgence for the evening, and sat down to read. Historical fiction entertained her and she found it a pleasant, if not totally accurate, way to study history. There were several authors whose accuracy was impeccable, and who were able to add just enough spice to keep her interest. She slipped the slim reading glasses down on her nose, leaned back in her comfortable chair and opened her novel at the bookmark.

Before she had even finished the first page her phone began to ring. She considered letting her answering machine pick up, but thought it might be important. She reached for the phone, "Rebecca? This is Justin. I have some good news for you."

"Great I could use some good news. Can you tell me on the phone?"

"I'd better not."

"Why don't you come over to my place. Do you know where I live?" she asked realizing that her relaxing evening was just shot to pieces. She gave him directions and began to speculate on what 'boy wonder' had found out. He should have been taking it easy today too, but she was secretly glad he had stayed at it.

Twenty minutes later came a knock on the front door. Her house was situated in a nice residential neighborhood on a cul-de-sac. It was an older part of town than where Dr. Sharp lived but it made for a peaceful setting. A backyard hedge and some large trees afforded her a significant measure of privacy as well.

Justin was at the door in a t-shirt that read "OXFORD" and faded denims.

She tipped her head and squinted at Justin, "I thought you went to the University of Washington?"

He got a slightly puzzled look on his face then glanced down at his shirt. Smiling he said, "Oh this," pointing to the word 'OXFORD,' "I spent a semester studying history there. It was a great way to see England before the dollar tanked."

Currency devaluation had made European travel unappealing in the past few years. "I see. Did you pick up an English accent or habits?" Rebecca asked.

"I'm lousy at accents but I like calling the trunk of my car a 'boot,'" he countered. "I liked living there but don't expect to visit

England again soon on my salary."

Letting him in she asked, "What do you have that couldn't wait until tomorrow?"

"I found out who our victim is," Justin said taking a seat and pulling out his notebook computer. "Do you have wi fi?" he asked.

"Wi what?" she replied. "Oh you mean internet? No I just use it at work."

"Too bad. Well here is what I have found out so far." Justin gave her the name and address in Chicago. He had saved a copy of the online map and was able to show Rebecca the location of Connie's place in relation to Alicia's apartment. "I haven't found out where she or Alicia worked yet so I guess we'll have to ask the Chicago PD." He chose not to mention his foray into the hacking world. It had been exhilarating, but unfruitful and highly risky. Justin thought he knew what Rebecca would say about him making such a bold attempt.

"Justin. I am impressed. Great job! How did you get all that done today?" Rebecca was truly excited. She felt a little guilty about her initial attitude toward this young man. She was beginning to see the assets he could bring to this work.

Justin told her about looking through the evidence and finding the clothing label. "I didn't really expect to find anything helpful. It was just that she shopped at this exclusive store. If it had been a large chain or had had no label the search would have been a waste of time."

Rebecca scowled. Looking at evidence was the crime lab technician's job. "Why didn't the crime lab folks tell us about it first?"

"They were busy trying to clean up that diamond," he said in an effort to deflect her barbs. "They might have found it sooner, but I thought of it first."

Rebecca stopped frowning and reached over and gave Justin a little hug. "I'm glad you're working with me," she said.

Justin's cheeks colored a little, mildly embarrassed. He wasn't used to getting hugs from anyone, let alone his partner.

"Do you know what I want you to do now?" Rebecca asked.

"No, what?" he asked surprised.

"Go home. Forget the case for the rest of the evening. Have some fun and meet me first thing in the morning at the office. There's nothing else we can do tonight. Okay?" She said this gripping his forearm with one hand.

"But shouldn't we..."

"No 'buts.' Go home. We both need to relax and give our brains a rest."

"Sure. I guess I can do that. I am tired and I really don't know what else I could do anyway. I'll just write up what I've done ..."

"No. Write it tomorrow. Good night." Rebecca literally pushed Justin toward the door. "Have *fun*. I mean it."

Justin nodded as he hurried toward and then out the door. He waved at her still smiling face thankful for her interest, but not sure exactly what he should do to have fun.

31

Very Early Monday Morning

Dan lay in his damp bed in a cold sweat. His fitful night had, again, been filled with wild dreams. He had thought he heard screams and moaning in the night, but when he opened his eyes and listened all he heard was dripping water in his cell toilet. The sound of the drops echoed through the cement block rooms, but there were no human voices. He had no watch, but thought it must be close to six o'clock.

Would Riley be there like she had said?

He felt dirty but he doubted they would let him clean up first.

He sat, elbows on his knees and head drooping almost in a stupor while he awaited his release. Feeling like he couldn't leave this hateful place soon enough, Dan tried to think about what to do first once he was out, but his mind was a jumble and he couldn't get things back in order.

Sensing someone's presence, Dan looked up and saw a figure in the cell doorway. It was too dark to make out the features, but it wasn't his lawyer. "Who's there?" He called out.

The figure spoke softly from the grate in the door, "What were you doing, Dan?"

The voice was familiar, but he didn't recognize its owner. "What do you mean?"

Pete Sears, the assistant district attorney stood, just outside his cell. His eyes were burning through the open grate of a window as he spoke to Dan. "What were you doing that day? Why were you on the bike path? Did you kill her Dan? Did you do it?"

Dan now realized who was there. His self confidence returned and he sneered, "Wouldn't you like to know? You can't ask me questions without my lawyer. I guess you have to let me go don't you?"

The ADA was still quiet, "I just want to know the truth."

"Well I guess you should have tried harder," Dan shot back.

"Sure. I think you'll realize you should have told us more too. You're being an idiot. Do you think we won't figure it out anyway? Just be careful crossing the street." Then almost in a whisper he added, "Too bad. Now you won't even get your 'day in court.'"

The last few words made no sense to Dan. "What do you mean?" he asked. "Why won't I get my day in court?" He looked and saw that there was no one in the window now. *Was it real or a dream?* He wasn't sure now, but whatever it was left pure dread in his heart?

He lay back, again, even more confused. Still tired, he drifted into disturbed sleep. He was startled awake after what seemed like only a minute later. Another voice came from his door.

"Hey Dan!" It was the cheerful, bubbly voice of Riley Peters. "I have some papers here. Do you want to get out of here or lie there like a lump?"

Dan was still shaken by the conversation he had during the night, but Riley's sudden appearance made him feel certain that it had only been a trick of his mind. "Did you see the Assistant DA just now?" he asked.

"What? I doubt he is even out of bed yet. Of course not. Why would he come now? You're getting out of here." Riley gave him a curious look as the guard opened the door. This time they did not handcuff or shackle his wrists and ankles. After all, what was the point?

His fancy lawyer had brought his "get out of jail free" papers.

Dan still pressed the issue. "I think he was here just now. He talked to me."

Riley looked at the guard. "Was ADA Sears here just now?"

"No ma'am I haven't seen him," came the reply.

Looking back at Dan she said, "See? What is that all about?"

Dan was miffed but shrugged it off, "I guess it was part of my dream. I didn't sleep well last night."

"Who can, in a jail?" Riley answered

"Let's go," he said. The guard led them to a small office where Dan was given back his few possessions, minus the gun, taken from him at the time he had been picked up. "What about my revolver?" he asked.

"You have to wait thirty days to get it back." The man behind the desk handed him a paper. "Fill this out and return it after thirty days and you can come back and pick it up."

Dan grabbed the papers disgustedly. He didn't expect to use the revolver, but liked the security he felt with it. Nevertheless, he didn't want to make a scene about it. He also knew he wouldn't return for it.

Next, he stepped into the bathroom to change clothes. He was getting nervous about leaving the jail now. He had had no communication from his uncle and didn't know if he should call him or just drive back to his place in Chicago. That reminded him that he needed to find out where his car had gone. He had left it in the rental car parking lot. He donned his jeans and the t-shirt he had worn and pulled on his tennis shoes. He had no socks.

As he stepped from the bathroom he asked, "Where's my car?"

"It would be at the city impound lot," came the flat reply. "It'll cost a hundred bucks to get it out and they only take cash."

"What! Where am I going to get a hundred bucks?" Dan almost shouted.

The police sergeant behind the desk just smiled and said, "Not my problem," as he handed Dan his wallet and a pen to sign the log.

Riley was annoyed at both her client and the policeman.

"Where is this impound lot?" Dan was asking.

The sergeant reached beneath the counter and pulled out a faded copy of a map.

"This map shows how to get there. It's on the west edge of town."

"Great! And how am I going to get there?" Dan asked.

"I don't care. Call a cab, buddy. You're outta here." They began to walk away when he followed up, "And hey, have a nice day." The officer turned his back and returned to a desk piled with loose papers.

Riley glared hard but got no response. "All right. I have to get back to Omaha, but I'll drive you to the lot. I guess I'll have to float you the money too. I'll add it to your bill."

Dan wanted to give the policeman a piece of his mind, but he didn't want them to have a reason to put him back in a cell. They walked together the rest of the way out in silence. Riley led him to her Lexus and touched her key pad. The "bleep" sound indicated that the lock was released and Dan could get in.

He marveled at the car. "I figured you were a good lawyer, but I had no idea." He walked around the sleek vehicle whose color was called "matador red mica." He lightly touched the hood and looked up at Riley. "I want one of these." Then he sighed realizing the futility of such hopes. He was destined for an hourly wage and a lower middle-class life. He gently opened the door caressing the metal as if he might damage the surface. He sat in the camel leather seat and pulled the door closed with a satisfying "thunk" and merely shook his head. He decided that lower middle class was still better than jail.

Riley spoke little as they left the lot and pulled out onto the street. At last she said, "I'm glad you were able to get out. I have to admit it wasn't anything I did. The police wanted you to stay, but the assistant district attorney insisted on the release because he didn't have enough to prosecute. It is a little strange since it involved a murder, but I don't think they were convinced of your guilt in that. They could still have arrested you for breaking and entering, but the evidence there was sketchy too."

"I can't figure out how they knew I was there," he almost whined. "I planned everything carefully."

"Someone saw you. It's as simple as that," she answered shrugging her shoulders. She looked at him and smiled, "Unlucky break."

"Huh," he grunted, "In Chicago they wouldn't have called the cops. They'd have been too scared."

Soon they arrived at the entrance to the impound lot. It was no more than a field of parked cars from fancy sports cars to wrecks. Riley drove up the gravel entrance road toward a white building that she took to be the office. She vaguely noticed a large pick-up truck that had been behind them that had not turned in at the same time. Curiously, it was now parked along the road they had just driven on.

Pulling up to the building Riley and Dan exited the Lexus. They could hear engine noise coming from the rear of the lot where a tow truck was apparently depositing a new acquisition but they saw nobody near the office. Neither of them was paying attention to the pickup in the road and they began to cross the rock parking area toward a low white dilapidated building with a crooked sign flickering the word, "OFFICE."

Dan had gotten out of the car first and, part way across the lot, stood waiting for Riley. He turned his head to say something to her when they both heard another engine roar. Their heads turned simultaneously in time to see the fast approaching pickup truck. Dan had a clear view of the face of the driver. His eyes widened and he screamed,"NO! NO! NO!"

In a fraction of a second Riley saw his expression and as if in slow motion she whipped around and tried to flee. The loose rocks caused her to slip and, as she moved, she fell down onto the gravel. Dan, on the other hand, faced his fate without even putting a hand up. His body flew over the nearby fence and bounced lifelessly onto an old Impala near the building.

He had uttered no more sounds and did not move again.

Though Riley had started to run, as a result of her fall, she had not moved far enough away to avoid being struck. The truck ran over her torso with the front tire and her legs with the rear. The driver attempted to back over her but, still conscious, she pulled herself forward just enough to be out of the path of the truck. Without any further attempts at Riley the truck spun its wheels wildly and sped out of the lot quickly disappearing down the country road. Riley had seen that it had been a large black truck but soon, due to pain and shock, she was only able to mutter for help as her vision blurred and the world began to swim away.

No one had been in the shack at the time of the attack, but the manager of the facility had walked around the corner of a row of cars in time to see the truck make its attempt to back up over the woman. He noted that there was no license plate and only had a glimpse of the driver. What he thought he saw was a short man with dark glasses and longish hair. He couldn't get any clearer view. At first Dan's body was not in his line of sight and he rushed to the pretty young woman who was pawing the gravel in the parking lot. She looked up at him with glazed eyes and whispered the words, "Help Dan!"

Dmitrios, the manager, looked over his shoulder. The tow-truck driver was running up, now, having heard a shout. Dmitrios now yelled.

"Look for some guy. She said 'help Dan.' I call ambulance and the police." He carried a cell phone which he almost never answered. He liked feeling that he had important calls to make.

Dialing 911, for once, he was right.

32

Monday

Every Monday morning the whole office seemed to be in a panic to get organized. Officers coming off their shifts were yawning and pressing for the new shift to get their act together for the morning briefing. Clerks were busy going from cubicle to cubicle, dropping off memos. Everyone was preparing for their own assigned tasks with no one merely milling about.

It had always been this way, but today Rebecca was acutely aware of the "organized" chaos. She didn't know why, but she felt that she walking in slow motion in comparison to the droning activity around her. Something seemed wrong, but she couldn't put her finger on it. Walking through the melee was like wading through knee-deep water to reach her desk. Setting her purse down she spotted a small piece of paper on her blotter which hadn't been there the night before. She picked it up and the color drained from her face as she read. Her anger began to build and she rushed out of her office once again. This time her appearance and demeanor had altered so greatly that each person near her stopped what they were doing and stared.

Justin spotted Rebecca as she stepped from her office. He smiled and was about to say something witty when he also noted her countenance. It told him "hold your tongue."

Rebecca handed him the note and said, "Come with me."

He obeyed without a word or comment. As he read the note he was similarly stunned and thought he knew now where she was headed. The pair strode into the office of the assistant district attorney with Rebecca in the lead. She grasped the note from Justin's hand and thrust it at the ADA.

"What do you mean by this?" The words were almost a whisper. Her anger was so great that she feared she would shout so kept her voice tight. "How could you do this without even consulting me. I am the lead detective on this case!"

Pete Sears, the assistant district attorney, had been initially taken aback by Rebecca and Justin's sudden appearance. Now, however, he took on a smug expression. "You knew you had forty eight hours to build a case. I saw that we didn't have much on him so I let him go."

"This is a mur-der investigation you ..." she said, her rage barely concealed. "His testimony is vital and you just let him leave? We could have at least charged him for breaking and entering."

"Cut the crap, Rebecca. He would have made bail by eight this morning even then." Pete pushed himself back in his seat, "Don't yell at *me* because *you* didn't have any evidence. I did what I saw as the right thing ... by, the, law!"

"Well, by the law, his forty eight hours weren't up until nine and I could have at least asked him a few more questions. He's already gone, according to your little note." Rebecca's wind was slackening, but her face was still flushed and she was still angry. "You're boss will hear about this. You had an obligation to inform us of your intentions."

"I won't dignify that with an answer. Now, if you will excuse me I have work to do on cases I *can* win. If you had done your job maybe we wouldn't have come to this." The last comment stung. Ultimately it was her responsibility to get the evidence and it was a card Sears could play to defend his position. Frustrated, she looked at Justin. She was about to make a suggestion when, at that moment, both Justin's and Rebecca's phones rang.

They simultaneously looked down at their belts and reached for their phones.

Rebecca saw that it was a text message. Justin quickly read his, then both glared at the ADA. Justin who had remained silent was first to step forward. He stuck his phone's display in front of Pete Sears face and said, "I hope you're happy now with your decision."

The message on the screen read, "911 call for impound lot. Randizzio dead at scene lawyer critical Hit &Run."

Sears read the message. His face instantly grew white as a

ghost. He choked and all he could say was, "Oh, my God."

All Rebecca could do was shake her head.

"Rebecca how was I supposed to know?" he pleaded.

She and Justin, now more slowly, left the room, without looking back at Sears. Had she turned, she would have seen that his face was now white as a sheet.

****

Jack had hung around the hospital all day Sunday, but Kathy had been very drowsy. She had awakened a few times and had stared around her, but he could see the nurses were concerned. Her earlier alertness had surprised them, but her current somnolence seemed more ominous. Jack knew that any brain surgery had the potential for being disastrous but, he thought to himself,

"Hadn't she awakened and they had seen that she had no deficits?"

Mack had also stopped in. This was nothing new to him and he tried to sound optimistic to Jack. Nevertheless, he had reiterated the risks of the procedure and he had been very sober about Kathy.

"Don't get your hopes up and don't be impatient." Mack had told him that his first neurosurgery attending physician had given him that advice on his first brain cancer case.

"Some patients do great and some crash. We're doing our very best for Kathy," he had said gently as he had noted the concern on Jack's face and advised Jack to get some rest.

Jack had finally taken his advice.

On Monday morning Jack woke early as usual and then remembered that he was on a leave of absence from work. Not one to sleep in, he got up and decided on an early morning walk instead of waiting until later. He put on some jogging pants and wore a light jacket over his t-shirt. This time of year it could get below freezing at night.

The air felt crisp as the sun peeked above the rooftops. There was still no frost, but it would soon come. During the previous week the red maples in his neighborhood had started to changing color and now seemed like balls of fire as the first magenta rays ignited them. Jack, heartened by the beauty and freshness of his walk, was invigorated by the exercise and found that he was able to think more clearly. As he considered Kathy and her plight he made a decision. The issue of being in love with her was still uncertain, but she now had no husband and her children had jobs and lives of their own. If she needed help for whatever time she had left he would do his best to be there for her, at least as a friend. If Kathy needed full-time assistance he could help pay for it if she couldn't. They would choose another physician for her regular care, as she had requested just a few days earlier.

Jack continued his walk as the light changed from orange to bright yellow. Traffic sounds were increasing as cars made their way out of his suburban neighborhood. A new week for work and school was under way for many people. It was as if the houses themselves were waking up as garage doors opened and children began making their way to the bus stops.

Jack arrived back home after about thirty minutes and walked around his house to be sure the gardens were maintained. Most of the perennials were past their prime, but still green. It wouldn't be long, though, before he would have to start trimming them back and cleaning things up. He left some of the bigger plants alone in the fall, waiting for springtime to clean out the dead foliage. He took in his whole yard and saw that everything needed water too. It had been typically dry for a few weeks, so he grabbed a hose and began the chore of moistening the soil throughout the garden beds.

Satisfied that the garden would survive another day, Jack went inside to make his coffee and clean up for the day. He looked at his watch and saw it was only seven-thirty. Without going to work he realized that he had a lot of day and not much to do. Maybe he could actually relax.

Jack could hear the phone ringing as he entered his garage and trotted up the steps. He reached the desk phone just as the answering machine started its message.

"Hello, wait a second," and he and his caller waited for the voice from the recorder to run through its lines. "This is Dr. Sharp," he said.

"Jack! Turn on your TV," came the commanding voice. Jack recognized it at once as his lawyer, Sam Boniface.

"Why? What's going on?" Jack queried as he moved toward the television.

"Go to the local news. You've got to see this story." Sam was evasive, but Jack could read the urgency in his voice.

Jack carried the portable phone as he waited for the set to turn on. He immediately turned to the local channel where the female announcer was saying, "... was struck down by a hit and run driver this morning shortly after his release from custody. Police aren't speculating on the identity of the driver, but it has also been learned that his lawyer was injured in the accident. The lawyer, Riley Peters of Omaha, is currently in surgery at Lincoln Regional Hospital and her condition is unknown at this time. We have a reporter at the scene." She turned toward a monitor and asked, "John what is the story from there?"

"Thank you Charity. Local police aren't saying much about the hit and run which happened here at the local impound lot." The camera view left the reporter's face and panned over an area filled with cars, then opened back up in the parking lot of the business. "The owner says he heard a roar and saw a truck speeding from the lot just an hour ago. Police say they are looking for ..."

Jack turned away and got back on the phone. "Okay, Sam I watched it. What has that got to do with me?"

"Jack didn't you hear who was hit?"

"No I was too late. I recognized the name of the lawyer, though. I hope she's going to be okay," Jack answered still not understanding the concern.

"Jack, the other victim was Dan Randizzio! The guy who was in your house. Don't you get it? He was killed just after being released."

The light came on for Jack at that moment. "Released? They just arrested him two days ago."

"He was never actually charged. They may have had no choice but to release him without more evidence," said Sam. Now Jack was getting agitated, "More evidence? He was in my home. He planted evidence here! Why isn't that enough?" He hesitated. "But now he's dead?"

"That's my point. You're still in danger Jack," Sam said. "I'm going to talk to the police about getting you some protection."

"Sam I don't need protection ..."

"Shut up Jack," Sam said firmly. "You don't know what you're into here. For all you know this guy could have been here to kill you and not just plant evidence. And there's clearly someone else out there capable of killing."

"Are they sure it wasn't an accident?"

"Did you hear them say, 'hit and run'? He was a loose end Jack. They may think you are too."

Jack sat dumbfounded for a moment, remembering the shootout just two days earlier, then said, "All right Sam. You call the police. I need a shower and then I'm going to the hospital. Okay?"

"Okay. And Jack?"

"Yes?"

"Don't let anyone in and watch your back. Keep your phone charged."

"Sure Sam." He hung up the phone and began to wonder what was happening. Just minutes ago he had been contemplating a relaxing day off. He had a whole day to enjoy. Now was he in danger? He couldn't wrap his mind around what was going on. Once again circumstances seemed to be spiraling out of control. He shook his head but, thinking twice about it, he went around the house and made sure the windows were latched, garage door down, and the doors locked and bolted.

Then he went up to take his shower.

33

As they finished visually examining Dan's lifeless body, Rebecca stepped up to the uniformed policeman and asked if the manager was inside. He answered that he was out back having his fourth or fifth cigarette.

"He might also have sneaked a couple swigs of bourbon," he said.

She thanked him and she and Justin walked together around the side of the office building. It wasn't exactly falling apart, but the building looked as if it had been thrown together quickly. There were gaps in the paint where the brush had completely missed the siding. The trim had been painted at least two slightly different shades of ivory and the rows of shingles were uneven. The building sat on concrete blocks with a space between the floorboards and the ground of at least eighteen inches. Rebecca doubted that the building construction met any of the local codes.

They could smell the smoke before they saw the proprietor. When he came into view his face was slightly obscured by a recently exhaled cloud of acrid bluish smoke. He looked over. With a foreign-sounding accent said,

"I already give statement to police." He was clearly nervous and Rebecca could see his hands shaking. She heard his accent, but she wasn't sure what nationality.

Justin went forward first and held up his badge case. "I'm Detective Justin Samuelson and this is Detective Rebecca Sweate. We just want your perspective on what happened. We aren't here to cause you any problems."

"Right here! It happened here! I see drunks and punks waving knives, but no one gets killed here before." He was nearly weeping.

"Sir I know it's hard, but we have no reason to think you're in danger. Can you tell us what you saw? By the way what is your name please?" Justin gently asked. Rebecca was impressed by his tactfulness in the difficult situation.

"I Dmitrios Favos. I come from Crete twenty years ago. My

family is still there. I get no living there - only olive oil. I come to America, 'The land of opportunity.' Look around. What opportunity? I take cars away from people who have no money or break the law." He stubbed out his cigarette and sat down hard on the concrete step near his back door. "What did I see? I hear a roar and when I come around car see big black truck spinning tires to get out of my lot."

"Could you tell what kind of truck it was sir?" Rebecca asked.

He looked curiously at Rebecca. "Pretty woman detective. Tell this young man to go away and I'll tell you whatever you want," he said with a leer and a smile that told her all too much.

"Just tell us the facts Mr. Favos," she spat back

"Okay. Sure," he said shrugging, "I don't know for sure, but maybe one of those new foreign trucks. Toyota? I don't know new models. It was new, though. No license and no sticker in the window. I think stolen. What you think?" Dmitrios was no longer shaking, but his words were becoming a little slurred.

"Did you see who was driving the truck?"

The plump little man turned his head slightly as if trying to see something. He was swaying a little now too. "Small like me. Dark glasses. Hair to ... here." He made a motion with his hand at the base of his neck.

Rebecca caught sight of a bottle of whiskey by the steps. "Sir this interview is over until you're sober. We can talk again later, maybe down at the station. In the mean time please don't talk to reporters. You wouldn't want to hamper our investigation would you?"

Now that he had been found out he reached down and picked up the half-empty bottle. He unscrewed the cap and took a long pull of the amber liquid.

"No problem. I go take a nap." He stood and disappeared through the door letting the screen outer door slam.

Justin said, "This was a waste of time."

Rebecca was not quite as morose. "Not totally. If it was a Toyota there aren't as many around here as Fords and Chevys. Let's look at the crime scene."

They walked back around and could see Dr. French standing with his back to them as the body of Dan Randizzio was zipped into a black vinyl body bag. Small spots of blood remained behind and bits of broken glass were lying in the gravel. Crime lab personnel were gingerly picking up these flecks of plastic and glass and photographing diligently.

When Rebecca and Justin had arrived it was clear that their former prisoner was dead. He had lain unmoving with arms out-stretched and both legs bent in unnatural directions. His face had remained unmarred but she believed he must have had massive internal injuries as well.

Justin spoke to Dr. French, "Any idea what actually killed the guy?"

Dr. French appraised the young detective. "Well, young man what do you think? A three ton motor vehicle struck him in the mid-section fracturing both legs and pelvis. It most likely ruptured most of his internal organs." At that he walked away shaking his head.

Rebecca wanted to chastise her young partner but the look on his face told her that he already felt chastised by the doctor's tone. She asked a nearby policeman, "Where was the lawyer after the hit and run?"

He pointed to the south. "She crawled to the edge of the road. Maybe she thought the truck would come back and was trying to get into the grass. She was talking but the paramedics couldn't understand her when they arrived. They tried to stabilize her then life-flighted her out."

Rebecca stood and twisted around to see the whole scene. She could see the car around which Dmitrios would have come to spy the truck. There was a patch of mud and standing water in the driveway with flags around it and the crime scene specialists were already looking at tire impressions. "Well I guess we've gotten all we can here."

Justin nodded, "I just can't figure out how the killer knew they would be here."

"Maybe he followed them from the courthouse," Rebecca answered.

"Okay, then how did he *or she* know they would be released?

We didn't even know that," Justin fired back.

"Hm. Why did you say 'or she'?

"Jealous girlfriend. She came to pick him up and saw him with a beautiful woman. She put two and two together and flew into a jealous rage," Justin said shrugging his shoulders.

"Interesting theory but weak," she answered.

"Hey give me credit for being quick on my feet," Justin said, smiling.

"You're right. We can't discount any theories at this stage. But I think this death is related to the other murder and that makes this homicide a murder too. What do you think?"

"You are probably correct," Justin sighed, mimicking the accent of the manager from Crete.

Rebecca said sardonically, "We need to find out who knew about the release. Do you want the ADA or can I have him?"

"I'll check with the jail guard and see if anyone visited him."

"Okay. Let's get back. Great way to start a week!" Rebecca said, as she started walking toward the car.

****

When Alicia woke it was still dark. She was thrashing about in her bed. Her leg was dangling over the side and she was sweating. She knew she was awake, but was afraid to open her eyes. The dream had come again. But this time things had been strangely different. She could hear Connie calling for her to run. She saw the person with the gun. Again they lifted the gun, but this time the person looked straight at her. She gasped. The face was there this time.

It took a few minutes for her heart to stop racing. Why hadn't she realized what she had seen any sooner? It must have been the shock she decided.

Alicia looked around the room. She slipped from her bed and stepped to her window. Outside there was a faint glow on the horizon. Then, in the sky, she saw streaks of light appearing. They grew as she watched. She hugged herself and put the dream, once more, from her mind. She thought more about Sunday and church.

After the service they had had a wonderful pot-luck meal. She had chatted with people who had treated her like she had belonged there. As she recalled more, Alicia got back in bed and lay, staring at the ceiling watching the sunbeams play over the wall. Her eyes once again traced the ceiling pattern imagining different figures in the design. It reminded her of her childhood visits to her grandmother's home. Her bedrooms had the same kind of ceilings with patterns not all that different from these. She had loved that old house.

Alicia decided that someday she would like to live like this. She, nevertheless, feared that she would not live long, but wanted the peacefulness of this kind of life. The thought of having to leave this quiet place saddened her. She rose, put on the robe Missy had loaned her and once again peered out the window into the gathering daylight, and could see the fields stretching away into the distance. A few flies buzzed around the edge of the glass. There were large combines already working the last patches of unharvested grain. The dust rose behind them like clouds of smoke drifting lazily in the early morning calm.

The few days she had been running felt like weeks. She was aware that she shouldn't stay in one place any longer. Danger might follow her here and these nice people might be drawn into it with her. To bring such trouble to this quiet farm was the last thing she wanted. Thinking once again about the day before and the happy people at the church she remembered the sermon about the prodigal son. She had identified well with the main character of that story. It was a story she had heard before, but had not known its meaning. According to the pastor, the story was as much about the father as about the son. In it the father had waited patiently for his son to return and had loved him in spite of his having squandered his money. Alicia deeply missed her long dead parents and realized that she had wandered away from her aunt and uncle much like the prodigal son only she had yet to go back to them.

Would it even be possible now?

Alicia's mind returned to her own troubles and she decided that she had to leave soon. She changed plans to actually go to Minneapolis, though she still didn't know what she would do there. It was a large enough city maybe she could be inconspicuous. Alicia now felt that returning to Chicago was not worth the risk. She needed to stay out of sight until the people in Chicago forgot about her. She felt anger because she hadn't personally done anything wrong. She hadn't taken the diamond. That had been Connie. Surely, they should just forget about her. Reality hit, though, as she also admitted to herself that as a witness to her friend's murder they might still feel a need to silence her. How long would they pursue her? Connie had warned her that these people had friends in high places including even the police departments so she was afraid to go to the police.

Alicia descended the stairs. She could smell the coffee brewing and wondered what time it was. Seeing herself in the hallway mirror she quickly pushed hair back trying to look more presentable. She entered the kitchen and said, "Hi" as Missy turned her head.

Missy said, "Hello sleepy head! You are a good sleeper. Are you hungry?"

"Okay, maybe a little something. I didn't really sleep that well and I usually don't eat breakfast," Alicia answered.

"Don't eat breakfast! It's the most important meal of the day," Missy said, smiling.

"I need to take a shower. Okay?" Alicia said.

"All right. I'll have a little something for you when you're dressed. Your clothes are clean and folded over the couch in there." She pointed to the living room.

Alicia said, "Oh thank you. That was awfully nice." She picked up the blouse and jeans on the back of the couch and went in to take her shower.

After a lengthy, steamy shower Alicia dressed and put on a little make-up. She returned to the kitchen where Missy had laid out a plate with an egg, some bacon, and a glass of orange juice. "Now I know you don't eat breakfast, but you need your strength."

Alicia didn't argue and found that the sight of such a hearty meal had stimulated her appetite. She sat down and took a sip of the orange juice. Missy sat across from her coffee mug in hand.

"Honey, why don't you tell me what's wrong? I don't mean to pry, but you don't seem very happy. How can I help?"

Alicia swallowed her bacon and looked away. "I ... can't tell you. It isn't safe."

"Isn't safe? Hun we're as safe out here as you can get. You can see trouble comin' a long way off out here."

"But not this kind of trouble. I'm sorry, but I can't say more. I plan to leave today and I'll be out of your hair."

"I thought maybe you were thinking of going, but I would sure like to see your troubles solved." She pushed a piece of paper across the table. It had a business card stapled to it and a phone number written at the bottom. "This is my business card and my cell phone number is on that paper. You call any time. You can talk to me. Okay?"

Alicia gingerly picked up the paper. She looked at it and tears formed in her eye as she ate in silence. When she had finished she said, "You've been

"You've been so kind and good to me. I'm sorry I can't say more, but it won't help." She rose and slipped the paper into her pocket. "I need to go. Will you say good-bye to Roy for me?"

Missy stayed seated. "All right," she answered evenly without emotion. "He won't be too long. You could say good-bye yourself."

"No, I really need to go," she was firmer now but not harsh. Without another word she returned to her bedroom and gathered up her few remaining items. She found her car keys on the night stand and just looked at them for a second. Her cell phone was placed next to where the keys had lain. It had been plugged in and was fully charged. Alicia didn't know when that had been done. She didn't want to give up this peacefulness, but knew that it couldn't stay peaceful forever as long as she was hiding. She packed the charger and dropped her phone in her purse, forgetting to notice if it had been turned on or off.

Alicia left after a quiet hug from Missy. Roy had backed the car into the barn and as she started it saw that the tank was full of gas. She smiled and wished she could wait for Roy. He had been so nice to her. She put that out of her mind, though, and carefully drove around the yard of the farmhouse. Missy stood on the porch waving, a smile on her face. Alicia barely saw her through her tears. She waved back and kept going, turning out of the yard onto the road still not sure where she should go.

One of Alicia's first thoughts was of money. She hadn't solved the little problem of accessing her account without tipping off police or the "bad guys" where she was. She reached for her purse and pulled out her wallet. She remembered having about thirty dollars left. Opening the money pocket she was horrified to find it empty. Could they have taken her money when she was a sleep? She pulled onto the roadside verge and searched her purse in earnest. Lying just inside she found a bank envelope. In it was her thirty dollars as well as three crisp fifty dollar bills. She burst into fresh tears realizing just how special Missy and her father were. They had taken her in without explanation and given her a few days of peace and now this! She didn't know what to do. Part of her wanted to return and thank them, but she knew she had to keep going.

Someday she would find a way to pay them back.

Her immediate fears allayed she sat for a few minutes to ponder direction. She was beginning to wonder if she would have to run her entire life. Was she that dangerous to the people in Chicago? How would she know if it was ever safe? She remembered what the pastor had said in church.

"You can always pray. God will hear you." Feeling like she had no other options she put her head down right there and began to pray, "God if you exist please help me to know what to do. Where can I go? I want to feel safe again."

Alicia didn't know if she should hear an answer or exactly what to expect, but she felt better for having prayed. Minneapolis still seemed right to her. She put the car in gear and started back in the direction of the interstate highway.

She knew too that the first place to go would be a church. She wasn't sure why that idea was in her head, but now it made sense to her.

****

Missy went back inside with a melancholy feeling in her heart. She had known that Alicia was in trouble. Was she running from a boyfriend or was she pregnant? Had she done something illegal? She shuddered at that thought that she might have "harbored" a criminal. But she couldn't think of Alicia as a criminal. She had grown fond of the young woman and knew she had a kind inner nature.

Roy had come in, disappointed that he had missed Alicia and had decided to work on some of his machinery. Missy knew she wouldn't see him again until supper time. She puttered around the kitchen for a while then, about noon, sat in the living room having lost interest in cooking for a moment. She had a bowl of home-made potato salad and a glass of milk which she set on the lamp table. Turning on the local news, something she rarely did during the day, she put her feet up on the footstool.

As the picture came on the commentator was speaking about murders that had occurred in Nebraska. That seemed odd. They were hundreds of miles away and, unless it was quite dramatic, this kind of thing was not usually mentioned on her local station. She turned the sound up and listened, "... was killed by a hit and run driver shortly after being released from custody. He had been held in connection with the death of a young woman whose body was found last week. Police have learned her identity to be that of Connie Ridgeway." A photo of an attractive young woman was shown next and then Missy gasped.

"Police are also canvassing the area in an attempt to find the whereabouts of her friend, Alicia Winters, who has been missing since the murdered young woman was found. The photo they showed of Alicia was clearly several years old, but there was no mistaking her face. Missy couldn't believe it. Alicia had been right there. She had helped her while the police were looking for her. They thought she was missing, and from the report it didn't sound like they were thinking she was an accomplice, but were concerned that she might be another victim.

Missy thought. Why was Alicia running? Should she call the police? She had written Alicia's cell phone number down and, right then, decided to start out by trying to talk to her. Maybe she could convince her to turn herself in.

Missy picked up her phone and dialed.

****

Alicia heard her phone ringing in her purse. She panicked, realizing that she should have turned it off. *Who had turned the phone on anyway? Missy's actions again? Was it safe to use her phone?* She had seen television shows where they tracked people by their cell phones. She was afraid to answer so let it ring but checked the number before turning it off. She recognized Missy's number and wanted to talk with her. She decided to look for a pay phone.

Pay phones had become harder to find, but there were still out-door phones at some gas stations. Just ahead was a small convenience store gas station. It was early afternoon on Monday and there had not been much traffic on the road. At this station there wasn't a single car in the lot or at the pumps. Alicia pulled up to the phone and looked at the keypad. She had no change so went inside to break one of her smaller bills. She didn't want to flash the fifties around so she chose one of the five dollar bills. She didn't know how much she would need so asked for all quarters.

Once back at the phone she put in two quarters and dialed Missy's number. It took two more quarters for her call to go through. Alicia heard the ringing at the other end and anxiously waited for Missy to pick up.

"Hello?" came Missy's voice on the other end.

"Hi. It's Alicia. You called my cell phone, but the battery was almost dead so I'm at a pay phone," she lied.

"Okay," Missy hesitated knowing it was a lie. "Honey, you don't have to run. Please come back, let's talk about things."

Alicia was startled and took a second to answer. "What are you talking about?" she said genuinely uncertain.

"Alicia, your picture's on the news. The police are trying to find you," Missy said pleadingly.

Alicia stood mute for a long moment, "Alicia, are you there?"

"Yes, I'm here," she answered almost too quietly for Missy to hear. She couldn't believe her luck. Couldn't she get any breaks? Her face was on the news even here. She started to cry softly. How could she run now? People would recognize her. Someone would turn her in.

"What are *you* going to do?" she asked.

Missy said, "Hon, I'm not going to do anything yet. But I don't want to see you hurt or in more trouble. Come on back and we can figure this thing out."

Alicia was wary. She sniffed and said with bravado she didn't feel, "Is there some kind of reward?"

"Reward!" Missy almost laughed, "There was no mention of a reward. Should there be?"

"Well, no. I was just wondering. Look Missy, I'm ... in trouble and I don't really want you to get mixed up in it," she said at last.

"Well young lady from the looks of things you need help and being on your own may not be so good for you. Come on back. Let's talk. If you still want to run I won't try to stop you, but I bet Roy and I can help somehow."

There was another long silence then finally Alicia said, "I'll think about it. Missy you've already done too much..."

"Not enough by my count," Missy interrupted.

"No. You have. I'll think it over. Thanks." Alicia hung up the phone before Missy could say more. She stood looking back along the road on which she had come then got back in her car. She put her face on her hands and cried for a long time. She cried for her lost friend and for her own situation. Feeling totally lost she cried because of the kindness shown to her by people who had been perfect strangers.

Most of all, she cried out to God to somehow help her in her plight.

34

Rebecca's cell phone rang. She was driving, but decided to take the call. "Detective Sweate," she answered.

"Detective, this is Gus Wilson. Do you remember when you asked me to see what connection the doc had to diamonds?"

"Yes. I remember thinking it was just a shot in the dark," she said.

"Well, detective you shoot pretty well. I honestly didn't really expect to find anything either, but there's something here you will want to see," he didn't sound too pleased.

"I'm headed back to my office now. Where are you?" she asked.

"I'm here at the station. I'll find you. And one other thing. The doc's lawyer called and now wants him to get additional protection." He sounded sullen.

"Didn't we arrange it after the shooting the other day?"

Gus hesitated, "Well, we talked about it, but it was low priority."

"I see," she retorted. "Get it done. We don't need another dead body."

"Yes ma'am," Gus shot back.

"I'll see you in a couple minutes," she said and hung up without waiting for a reply.

****

Jack's day had started pleasantly, but a dark pall had been cast over it by learning of the death of the man he had known as Greg Connolly, the jogger. Jack had tried to understand in his own mind what all the pieces meant, but they didn't seem to fit together. He was pouring a cup of coffee when he heard a pounding on the front door.

"Who could that be?" he said to the air. "Use the doorbell," he said louder hoping they might hear it through the closed door.

He opened the door to find two uniformed officers at his door. "Two? Are you my protection detail?" He smiled and said, "Would you like some coffee?"

Neither of the officers was smiling. The first one with whom he was familiar, Mike Jackson, said, "Sir, Detective Sweate would like to speak with you further."

"She would? If this is about getting extra protection, that was my lawyer's idea." He noted that neither man nodded, and he slowly began to understand that he was going to be questioned again. "Until now she merely had one of you call me. Why the change in tactics?" he asked. When they failed to answer he said, "Okay. This looks serious or at least you do. Maybe now would be a good time to have my lawyer with me. Am I in some kind of trouble?" he asked.

"Sir, all I know is that she is asking you to come down. I don't know why she sent us or exactly what it is about. But she isn't just asking." His voice was even and there was no malice, but Dr. Sharp assumed he was used to avoiding any show of emotion.

He couldn't be sure if he was going to have a problem, but placed the call to Sam just in case.

****

Detective Sweate sat across from Jack who sat mute.

"Why do you suddenly feel the need for a lawyer?" she asked, raising her eyebrows.

"Why did you send two policemen to pick me up instead of a phone call?" he countered. "I haven't done anything wrong, but I've watched too many cop shows and read too many novels. The police can trip up anyone if they try hard enough. You must think I've done something wrong or you wouldn't have brought me down again. So I want a lawyer to make sure I don't say something dumb. I believe it is my right?"

"Of course. But bringing a lawyer into this now makes me wonder if you have something to hide," she said.

This brought a smile to the lips of Dr. Sharp. "Don't you see the problem with that? For me, it is a lose–lose proposition. If I don't ask for a lawyer you could get me to say almost anything making me look guilty of something. Or you might misinterpret what I say to you. If I ask for a lawyer you say it makes me look guilty. Either way you get someone looking guilty. I only know that I have nothing to do with this case except that I found the body of that unfortunate young lady."

At this point Sam opened the door and walked in. "What have I told you about answering questions before I get here?" he asked looking sternly at Jack.

"I haven't said anything. We were just sparring about the value of lawyers," he responded pleasantly. Jack turned and shook Sam's hand. "Thanks for coming. Sam you know I have nothing to hide so I don't mind answering questions. I just want you here to be sure I don't say something stupid."

"I hope I can help," then turning to Detective Sweate, Sam said, "Detective, why did you pick up my client? Is he being charged with any crime?"

"No, not yet, but we have some new questions," she said unable to hide the irritation. She had not wanted this to be an adversarial discussion, but it was turning out that way. She still had two dead bodies and was getting tired of not making headway. The doctor was her only other connection so far. He didn't seem worried and she secretly wanted to leave him alone, but she, nevertheless, pressed forward. Before her, on the table, sat a folder unopened. She said, "I am going to tape record this session. Any objections?"

Sam waved his hand dismissively and she began by identifying herself and those present. Justin was watching behind the double mirrored window. "Dr. Sharp I'm going to let you know something that we haven't put out in the media just yet. Is that all right?"

Jack didn't even glance at Sam, "Yes, of course."

Rebecca continued, "The young woman, whose body you found, was hiding something. The man who searched your house was undoubtedly looking there for it."

"What was it?" Jack asked benignly. This wasn't so bad. He was beginning to think asking for his lawyer had been a mistake.

"She stole a diamond and swallowed it to smuggle it away from its owner. We think she was going to sell it."

"It must have been valuable. Where did she get it?" Jack asked.

Sam scowled at him, "Jack, just let her talk without responding."
Jack just nodded.

"That's all right. I need answers so I'll give you some. We are not yet certain from whom," she said. Then she looked down at the folder which appeared to contain quite a few sheets. She opened it and took out the top page. "We also have information that you spent time in Africa about twenty years ago. Is that right?"

Jack nodded then glanced at Sam. Where was this leading? "Yes," he said more hesitantly, "I was a missionary for two years in Zaire. It's now called the Democratic Republic of the Congo. Why?"

Rebecca turned the document over on the table and took out another one. This was her bombshell. Most of the papers in the folder were worthless or blank to lend the idea that she held much more than she truly did. "We also have information that you had some dealings with diamonds while you were in Africa." The statement was delivered like it was of little interest. Rebecca was, herself, not certain where it would lead, but she was fishing.

Jack's expression changed from mild curiousity to panic then anger in seconds. "How did you ... ? Where ... ?"

Sam sensed the change and clamped a hand on Jack's arm. He looked straight at Jack and said icily, "Not another word." Then back to Rebecca, "I want to see these documents. What do they contain?"

"We'll see," she tried to keep her own composure. "Doctor, do you want to comment?"

Jack could barely contain himself. He was clearly very agitated. He tried to reach across the table to look at the folder, but Rebecca snatched it away. A police officer entered the room and was crossing to Dr. Sharp. Sam had reached over and grabbed both of Jack's arms. "Jack! Stop!" Then he said to Rebecca, "Twenty years ago? What's this about?"

Rebecca didn't answer. She merely stared at Jack. He was looking at the policeman who was ready to subdue him if needed. The anger left as quickly as it had appeared and Jack's tenseness left him. He lifted his arms in surrender and shook off Sam's grasp.

"All right. I'm sorry."

"Dr. Sharp, do you want to tell me about your connection to diamonds and how they connect you to this case?" Rebecca's voice was cold as ice. She had thought the doctor was completely cleared from this case. But now knowing he had been involved with diamonds she was no longer sure herself. She had known far stranger connections. Maybe this doctor had managed, so far, to set things up to make it look like he wasn't involved, but having uncovered this tidbit of information obviously surprised him.

Sam again said, "Jack. Enough." He then talked to Rebecca, "I want full disclosure of those documents. This interview is over. Let's go, Jack." He rose and touched Jack's arm. Jack now appearing slightly disoriented stood slowly. He nodded but turned to Rebecca, "You don't know ..."

"Jack!"

Stopping abruptly in midsentence, Jack's nostrils flared. He desperately wanted to say something, but Sam's caution had its effect. He shook his head again and left with Sam.

Rebecca leaned back in her chair with a blank expression. Both hands on the edge of the table she said, "Doctor, please don't do any traveling for a while. I still have more questions to ask. We can make it even more official if needed and you will have a police presence nearby. Just as you requested."

They reached Sam's car without either of the men speaking. They got in and Sam started the engine. "Jack, what just happened? What's going on with you? I've never seen you so angry."

A deflated Jack sat staring straight ahead. "I need to think. Take me home."

****

Back in her own office Rebecca was nearly as stunned as Dr. Sharp had been. She had expected some reaction, but not the outburst that had nearly come to a conflict. She looked across her desk at Justin. "What just happened in there? All we have is sketchy information about a diamond theft and his name is in the report. Why such a violent reaction?"

Shaking his head Justin asked, "Where did the report come from?"

Rebecca looked at the reference line. "From the FBI. They mention that the CIA was somehow involved in it, but the FBI had this one page document about the African situation because it involved a U.S. citizen."

"I doubt the CIA will give us any help. Have you ever contacted them?" Justin asked.

"No," she said with a low chuckle. "I rarely even call the FBI."

"It was long enough in the past, *maybe* they will be willing to give us more," Justin commented thinking.

She rose and stood looking out her window, "I don't know. Go ahead. Call the CIA. The worst they can do is tell us to jump in a lake."

Justin had begun to like the doctor. He was mystified by the recent events and hoped they were wrong about the doctor being involved. The information was, after all, twenty years old. Yet, like Rebecca, he was learning not to like coincidences and this was a strange one.

"Wait, Justin. Maybe I should make that call."

Rebecca then asked no one in particular, "What Pandora's box did we just open? Say, did you get a chance to speak to the guard at the jail to see if Randizzio had any visitors?"

Justin shook his head. "No, but I could go there now to see who was on shift. What about the ADA?"

Rebecca scowled, "He wasn't in his office this afternoon. I didn't think it was the kind of thing I wanted to discuss on the phone so I'll wait until he's back. His secretary said he had made a last minute decision to take the afternoon off, but expects him in the office tomorrow. I guess we have enough to think about today. See what you can find out."

Justin left without a word and Rebecca looked once again at the pile of paper that mysteriously grew each day despite her best efforts.

Nevertheless, she opened her rolodex file and found a card labeled "CIA."

35

Jack motioned Sam to the sofa in his living room. Handing him a glass of iced tea, he told him to wait a few minutes. Jack went to his den and took down a large album. Sam noticed that, though Jack had seemed upset in the police interview he now was more sad than angry.

He sat down next to Sam with his own glass of tea and the album. "This is one of my photo albums of my time in Africa twenty years ago. I worked there on a mission compound with another doctor. We had a fairly large hospital and worked in village health centers in the region."

"Yes, you've told me some things about that time and I think you've shown me some pictures," said Sam who was patiently waiting for Jack to tell what was on his mind.

As Jack browsed the pages he smiled as he spied faces of people he recalled and places he had visited in the photos. When he reached the last few pages he opened the plastic file page and Sam could see that there was an extra page tucked inside each of them. Jack slipped them out. "I've never shown you these pictures. No one has seen them."

The pictures on the new pages were different. They showed burned buildings. Smoke coiled around a blasted tree. Mangled bodies lying frozen in place on the ground. There was one photo of a much younger Jack Sharp standing next to a nun and another young woman, a church building in the background. The next page showed the same church with charred walls and a door barely hanging from its hinges. One photo depicted a truck filled with armed men standing firing wildly. In another there was a woman in the back of the truck being held by a man brandishing an automatic weapon. The figure was a little blurry, but still recognizable as the same woman who had stood next to Jack in the previous photo.

Jack walked to his front window. "That is what diamonds do. They kill and burn. The detective was right in one sense. I did have dealings with diamonds. But see what they accomplished? I thought I was doing a good thing Sam, and it all went wrong. Poor Sharon. All those innocent people." At this point Jack began to sob. Tears flowed. Sam had never seen his friend like this. He didn't know what to say.

Jack stood and wept, alone in his grief for a minute longer.

Then he said, "I promised never to discuss this. It was supposed to be kept secret and I was assured that my involvement would be 'forgotten.' I was not supposed to keep those pictures. The nun you see there, Sister Mary Elizabeth, ran a school in that church after the priest died. Sharon was her younger sister, a biological sister. She had been visiting for a few months then, and we met when I was checking on the local village health center. After she was taken, Sister Mary Elizabeth heard that Sharon had been killed."

"That village was fifty miles from my mission station." He walked over and pointed to the picture where they were happily posing. "When the shooting and burning was over I promised Sister Mary Elizabeth that, if I could, I would find a way to help rebuild her church and the village. I knew it wasn't enough, and she said she didn't blame me, but she has never answered my letters even though I have sent money. It was the diamond dealer who sent the soldiers, but I felt responsible. Sam, I was in love with her."

Sam finally found his voice. "Who was the diamond dealer?"

"His name was Jacques Levant, a Belgian or Frenchman. He called himself 'John Levy' and he disappeared after that, but I'll never forget his face. Look at the last page," Jack instructed.

Sam saw a photo of Jack holding the hand of the pretty girl, Sharon. There were several African children and a man wearing a safari hat and outfit. He was holding Sharon's other hand. "This is Jacques?"

"Yes. I believe he is the devil himself," Jack answered. "Yes that is the man. I do not believe in revenge, but if I did I would take it against that man. He stole more than just diamonds. He stole precious lives and cared nothing about them."

Sam was thinking, "Jack we can tell the police about this.

Nothing you have told me is incriminating. It shows that your African years have nothing to do with this."

"Does it? What do you know about diamonds?" Jack asked darkly. "This stolen one could be an African diamond like those Jacques stole. It's my fault he got them. People died because of the diamonds. Doesn't that also make me guilty?"

"Jack," Sam pleaded. "*You* are the only one accusing you of guilt in this." He said this motioning toward the photo album. "You are not the bad guy here; it was this Jacques."

"Sam, I was there on the Lord's business. I was supposed to be healing people, not finding romance and working with the "good guys" against diamond smugglers. I had no right to get involved." He picked up the album and replaced the spare photo pages. "Besides I made promises not to talk about it. Ever. Which is more important?"

"Okay, let me think," Sam said rising. He paced for a minute, "We can admit to the police that you were involved in Africa with diamonds. But only in a peripheral way in the twenty years ago. We don't fill in the details. But, Jack, they can subpoena your testimony and you will have to tell them. A judge could hold you in contempt if you refuse."

"Then I will be held in contempt. Sam I made a promise. It's bad enough that I've now told you. It wasn't just to this government. If any word about this got back to Bobito it would be nothing but trouble for Sister Mary Elizabeth. Even now, twenty years later." He turned and looked Sam directly in the face. Jack was clearly adamant. "Go ahead and give the detective that statement. But tell her that's all she will get from me. Tell her there is no connection between me and this diamond. This is merely a strange coincidence."

Sam stood and touched Jack's arm. "I'm sorry. I see that this is terribly hard for you."

He thought to himself, *"Maybe that explains, a little bit, why Jack has never settled down."*

Jack said nothing more and Sam found his own way out.

Jack felt old and weighed down by what had happened. After Sam left he sat, head in hands, for several minutes. His memories of

Sharon and their time together had come flooding back, unbidden. It had been so many years ago yet the memories, the fears, the anguish he had felt when he was told of Sharon's death were as vivid in that moment as they had been two decades earlier. The pressure of all that had happened was wearing him down and he was beginning to let it and give in to an old, long suppressed, desire. Almost without conscious effort he picked up a jacket and walked to his car. Before he really knew what he was doing he had stopped at a nearby liquor store, tastefully named "The Happy Cellar." He had passed the beer and headed straight for the whiskey, the good stuff. His new purchase in a paper sack, he drove back home. Jack was deliberately making his mind a blank because the memories had been too painful.

Once again at home he found a glass and quickly poured a large measure of the amber liquid into it. He was consciously trying to bypass all the safety nets he had carefully constructed since he last had gotten into trouble with alcohol. He knew where this path would lead but he chose not to think about it.

Picking up the glass he began to tip his head, the whiskey touched his lips, but he stopped abruptly. "NO!" He shouted, then, sobbing, more quietly, he said again, "No." With the glass in one hand and the bottle in the other he slid down the counter to the floor. Without putting the glass down he reached for his cell phone, attached to his belt. He dialed a familiar number and after only a few rings his call was answered.

"Hello?

"I almost blew it."

"But you didn't?"

"Not yet."

"Why did you call?"

"You know why."

"Pour it out Jack. All of it. Now."

The instruction was given in a firm but sympathetic voice and Jack stood obediently, cell phone still at his ear. He threw the cup full of liquid into the sink. Next he poured the thirty-dollar bottle of whiskey after it rinsing it down with water from the tap.

"Is it done?"

"Yes."

"You going to be okay?"

"I don't know."

"Call me again tomorrow. Okay?"

"Sure... thanks."

"You'd do it for me."

Jack felt drained. He set the glass in his dishwasher and tossed the empty bottle into the trash. He was stunned at how close he had gotten to throwing everything away. He dragged himself to the bedroom where, he knelt by his bedside.

"Lord, forgive me and thank you for protecting me. It wasn't my willpower that stopped me tonight. You gave me the will and the strength to call Sid." Jack stayed there quietly for several minutes and finally, decided to take a shower. He hadn't done any work but felt dirty and tired. His day was not yet over and he needed something to refresh him.

He rose, sober for one more day.

36

James Rizzo was miserable. He had begun to see the gravity of his own situation. He was now responsible for ordering the deaths of two people, one of whom was even a relative. If these facts were ever to become known he knew he would probably go to prison for life, but worse he would be totally banished from his family. How could he have done it? He had known his error in letting the girl get away with the diamond, but now he was in trouble from every direction. He owed the Leader a great deal for gaining him his current status, but with the murders he had ordered, in his own mind, that debt was now paid. He needed to find a way to extricate himself before it became even worse. He was beginning to see that the big money he stood to gain may not be worth the price it was exacting from him.

James was normally a confident, ruthless businessman, but the recent events had shaken him. In all of his previous shady dealings he had never done anything like this. He was beginning to realize that maybe he wasn't so ruthless after all. Nevertheless, he was astute enough to know that he could not allow the Leader to see any chinks in his armor or it would be the end for him.

James entered the board room and noted that the other members were already there. He nonchalantly gazed around the room taking in its opulence as if he was unconcerned. His true feelings were far from being relaxed, however. Had they been talking about him? He steeled his facial features and covered his feelings, as was his habit, with his impenetrable mask and said, "All taken care of sir. Where do we stand?"

The Leader's eyebrows rose. Then a smile came to his lips, "No regrets I trust?" He didn't wait for an answer. "You'll soon be an extremely rich man if you continue to do what you are told."

"Of course sir," James responded. "It seems, though, that so far I have taken all the risks. When will our business be concluded?" James answered with a hint of annoyance in his voice covering the anxiety he felt.

"It won't be long. Don't be impatient!" The Leader was moody and short. "There is still a loose end out there. Malcomb, why haven't you taken care of that girl yet? She must have the diamond. Do I need to get somebody else?" He said as he scanned the three faces before him.

"She has just dropped completely off the radar," answered Malcomb. "I've had my people working on finding her and she hasn't used her credit or ATM cards. Her car hasn't been seen. She hasn't called anyone, including her family. She must have left her cell phone turned off. If she turns it on, though, we will be on it immediately." Malcomb shifted in his seat, "At this point, sir, I don't think she is a threat any longer since she's gone cold."

The leader stood, his face taking on a dark appearance. "Not a threat?! She knows too much, thanks to our brother James and his bumbling nephew."

He swept his gaze and his hand in a wide arc toward James. Then he smiled maliciously.

"And what she knows could derail everything I have worked on for years, and what if she has the diamond after all?" He paced and fumed, but said nothing for several minutes. Then, more calmly, he said, "James, you've been successful lately. Why don't you help Malcomb out and find out where she is?" His gaze was like a laser beam pointed at James' eyes. James could not bear his look. "Because if she isn't found I think we will have fewer ways to divide the spoils."

"Sir, I could keep on trying. I haven't checked on any activity today. Maybe she'll yet get careless or overconfident. I haven't checked with everyone yet," Malcomb humbly replied.

"I think you've done enough. You haven't accomplished any-thing. Tell me why I included you in this deal?" said the Leader with a sneer and a hint of menace in his voice. "Give what information you have to James and help him find that girl. I think I'll give him some of your percentage too, unless he fails."

Malcomb was afraid to say more and only nodded. He glanced down at his computer monitor and found a text from James already on the screen listing the location for Malcomb to send his information.

James was feeling sick. He didn't want another death on his hands. He knew that once the girl, Alicia, was found, Antony would kill her and any witnesses. James had lost his own lust for power with the death of his nephew. He knew, however, that he was as good as dead if the Leader sensed he was failing in his task. He only hoped the girl would stay hidden and not surface. Nevertheless, he made a feeble effort to dodge the assignment.

He said, "Okay, but what about Cindy? Why isn't she helping with additional resources?"

"You just look after your own business," came the leader's tart reply. "Cindy has her assignments and you don't need to know or worry about them." He sat and shuffled some papers in front of him. He picked up one that had a month-long calendar printed on it. "Our business will be completed one week from today."

The three other members stirred. They looked at each other in astonishment. "I know you thought it was a month away, but I have moved it forward. Since you can't seem fix this little problem, we have to press on to avoid potential complications."

This time it was Cindy who protested. "You didn't tell me. I won't have the security set up or the intel finished that quickly."

"Yes you will! You have no choice. Push harder, people. We finish next week. I have already been in touch with our ... partners." His face was like pewter. His jaw set. He looked back and forth at each face looking for defiance. "You will need your own security arrangements completed by then too or you will be left out in the cold."

The Leader was known to each of them and the rest of the world as 'Mark Antony.' It was, of course, a fictitious name borrowed from the Roman emperor, but none of them knew his real identity. He had amassed a vast amount of wealth, but seemed never satisfied with it and he liked the way it got people to do things for him. Antony knew that he would need to relocate his assets and find a new nation of residence once his next feat was completed, but that didn't bother him. Things would get hot for him here, but he hated Chicago anyway.

Moving around from country to country was nothing new to him, though he had stayed put longer this time than usual. His partners knew that they were involved in a risky deal, but didn't know just how likely they were to fall victim themselves. Once their business was done there would be local and, probably, international pressure to find them all. Adding more pressure now might be unproductive, yet Mark Antony needed the diamond back and he wanted the girl permanently out of the way. She was a major liability that could still lead back to him. He was not about to let that happen.

Antony had tried, too, to find the girl on his own. This was a fact that he had kept hidden from his compatriots. So far his own sources in the Chicago police and in Nebraska had heard no more about the girl than he. Pushing James a little harder could increase the chances of finding her. He had been very successful lately despite his earlier lapse that had led to this whole fiasco.

Antony addressed the group again without looking up at them. "You may all want to consider finding a new location to work from after this is all over. I, for one, plan to set up shop some place where a few hundred thousand would make you seem wealthy and a few hundred million would let you live like a king. But ... if everything goes as planned no one will be the wiser and you can keep working right here in Chicago. Any connection to me will be wiped out and untraceable by the time we get our money."

This brought out actual murmuring. He interrupted their speculations, "Until next Monday then." Mark Antony stood with his brief case in hand. He turned without another word and stepped out of the room through a door which had been well hidden in the mahogany paneled wall.

James sat stunned though his face remained impassive. The other two were still talking together excitedly. To them it seemed to be an adventure, to him a nightmare. A member of his own family lay dead. He could be implicated in two murders and now he had become solely responsible to provide information for a third. He had not previously considered leaving town or the country. What of his family, his business? He suddenly realized that the stakes were higher than he had ever imagined.

James lifted his own brief case and stood. He smiled weakly to the others and bade them goodnight. They were discussing countries; he was contemplating suicide. He acted confidently, but as soon as he reached the hall he could barely stand. Was it the better way out?

It didn't take long for him to realize that his own death would not stop anything at this point and what he had already done could not be undone. He had once been drawn to money but could see clearly now how false was that desire. Should he just go to the police and get it over with? He was afraid that would, likewise accomplish nothing. Antony would probably have him killed before he could say anything of substance. Who would believe him? He would receive the blame for the murders leaving the Leader and the others free as birds. They would just change their plans and he would look like a murderous fool.

"I have to continue just like I am supposed to," he thought to himself. But, as much as he had wanted the money, now he would look for a way to throw a wrench into the works.

Maybe he could still save one girl's life.

****

Alicia felt a sense of dèjá vu as she found herself driving back into the yard from which she had left earlier in the morning. After her call to Missy she had begun driving toward Minneapolis again, but realized it was no use. She had found driving impossible as tears obscured her vision. Pulling off the road, she had spent long minutes soul-searching and, finally, had become resigned to the fact that she was out of choices. If she kept going someone was likely to recognize her making her situation even more dangerous. If she returned to Missy and Roy, they would take care of her and she could hide out here a little longer.

She parked the car and got out. Missy was on the porch in the same place where she had last seen her. There was a new chill in the air and she could see Missy wrapping herself with her arms.

Missy, trying to hide the happiness she was feeling motioned to her.

"Come on in girl it's gettin' cold out here."

Alicia waved and quickly trotted up to the house. She felt a lightness in her heart that hadn't been there for a long time and she could feel tears again forming at the corners of her eyes.

In the welcoming kitchen once again with a steaming mug of coffee Alicia shrugged her shoulders. She looked away from Missy's piercing gaze. "I'm not sure where to start. I don't totally understand what happened myself." She stopped and took as sip of her sweetened coffee, the mug held in both hands. "I had a friend who was killed."

"Killed how?" Missy pressed, remembering the news report.

"Murdered... and I was there. I saw it happen," she said.

Missy turned at this and put down the pan she had been holding. "You saw it and you didn't go to the police?" she asked.

"I was so scared," her face had turned ghostly white. Bottled up feelings began to spill out. "It's what I've been dreaming about. At first I couldn't remember but now... I was with her and we were talking and laughing. She stopped for something and I kept going a little way. I looked back and saw someone else with her. I saw a gun, and then a loud bang, and I knew she was shot because..." At this point she couldn't maintain her composure. She put the coffee down and buried her face in her hands deep sobs racking her body. She began crying in earnest and could not continue her explanation.

Missy was sympathetic and moved over to her. She sat down next to Alicia and held her close. "It's going to be okay. Sh, sh it'll be fine." She rocked her and held her for several minutes while days of fear and sorrow drained away.

After a few moments Alicia was spent. She sniffled and whimpered a little. Missy released her and got her a box of tissues. Loudly blowing her nose, Alicia attempted to continue the tale. "I know she was shot because she flew backwards and landed hard on the ground. Then comes the part I couldn't remember at first. The killer turned toward me and aimed the gun. I thought I was going to be shot. I got really scared and then I saw it. That face. I know the face of the killer."

Alicia was quiet for another minute. She took a sip of her coffee then began her tale again. "The killer was a woman. I turned and ran and she shot at me, but it was dark and I was wobbly so she completely missed."

"A woman!" exclaimed Missy.

"Yes. After shooting at me I ran around a corner. Instead of chasing me when I peeked back I saw her take out a knife and she kind of went crazy. She stabbed Connie lying there..." she broke out in fresh crying, but tried to continue, "she stabbed her over and over and over. I was, like frozen. I couldn't move at first. I don't know why, but she just kept on... She was my friend!" She covered her eyes fresh tears beginning anew.

Missy was close again and touched her lightly on the arm. "How did you get away? Didn't she see you?"

"I don't really know, but when I saw what she was doing I think I hid. She was too involved to care about me right then," Alicia said.

"Why didn't you just go to the police?" Missy tried again.

"I don't know. We... Connie, had taken something," Alicia said at last.

Missy cocked her head at this and the question she had in mind was obvious.

Alicia looked at her. "It was wrong, but..." she said now trying to justify herself. "It was Connie's idea and she said it would be worth a lot of money."

"What did you take?" Missy was growing impatient now as Alicia delayed completing the story.

"I've never done anything like it before. She didn't believe they would notice for a while." She looked at Missy and saw the impatience in her eyes and said evenly, "It was a diamond. A big one."

"A diamond?" Missy was taken aback, but not shocked. She hadn't known what Alicia had been involved in, but had known, from the news, that it had culminated in murder. Missy pondered this a moment. When Alicia did not continue she said, "Well, little lady, you need to tell the police. There's no sense in running. Even if you had stolen the Hope diamond, it's not as bad as murder."

Alicia stood up, "I knew you would tell me that, but you don't understand. It isn't safe,"

Missy sensed her reluctance, but putting up a strong front said, "You're safe here. No one is coming after you here. We can call the sheriff and maybe he'll let you stay here until things get sorted out."

"Connie didn't tell me much, but she said we couldn't trust anyone who was even close to Chicago. We were on our way to Denver. I don't think I can trust your sheriff or anyone else. Don't you see? They killed Connie over a diamond and I saw it. They'll want me dead too. The police can't stop that."

"Why don't you think they can help?" Missy asked with genuinely curiosity.

"You don't know these people. I guess we didn't either. Connie said they were very important, into a lot of things, and were well connected even with the police. But she thought they wouldn't bother with one little, well, not so little, diamond. It shouldn't have gotten her killed. Besides, we were a long way away from home and they still found Connie. They might still be looking for me too. If we go to the police they could hear about it and I don't think the police can protect me, or you if they find me here." Alicia was almost frantic with worry now afraid because she had confided in someone.

"All right. All right, honey. They aren't going to find you here. Not if we can help it," assured Missy. Missy saw the fear in this young woman's face and realized that she could not dispel it with mere assurances. "As long as we keep you here at the house no-body's going to see you. We'll figure something out. Can you tell me more about your friend, Connie?"

This last request calmed Alicia down somewhat. She sat up straighter in the chair and took a sip of her, now lukewarm, coffee. Pushing a loose strand of hair out of her face she glanced at the dark window. The gloom which had been pressing down upon her seemed to lessen just a little. Then she began by describing her meeting with Connie at lunch one day at a deli near both of their office buildings. They worked only a few blocks apart. Connie had just started seeing this body builder named Dan who was somehow related to her boss.

Alicia reluctantly gave Missy the details of how Connie had seen the diamond at her employer's office while waiting for Dan one evening. The boss had been in a meeting and she had heard some of what had been said.

"Connie said she thought it had something to do with selling diamonds." That got her looking around the office and she saw some rocks in a glass case along one wall. "There were all kinds of beautiful diamonds sparkling. She said that in the middle was a wooden box with bigger stones sitting on it."

Dan, her boyfriend, had seen her interest and told her that the rocks were actually more valuable because they were big and uncut. "Connie said they didn't look like diamonds, but I guess they look like chunks of glass until they are cut and polished."

Dan said that the case was specially made and even a bullet couldn't break the glass. He actually took out the box and let her look at the diamonds. "She said the devil put it in her mind to take one of the rocks when Dan had turned his head. She figured no one would know what it was if they saw it. She didn't take the shiny cut diamonds but one of the bigger plain-looking stones. I don't really know why she took it. It was crazy, but no one seemed to notice right away so she thought she was okay. Now I wish she had just left it alone."

Alicia went on with the story. "It was strange. Connie went to work for a couple of days. She got nervous, though and realized it was a mistake. She went up to the office to try to put it back, but the boss walked in on her and she had to do some fast thinking. She stuck it in her mouth and acted like it was gum. It worked, but her boss thought she had come up to his office for 'other reasons.' She said he came onto her and invited her to come to his office later. She didn't want that and she was even more scared so she got the idea of wrapping the diamond in her gum and swallowing it. She left work, but I think it made him suspicious. He must have checked out his diamond case."

"When Connie told me she wanted to take a trip she didn't tell me about the diamond at first. She just said she wanted to take a quick trip to Denver. It sounded like fun and I was able to take a couple of days off work so I agreed to go. When she told me about it on the road I was furious, but she said it would be worth a lot of money. It didn't seem too bad after that. After all, I hadn't stolen anything. We never thought we were in that much trouble. Connie didn't think anyone had figured out that she had taken the diamond, or at least she didn't say that to me. I've never even seen this diamond. Connie had already swallowed it."

Alicia stopped here and asked Missy if she could have some toast. Missy stood and refilled her own coffee cup, picked up the bread, and stuck two slices into the toaster. She didn't say a word while the toaster heated. Once it was done and Alicia was buttering her toast she resumed the tale.

"Since we would be traveling right by my aunt and uncle's town I suggested that we ask to stay with them. When I called, Aunt Olivia liked the idea so we stopped there, but didn't really get around to unpacking much. Connie wanted to go out to eat because she thought we should celebrate. My aunt was a little put out because she had started some dinner, but we went anyway. We ate at a nice new place and drank a bottle of champagne. I wasn't too bad, but Connie was a little tipsy so I figured that I should drive. It was kind of dark when we left the restaurant and we had trouble at first finding the car." Alicia hesitated and nearly crying again said, "I don't know how, but they must have been following us all the way. She was just waiting for a time to kill Connie."

Missy looked up mildly startled, "Alicia, you said 'they.' I thought there was only one killer."

"That's right," said Alicia, "One..."

Recognition struck Alicia's face, "There was one killer, but now that you mention it, I remember someone was coming down the sidewalk. I only caught a glimpse of him as I ran around a corner. He was a big guy. He must have been with her because he went up to her but I didn't stay to watch."

Missy said helpfully, "Maybe it was a bystander trying to help."

"No. I don't think so. It's just something about the way he came up and was there. He didn't say or shout anything. The car was just around the corner. I got in and took off. I was too scared to do anything else."

Missy had one question. "What were you planning to do in Denver?"

"Once Connie passed the stone she figured we could sell it. Denver's big enough that we thought we might be able to find a way to sell it for a lot of money. We weren't thinking very far ahead, unfortunately. Oh, Missy! I'm so scared. I just don't know what to do. What a mess!"

Missy consoled her and thought a while. "On television they mentioned the murder, but they didn't say much. There's been another killing too, but they didn't mention any diamonds. They showed your picture like you were a suspect or something."

Alicia sniffed, "Another death? Who?"

"It was a man the police had in for questioning," Missy answered.

"See! They got to him didn't they?" Alicia squeaked.

Missy was thinking, "If Connie swallowed the diamond the police will find it when they do an autopsy."

Alicia said, "I don't know. Connie coated it with gum hoping it would go down more easily."

Maybe the police still don't know about it then," Missy said. "We should try to find a way to let them know you're okay and tell them about the diamond."

"No. If we do that they'll find me for sure. I told you, I don't think they will protect me either."

Missy thought again, "You really are worried aren't you? It's just hard to believe. But, considering this second murder, you may actually be right. Okay here's an idea. We can't call on a phone because of caller ID. They'd find us here. Email is out too because that can be traced." She then grinned and put her index finger up in a gesture of triumph, "I know, I have a friend in Seattle who might just help us out. I could call her and she could send an actual letter. They couldn't tell who sent it because it could only be traced to the zip-code location."

Alicia was alert now. This idea made sense, "But it will take days for the police to get the letter." She considered this idea, "I guess it's not such a bad idea though. Can we call her?"

Missy got out her address book and made the call to her friend, "Hello, Carol?"

Carol Russing had answered on the first ring, "Missy is that you? Hello yourself."

Missy filled her in on the basics of the problem and what they needed.

Carol had listened intently and now answered, "Ooo Missy. What are you into? This is pretty exciting, but you be careful. Say, instead of mail why not send a fax?"

Missy said, "I can't send a fax. They would figure out where it came from."

"I know, but if I send a fax from a public place like ... the library they won't know who sent it. They will only be able to find where it came from. With a fax the police will get the information right away."

Missy relayed this to Alicia who brightened, "That's a great idea. Why didn't we think of it? Are you sure it is safe and they won't be able to track it back to you?"

"I don't see how," she thought a second, "Just to be sure I'll go to a library in another town like Kent. I'll pay them with cash. It's about as safe as I can get," mused Carol.

They agreed upon this course of action and discussed the wording for a few minutes. Missy told Carol to send it to a Detective Sweate who was named in the news report .

Then Carol said, "Okay. I'll get this ready and head to the library. Consider it done. Only one thing though."

"What's that?" Missy asked puzzled.

"You have to let me know how things go. Okay?"

"Sure, Carol. I'll let you know. Thanks a heap. Take care," Missy said as she rang off. Turning to Alicia she said, "Now we've got chores to do."

38

Jack still had things to do. He had almost derailed his relationship with Kathy before it had ever gotten started. If he had taken that drink he didn't know if he could have stopped again. Nevertheless, now he intended to go to the hospital and see how Kathy was doing and didn't want her to become worried about him. He had to block out what was happening in his own mind and say nothing about it to Kathy or her family.

No one from Kathy's family had called him nor had anyone from the hospital paged him so he felt comforted that all was well. He poked his head out the front door and looked down the cul-de-sac. There were no strange cars or trucks, even the media had been leaving him alone, though with the latest developments that might not last. He checked his windows and doors, all securely locked. In his garage, he locked that entry door as well. He was taking no chances. Next he did something he had seen in a spy movie. Taking a small piece of paper, he slipped it between the door and the jam. If someone opened the door it would fall to the ground. When he returned he could then tell if someone had opened the door and could be waiting inside. Even locked he knew, from recent experience, that the garage entrance was the easiest way into his house.

Jack's drive to the hospital was uneventful. He flashed his ID badge, with its embedded computer chip, at the entry pad and the barrier rose as he entered the hospital physicians parking garage. Parking in his usual spot, he smiled to himself. He found it interesting that most people tended to park in approximately the same place each day even though there were no assigned parking places. Jack picked up his stethoscope out of habit and exited his car ambling alone through the parking area. His earlier feelings of distress had abated significantly. Part of the way to the hospital entrance it dawned on him that this place would be an easy location for a "hit-man" to "take him out." The idea made him hurry to the hospital door where he found himself a little shaky and in a cold sweat, wondering if he was becoming paranoid.

At the check-in desk he logged onto the computer and printed out his patient list. Even though he was off work he wanted to see who was currently in the hospital. One of his patients was in the cardiac unit. He decided that, if he felt he had time, he would stop and see how they were doing.

He found Kathy's name as expected and she had not been moved. Accessing her medical record he checked recent lab and x-ray reports. There was no report yet available, officially, on the pathology of her tumor. On his way to the ICU he greeted several nurses and doctors. It seemed almost like any other Monday.

It was already the middle of the evening, thanks to his trip to the police station, his discussion with Sam and his bout of temptation. Nevertheless, Jack found no family members at Kathy's room. The nurse was attending to another patient at that moment so Jack walked up to the door without speaking to anyone. He saw Kathy lying peacefully in the bed, head swathed with a bandage. The room was dark, but her features were dimly lit by glowing lights from her intravenous pumps and monitors. Her eyes were closed, and she seemed relaxed. Jack stepped close to her and slipped her hand in his without saying a word. Her eyes fluttered then he could see them open slightly.

"Jack?" she whispered. "Are you still here?"

He smiled, "I've just arrived. I haven't been here all the time."

"What time is it? What day is it? I'm in such a fog," she said as she closed and reopened her eyes. She started to stretch then seemed to remember her circumstances, "Ow," she said as she brushed her forehead with her hand. "What did you do to me?"

Jack wasn't sure if she was really uncertain or being facetious. "Do you remember where you are and why?" he said.

She seemed to think a while, "In the hospital. Did I have surgery?" She didn't wait for an answer and said, "It must have been on my head because it hurts."

"Yes it was your head. Do you remember why?" Jack probed.

Again she pondered the question. "I think I have a tumor? How long have I been here?" she asked.

"Yes. You *had* a tumor and you've been here about four days. You got sick when we were eating breakfast at a restaurant and we came to the hospital. Dr. Clark operated on your brain two days ago and you are just starting to wake up, though yesterday you were awake for a short time?"

"I kind of remember that," she smiled shyly. "I have been having some interesting dreams and you show up in a lot of them." She squeezed his hand pulled it up to her face. She rested her cheek on the back of his hand and sighed, "Jack you've been more than a friend to me. I know you've been here. I was awake at times and I could see you standing by the door or at my bedside even when I couldn't talk."

Jack said, "Well when we were at the restaurant you said you wanted another doctor so I decided I would have to try harder."

"I didn't say that!" she said incredulously.

"Amnesia? Good because I still want to be your doctor."Kathy tried to laugh, but found that it also induced pain.

"I want you around too, but are you sure you want to be saddled with a sick old lady?" she asked.

"'A', you're not old. And 'B', I don't think you would be much of a burden."

Kathy closed her eyes and Jack thought she may have drifted back to sleep. Her face showed contentment and all she said was "Mmmm."

After a moment she smiled a beautiful smile and said, "I want a real date."

"Hm. I suppose that would be okay. I might want to wait until the bandages come off, though" he said with a chuckle. He was showing lightness of heart he didn't feel at the moment.

Kathy scowled, "I'd punch you if I could."

Just then the nurse came in. She only heard the last comment, "Are you bothering my patient sir?" she said defiantly.

Jack turned and she saw who he was and her hand flew to her mouth,

"Oh! Dr. Sharp I'm so sorry. I didn't know it was you." Then she mockingly put her hands on her hips and said, smiling this time, "*Sir*, are you bothering my patient?"

Kathy answered this time, "No, nurse, he is being sweet. He is filling me in on my last few days."

"You still need your rest. But it's okay to stand there and hold hands." Then conspiratorially she said, "I won't say a thing. By the way its nice to see you fully awake. Do you need anything?"

"Can I have some ice water?" Kathy asked.

"You're still NPO, but I'll check with Dr. Clark. If it's okay with him I'll get you some ice chips."

Kathy's alertness improved rapidly and she was able to sit up a little later on. She was allowed to have clear liquids to drink and some of her intravenous medications were changed to pills. Dr. Clark came by about nine, having been in surgery all day. He let her know that the preliminary pathology report was available if she wanted him to tell her.

She glanced at Jack, "I think it is as good a time as any to tell me what you have found, Dr. Clark."

Mack's face grew dark, "I'm afraid I was correct in my initial assessment. Your tumor is a malignant glioma. We can't be sure we get the whole tumor even when using microscopes. The problem with malignant tumors versus benign is that they are even more likely to recur or start somewhere else in the brain. It can have cells invading the tissue around it. If we operate too extensively you are left with much greater deficits. We will need to follow this surgery up with radiation to complete the treatment."

"Will I need chemotherapy?" Kathy asked having grown even paler with the news.

"It is possible, but not likely. I'll have Dr. Montavy stop by and look things over. He is one of the best oncologists, around here, for this type of problem. If he thinks you should have it I recommend following his plan." Dr. Clark left the room, wrote a quick note and was gone.

"He is such a nice doctor," came Kathy's comment, "and good looking too."

Jack, who was still mulling over the diagnosis, was taken off guard by her comment. He looked up to see Kathy's impish grin.

"What? Good looking? Hey, just because he's ten years younger!"

"I wondered if you were paying attention, *doctor.*" With that she reached up gently pulled Jack's face toward her. She gave him a light kiss on the lips. Getting the diagnosis of a deadly disease seemed not to have fazed her at all.

Nevertheless, the report confirming that the tumor was malignant sobered the mood between them. Despite her early wakefulness she tired quickly and soon was ready to go back to sleep. A few of Kathy's family members arrived about nine-thirty, but she was already sleeping.

Jack was sitting in the chair by her bedside when Frank appeared at the door. He made a small gesture of greeting without speaking so he wouldn't disturb his mother's sleep.

Jack rose and met him in the corridor. They shook hands firmly. "When the nurse said Mom was asleep I told the others to wait downstairs."

"Your mother is strong, but this has tired her out." Jack told Frank about the diagnosis, which came as no surprise.

"How much longer will she be in here?"

"I don't know. She might be able to go home in a few days if she continues to improve, but there are many other treatments ahead," replied Jack.

Frank told him, "Our church has been holding an all-night prayer vigil for her. Different people go to the church to pray. I know it doesn't change the diagnosis but we believe God can do anything."

Jack nodded. He had seen "miraculous" cures. He had also prayed for healing for patients and believed God could do it. But, unlike faith healers, he did not promise a cure. God's plans were known only to Him and Jack did not presume to try to force his will upon God. "Frank, that is a great idea. I hope He does completely heal your mom and I'll be praying for her too."

Jack then took the opportunity to talk with him about his relationship with Kathy. "Frank, I have known your mother for many years. I have admired her and we have remained friends. I think that friendship has been made stronger recently, especially the last few days. I feel very close to your mother. I want to be there for her. It is kind of awkward because I feel I need your permission, but I would like to date your mother."

Frank listened carefully. He made a face and stroked his chin. "Hm. Let me see. You're asking my permission? What does Mom think?"

Jack said, "I believe it's a mutual feeling."

"I see." He feigned uncertainty. "Well, I'll have to check with my brother and sisters, but..." then he removed the somber mask and smiled. "Dr. Sharp don't you think we've already been talking about you? We were kind of hoping you would stick around. We know Mom likes you and we've really appreciated your presence this weekend. We have actually been hoping it wasn't just professional concern."

They shook hands again then Frank reached around and gave Jack a powerful hug. When he released him he had small tears on his cheeks, "Can you tell me, though, how much time Mom has? This all sounds great, but in light of her condition will we have her with us much longer?"

"Frank, no one knows the answer to that. It depends upon the success of the surgery and other treatments. She may have years, but it could also be only months before the tumor comes back. We'll just have to pray for healing and hope that God answers 'Yes,'" Jack said.

39

Tuesday

With a new day came a sense of hopefulness for Rebecca and Justin. Rebecca had made a few inquiries and was told that the CIA might send a man over with information about the Africa business. They wouldn't share anything on the phone, however. In fact, they didn't really tell her that they had actual knowledge of the affair, but had shown interest when she had mentioned the doctor's name. Even receiving a response had surprised her and she was anxious to learn more.

The challenges they faced had become greater as they had lost a witness and possible suspect with the death of Dan Randizzio, and had another murder to solve. The whole force had been working with the description of the vehicle used by the killer. If they could find him, they might be able to wrap up two murders. However, there was a deeper current that was still a mystery. *Diamonds! How much money was actually involved? What was going on that was worth killing two people?* These questions and more rolled around incessantly in Rebecca's mind as she tried to piece together the evidence they had.

Time kept moving on against them, but they were still hopeful that the killer had remained near by. Whoever it was would not take a chance getting out on the highway with the same truck. Unfortunately the impound lot manager had not seen the driver clearly, but the killer did not necessarily know that.

Rebecca said, "I think our guy is going to ditch the truck and lay low. But he could try to leave town some other way. That lot is near the airport and the bus station isn't that far away. She stomped her foot and hands on hips said, "But we don't have any description to use to find this guy."

"Given the ruthlessness of this killer do you think we should put some protection out at the impound lot in case the killer tries to clean up 'loose ends?' It might actually net us the killer."

"Good idea, Justin." She picked up the phone and spoke to dispatch, "Keep a cruiser in the area twenty four seven for a few days... Yes that's right... thank you." She hung up and motioned to Justin to sit. "Okay what next? Any more word on our missing girl?"

Just then a young man wearing a light blue shirt and open collar came into the conference room where Rebecca and Justin were musing. "Ma'am? Are you Detective Sweate?"

Annoyed she looked over, "Yes, I am.."

"Ma'am we just got this. It's a fax and I think you will want to read it."

Rebecca approached him and snatched the page from his hands. "Who are you and who's this from?"

"My name is Roger Whitmore, ma'am. I'm new in the communications department. Sorry, we couldn't tell who sent it, but it came from Seattle, Washington," he said somewhat nervously.

"Seattle. What does that have to do with this? Are you sure you're in the right office?" she nearly handed the sheet of paper back to the fresh-faced clerk, but decided to look it over first. Her eyebrows went up and she smiled briefly. Rebecca looked back at the young man.

"Who has looked at this message?" she asked trying to keep the urgency out of her voice.

"Mandy took it off the machine and handed it to me. She thought I should throw it away, but I heard that you were working this case so I brought it to you," he said becoming a little annoyed at the grilling.

As she handed the paper to Justin she said, "You did great work." She thought for a second then to the messenger, "Please get Mandy, whoever she is, and quietly bring her here. Don't talk to anyone about this fax. Understood?" she said with a glint in her eyes.

Roger began to smile back, "Yes, ma'am. Mandy works in the same department. She is training me. I'll be right back." He saw that he had done something right today; lately his track record hadn't been so good. Trying to look nonchalant, Roger returned to the communications room. He moved up to Mandy and tapped her on the shoulder.

"Mandy, may I talk with you?"

Mandy looked up and was about to scold him for taking too much time when she saw the odd expression on his face. He had his hand out in a gesture of conciliation and he was looking intently at her.

"Um, sure. Just let me log off." She entered a few keystrokes on her computer and the screen changed to the symbol for the local police department. Mandy stood and they walked into the hallway.

"Mandy," Roger began, "You know that fax you got?"

"You mean the crazy one from Washington that I told you to file away? What about it?"

"I showed it to Detective Sweate and she wants to talk to us both about it right away. Did you mention it to anyone else?" he asked.

"You did what?" she nearly shouted.

Roger tried to quiet her and moved her farther down the hallway.

"If I'd known you were going to pull that kind of crazy stunt I would have pitched it myself," she scoffed. "It's probably just another crank lead. Who in Seattle would know anything about what's going on here?"

"I don't know, Mandy, but listen to me. Detective Sweate is taking it seriously. She wants to see us right away so let's go." He put his hand on her elbow and directed her toward the conference room. Mandy, surprised by his apparent new-found confidence, at first resisted then followed out of curiousity. She had, until now, seen him as a weakling hardly fit for working in a police station.

Rebecca was talking excitedly with Justin about the missive in his hand. "I think we can accept this as genuine."

Justin countered, "It is unattributable. It came from a thousand miles away. It only gives a general description anyone could have made up. It could have been anyone who has read about the case online or in a paper."

Just then they realized they had company. Rebecca said, "Come in you two. Please close the door. Did you tell anyone where you were going?"

They answered in unison, "No one, ma'am."

Rebecca scowled, "Okay. First you may say 'Rebecca' in here or 'Detective Sweate,' but no more 'Ma'am' please." This helped to put them at ease. "Let's all sit down."

The two young office workers were surprised at this. They were used to getting a dressing down from senior officers but, instead, found themselves being asked to be included in the current discussions. "You're Mandy?" Rebecca asked looking at the pretty young woman. She had very dark, short-cropped hair and was conservatively dressed.

"Mandy Chatzi, Ma... Detective Sweate. I've been training Roger. I told him it was probably a hoax, but..."

"That's okay. He may have acted a little rashly, but I think he did right by bringing this to me. Did *you* tell anyone else about this fax?"

Mandy looked at Roger questioningly, "No. I didn't put much stock in it. Do you think it has bearing on your case, ma'am?" She put her hand to her mouth and said, "Oops."

Rebecca smiled glancing at Justin, "It could be important. It is also important that you not mention it to anyone. I mean ANYONE. Okay?" If someone asks if you have heard anything new refer them to Detective Samuelson or me, do not give out this information. Not even to the DA. Understood?"

They were both nodding their heads. "You did great work. I'll be sure to mention it to your supervisor," Rebecca said. She shook Mandy's hand and patted Roger's shoulder. "If any more faxes come from our mystery writer get them to me ASAP, Okay?"

They looked at each other and nodded. As the two left Rebecca's office Roger couldn't resist poking Mandy in the ribs as if to say, "I told you so."

Rebecca looked at Justin, "Well, do you agree that it is important?"

"Yes. We haven't mentioned the diamond to anyone. The rest of the things on this fax could have been made up, but the information about the diamond fits perfectly. This came from our missing girl."

"Notice the height of our killer, 'not much taller than Connie.'

The kicker is that our killer was a woman! We have focused on a male. There's no way it could have been Dan Randizzio, though he was somehow involved. Why else would he have been killed? We have to find Alicia Winters for her own sake. She'll be going after her next. I can feel it. Can you see if she has flown out of nearby airports in the past few days?" Rebecca asked.

"I can do that, but I doubt she's really in Seattle. If she wanted us to know this without giving up her location she could have called from a pay phone or cell phone in Seattle." He was on his computer doing a reverse look-up on the Seattle fax number. "This fax came from a public library. We are really no closer to finding her, but at least it appears that she is alive. She's being very smart and wants to communicate with us. The thing that worries me is her concern that she can't even trust us."

"She must believe someone even in our department is in on this. I have to admit it looks like that is possible. The killer knew when Dan Randizzio was to be released! Why kill *him* unless he had additional information that could compromise the true killer?" Rebecca motioned to Justin that they should go back to her office. She said nothing more until they were safely inside with the door closed.

"We need to let our officers know that we are now looking for a woman, not a man," said Rebecca at last.

"Are you going to inform the chief about this fax?" asked Justin. "Otherwise how will you explain our interest in a woman killer after picking up Dan Randizzio?"

Rebecca shook her head, "He isn't going to like it. I'll have to tell him, but I want the fax kept quiet. I could say that, once our lot manager sobered up, he 'thought' it was a woman. The fewer people who know we have a source and are in contact with Alicia the better. Let's review our facts again."

They pored over the information they had received and reviewed the role of every person they had interviewed. Their conclusions were the same. The death of the young woman was personal, given the knife wounds, but the diamond had some significance they did not yet understand. Justin said, "People have been killed for less. Do you think this diamond could be very valuable?"

"Sure, but someone went to supreme effort to track her down then to go after Randizzio."

"Your angry girlfriend theory may be closer than we thought," said Justin.

"What?" Rebecca was startled and a vacant look came on her face. Mulling over the idea she then said, "You're right. If our killer is really a woman that changes almost everything. Was she the owner of the diamond?" she stood again and paced. "I don't think so," she said answering her own rhetorical question. "This has the earmarks of strings being pulled by someone in authority, but it is still murky. There's something big here. And where does our good doctor fit in?"

Justin remained pensive. "Maybe he knows this female killer. He knows we have the diamond."

Rebecca said, "Great. That's right. Could he have arranged the fax?"

Justin put up his hands. "Too many 'what ifs.' Do we need to find Alicia?"

"Maybe not immediately, but call Seattle and check out that library. Otherwise we won't waste valuable effort trying to track her down yet. If this fax is really from her she may give us more information and we can't be one hundred percent sure that this wasn't coerced from her." Rebecca bit her lip and paced the room.

"Okay let's assume this fax is legitimate. She finds a way to give us the killer's description and that she is okay. She warns us about the diamond. Let's get the description on the wire now. Our diamond expert should be here today. I'll go talk to the chief."

"Do we let the aunt know that she is alive?"

"I don't think that is a good idea yet. All we have is the fax. It isn't proof of life. Let's get going.

40

"James, it's Malcomb," came the voice on the other end of the phone. "We need to meet," Malcomb said with no apology in his voice. "James?"

Annoyed at the interruption of his thoughts James belatedly said, "Fine. Don't mention it on the phone. Send me the location for the meeting by email while I sit here and wait for it." He hung up disgusted. Malcomb didn't use his brains sometime. They had decided upon some simple security measures and Malcomb paid no attention. For all they knew the FBI was listening in on them. He checked and in less than a minute there was an encrypted email from Malcomb instructing him to meet at a local Starbucks.

"Nothing like an obscure place," James muttered to himself sarcastically. So far Malcomb hadn't sent him any information and he hoped he would continue to delay. Then he would have an excuse for not finding the girl. If they didn't find her in time she would probably not receive her death sentence.

At the coffee shop James ordered his favorite latte combination, hazelnut and Irish crème with a dab of chocolate, and found a booth in the back corner. There weren't many people so it seemed secure enough.

Malcomb walked in looking happy as a lark. He waved and strode straight up to the booth. "Hey, Jimmy."

"My name is not 'Jimmy,'" he hissed at Malcomb. "Now order a coffee like everyone else and come back over here quietly!"

Malcomb scowled, but did as he was told. Back in the booth Malcomb handed a thick manila envelope to James. "Here's everything we tried that didn't work."

"That's why we had to meet so urgently?" James said in genuine bewilderment.

"No, but this is." Malcomb held up a small slip of paper with lettering on it. "This is the location of a cell tower near where Alicia last used her phone. It is in northern Iowa." His grin was dazzling. "We found it just twenty minutes ago. Her phone was on yesterday for about an hour and she received one call."

"Malcomb if you had just emailed me I could have sent my field agent to check it out." James was already breaking out his notebook computer.

"I had to tell someone else first and he told me to tell you in person."

"You mean the Leader already knows about this?" James said desperate to keep the panic out of his voice. James had hoped that once the search for the girl was in his hands he could control it. He wanted to slow it down just long enough to allow the deal to be done. James had hoped that Antony would decide to leave her alone once their business was finally concluded. Now he would have to pursue this lead as Mark Antony would not be patient. James sat mute for almost a full minute. "Fine. Get out of here. I need to get my agent up there and track her from there. It could still take time."

"I imagine so, but I also know that our precious leader is impatient to find that girl. So now it's your problem because you're so *good* at your job." Malcomb smiled again and almost laughed as he stepped lightly out the door.

James just sat. What would he do now? He had little choice, as he would have to continue the search or face the wrath of Mark Antony. He sent the information to his operative via his own encrypted email. She was generally very good, though she had obviously made a few mistakes in Nebraska. She had managed to evade capture, just barely. Nevertheless, he had little doubt that she would learn the girl's whereabouts soon. It would bring him no pleasure to have found the girl, but at least he didn't have to send the "kill" instruction. This time he felt certain that dear Mark Antony would see to it himself.

Then he struck on an idea. Once they found the girl if he could somehow delay informing the Leader long enough he might be able to move her to safety. If he warned her she could stay ahead of the Leader then the shortened time to their deal would work toward Alicia's advantage. He almost laughed as he realized he would be working on both sides. Yet, another life was in the balance. That was not funny. James knew he would have to tread cautiously with his agent. She was well trained, but he couldn't be sure of her total loyalty to him.

James feared contacting the police directly, knowing that the Leader had inside sources in many places. One word to the wrong person would put his neck on the chopping block. He stood and took the last sip from his latte wondering if anyone was still tracking her cell phone. If she turned it on again and he called her cell phone he could warn her directly. But what if she didn't turn it on? He couldn't go himself; he needed an outside party. Someone interested, but not directly connected.

James had not been able to sleep the night before as he was still pondering his role in all of this. *How had he let himself get so involved? Was the money really worth this?* Outside, the wind was biting as it whipped through the Chicago high-rises and he had to walk a block to get to his car. His lightweight jacket helped shed the wind, but it did not keep out the cold. Wrapping his arms tightly around himself he decided he would have to exchange it for his heavier wool coat when he got home.

He approached his car thinking hard. As he pressed the unlock button on his remote an idea popped into his head. He stopped and looked around at the busy sidewalks and for the first time is several days he smiled. He remembered reading in the internet account of the murder about a doctor who had found the body of the other girl.

What was the name? Short? No, Sharp! Dr. Sharp was the name. He would do some checking, but he might prove useful. James had felt sluggish and deeply fatigued, but now found new vitality. He had grown weary of his part in this affair, but he was now determined to find a way to help the girl and do his best to extricate himself.

****

Armed with their new information Rebecca and Justin were hopeful for a break. They had a witness who was out of reach, but apparently safe for the moment. She was in hiding and had not given them much to work with yet, but perhaps she would give them more. Rebecca breathed almost to herself,

"Stay safe, Alicia."

A uniformed officer appeared at her door as she was about to check with the front desk to see if the diamond expert had arrived.

"Ma'am, we have found the truck we think was used in the hit and run."

Rebecca felt elation, but didn't show it. "What is it with Ma'am these days! Do I look like I'm fifty?"

"No ma'am, I mean Detective," the officer said, grinning.

"Thank you," she said in surrender. "I like good news. Let's get forensics on it double quick. Maybe we can pinpoint the identity of our killer. Where was it?"

"It was parked two blocks from the bus station. There were a couple of parking tickets on its window so the driver may have gone straight to the bus terminal from the hit and run."

"Okay get that new description out to the bus station and check with everyone there to see if they saw this woman."

"Yes ma ... Detective," he spun on his heel and left the room.

Beyond him, Rebecca saw Justin walking down the hall with a well dressed middle-aged man in tow. She assumed that this was their diamond expert. His suit would have cost her a month's salary, but he looked good in it. He had a truly chiseled jaw and she could tell, despite the suit, that he worked out. She had had a much different mental picture of their expert. In her mind's eye she had been expecting a short, balding, older man with "Coke-bottle" glasses.

She stood as he entered the office and found herself going around her desk to greet this good looking gentleman. "Hi, I'm Rebecca Sweate," she said with her hand already extended.

His smile could have gotten him a role in Hollywood, "Robert Carmichael," he responded with a velvety voice. He took her hand and shook it looking directly into her eyes. As he did so he let her hand linger just a second before releasing it.

Rebecca felt internal alarms already blaring. She forced herself to "get objective" as her former boss had taught her. They needed this guy's mind, not his good looks. "Are you our diamond expert?" she said asking the obvious question.

"I specialize in diamonds. Expert? I guess you could say that too. I work independently, but have performed services for the FBI in the past. They have vetted me and trust me as well as anyone. There may be a few out there with greater experience who could still teach me some things." His explanation was more than she had needed, but Rebecca was pleased with his forthrightness.

"We greatly appreciate you taking time to help us with this, nonetheless. I'm sure that we have no one here with the level of knowledge you possess. Shall we go see the stone?" She said.

Justin cut her off by saying, "We've already been to the lab."

"Oh. You should have let me know."

"I asked to be taken directly to the stone. I am on a tight schedule. You understand."

"Sure," Rebecca answered casually but shot a "look" at Justin. Chagrined Justin laid the case, bearing the diamond, on the desk.

"What you have here," Robert said gingerly raising the stone, "is a large native diamond. It appears nearly flawless, though there are some spots of some sticky substance stuck to it. Based upon the planes it contains I could cut this diamond into a dozen very nice stones."

Rebecca was mystified, "Why wouldn't you make it one stone?"

Robert Carmichael laughed. Smiling he said, "Detective Sweate, a stone that size would certainly be valuable, but who could own it? Besides there are planes which would make the quality of a large cut diamond less than perfect. However, smaller stones could be cut with near perfect quality. Which would you rather have, a single large diamond which is hard to sell or many smaller, nearly perfect stones, each fetching a very good price?"

"I see," Rebecca said genuinely curious. "What would be the value of those stones?" she asked.

"Oh, that is hard to tell. Each stone could be anywhere from one to three carats. We might be able to get a four carat diamond. Let's say a perfect one carat stone could sell for twenty or thirty thousand and go up from there. You do the math. Your native stone here could be worth millions if cut by the right person. May I ask where did you get this?"

"You may ask," she said, but did not answer him. "Just say it is part of an ongoing investigation."

Robert's friendly demeanor turned dark, "That's not very friendly, detective. Can you tell me if there are more of these?"

"We believe that it is possible, Mr. Carmichael." Rebecca was ready to move along.

Justin asked, "Can you tell anything more about the stone such as where it came from?" He was tired of the mind games going on between Rebecca and this expert. So what if he was muscular, good looking, and obviously well off?

"Justin, good question. No. I can't say exactly where it came from, but we all know these types of stones came from Africa. Possibly South Africa, though it may have been originally mined in the DRC or Congo as it was once called. It could be a so-called 'conflict diamond' as well."

"Conflict diamond? You mean like in the movie?" Justin asked.

Robert let out a small laugh, "A fairly inaccurate portrayal, but, yes, that is the idea. A miner finds a stone and hides it. He later sells it for basic needs. This sale would be to a disreputable dealer and the miner would receive a pittance. The local dealer likewise cannot sell the diamond on the open market so he sells to someone who can smuggle it out of the country. He may have made ten or twenty thousand dollars for a stone like this. The smuggler gets this stone and probably several others across the borders to another country and from there to someone who can cut the diamond. Often the smuggler is working with a local warlord. The profits from the sale probably go to purchase weapons and ammunition or just to line his pockets."

"In the past, this was a much greater problem. Today the practice is much better controlled. Diamonds must be certified and conflict diamonds are less common. The diamond market is very tightly regulated too. If a large number of diamonds were to come into the picture it could topple the market price. A few, even like this one, would likely not be a problem. They would be easily absorbed." He returned his admiring gaze to the stone. "I am amazed that this diamond has not already been cut. However, there was another thing we found by looking closely under the microscope." He held the stone before his magnifying eyepiece as if trying to see a tiny detail. "It appears someone has marked this diamond. There is a series of numbers etched into the diamond."

"I thought diamonds were the hardest substance on earth," said Rebecca. "How could they mark it?"

"These days lasers are used for marking diamonds, but not usually until they have been cut. These numbers could be part of a series that could help you identify its owner."

Rebecca said, "So whoever owns this stone has enough others that he had to label it and document its existence. Could that be a legitimate source? Perhaps the diamond was stolen from a major diamond company."

Robert said, "I doubt it. They wouldn't have left it in this uncut state long because it would be worth much more once it has been cut. Why mark it in the 'uncut' state?"

Rebecca walked up to him with her hand out. "Thank you Mr. Carmichael for taking time to give us a lesson in diamonds. We may need you to testify at some point. Can I walk you out?"

"Of course. I understand." He shook her hand and took out two business cards, one for Justin and one for Rebecca. "I answer my cell at all hours."

Justin took his arm and said, "I'll escort you back to the lobby." Then he said to Rebecca, "I'll be back in your office in a minute. Okay?"

"Sure, Justin," she answered taken aback. She stepped to the door mulling over what they had heard.

Was it just the value of this diamond that had gotten two people killed? She knew that people had certainly been killed for less.

PART THREE

41

Mark Antony paced back and forth before the large window of his top floor apartment. He had heard from Malcomb, but was still waiting to see if James had come up with anything else. He was basically pleased with the way things were going, but was still annoyed at the snag they kept hitting with regard to this elusive girl. *How could she continue to stay hidden? She's a mere amateur.* Nevertheless, now that her general whereabouts had been determined he was confident that they would know soon exactly where she was. He had direct contact with the agent whom James thought was his own. She went by the name of Tonya, when she was working. She was, in fact, his common law wife. Her, given name was Delia and she had her own axe to grind with this girl. He knew that Delia would undoubtedly let him know as soon as she found the girl. Yet she would probably call James out of a misguided sense of loyalty toward him since he was her "employer."

Antony had decided that he wanted to do this job personally. Tonya would not be happy to sit on the sidelines, but she would have to understand. Antony was now becoming worried about his partners. Malcomb might be a good business man but in this business he seemed incompetent. James had been sullen at their last meeting. Should he continue to trust him? Only Cindy seemed to be remaining sharp. She had nearly completed the arrangements for securing their meeting location despite the change in the time-table. He had moved the deal into Iowa since it seemed that he would be traveling there soon anyway. He would inform James and Malcomb where to go to pick up their "cut" as soon as he had taken care of the girl.

Antony now needed to speak to their business partners and was steeling himself for the conversation. They had managed, somehow, to set up this meeting via a secure satellite network emphasizing to him that their own government contacts were higher than his. These men known as "The Five Diamonds" wanted him to show them a few of his samples before buying. Mark Antony stood facing his ninety six inch LCD screen television monitor. A mini-cam tracked his movements allowing the other party to see him as well. He was wearing a new perfectly tailored suit and had made every effort to appear relaxed. The screen was activated and all he saw was an empty desk. This surprised him, but he remained standing before the screen and camera. A voice then came over the speakers.

"Mr. Antony. Are you disappointed that we do not appear on the camera?"

"I had hoped we could meet on equal terms. But this is your network and your show." He had recovered his composure quickly, but was certain they had noted his discomfort. Swearing silently he realized he had been set up for this. These business partners could see him, but he could not see them. "What can I do for you?" he asked benignly.

"I am Yo Wang. We have spoken before. You know basically where we are from, but you do not need to see us face to face until we are ready to finish this... transaction" This did not answer his question, but anticipated his real interest. "We, on the other hand wanted to see you. And we want to see some of your samples. We have trusted you up to this point, but we do not desire to risk ourselves for mere baubles."

A slow grin spread over Antony's face. He knew he still held the higher cards because this "partner" desperately wanted his merchandise. "I am prepared to show you what you want."

Antony moved over to a low table placed within the mini-cam's field of view. He opened a drawer and pulled out an ornately carved wooden box. It was not heavy, but he lifted it out with reverence. He glanced toward the camera, "Here is what you want to see."

He then reached over to another camera set up on a tripod near the table. He switched it on and pressed a button on a remote lying on the table. This camera focused directly upon the table's surface. Antony opened the box and took out four stones each about the size of a nickel. Their appearance was unremarkable, but their presence brought a low murmur from his audience. Mark then did something interesting. He slipped a small object from his pocket. It looked like a small penlight. As he squeezed a bright white light shown from its bulb. He used this light to transilluminate each stone. Now he could hear the other men speaking excitedly. He could not understand their language, but waited for their approval.

Yo Wang spoke, "Amazing Mr. Antony. You have what we were hoping for. But where is the fifth stone?"

He hesitated, then spoke, "I may need to keep one or two of the uncut diamonds for my own security."

At this Wang said, "Mr. Antony we had an agreement. All the stones!"

"What's one or two more or less to you considering the total number of smaller stones? Besides I'm the one who will have to disappear." He had taken a calculated risk. If he didn't keep to the deal they could leave him dangling. He believed, however, that avarice would win out. These men, The Five Diamonds, wanted what he had and it was nearly within their grasp.

"You are sure that the entire lot is untraceable?"

He hesitated uncomfortably. "Untraceable, yes, but I have had the large ones specially marked."

"What do you mean, 'marked?'"

"Each stone has a plane that will be destroyed when the diamond is cut. I have had laser imprinting done to identify the stones. Each has a unique number."

This last statement caused quite a stir among his audience. He could here the conversation, but he could understand no Mandarin.

"You surprise us, Mr. Antony. This changes our timetable even more. First you move up the meeting. Now, because you have marked the diamonds, we must begin cutting the stones or risk having identifiable diamonds in our possession. Perhaps we should just move on to another market."

The television screen began to fade and Antony, thinking quickly said, "I don't believe there is another market." He did his best to avoid appearing smug. "The markings are of no concern. They were only for my own benefit. No one else knows about it or has the numbers."

The screen stopped fading then he heard, "Very well. We know you are taking some risks but we are very disappointed at the reduction in number. We will merely reduce the offer by five hundred thousand unless you bring the fifth stone."

Antony's face became red he was furious at this, but he tried to remain calm. They had called his bluff, but even the reduction left him with more money than he could ever spend. He put on a show of reconsidering. He didn't want these men to know that he had lost a marked stone already. "Understood. I have a change in plans. For security reasons we need to move the meeting site."

"Another change Mr. Antony?" Yo Wang laughed, "It is of no concern since we didn't know the original site anyway. Go ahead. Where do we meet?" Wang said in perfect English.

"Adventureland in Des Moines Iowa. Monday next week. I will send you the exact GPS coordinates for the site by encrypted email." Antony spoke firmly and without hesitation.

There was now additional laughter on the other end of his satellite connection. "Are we to enjoy an amusement park Mr. Antony? Isn't that rather public?" Wang responded once the laughter had died down.

"Not exactly. It's off-season. There won't be many people around, especially on a weekday. How many will you be bringing with you? I need to know for security arrangements," Mark Antony inquired.

"There are five of us, but of course we will have our own security," came the reply.

"Your guards may only come within one hundred yards of the appointed location," Antony stated firmly.

Again there was murmuring and an angry retort, "You presume much in telling us what we can do!"

"Do not cross me, sir," Antony said almost in a whisper. There was silence for a moment. Then Antony intoned, "I will send you the account number for the transfer. Bring the bonds for the transaction and the other half you may transfer when you are safely out of our country as we previously agreed." There was still a stony silence from the other end of the line. Antony nervously continued, "Well gentlemen unless there is something more I have additional arrangements to make." They clearly didn't like being dictated to, but that was exactly why Mark Antony had tried to re-take the momentum.

"I'll see you next Monday." Antony then severed the connection. He knew this would irritate the men, but he was angry and getting close to losing control himself. Mark Antony didn't want to be seen as weak. He opened his notebook computer and typed a short note to Cindy detailing the arrangements. He was miffed at the loss of five hundred thousand dollars, but split four ways it wasn't much in comparison to what they would gain. Besides he could make James take a bigger loss since he had caused the trouble. Antony had long been planning for this day, but was starting to feel a little uncomfortable. With all the years of planning for this final deal, there should not have been even a slight bump in the road. Now they had not only had to kill two people, but they had lost one of the diamonds. At least the buyers had not cancelled the deal as a result of this. There was still a loose end out there he intended to tie up soon.

The last thought prompted him to send an email to James.

"Where are we in finding that girl?"

42

Rebecca had slept well for once without nightmares; in fact, she could not remember dreaming at all. Rising from her bed this morning, she actually felt rested. Her "go to work" ritual was on "automatic pilot" and before long she found herself seated, once again, at her messy desk.

Wednesday, had arrived and she felt no closer to solving their case. This should not have surprised her. Murder cases often took months of steady police work to establish alibis find witnesses and run the suspects to the ground. But she was impatient for some reason. She worried about the safety of their one remaining witness and some inner voice kept pushing her, believing that time was more important than usual.

Nevertheless, the day was nearly half gone before Rebecca and Justin could discuss the case. The CIA man had not shown up yet and hopes of finding Randizzio's killer nearby were also quickly fading. As so often happened in investigations, the whirlwind of activity became a dogged grind of sifting details. Justin had spent the first part of the morning relooking at their evidence. Rebecca secretly suspected he was at the crime lab getting "help" from pretty young Cindy. That thought made her smile. Maybe there could be a relationship there, though she had found out the hard way that dating within the department can be dangerous to the relationship.

She met Justin back in the conference room. He was already standing in the room looking at the timeline they had drawn.

Opening the discussion he said, "I didn't really find anything else that helps us out at this point. They have that diamond completely clean now. I am still surprised at how dull it appears as a raw stone."

"That surprised me too. They must be hard to find and tell

301

apart from other stones in the mines." Rebecca was pensive, her mind drawn to what little she knew of Africa. "I can't imagine a life of digging for them day after day."

Justin shook his head. "Makes me glad I live here."

She and Justin bantered back and forth about the reasons for the killings and the possible role of the diamond. Rebecca said, "I think we should get the doctor back in and find out more about his connection with diamonds. It is just too much of a coincidence that he found the body."

Justin answered, "Shouldn't we wait for the CIA? They obviously know about him and haven't done anything about him."

"Justin, the CIA isn't supposed to *do* anything in this country,"

"I know, but they could tip us off if they have concerns about the doc. I think we should see what they have to say. Up until now he has been cooperative and he might still be able to help us," Justin said.

Rebecca noted that Justin had become much less timid over the past week. He spoke his mind was more willing to contradict her. Though she was facing away from him, toward the wall, she smiled. "All right, Justin. You seem to have some pretty good instincts."

They had lost the trail of their female killer. No new faxes had come to light. In other words their progress had come to a screeching halt.

"I don't like this," Rebecca was saying to Justin. "We were making headway and we were finding out new things, but now we have hit a brick wall. The ADA wasn't in his office again today. Now he's apparently sick or something. If he's not back tomorrow I'm going to the District Attorney."

"What will you say to the DA? She probably knows about his absence," Justin said openly curious. His eyebrows went up, "Oh, I forgot to tell you. I also spoke to the guard who was on duty during Randizzio's last night in jail. The only "official" visitor who went into the cell was his lawyer. He said she had been happy- almost bubbly. He could describe what she was wearing and the color of her lipstick, but for some reason didn't know why she had come down for the visit."

Justin was now getting a little more excited. "But there is more about the night that the guard had to tell me."

Rebecca's brows furrowed, "The guard? What do you mean?

"Well, he told me that the ADA, Sears, was down at his cell for a few minutes. The guard says he just stood at the door and talked to Randizzio in his cell. He didn't go in. One thing that was weird, though, it was like three AM," Justin answered referring to his notes on his PDA. "He said he overheard the end of the conversation because they were getting loud." Justin read, "The ADA said, 'You're being an idiot. Do you think we won't figure it out anyway?' Then it was garbled for a while and he remembered the very last thing. '... or at least we would have. You're getting out in the morning. Be sure to be careful crossing the street.'"

"The guard was sure? That seems like a lot for someone to remember," said Rebecca doubtfully.

"Yeah. He said he has nothing better to do so he listens in when he can."

"Remind me to talk more quietly down there. What do you suppose Sears meant by that last comment?'" Rebecca asked.

Justin said, "I'm not sure. It sounds like a taunt, but it is odd that he would mention 'crossing the street.'"

"It could mean he knew something was going to happen to Dan Randizzio," Rebecca countered.

"You don't really think the Assistant District Attorney had anything to do with that do you?" When no answer was forthcoming he said, "You do, don't you?"

"Well someone leaked the information," Rebecca said.

"Whoa! You'd better keep that to yourself until you have some proof," Justin said.

"Oh, I know. I doubt we will ever be able to prove that either. It just seems that someone is a step ahead of us all the time. We could check his phone records but that would take a court order and more evidence than we have at the moment. I can keep my eyes open, though. It also gives me more reason to find him and have a conversation." Rebecca made a few notes of her own. "I think I'll call the CIA again. I want to try to find out when their intrepid agent will bless us with an appearance."

This brought a smile to Justin, "Go get 'em boss."

****

Jack was coming back up his street from his morning walk when Randy spotted him. Normally quiet, Randy ambled down the sidewalk to meet him. "Hey, Doc."

"Hello."

"Are you all right? I've seen that guy twice at your house lately. I saw the police here a couple of times last week. There's been a lot of activity going on at your place." His manner wasn't unpleasant, but Jack hadn't had many conversations with Randy and didn't know what to think of this interest.

"Thanks for asking. I think it will calm down now. I appreciate your keeping an eye out and you may have actually saved my life." Jack reached over and shook Randy's hand.

Randy surprised replied, "Really." He actually smiled, "I didn't know it was that serious. Was that the same guy on the news who was killed the other day?"

"I'm afraid so."

"That's creepy." Randy shifted from one foot to the other. "Doc, do we have to worry about anything else now?"

"What do you mean?" asked Jack.

"Are you going to get any more visitors like him and is it going to be dangerous around here?" he said with a hint of anxiety in his voice. Randy and his wife had two young children.

Jack put a calming hand on Randy's shoulder. "I believe the worst is over, but your sharp eye and wits are a good combination. If you see anyone traipsing around here will you call me or the police right away? I'll get you my business card with my phone numbers on it. Okay?"

"Sure, Doc. I'll watch out." He almost smiled again and reached over to shake Doctor Sharp's hand. "What are neighbors for?"

Jack was getting a little chilled standing in the cool morning air. Turning back toward his own house he breathed in the fresh crisp air. "Man, I love it here." He said to no one. He walked back and surveyed his lawn and house. Things looked a little unkempt, he decided. It would soon be time to get the mower out for one last mowing.

Back inside, Jack started the coffee pot and sat to read a few chapters of his Bible. His recent experiences had made him think of more eternal things and he had neglected reading. He had been reading through the Bible regularly for years and had read through it many times. He didn't usually try to finish in a year, but took a more leisurely pace. For him, reading every morning was like checking in with the boss before beginning the day.

This day he felt especially alive.

Having showered and dressed with a plan to visit Kathy, Jack put on some new cologne. He carefully checked to see that he had shaved well. Stepping back he looked at the color combination he had chosen to be sure it was appropriate.

"I need to shop for some new duds," Jack muttered to the mirror.

****

Jack entered the hospital room carrying a bouquet of flowers. Kathy was sitting up in bed, but had her eyes closed. Opening them as she heard the rustling of the bouquet a broad smile formed on her lips, "Good morning. Oh, flowers, something new." This was said facetiously as Jack could see at least a dozen larger and more elaborate floral arrangements tucked here and there in her room.

Jack laid the flowers on an empty spot near the sink, "Better late than never." He moved close to her and was pleasantly surprised as she lifted her arms to embrace him. They held each other briefly and he was even more pleased as Kathy kissed him lightly on his cheek.

"No public displays of affection," came a voice from the door followed by snickering laughter. Kathy's nurse entered and said, "Dr. Sharp, nice to see you."

Jack felt a little embarrassed as he and this nurse had dated in the past. Her name was Julie and, while they had had some fun, the relationship had ended with them parting as friends. Julie was now engaged to be married to a much younger intern.

"Hi, Julie. How are the wedding plans?"

With another, more pleasant laugh, Julie said, "My parents are still in shock. They thought I'd never get married." The look she gave him held something between mischief and reproach. "I'm doing most of the arrangements myself, but Ahmed's parents are going to come from Turkey a week early to help with things. They have never visited the United States."

"Wow! That should make things interesting."

"Yes it will. I don't know if they are ready for an *American* wedding. But enough about me. How's our patient?" asked Julie, skillfully changing the subject.

Kathy had sat listening to the conversation. "I want to hear more about your new in-laws to be."

Julie wrinkled up her nose and conspiratorially said, "I'll catch you up when 'you know who' is gone."

Kathy looked at her nurse, "It sounds like you have some inside information about a certain doctor. You can fill me in later."

In mock irritation Jack stood with hands on hips and said,

"Hey I'm in the room too!"

Changing the subject, Kathy smiled at Jack. "I get to go home soon."

"Really? Great!" intoned Jack. "Have you been up and around? Has physical therapy been in?"

"Yes and yes. Since you weren't here to hold my hand I had a very handsome young man help me and we walked the halls already this morning. I have spoken to home health and they'll check on me. Doctor Mack won't let me drive. I get fuzzy-headed sometimes. The kids are going to take turns getting me to the radiation oncologist and oncology appointments."

"It sounds like someone has been planning ahead. I could take you too, you know." Jack said.

"Don't you have a job?" she smiled mischievously. "They have been great about everything. The only thing I'll miss is the food."

"The food?" Jack was a little uncertain, "I thought you didn't like hospital food."

"That's just it. It was helping me lose weight." They both laughed. Jack noticed that Kathy seemed much more 'with it' than even before surgery as if removing the tumor had wiped away some dirt from her mind. He decided that he should ask Frank if he had noticed it too.

Julie said, "I have to move on since you are so well taken care of." She waved and, with a wink at Jack, was out the door. Jack slid one of the recliner chairs closer to the bedside. He was finding out how easy it was to just sit and talk with Kath and soon they were lost in conversation.

****

"Whew! I thought pitchforks were something that belonged in the 'Wizard of Oz.'" Covered in dust with bits of hay stuck in her hair Alicia put her fork down and leaned on it. She pulled out a handkerchief loaned to her by Missy and wiped the hay from her forehead. The overalls she was wearing were several sizes too big so in addition to being tired she felt awkward and bulky. Directing her comments up toward the ceiling she said, "My arms feel like spaghetti." Then changing the subject, "When do you find time to do your redecorating job?"

Missy was busily moving the hay into the free spaces of the loft. The old barn, once a bright red, now desperately needed a coat of paint. What paint remained was peeling badly, though the wood was sound and it had a relatively new roof. The structure provided shelter for two horses and some of the smaller farm implements. Roy had bigger pieces of equipment which were housed in a more modern metal building across the yard. Even though he rented out most of his land, he liked to get into the field and work on a few acres.

As she worked Missy replied, "That's my off season job. Once harvest is in and we've taken care of the financial stuff I get busier with redecorating. Everyone around here understands the schedule, so it's not too bad."

"But you still have to do chores all winter don't you?" Alicia felt guilty taking a break, though she was growing weary, so she again began moving hay. Roy had ingeniously made a kind of elevator with weights and pulleys. Hay was loaded onto a plywood platform. The operator then released a weight near the wall and the platform rose to the loft level. Since there was no motor involved it took practice putting the right amount of hay on the platform to allow the weight to raise it. If there was too little the platform shot upward and spilled most of the hay. Too much weight and she had to assist the weight and raise it by pulling another rope. Alicia marveled at the way Roy had managed to become self-sufficient and energy efficient even in this little thing.

Earlier, they had pulled up tomato plants in the vegetable garden. Missy had about fifty of these. Since there had been a killing frost the leaves were now shriveled and the tomatoes greenish and yellow blobs of mush. There were still potatoes to dig, but Missy said they would be able to dig those well into the winter. They had spread a layer of straw over the potato patch as insulation from the cold to come. The only chore left for the vegetable bed was to plow in the finished areas and let it rest for the winter.

As Alicia worked she became puzzled. Fifty tomato plants produced hundreds, possibly thousands, of tomatoes. "Missy, what do you do with all the stuff you grow in you garden. Isn't it way more than you and Roy eat?"

Missy slipped her gloves off, mopped her forehead and laughed, "I wondered when you'd ask that. We do produce a lot more than we can use, but you would be surprised how many tomatoes you go through in the winter. I can them and freeze some. I make tomato juice, sauce and even some salsa. But for that I would still only need a few plants. We haul fresh vegetables and some canned items to the food pantry in Des Moines and sometimes I sell a few things at the roadside stand near town. Its just one more thing Roy feels we should do. God has given him this fertile land and he hates to let any of it go to waste." She motioned to Alicia to follow her as she started back to the house.

As they walked Alicia shook her head. "Do you ever just take it easy?"

"Honey, do you see me rushing around? I work hard, but we

are meant to do work. I like to sit and read and I do that at night and Sundays. Work fills my days up. Without it I would probably feel lonesome and I would remember the past more and it would hurt more."

Alicia realized she had touched a tender spot in Missy's life. She wanted to learn more, but was wise enough to not press the issue. She would let Missy tell her more about herself when the time was right. They had reached the porch and they sat. Alicia changed the subject, "What do you do for fun around here?"

Missy paused. She had come close to opening her heart to Alicia, but she wasn't sure she dare rend that wound open again. It was wonderful having another woman to chat with and she didn't want to alienate her at this juncture.

"You have to define fun," she said relieved at the shift in direction.

"Do you go dancing or movies or dinners?"

"Dancing! You are dreaming. There are some places to dance in some of the towns around here, but they're for you younger folks." Missy got a far away look in her eyes, "I don't take with goin' to movies because you can't do anything while you watch. If it's any good I can wait for the DVD and then watch the show on the television."

"Are there any nice restaurants in the area?" Alicia queried.

"There used to be a steakhouse in Mason City, but it burned down two years ago and hasn't been rebuilt. There are several fast-food outlets there, and we go to Des Moines sometimes for a nice meal. Where are you heading with all this?" Missy said.

"I don't know it just seems that you don't get out much and maybe we could do something about that," said Alicia.

"Get out! With your face plastered all over kingdom come! Now is not the time for that Alicia. I get out enough for my pleasure. Maybe when this all blows over we can do something like a dinner, but now is not the time." Missy shook her head. This young woman was in trouble and the last thing she needed was to get out into public. "Don't go getting' itchy feet and try to go somewhere."

Alicia was stymied. Missy was right. She didn't dare do anything to attract attention. She had returned to the farm for that very reason. Yet she had it in her heart do something for Missy.

"I'm sorry. I know," she said as she struck on an idea. "I can't go into town, but you and Roy can. Let me make up a list of things for you to pick up and I will surprise you!"

Missy, scowled a fake scowl then smiled, "All right. That seems reasonable. You go right on and make your list. I've got to clean up and get dinner started. I can go into town tomorrow, okay?" She rose to go into the house.

Alicia noticed that the breeze had become even sharper. She stood and said, "Sure- tomorrow will be fine. I'll work on the list tonight. Did you notice how cool it got?"

"Yes. I heard that a cold front is moving through. We might get snow tonight or tomorrow. It's comin' early this year. I'm glad we got so much done this mornin'. Thanks for the help." They stepped up onto the porch together and Missy opened the door. Alicia looked back over her shoulder.

The gray featureless sky and cold breeze caused her to shiver, but she was also feeling a chill that went even deeper.

43

Rebecca had a deli sandwich in one hand and was taking a sip from her diet drink when a voice reached her ear from behind. She didn't like being approached from behind and her whole body tensed as her training began to take over.

The male voice said, "Detective Sweate fancy meeting you here."

Prepared to drop her sandwich and draw her weapon, she made a subtle move to her left and cautiously looked over her shoulder to her right. Standing just to her right and behind was a man who could easily pass for a local executive in his well cut dark suit. The slight bulge under his left arm and his short-cropped hair, however, gave away his true profession. Rebecca did not know him, but immediately decided he was friend, not foe, and completed the turn toward him without touching her weapon. She was angry now, but tried to maintain her composure.

"Don't you people ever just make appointments?"

Clearly enjoying the moment, the younger man replied, "We're not having this conversation. Right? We just bumped into each other like old friends."

"Sure and I'm not eating this sandwich. But let me see some ID."

"You asked for information," he said opening an ID case and showing to Detective Sweate. "I can provide what you need. Under those conditions."

The young man had much the same build as the late jogger. Rebecca thought he probably played college- or maybe even professional football. He turned to pay for a similar deli sandwich and drink at this outdoor kiosk frequented by many of the local office workers.

"Of course I want information. I just don't know why you're pulling the 'cloak and dagger' routine."

They found a table and sat opposite each other. The young man smiled, "You also don't know what a hornet's nest you stirred up. This guy has been out of our sights for a long time. We're curious about why you need the information and it's making someone upstairs a little nervous."

"You mean they don't want you to talk to me?"

"Let's just say I'm being your friend. But I need you to reciprocate. You know we aren't allowed to do any local surveillance."

"And you never investigate U.S. citizens, right?" she said sarcastically.

He only smiled at that. His hand went to his left lapel, a movement that caused Rebecca to tense automatically. He stopped opened his palm in a gesture of conciliation. "I'm just getting something from my pocket." His eyes glinted, "I really make you nervous don't I."

"Too many spy novels," Rebecca replied letting out her breath. "What's your name, agent ... ?"

"Just call me 'Tom' okay?" He slipped several folded sheets from an inner pocket and held them in front of him. "I can give this to you, but we need a few things too."

Rebecca tried to dodge this and use the direct approach, "Do we need to be looking harder at the doctor?"

Tom again smiled, "Do you want these? I ask the questions."

Rebecca stared anger building again, "All right," she wanted to say more, but her investigation needed a boost and she knew that antagonizing this man, who was obviously a CIA agent, would probably get her nowhere. "What do you want to know?"

"Good. Has Dr. Sharp been out of the country lately?"

Rebecca's eyebrows went up. Maybe they were suspicious of the doctor. "Not as far as I know."

"Okay, tell me how he is involved in your case."

Rebecca hesitated, but could not see how this would harm her own investigation. Much of it was already in the public record. She laid out for the agent how the doctor had come to be involved, mentioning some of her suspicions, but not every detail of their investigation. She touched on the diamond, but not the size or how they had found it.

The agent sat attentively and when Rebecca had finished he nodded. "Good. From what I know about the doctor you probably don't have to worry that he is a murder suspect. You'll find what you need about him and his connection to diamonds in this."

He slid the papers across to Rebecca, still folded.

Rebecca looked down at the pages and carefully unfolded them. She began to read then glanced up. Tom, or whatever his name was, had managed to make his exit without her even noticing. She scowled and said aloud, "How... ?"

The voice came from behind her again. "Don't look around. By the way, keep looking at your ADA. You may find something interesting."

Rebecca, despite the warning, turned in her seat. All she saw was the retreating dark suit quickly lost among the smattering of customers near the kiosk.

"Spooks!" she said disgustedly. She pushed the papers into her purse and rose, having completely lost her appetite.

As she stood, the breeze bit through the thin jacket that she had put on to walk to lunch. The novelty of her interesting encounter had worn off and the cold was becoming more noticeable. Rebecca didn't like the changing weather. Winter was not her favorite time of year preferring hot sunny weather like in Florida where working up a good sweat on a run was her idea of a good time. Gloomy winter made her start looking at brochures for Caribbean cruises, though she had yet to take one.

She looked in her purse then clutched it close to herself, as if she needed reassurance that the papers were still in her possession.

What could they contain that caused the CIA to want to suppress them?

She approached a side door into the city-county building where her office was located. Holding her badge to a card reader she heard the satisfying click and pulled it open. While the main entrance and the edifice itself had been stylishly designed, the architect had failed to use any imagination on this, more mundane entrance. It was like a small mud room with plain concrete block walls and a stairway leading up. An imposing steel door lay just ahead with another card reader blinking red to the side. This led to the judicial section of the building and through a small window could be seen the lavish wood paneling along the walls. Rebecca began ascending the steel and concrete steps as her badge did not gain her access to this "important" part of the building.

As Rebecca passed into her section she spotted Justin on the phone along one wall. She caught his eye and motioned for him to follow her to her office. She saw him say a few last words then he slipped his phone into its case and began walking her way.

Leading him into her office and closing the door she slipped the papers from her purse and sat down. As she scanned the pages Justin stood with curiosity part of the way between the desk and her door.

"I thought you wanted me to come in with you."

Rebecca glanced up, "Oh, sorry. I'll give you this page when I'm finished reading." She looked back down with no other explanation.

Justin, amused by this, leaned back against the door, waiting.

In a few minutes Rebecca, still looking down, thrust the paper toward Justin. He stepped up and took it from her hand.

"Am I allowed to ask what this is?"

"Just read then I'll explain."

The room was silent for several minutes while they read the documents. Justin had finished the first page before Rebecca was half way through the second. He laid it on the desk, jarred by its content, and waited patiently for the second page.

Pulling up a chair Justin quickly finished reading once Rebecca had handed the last page to him. "Where did you get this? The CIA still hasn't called back as far as I know."

"Apparently, they like being dramatic," Rebecca said sarcastically. She related her encounter with agent "Tom" and the desire for secrecy.

"Well, yeah! If it got out that the CIA used missionaries, like Dr. Sharp, there would be real problems."

Rebecca said, "I think this is an isolated situation. They had him cornered according to this…"

"I can't believe they wanted you to have all this," Justin said incredulously.

"At the moment I don't intend to disclose any of it. It's totally non-attributable. The CIA would deny it. Agent 'Tom' said he wasn't supposed to give it to me so we'd get him into hot water."

Justin stood and began pacing, an action he had picked up from Rebecca. "So can we trust it to be true?"

"We can't cast doubt on everything, Justin."

"Okay. Say it *is* true. So Dr. Sharp tried to help the CIA to nab this diamond thief in Africa, but everything went sour. According to that second page they basically left him to pick up the pieces and his girlfriend got killed in the process. Maybe he's bitter and trying to get some payback."

"Does he come across as vengeful to you? They told him that she had been killed, but here it says that it was never confirmed. All they knew, for sure, was that she was abducted. So let's see how that fits in with today. We are dealing with an uncut diamond stolen from someone in Chicago. The owner of the diamond didn't like that and killed the girl to get it back. They got the girl but missed the diamond. Hopefully they don't know we have it. There's still a girl missing, though we know she is alive..."

"Or was a day or two ago," interjected Justin.

"Right," said Rebecca with finger on chin. "Whoever is trying to find the stone has money and connections and is now responsible for two murders and a serious assault on the defense attorney, you and the doctor." She looked up and emphasized the next statement, *"And the ADA is somehow involved."*

"What?"

"The last thing the agent told me was to look deeper at Sears."

"Good grief!" muttered Justin. "Who else is dirty?"

"Hopefully no one. We need to find Sears. I'll talk to the chief and then the DA. We don't have enough evidence to convict him, but he may know who is behind all this or at least have valuable information for us, if we can find him and get him to talk. Do you want to talk to the doctor again? Maybe we can patch things up. I think he will be more likely to talk to you."

"You do? Hm. Okay. I can see now why your mention of diamonds got him riled up. Maybe he feels guilty about his girlfriend's abduction. I'll call him in the morning. I have some digging to do first."

44

Thursday

Thursday arrived for Jack more quickly than he wanted. He had thought that by taking time off from work he would be able to sleep in a little, but his phone was beeping at him and in the pitch dark he first managed to push his alarm onto the floor before picking up the receiver.

"Hello," he croaked, his vocal cords not awake yet . He half expected the hospital to be calling about some new disaster, but instead came an unfamiliar male voice.

"Dr. Sharp?" said the voice.

"Yes. Who's this?" Jack replied sleep quickly fleeing and his mind clearing.

"Let's just say 'a friend.' I understand that you have been in some hot water lately and I think I can help." The voice was strong with no apparent accent. Jack couldn't place it at all.

"I'm not in any trouble," answered Jack.

"Oh? All those trips to the police station mean nothing?" said the man.

Jack was silent.

"Whether you are in trouble or not I can help with the investigation you're involved in. Are you interested?"

Jack's eyes widened. He had hoped that his involvement had ended, but this caller was raising doubts. "What do you mean? I'm not involved in the investigation." He decided to remain cool and get information.

"I don't have time for games, Dr. Sharp. Are you interested or not?" There was a new hardness in the voice and Jack sat a little straighter.

"Okay. I'm interested. What do you have to tell me?"

"That's better. I know where the girl is." This revelation came as a shock to Jack who had no idea where the police were in this part of the investigation.

He tried to stall for time to clear the cobwebs from his mind, "What girl?"

"You know who I'm talking about. The one who is still alive, for now. Alicia Winters."

"Why tell me? I'm not the police. Let them know," Jack replied uncertainly.

"That is not possible. Doing so could, in fact, spell disaster. If I tell you then you must not tell them either or she will certainly die."

The man was matter-of-fact about the information as though her death meant little to him.

"Are you trying to blackmail me?"

"Oh no, Dr. Sharp. I'm trying to save the girl. I want nothing in return. But by going to the police the wrong people will find out where she has gone and they will finish what they tried to do already. How do you think I know about your own problem?"

Jack said, "Are you saying the police are corrupt?"

"Let's just say they have been compromised."

Jack was thinking hard now trying to decide what he should do. Should he try to reach the police on his cell and get them to somehow trace this call? That would be ridiculous. They could not get there in time. Should he mistrust the police as this caller said? They hadn't been all that kind to him, but he had assumed that they were just doing their job.

"How do I know you will tell me the truth?" asked Jack, stalling for time to think.

"You don't. No more delays. Do you want the information or will you let the young lady die?"

Jack thought back to the body of the young woman lying in the ditch. He didn't want to be responsible for another death if he had the power to prevent it. He stroked his forehead noting the beads of sweat beginning to form there. "What do I need to do?" he asked making up his mind.

"You need to warn her and get her to a safe place," was the answer from this mystery man.

"If you know where she is, why can't you just call her and tell her to leave?" Jack was feeling anxiety rise in his stomach.

"You don't understand your adversary's capabilities. Phones are risky. I'm taking my own life in my hands by calling you, but you are an outlier. No one else will think of you and you will have at least a few hours' head start if you move." The volume of the voice had risen slightly as if by speaking louder Jack would act more swiftly.

Jack made a decision, "All right. How do I find her? Can't I just call her?" He flicked on the light and found a pen and a note pad.

At the other end of the connection James smiled slightly. His plan to help the girl and remain safe was working. "Here's her cell phone number, but she has kept it off. I doubt you will be able to reach it." Next he spoke succinctly and revealed the location where he thought Dr. Sharp could find the girl. He knew he could still be wrong, but being certain would necessitate sending someone else to check. If Dr. Sharp found the farmhouse and there was no one there he would be no worse for it.

Locating the farmhouse where Alicia was staying had been a feat of both ingenuity and a little luck. He had been able to find the exact Global Positioning System coordinates of the phone called by Alicia. That, of course, didn't mean Alicia would go there. However, he had called in a favor from a satellite mapping company. This favor had cleared his account with that man because having a satellite directed to any location took special clearance and an excellent reason. Thankfully one satellite was "viewing" an area not far from Iowa. He had gotten some unusually high quality pictures and sent them to James. In the photos a car could be seen parked in the yard behind the barn. A little digging had proven that to be the same model as Alicia's car. If the photo had been taken at any other time the car could easily have been missed or moved, but it indicated that she had probably been at that spot on Monday. He was now only guessing that she was still there. James would tell Antony about the girl's cell phone calls, but would not mention the car or the exact location. The Leader would have to do his own recognizance. That should give Dr. Sharp sufficient time to get the girl out.

Once he had imparted the information James said, "Good luck, Dr. Sharp. Save the girl." He then hung up without waiting for a response.

Jack sat staring at the receiver. The call was over and now he was stunned at what he had just agreed to do. *I should just call Detective Sweate.* His thoughts were confused. The caller had said some of the police might be working against the girl. His gut feelings also told him that this could be true. How had the caller known of his association with the case? Maybe there really was a "mole" in the police department? What was there to lose? He was on a leave of absence from work and the drive to northern Iowa would only take half a day.

Jack stepped out of bed and went into action.

"If I'm going to do this, I'll do it right," he said aloud as he approached the shower.

****

Justin was trying to call Dr. Sharp, but the line was busy. He tried the cell and got voicemail. On the third try of the house phone he heard the click and whir of an answering machine. He checked his watch and saw that it was only six AM. Was Dr. Sharp just avoiding phone calls? A new dread had crept into his thoughts.

What if the doctor was a new victim?

****

Once dressed, Jack hesitated. He looked at the picture hanging over his bed and thought briefly. Shaking his head he moved to the wall and reached behind the photo. It appeared to be covering an electrical panel, but by pressing a small catch the photo and a section of the wall swung away. Neither the police, nor the jogger had identified this secret panel and he had not been inclined to point it out to them. He immediately began turning the dial of a small wall safe hidden there.

The safe held only a few objects. There was a small jewelry case and several envelopes, but at the back he found what he had gone to the safe for. The safe held a 9mm Beretta semi-automatic

319

pistol and two fully loaded magazines. He picked them up and checked the weapon as he had been trained. It was in excellent condition as he regularly cleaned it. He was proficient in its use and comfortable with its heft, but he had only fired it at a range. He had not needed a weapon for many years. He also withdrew one envelope and quickly wrote Sam's address on the front. It contained changes he had recently made to his will.

During his years in the military he had been taught how to use many different weapons, but as a physician his responsibility was to defend his patients' lives first and then his own. He was never supposed to be in an offensive position as this would have violated his Geneva Convention status. As a "doc" in Special Forces, there were a lot of gray areas when it came to the rules and he had been in more than one firefight.

Jack had a permit to carry and conceal the weapon and practiced on the firing range regularly. Nevertheless, he still hoped he would never need it.

He descended the stairs and entered the kitchen. He ate a hasty breakfast then noticed the light blinking on his answering machine. He rinsed his dishes and pushed the "play" button on the phone as he began assembling a few items for food on the road.

The message played, "Dr. Sharp, this is Detective Samuelson. I really need to talk to you about some new information. Could we get together today? I don't need you to come down to the station. We could talk at your home. I'll tell you what. I'll head over there this morning and we can talk before the day gets too far along. I'll see you soon."

"Great!" Jack said aloud, "Just what I need." He finished making a sandwich and was packing up a cooler when the doorbell rang. He noticed the Beretta on his table, quickly slipped it into a desk drawer, and then walked to the front door.

Justin was standing outside waiting patiently. When Jack had opened up he said, "Hello Dr. Sharp. I hope I'm not intruding. I really needed to talk and was hoping we could just do it here. Is that okay?"

Jack was incredulous, "I can't believe you people. You just left me a message. Couldn't you wait for my answer?"

Justin smiled, "You didn't answer the phone so I wasn't even sure you were here, and I confess, I was a little worried."

"Worried? About what?"

"You know. With two people already murdered and the attack on us the other day, I was just a little concerned that something could have happened to you."

With that Jack became incensed. "Do you expect me to believe that you would consider me a suspect one day and a victim the next?"

Justin put up his hands in surrender. "Okay. You've got a point, but I am glad you're ok."

Calming down a bit, but anxious to get going Jack replied, "I was probably in the shower when you called."

"I see." Justin began to step into the house even though Jack had not actually invited him in.

Jack stood aside and shook his head, "Please come in," came out somewhat sarcastically. "I am in a bit of a hurry, though. What is this about?"

Justin went into the living room and sat down. Jack was surprised at this young detective's boldness. Until now he had thought him more a "geek" than a detective.

"Dr. Sharp, we have been talking to the CIA."

The revelation stunned Jack. He stood gaping at the police detective. "What?"

"I'll be frank with you Doctor. We know some things about your time in Zaire. We were concerned about your involvement with diamonds and how that might relate to this case."

"Diamonds?" came Jack's bitter response. "I'm sick of diamonds. I have hated them for years. Talk to me about lives. Ask me about burned villages and dead friends. That is what the lust for diamonds leads to."

Justin paused, "Tell me about it."

"I don't have time."

"Why? What are you hurrying to do?" Justin asked sincerely.

Jack was perplexed. He had a task to accomplish, but felt impotent to carry it out and now he wanted to know what information this young detective had been given about his past. Jack didn't know whether to trust him or just walk out and drive to Iowa. He did some mental gymnastics in the next few seconds as he stood mute and decided that Justin was not likely to be the turn-coat mentioned by the caller. He was too wet behind the ears, but would he believe Jack that one existed?

Jack stole a glance at his watch and made a decision.

"All right. I trust *you*, but you have to keep this to yourself."

"I can't promise that. I'm with the police department."

"I can just leave unless you plan to arrest me," replied Jack.

Now Justin had to think quickly. "Okay. I won't say anything for now unless it implicates you in one of the murders."

Jack smiled malevolently, "If I were a murderer you would be in big trouble right now. But I'm not." He picked the same photo album which he had shown to Sam earlier that week and motioned for Justin to sit. "You tell me what you know then I'll talk to you."

Jack let Justin browse the photos, but did not speak as Justin related the CIA's information.

"That's pretty accurate. Here's the rest of the story." Jack quickly told of his involvement with the mission in Bobito and of his relationship to the young woman, Sharon. He did not break down emotionally this time as he told Justin about how they had been betrayed and the abduction and assumed death of Sharon.

"That was all for diamonds. But there were hundreds maybe thousands of stones, not one big one. It has nothing to do with your case now."

"Maybe not," said Justin calmly. "Yet there is certainly more to it than just the theft of a single stone. Two people have died and we believe there is someone involved in our own department."

This last revelation surprised Jack. "You too?"

"What do you mean?" It was now Justin's turn to be surprised.

Jack sighed. "Now you have to keep your side of the deal." He told Justin about the earlier phone call.

"Good grief!" Justin exclaimed, "You can't do this alone."

"You promised," said Jack. "If you talk to anyone at the department it could get leaked to whoever is killing these people. Give me half a day. Let me get this girl and get away from the place she where she is holed up." Jack stood and moved to the kitchen. He didn't care now if the detective saw his weapon. He retrieved it from the drawer and picked up the cooler. "I have to go or there won't be time to get there."

"You need some kind of back-up."

"Look. It may have been stupid of me to trust you but I do. You need to trust that I know something of what I'm doing. They, whoever 'they' are, have found this girl and she isn't safe right now. I don't know how I'm going to keep her safe, but the fewer people who know about me the better," Jack was fired up. He locked the front door. Justin followed him into the garage like a puppy following its owner.

Jack turned. "Don't send anyone after me and don't try to call. I'll turn my phone off. If I need help I'll call you and only you. Understood?"

Justin stood back as Jack closed his car door. "Okay, Doc. I guess there's not much I can do and if I try to stop you it just makes it worse for Alicia. Maybe I can figure out a safe place to go."

"All right. I may call if I need one." He backed out of his garage and Justin made his way to his own car.

As Justin watched the doctor's car turn the corner he shook his head and said out loud, "What am I doing?"

****

Before he turned off his cell Jack opened it and pressed speed – dial for the hospital. "I would like to speak to Kathy Sanders please," he said when the phone was answered. "Yes, I'll wait." He looked at his watch and realized it was still very early. He hoped that she was awake.

"Hello?" came her sweet voice without a trace of sleepiness.

"Kathy, I have a ... family emergency I have to look into. I'll need to take a short trip so I won't be in to see you today and maybe not tomorrow either. I'm sorry." He cringed at having to lie to Kathy.

Kathy's disappointed voice came back, "I'm going home later today." Then, after a pause, "It must be important. When will you be back?"

"I should be back for sure by Saturday. I'll try to wrap everything up as quickly as possible. Kathy I'm sorry," he repeated.

"You said that," she replied. He couldn't tell whether she was a little annoyed or a little disappointed. He hoped it was the latter.

She then added, "I suppose I will have to get used to your rushing off to one crisis or another." Now Jack could almost see her half smile as she spoke. "You just get back as soon as you can. And Jack..."

"Yes?"

"I love you."

Jack's breath went out of him. He hadn't heard those words for a long time. In fact, Sharon had been the last one who had spoken them in his ear. He managed to croak back, "I love you too." Then he gently laid the receiver down turning off the phone as he pondered the events of the very early day.

****

James breathlessly entered his condominium in downtown Chicago. He had nearly run the block from the "el" station to the noisy pharmacy, where he had found the pay phone which he had used to call Dr. Sharp. He quickly assembled the documents he had used to establish the girl's location. James doubted that the Leader would know about his map company connection but he didn't want any of the evidence to be in his possession in case he had a "surprise" visit from the Leader.

He grasped the papers and opened the glass doors on his fireplace. He had seldom used this feature of his townhome, but it served this purpose well. Shredding was fairly effective, but burning completely destroyed the "evidence." Leaning forward he opened the flue and next ignited the corner of the large format photograph. Flames leapt up from the small pile of papers and in a short time there was nothing but ash. He stirred them around to reduce any tell-tale sign of what had been done. Laying some kindling on the grate he lit that as well. Once he had an adequate flame he placed a few small split logs on the burning wood. The ashes and heat from the additional fire would completely erase all signs of the documents.

James again fingered his cell phone. He plugged in his encryption device and hit speed dial. He heard the familiar whir of the encrytor then voice of Antony was on the line, "Yes?"

"I believe I have narrowed down the location where the girl may have gone," he said evenly.

"Narrowed to what kind of distance?" came the icy question.

"I believe she is somewhere east of Mason City, Iowa. Probably within twenty miles."

"Is that the best you've got? It could still take days to find her." Antony was impatient and irritable.

"Sir, please let me finish," he tried to sound confident, but was beginning to feel his resolve wane. "We tracked a call to her cell from a spot that appears to be a convenience store on highway 122 east of Mason City, the 'Stop 'n' Go' shop. We also know she went east from there because while the phone was still on we could find signals from the next cell tower to the east. It never went further east and it was stopped for a while in one area before the signal disappeared. I can send my agent to canvas the area to see if she has been seen."

"No! I'll take care of it," Antony paused. "Wait. It might be good to have your agent in the area, though. I might need to reach her."

James was stunned that the Leader knew that his agent was a woman. "Do you know my agent?"

"Don't interrupt! I have my own resources too. In the mean time if you get any more precise location call me immediately. Understood?" Antony had not questioned James' inability to locate the girl's car.

"Yes sir. I'll keep working on it, but without a cell phone signal it won't be easy."

Antony was now smiling. "I have her," he thought to himself. Aloud he said, "She was careless once maybe she'll be careless again. I'll see you next week as planned." The call ended abruptly. Antony typically kept his phone conversations short, despite encryption, to lessen his exposure to tracking and bugs.

James stared straight ahead. He unplugged his equipment. There was nothing else he could do without significantly increasing his risk. He hoped he had delayed Antony somewhat. Nevertheless, he had no doubt that the Leader could find the girl now without further assistance. It might still take him a few days. If his calculations were correct, and the doctor had gotten moving, he should be able to get there well ahead of Antony. He hoped he had not underestimated the Leader for his and the doctor's sakes.

45

Alicia and Missy had coffee together as they prepared to begin another day's chores. The barn work was done and now Missy wanted to put the finishing touches on her vegetable bed.

Alicia sat sipping her hot brew as Missy told a funny story she had read in the Reader's Digest. Alicia's eyes were bright and she felt more relaxed than she had for a long time. She said, "Earning a living is necessary, but I am beginning to really enjoy being on a farm."

"It'll grow on you. We oughta start thinking about the future for you."

"I don't know what to do," said Alicia. "I like it here, but I could be putting you in danger."

"Nonsense, girl. No one knows you're here. How could they? No, we're okay for now, but you can't stay cooped up here forever." Missy rose to refill her own cup. "More?"

"No thank you. You're right, but I'm just nervous." She smiled pleasantly up at Missy, "Things are too good."

"That's never true. God can make things good if He wants to. Enjoy it, don't be afraid. Besides, Roy has been keeping an eye out and he has a few friends in town who can let us know if anyone comes snoopin' around."

Alicia was surprised. "You aren't perfectly sure we're safe are you?"

"Say I'm cautious. He won't talk to the sheriff unless it's really necessary, but we can get help pretty fast if we need it. Folks around here help each other out without askin' too many questions."

Just then Roy walked into the mudroom in the back of the house. "Missy, you won't be able to do much in the garden. It's starting to git real wet out there. We could do some work on the harrow. I got two new disks to mount and I could show Alicia, here, how to grease the fittings then we can put 'er away for the winter."

Missy glanced out the window and saw that the slate gray skies had begun to lower and a fine mist was driven by an easterly

327

breeze. Moisture coated the dry vegetation in the front yard and fog was developing at the bottom of the pane of glass.

"Storm's aheadin' here from the Dakotas. We'll see snow tonight." Roy was matter-of-fact in his pronouncement and Alicia wondered if he had some special knowledge or if he had watched the weather channel.

"Okay," said Missy lightly, "Let's get to it."

Alicia picked up a pair of worn leather gloves and exited the kitchen with Roy and Missy. Her heart was light despite the weather prediction. They walked out into the yard and Alicia could tell that the weather had changed significantly. It felt as if the drizzle could change over to freezing rain or snow. She could see her breath and felt the penetrating cold of the weather even through her top coat.

Inside the large metal building Alicia took note of the imposing machines. She had heard of farmers being injured by power take-offs and combine accidents. Up close, even when shut down, these monstrous vehicles seemed menacing. This was the first time she had been so near to them. Several had the familiar green and yellow coloring, but there was a bright red tractor parked next to the outer door. Attached to its rear hitch system was a trailer which appeared to be folded up in the middle. Roy referred to this as the harrow. Stacked vertically and spaced evenly was a row of metal disks that looked like so many large Frisbees. Alicia could see, though, that they were shiny and had been keenly sharpened. In the center of the right "wing" of this was a gap where Roy began loosening some bolts and fittings. He glanced over his shoulder and saw that Alicia had nothing to do. Seeing her pretty face he thought twice about getting her too messed up with a grease gun and said, "Girl why don't you grab that broom over there and sweep out the building?"

"Okay," she answered. She found the wide push broom, but scanning the building she was distressed by the sheer magnitude of the task. Determined not to complain, however, she headed for one corner without a word. She would work her way to the center of the large front overhead door where she could sweep any debris out to the yard.

Alicia found the work satisfying despite the monotony. There was plenty of dirt and field debris to sweep up. As she moved along, seeing one area swept clean left her feeling useful. Every so often she heard a bang or a clink from where Roy and Missy were working, but she was mainly alone with her thoughts.

She tried to think through what she should do to stay safe, but she couldn't think of anything better than remaining exactly where she was. All her trouble would surely blow over and she would be able to return to her former life. Yet she was beginning to wonder if she really wanted to go back to it. This place, this farm, was such a peaceful haven that going anywhere else seemed foolhardy. Missy and Roy had accepted her without hesitation and without prejudice. They did not expect any more from her than they did from themselves.

Soon the father and daughter were doing something under the hood of the combine and Alicia kept moving dirt toward the huge overhead door. Her plan was to make one big pile then open the door to push it all out at once. She had seen the two buttons marked "up" and "down" along the side wall. Trying to be self-sufficient, she didn't ask Roy if he had a different recommendation and she reached for the top, green, button.

****

Justin muttered to himself as he ascended the steps to his office level. "How am I going to explain this one?" He furtively glanced around the, all but deserted, room as he slipped by each desk. Justin had nearly maneuvered past her door when he heard Rebecca's voice.

"Justin?"

He stopped dead in his tracks and tried not to show his nervousness.

"Yes? Oh, hi Rebecca."

Rebecca's eyebrows went up. Justin seemed oddly nervous this morning. "In to do some catch-up?" At this he nodded and she continued, "Did you get hold of Doctor Sharp this morning?"

Now was the moment of truth. Should he lie? "I got his voice mail when I called... I'll get in touch with him later." There, he had skirted the actual truth and had not, in fact, lied.

She eyed him warily, "Are you okay?"

"Yeah. Just not enough sleep these days"

Rebecca half-turned toward her door then added, "Well, why don't we go over things once more sometime before you head back out?" She smiled briefly at him and returned to her office without another word.

Justin felt sweat forming on his forehead and his hands felt oddly clammy. Had she caught that? *I'm no good at lying.* He reached the safety of his desk and now wondered why he had even come in. Knowing he would run the risk of having to talk to Rebecca he had thought working on paperwork would distract him from the fear that he was breaking several rules, and possibly the law, by not reporting what Dr. Sharp was doing.

Rebecca can't be the leak. She says it could be the ADA. Is that a dodge to get my eyes off her? What do I really know about anyone in this department? But if I don't tell her and she finds out she might think it's me!

The last thought shook him. He needed at least one ally in this department. Rebecca had treated him, if not like an equal, at least without condescension. They had worked well together so far and he wanted to move up the promotion ladder. He would need her support for that. Justin put his head in his hands. *How could police work be so stressful?* He put his hands down and pushed himself back. After a moment he stood, having made up his mind, and headed back toward Rebecca's office.

Rebecca was busily scribbling notes on a pad when Justin appeared at the door. It was a few moments before she noticed his presence then she looked up, "Justin? I thought you had work to do?" She noted the look of concern on his face and tilted her own to one side and leaned back in her chair. "You have something to tell me." It was more a statement than a question.

Justin bit his lower lip looking like a schoolboy caught writing graffiti on the bathroom wall. He forced himself to look directly into Rebecca's eyes.

"I did talk to Dr. Sharp this morning. He asked me not to mention it yet because he is afraid of a leak in our department and that we would stop him."

Rebecca wasn't immediately angry. Curiousity won out, but she could feel her insides begin to roil. In almost a whisper she said, "You said you got his voicemail."

"Yes. I did get the voicemail, but then I went to his house."

An expletive escaped her lips and her eyes flashed. With a voice full of venom she spat,

"Close the door! I can't believe this."

Rebecca wanted to yell and berate this young man, but reined in her anger in order to avoid attracting too much attention. She stood and began her usual pacing. Her anger cooled slightly and she stopped after a moment and stared at Justin. "We'll discuss that little problem later. You will tell me everything he said." It came out as almost a whisper and Justin felt the hairs on the back of his neck stand up.

He gulped involuntarily and began, "Okay, but not here." He involuntarily looked around the office then wrote on a pad of paper, "He knows that someone in our department is passing information to someone else."

Despite her anger at Justin, Rebecca caught the caution and quickly adapted to the situation. She remained seething inside, but put on a calm exterior. "Let's go," she said without taking her eyes off Justin.

Justin led the way out of the building without speaking another word to Rebecca. They got to his car and once in, with the doors closed, Rebecca glared at him and said, "You had better tell me everything or you'll be working parking meters in North Dakota."

Justin understood the threat and now almost regretted going to her. Nevertheless, he also knew that it was better to just get it over with. He would have had to let her in on the information eventually. He had never seen her filled with so much anger and he was genuinely fearful.

"Look, I went along with him because he is taking a risk himself."

"I don't care about his risk. What did he tell you?" Her face was not as tense as he had seen it earlier, but he didn't hesitate further.

"The doctor thinks there is a connection in Chicago but isn't sure. He wanted me to not tell anyone because he said that he trusted me."

"Did you somehow think *I* was the leak?" came Rebecca's angry rejoinder.

"No... of course not. I was afraid someone else might be, though, and the more people who know something ... "

"I can't believe this," she repeated, rolling her eyes toward the ceiling of the car. "All right, look, I'm no mole and I am your superior. You tell me and we decide this stuff together, got it? Now spill it all."

"I'm sorry ... "

"Now!"

Justin had already heard her anger, but was still startled by the forcefulness of her speech. As if reciting his lessons he drove out of the parking lot and explained to her about the doctor's early morning phone call and what he had said he planned to do.

Rebecca ran her hand through her hair, clearly agitated. She stared out her window not talking at all. When Justin had finished his explanation she placed both hands on the dashboard and hissed, "I'm glad you have such faith in this doctor because if he is playing you we may have another death on our hands. Now he's out of town and you don't know where he is."

"He should be near Des Moines, by now."

"If he told you the truth."

Now Justin's face flushed. "I have to start trusting someone in this case. He seemed a good choice. He's been a doctor, trusted by patients, in this community for twenty years. If what he has said *is* true he is as much a victim as those who were killed. When will you trust me or my judgment?"

Rebecca was taken aback by his vehemence. Her own anger faltered and she straightened, remaining mute.

Justin continued, "If I screwed up it's too late. I want to follow through with this. If he doesn't call I'll go to Chief Barton myself. He'll probably want my badge."

Rebecca's silence continued as she pondered the new information. She wanted to keep up her tirade, but she was tired. She realized her anger wasn't all directed toward Justin. The case was frustrating because she felt always about two steps behind. Here, at last, was a chance to be up front, if Justin was right.

"We still don't have any idea who is pulling the strings do we?" she asked.

Justin relief in his voice, said, "I'd hoped you would wonder about that. I have been working on that since I found out where Connie, the deceased, worked." He turned into a parking lot and found a spot to park. "Come in with me and I'll show you what I've found."

Rebecca noticed that they had parked near a local coffee shop. "Coffee?"

They have free Wi Fi here."

"Wi ... ? Oh I remember. I barely know how to use a mouse."

"A lot of coffee shops have it." He opened the door for her and motioned her to a booth. "Do you want a latte?"

Now more curious than angry, Rebecca was allowing Justin to lead for now.

"No, just black coffee."

Justin ordered a grandé skinny vanilla mocha latté sans whipped cream for himself and a large black coffee for his partner.

Setting their cups on the table Justin took out his notebook computer. He sat side-by-side with Rebecca so she could see the screen too. He logged onto the internet and found a page to show her.

"The business where Connie worked is called "Matchless Enterprises." The CEO is a man named James Rizzo, but I couldn't find the name of the actual owner. I looked at him and this business dozens of ways. I tracked their profits and what they make..."

"What do they do?" Rebecca interjected.

"They manufacture precision lathed parts for other companies and the military. They have plants in Des Moines, St. Paul, and Fort Worth. They aren't too big, but their profit margin is significant. Like I said I looked at their business several ways. I even looked at photos of their building. I stumbled on something when I zoomed in with a satellite picture..."

"Satellite? And where did you get permission to use a satellite?"

Justin laughed out loud. "You really need to learn about this stuff. I just used 'maps' on the browser." He changed the screen and showed her how easily he could zoom in on their own building.

"Amazing! You can do that for free?"

"Yes, though the photo is as much as six months to a year old. Anyway when I looked at his building, like this," with a few more keystrokes he changed the satellite view. "Notice the unique appearance of the roof of his building."

Rebecca could see that most buildings had air handlers or small sheds with elevator equipment on their top floor. The building Justin was showing was different. For one thing the roof was painted a brilliant white and in the very center was a large shining disc.

"Do you see what I mean?"

Rebecca nodded.

"Now if I back out just a little..." He zoomed out slightly.

Rebecca exclaimed, "There are three more just like it!"

"Bingo! That's what I was trying to tell you. Notice the symmetry of the buildings in where they are located?"

"So tell me you already know who owns the other three buildings." Rebecca said now very impressed with her younger partner.

"Well, no. I still don't know the owner or owners, but it is very interesting that all four buildings look alike. Unfortunately they all are different kinds of businesses and there doesn't seem to be any other connection. But do you know what those big round things on top of the buildings are?"

"What?"

"They are large plexiglass representations of diamonds."

"Diamonds? The connection to our case?"

"Maybe. I don't know if I can get much more information about the companies. I didn't actually follow the rules to get some of this."

"Justin. What am I going to do with you?"

"I had to hack in to find employee names, but I haven't broken in since then. I found out the names of the four companies and their CEO's," said Justin.

Rebecca was pensive, "If we want to pursue connections

between these companies it will take warrants and we don't really have probable cause yet. I doubt we have enough to get warrants for all four companies. Do you have photos of the CEO's?"

"Those are on their public websites."

"Okay can you put together a file of "public" information on each of the companies and print it out?" Rebecca had calmed considerably and was now in planning mode. "I'm not sure what we can do with it yet, but I want everything I can get if the opportunity presents itself to act."

Justin reached and picked up his case. He removed four file folders and laid them in front of Rebecca. "I didn't know what else to do either. It doesn't help us solve the murders."

Rebecca leaned back now smiling, "No. Not yet. Good work, but don't think you're of the hook. I'm still unhappy with your antics this morning." She glanced over the files, "My gut says that the diamonds on those buildings and the diamond from our victim are not just a coincidence."

"Funny. My gut said the same thing."

****

Antony, dressed in untypical casual garb, ducked his head as he approached his helicopter, with its rotors still spinning menacingly above. The noise was deafening even with the spongy hearing protectors. Once on board he donned noise-reducing headphones which cut the roar to a gentle hum.

A slightly tinny voice crackled over the headset, "Sir, are you ready to take off?" He responded with a thumbs-up gesture and the assistant slid the side door closed. In moments they were rising then banking as they passed over the suburbs of Chicago.

Antony glanced down unable to quench the feeling of pride he felt as he viewed his four buildings. *He* had built those businesses with the money he had acquired with his own hands. *Some of it even legally.* For some reason his last thought seemed outrageously funny and he began laughing.

Overhearing the laughter on his headset the pilot asked, "Is everything all right, sir?"

Smiling he answered, "Fine. Just get me to Des Moines quickly."

"Yes sir," came the response. The nose of the helicopter dipped slightly and as they climbed they also picked up horizontal speed. Antony could see familiar areas of suburban Chicago pass beneath them and then wisps of haze intervened. Suddenly all was gray around them as they passed into the cloud layer. He sat back trying to be patient already planning his next steps. He preferred to take the girl alone, but first he had to find out exactly where she had holed up. Since learning about the general location of her phone he had predicted that she had found a family who had taken her in. James' agent, who was also his agent, was already searching for someone who might have seen her.

Just then the pilot's metallic voice came over his headset again.

"Sir, there is a call being patched through for you on COM 2. Just press that button on the panel next to you."

Antony turned his head and saw the panel with several labeled buttons. He jabbed the one that was marked "COM 2" and stated, "Yes?"

A pleasant female voice came on the line.

"Antony, are you coming this way?"

His own pleasure showed on his face though the pilot was too busy concentrating on his flying to notice.

"Hello, dear. How nice to talk to you. When will I see you?"

"Well if you'd get yourself up here, it should be pretty soon."

"What have you found?"

"She stopped at a minimart Monday and the attendant saw her go back the way she came."

"He's sure it was her?"

"He's sure. He said he couldn't forget that pretty face and he won't forget mine soon after the tip I gave him. I'm driving toward a little town ahead to see if anyone there knows if she is staying in the area. How are you getting here?"

"I've got a car waiting in Des Moines. How long from there?"

"About an hour-and-a-half. You could just go with me."

"No! We can't be seen together yet. Besides I want to do this myself. Once you've found her I'll take care of everything else.

Why don't you plan to meet me at the suite in Des Moines? You can go with me to the deal. I can't wait to see James' face when he realizes who you really are."

That brought laughter from the woman on the other end. "He thought he was getting a free lance hit man, or woman. That will be priceless. All right. Here's that little town now, so I'll call you later."

"Okay." He severed the connection and sat back, eyes closed, for the remainder of his flight.

****

Jack had passed a town where the water tower had a large smiley face. Despite himself he had smiled in return. He wondered if that wasn't the effect the townsfolk had wanted. Every time you thought of their town's name you would think about that water tower and smile. Not a bad piece of advertising.

He was coming upon the outskirts of Des Moines and realized he didn't even know what to say to the girl. What if she didn't believe him or thought he was one of the bad guys? He gave some thought to how he would present himself, not wanting to mention the police, in case she was wary of them. He decided just to tell her the truth and hope she would believe him. If she did not he couldn't force her to go with him. Then he would have to call Justin.

As he thought about his conversation with the detective he felt his phone vibrate. Glancing at the screen he saw the now familiar number of the police station. With an exasperated expulsion of air, realizing that he had forgotten to turn it completely off, he said, "Great!" and flipped open the phone. "Hello?"

"Dr. Sharp." The voice was female and he recognized it instantly as being that of Detective Sweate.

"What do you want?" he said with irritation.

"Please don't hang up. I'm not trying to track you, but I know what you are doing."

"Justin!"

"I made him tell me. Look, I can't stop you and I won't call the local sheriff."

"How kind of you."

"I believe you. Okay? Truce? I want to help and I need your cooperation," her voice was almost pleading.

"I told Justin I would find a safe place for her."

"I know, but we still need information from her that is critical for this case. If you hide her away, we may not be able to solve it."

"No, but she'll still be alive. If I tell you where she's going to be what guarantee will there be that she'll stay alive?"

"Look..."

"No. You look!" Jack was heating up. "I am sticking my neck out, but I know that I'm a good guy. I actually believe that Justin and probably you are on the right side too, but who else in your department can you trust? Someone's dirty and I don't want to risk it. I'm getting off now and turning off my phone. Don't try to call again."

He didn't wait for an answer and shut down the phone. He had noticed that the battery was low. As he began the northward leg of his journey he rummaged through his glove compartment to find his phone charger. With one hand on the phone and one on the steering wheel and traffic building up he at last managed to get the phone plugged in. Then, eying his map, he accelerated by a few miles per hour impatient to reach his destination.

There was a haze in the dark gray clouds that held an ominous appearance and he kicked himself for not checking on the weather. He didn't know what was coming. It was pretty early in the fall for a big snowstorm, but even freezing rain or ice would complicate matters. He had an idea for a safe house for Alicia, but first he had to convince her that it was safe for her to go with him. What could he say that would give her confidence in him and allow her to trust him?

46

Delia liked the way she looked in heels. In her silky blue dress she knew she was overdressed for the little town she was entering, but she was beyond caring at the moment. She didn't plan to be there long and if anyone noticed her, so what? She and Antony would be out of the country in a few days. She had eluded capture so far and felt confident that she had nothing to fear in this backwater town in Iowa. What she did need was information. Knowing that, in small towns, everyone knew everyone else's business she figured her best chance would be to talk to someone there. She could be friendly if it helped or use other methods of persuasion if needed.

She passed a café with a crooked neon sign hanging over the door, bright in the afternoon gloom. She made a pass through town spotting a hardware store and a variety shop and pharmacy. She almost missed it the first time but out of the corner of her eye she saw a dress shop. It was a small 'hole-in-the-wall' building, but just what she wanted.

Making a U-turn in the middle of the wide lane, she pulled into an empty parking space. A sheriff's deputy's car parked at the café but she was not greatly worried. He was nowhere in sight and she had more firepower available to her than he did, if it came to that.

Delia's confidence in her abilities did not prevent her presence from being noted. Though the nonobservant deputy was busy sipping coffee and having a smoke in the corner of the little café, its owner, Matthew Johannsen, was very alert. He had taken note of the Mercedes sedan as it cruised down the street and was intrigued by the woman who got out of the car.

She was certainly dressed inappropriately for the weather and Johannsen could see that she was clearly out of place in this town.

****

Alicia was flabbergasted. She had worked all morning to sweep up the detritus of the summer and had piled it neatly near the massive overhead door at the front of the building. How could she have known that as soon as she opened the door the wind would undo much of her labor? At first Missy and Roy had been no help. They had practically fallen over laughing at her distress.

Roy had rubbed it in, "Some things ya' gotta learn the hard way."

Then they had both found brooms to aid her in cleaning things up and completing the task. This time they swept the conglomeration of dirt, leaves, bits of wood and sawdust out a side door away from the wind. She had thought she was getting the hang of working on a farm. She had no idea how much work it took just to keep things in order.

They were leaning on their brooms beside the door about to brave their way through the wind and mist when, above the noise, they were able to hear a car engine in the yard.

At first they all stood in indecision, then Roy, thinking quickly, whispered, "Ah don't know who this is. You go hide up there in the combine. We'll see who's in that car and come back if it's okay. Don't leave and don't come up to the house 'till we get you."

Alicia nodded as Missy and Roy looked hard at each other. She scrambled away to the big green and yellow monster. She had watched Roy climb all over it so she knew how to enter the cab. This she did with a gymnast's agility and sat wondering what would happen next. She craned her neck to get a view of the door without making herself visible, but both Missy and Roy had moved outside and closed the door. They had left the mercury vapor lights on inside, where they cast their harsh, sterile, bluish light across the chasm-like interior of the building. It was suddenly deathly quiet and she was unnerved by the aloneness she felt. Alicia could not hear the storm from her perch and there was no movement around her and she realized that she had not been alone very often since the moment Roy had shown up and "rescued" her. She didn't know what to do, but her thoughts went back to the Sunday morning sermon when the pastor had said,

"You can pray to God about anything, anytime, anywhere. He always hears you."

She couldn't remember ever praying before, except "grace" at mealtime. Now her fear motivated her to bow her head.

"God. I don't know if you hear me or not. I haven't been very good, you know. Please help my friends and protect me here. Help me to not be afraid." She opened her eyes. Nothing around her had changed, but she felt less anxious. She felt less alone.

Out of the corner of her eye she sensed movement within the building, though she hadn't heard any other sound. The realization came to her then that the cab of this large machine was so well insulated that sound didn't enter in easily. *I hope they didn't see me!* She stole a glance over the back of the seat and saw Missy's tightly pinned hair moving between the vehicles. In a moment Missy's head popped up outside the combine door.

Opening it, Alicia nearly knocked Missy back to the ground. Close to tears, she hugged her. "I was getting scared. I didn't know what was going on. I even prayed to God. Is everything all right?"

Missy just stared, stunned by all that Alicia had said. Finally she smiled and said, "Hon, come on down. There's someone here to talk to you."

Fear suddenly showed in Alicia's eyes. "I thought..."

"I think its okay. You just stay with me. We'll go together."

Alicia, now uncertain at the turn of events, was mute. She had trusted Missy and Roy.

Who could know she was here?

47

"Where are you?" The reception was raspy with static, but she could understand the question.

"In a little town east of Mason City," she spoke leaning against her car. "How about you?"

He glanced at his atlas, "I'm a couple of hours away. You should have made arrangements for me to start in Mason City."

"I told you, getting a car there would have been a problem. Besides, I don't think there is a rush. I don't believe our quarry is planning to go anywhere."

"What do you mean?"

"The dress shop lady was very talkative. She let me know where this young lady is staying and that she's even been to church here. I think she's found a roost."

Antony smiled without answering. It sounded like this would be easier than he had thought. "How many people are at this place and where is it?"

"Antony, since you're so far away and I'm nearly there, why don't you just let me take care of it? You wouldn't get your hands dirty and I get to do what I do best." Delia said. "In fact, I think that's what I'll do. I'll meet you in Des Moines tonight."

"But my plan was..." Antony stammered.

"Darling, you know that my plans are always better. Ta ta for now."

She clicked off without waiting for a reply, removed her bluetooth headset from her ear and glanced down at the feet protruding from beneath the hanging clothes. She had been careful this time to just disable the woman, though she might suffer more than a headache from the blow she had received. There was no need to kill her even though she had seen Delia's face. In a few days they would be out of the country and free.

Delia stepped to the door, noting the increase in rain. She glanced back over her shoulder then turned to flip the sign in the door to "CLOSED." Clicking the light switch the room went dark and she stepped onto the sidewalk.

She knew that Antony would be furious, but he would realize the wisdom of her argument. She had never been suspected in any of the jobs she had performed. If she approached the occupants of farmhouse in the right way she would come across as a "woman in need." Antony, a lone male, on the other hand would raise suspicions as soon as he approached the place.

"*Especially in this weather*," she thought. It was getting nasty out there and the roads might start getting slick. What if he got in an accident?

Antony was apoplectic. No one else ever told him what to do, but *she* could. She had always had an almost hypnotic ability to get him to do her bidding. *I made her what she is.* He pounded his fist on the steering wheel. He could see that his trip to Iowa was a waste of time. *But I love her.* He knew that she was the one thing that in the world that he loved more than money. Antony glanced up noticing that the mist he had been driving in was now a rain ice mixture. He could hear the pinging sound as ice bounced off the car. The road was still only wet, but two more hours and going farther north could lead to pretty serious road conditions. He admitted to himself that Delia was probably right, yet he was still angry. He had made this trip for one purpose and was set on seeing it through. Antony had no doubt that she could pull this off, but this was an extremely important time and he desperately wanted his diamond back and this insolent girl taken care of.

Antony pulled the car over to the side of the road. He hit the steering wheel again, but this made him feel like a child who couldn't get his own way. She had said that she was taking care of this whether he liked it or not. He would talk to her about it when they, at last, met up, but for now he had no choice but to reluctantly let her finish what he had started.

****

Missy led Alicia back to the house. The light rain now had bits of stinging ice in it that seemed to drive straight through her warm clothing. She had gotten warm working in the out-building and her damp clothing now drew heat from her body. The wind had picked up so that when she tried to ask Missy what was going on it seemed to whip the words away from her lips. Missy didn't turn around, but took her hand and drew her to the house.

They entered the back door and mudroom and Missy stomped her boots to shake off the moisture. Alicia doffed her coat and decided her shoes were too tacky and muddy to wear into the house. She untied and removed them laying them along the floor board heater in the cramped room.

As she entered the kitchen she saw a man seated in a chair facing away from her and Roy in front of him silently wielding a double-barrel shotgun. It wasn't pointed at the man, but he had a dark look on his face that warned, "Don't mess with me!"

"What's going on?" Alicia asked innocently turning to Missy.

Missy smiled, "Hon, this feller says he's from your home town. He says you're in danger. I know he's right but I'm not sure I'd trust him."

The man stayed seated, but nearly strained his neck in order to get a look at Alicia. He had his hands up in front of him to placate the gun-toting farmer as he said, "Alicia Winters?"

Alicia clung to Missy as she spoke to Roy, "Do you need that gun?"

"I don't know, but considering the fix yore in, I figured it was a good idea."

"May I speak?" came the voice of the man seated.

"He says he's a doctor. Go ahead." He made a little move of the shotgun still without aiming at anyone.

Jack noticed that the safety was off and that this man meant business. He was a perfect body guard for this young woman. Perhaps his own visit was unnecessary. "I've come here because I believe the people you are running from either know you are here or will find out soon."

Alicia's hand went to her mouth. "How?"

"The same way I found you, by tracking your cell phone."

"But I've kept it turned off ... Oh! It was only on for a short time. I ... How... ?"

"I don't fully understand the technical part either, but one of the detectives is a whiz-kid at computers and he found you." He stretched the truth knowing that it would be harder to explain what had actually happened.

"Who are you, then? And why are you involved not the police?"

"My name is Jack Sharp. I'm a doctor in Lincoln, and I'm afraid it was I who found your friend's body."

Alicia gasped involuntarily and leaned closer to Missy. "You found her body?" Memories of her friend flooded her thoughts and she was nearly overwhelmed.

Jack leaned on the table and gently said, "Yes. I got mixed up in this whole business when I was just walking down the bike path. For a while I was even considered a suspect until the police figured out that it wasn't I who had killed her."

Roy, who had remained silent up to this point asked, "That still don't explain why yore here now." He stood, backing into the living room, a little less menacing. There he leaned against the couch awaiting the answer. He was not reluctant to point his weapon at this stranger but he had made no threatening moves so far.

Jack said, "Look, there might not be much time. We don't know who *is* involved or when they'll figure out where you are, but I am helping the police. Only two of them even know where I am. They got your fax and are being cautious not to tell others about it. They thought you would be more likely to trust me. They've kept it a secret because there appears to be a leak of information in that department." Jack knew that the police would never involve an ordinary citizen like this; he had come of his own volition.

Alicia asked, "Then why are you here?"

"To get you to a safer place."

"But this is a safe place. Roy and Missy are taking care of me," she almost whimpered. Almost in a childlike voice she said, "I like it here."

Nodding to Roy, Jack said, "I admit. They have you well in hand."

Missy spoke, "I recognize his face from the picture on TV."

Roy and Missy looked at each other and nodded. "You sound like the real McCoy mister." He laid the gun against the wall, scratched his head, and rubbed his arm. Again he glanced at Missy meaningfully. "If they know she's here there could be more trouble."

Missy scowled, "We don't even know who 'they' are, but I am inclined to believe him. They've murdered two people already." She waved her hand absently toward the doctor.

Jack was gratified that they were beginning to believe him, but he wasn't sure they trusted him yet. They stood silently looking at each other.

Finally Missy said, "Well, let's all sit down for a little bit and warm up. I'll make some coffee."

Jack was anxious, but was afraid to apply too much pressure. He shifted in his chair while Missy began to set up the coffee maker. He related to them what he knew of the investigation including how the medical examiner had found the diamond.

Alicia told him what she could about the killer and how the whole thing had begun. She had warmed up to him, but still seemed in no hurry to leave the house.

Inside Jack was feeling a sense of urgency. He stood again and went to the window. Outdoors the ambient light had dimmed, though it was only mid-afternoon. There were occasional snow flakes mixing in with the liquid rain. The formerly dry front yard appeared to have a crystalline sheen as the rain began to freeze on the cooler plant material. It was only a matter of time before the road would also begin to ice over. If they didn't leave soon they would not be able to leave tonight.

Roy joined him by the window. "I don't think ya oughta go anywhere right now. You won't have ta worry about assassins because you'll be up to your eyeballs in snow before too long."

Safety concerns were on Jack's mind as well. He hadn't counted on bad weather and was angry with himself for not considering it. He had worked out a plan to take Alicia to a lake cabin one of his friends owned in central Minnesota. They had been fishing there many times and Jack still had a key. "Do you have cable?" he asked Roy.

Roy's grin was brilliant, "We got satellite with two different dishes."

"Let's turn on the weather channel." They did so and Jack's demeanor fell as they watched the satellite image. A massive low pressure system was moving quickly across the Dakotas into Minnesota and Iowa. Nebraska would get little snow, but they could expect four to six inches and Minnesota was about to get dumped on. Jack shook his head and ran his hand through his hair. He could see that his plan would not work for tonight, at least.

"Look, Doc, nobody else will get out in this weather either, good or bad..."

His voice was interrupted by the sound of the phone ringing. They all stared at it as if it was somehow alive. Missy recovered first and picked up the receiver.

"Hello? What? Just now?" It was then that she looked at the answering machine and noticed that the message light was blinking.

Jack paid little attention to the phone call. He took advantage of the break to rise from his chair and ask Roy directions to the bathroom. Jack learned that he had to retreat back through the mudroom to find it. At least he didn't have to use an outdoor privy. Jack was pleasantly surprised to see a large remodeled space with two entrances. It was brightly colored and sported a shower and generous amounts of tile. Through the door he was able to make out a little of the phone conversation and became alarmed when Missy said, "Coming here? Do you really think so? Okay."

This was followed by the beep as Roy began listening to a message on the answering machine.

Jack could hear the recording, "Missy, Roy!" Though Jack was unfamiliar Missy knew that it was the voice of the café owner, Billy. His anxious voice came loudly over the speaker. "Some fancy woman was in here in town. She hurt my wife at the dress shop. I don't know if it's the trouble you were worried about, but she lit out of here like a bat out of..."

Jack didn't have time to process what he had just heard. Suddenly there was a cold draft of air from under the bathroom door. The next thing he heard nearly made him jump. A glass crashed to the floor and he heard a piercing scream. Not sure what was happening, but thinking quickly he dowsed the light in the bathroom and listened intently.

He heard another voice, obviously female. "Easy. I just want everyone to take it easy."

He next heard Roy's voice, "How d'ya expect us to take it easy with that cannon pointed at us?"

Jack noted that Roy had spoken a little loudly. Perhaps it was to help him understand the situation. Someone, a woman, had entered the room and apparently had a gun. He looked around the bathroom for some kind of weapon but, as expected, there was nothing at hand but toilet paper and towels.

He next heard, "So you're the little thief who took my property."

"I didn't take anything. If you mean the diamond, Connie did that, and you already killed her."

"And I'm going to kill you. But first I want that diamond."

"No!" came a shout from Missy. She must have stepped in front of Alicia because the woman spoke next.

"Get out of the way! Do you want to die first?"

Jack realized that there was not going to be a long conversation. This woman sounded very serious and she was there to kill Alicia. He doubted that she would leave anyone as a witness, though, apparently she was still unaware of his presence. He also realized that she must have come in some back way because they would have seen her arrive in the driveway, even from the kitchen. The wind shrieked outside and he could imagine that the storm was continuing to build.

Alicia spoke next. "I don't have your filthy diamond. You've already lost it and there's no way you can get it back."

Jack quietly slipped out of the bathroom through the second door. The room it opened into turned out to be a main floor bedroom. Again he searched for a weapon as quickly and quietly as possible. If he could surprise the woman maybe this could still end without bloodshed.

"What do you mean?" came an angry reply, than there was an explosion of noise from the kitchen and Jack feared the worst. The next thing he heard was Roy, gasping and groaning. "You shouldn't have tried for that shotgun. Throw it into the living room."

He heard a thump and another groan. If she was still talking to him, at least she hadn't killed Roy, but this woman meant business.

Alicia spoke up. "Why do you want to kill us?"

He had located nothing there, either under the bed or in the closet that would serve as any kind of protection or weapon. Standing near the door of the bedroom Jack could hear the conversation fairly clearly now.

There was scraping of chair legs against the kitchen floor. "All of you sit where I can see you. I don't mind telling you what's up. You won't be telling anyone else but first, where's the diamond?" The woman's voice dripped with anger and loathing. In his mind's eye Jack imagined an evil hag. He had not yet seen her and was afraid to peek around the door frame in case she happened to look that way. Then he spotted the shotgun lying on the living room floor, muzzle toward him. Roy had dropped it in front of the couch. The living room was in darkness. Only the kitchen lights were on.

Jack could see the woman's back toward him. She was well dressed with a long tan coat. She wasn't tall, but he glimpsed the gun in her hand and could tell that she knew how to handle it. He contemplated trying to sneak out the back door and go for help, but realized that was foolish. Even if he got away this woman would do her dirty work long before he could return. The shotgun was his only hope. He sent a quick prayer toward heaven knowing he could be there soon.

Jack gauged the distance to the shotgun. If he belly-crawled slowly enough he would be partially obscured by the back of the couch. The woman was facing away so, as long as he didn't make any noise, he could be successful.

Could he crawl ten feet just behind her without her hearing it? The storm outside provided some cover, but he would need a distraction at the last minute so he could stand up and take her by surprise.

"That diamond was special to me. That idiot James was keeping the entire set of especially large stones, but they belonged to me. I couldn't believe it when I found out one of them was stolen. Where is it?" she demanded.

Alicia didn't hesitate. "Connie had it all along. She swallowed it." Her reply was defiant without a hint of fear. "You killed her!"

The woman's confidence flagged. "Swallowed? She had it all along? I don't believe you. It was far too large a stone for someone to swallow. Is it in your purse?" She swore and must have pointed the gun because Jack heard a gasp from Alicia.

He thought fast and came up with a plan for a distraction. Timing was critical and he hoped it would all work. He went on his stomach on the floor and began his stealthy crawl to the gun. His Special Forces survival training came back to him unbidden and he could remember doing something similarly across dried grass and leaves. In those days he had made it within a foot of his instructor without being heard. Of course he had been younger and in much better shape.

He hoped he still had the skills.

"I can make it painful. Tell me the truth, where have you hidden it?"

Missy's shaky voice chimed in next. "She is telling the truth. She doesn't have it. Her friend coated the diamond in gum and swallowed it. You've got to believe her."

"Shut up!"

He heard Missy say defiantly, "You need to let me dress Roy's wound. He's going to pass out if it doesn't stop bleeding."

Jack could hear the sneer in the woman's voice. "It isn't going to matter. Do you want me to end his bleeding right now?"

"No! No. Please. We don't mean you any harm."

"I don't care. You've interfered. I can't let you live." Jack realized he had guessed correctly. This woman would not leave any witnesses.

"I got a little sloppy in Nebraska. That lawyer shouldn't have survived and, unfortunately I missed the doctor, but I got the ones I wanted."

Alicia kept her talking. "What kind of deal are you doing?"

Jack heard the woman shifting around in the kitchen. With his face to the floor he couldn't look up or see her. If she turned toward the living room she was sure to see him. He closed his eyes and prayed silently that she would not look at him.

He was inches away from the shotgun. He could now reach forward and touch it. It was time to put his distraction plan into effect.

"Oh, we are meeting with some Chinese business executives to arrange a little sale. We've been sitting on quite a few diamonds for years. No one is looking for them any more so we'll get millions. That's all. Millions. I might even retire." She laughed and Jack heard Missy scream again as the woman pointed her weapon.

Just then the telephone rang. There was sudden silence. It rang again.

This was it. As the woman began to give directions to Missy to answer the phone Jack reached over and gripped the barrel of the shotgun with his right hand. He heard the third ring as, ignoring a sudden pain in his knee, he leapt to his feet hoping his sense of direction was good. He spotted the woman as she began to turn her head aware now of his presence. One foot on the couch he vaulted over the back swinging the gun, back-handed, like a tennis racquet. To Jack it was happening as if in slow motion. Out of the corner of his eye he saw the shocked expression on Alicia's face. Missy was looking at Roy and Roy was smiling in a curious way.

Jack knew he was no Olympic hurdler, but he cleared the back of the couch. With all his attention drawn to the woman he brought the, butt of the gun down on her head just as he heard another explosion.

He felt a gut-wrenching punch to his torso and his breath went out of him. His left arm went numb then everything went blank.

****

Justin stared at his telephone screen. He wasn't sure what to make of the message. He had been speaking to Rebecca when his phone had vibrated in his pocket. Rebecca eyed him with a question, but before he answered her he shrugged his shoulders and began to dial.

The phone rang and rang. He hung up and tried again. This time it was picked up by a woman. "Hello?"

"Hello. Is Dr. Sharp there?" Justin asked.

The voice faltered, "Who is this?"

"My name is Justin Samuelson. I'm a detective and just received

351

a text message asking me to call your house."

"Dr. Sharp can't come to the phone and I'm not the owner." There was a long pause, then, "This is Alicia Winters." Justin nearly crowed. He gave a 'thumbs up' to Rebecca. "What's happening?"

Alicia was now crying, "Dr. Sharp just saved our lives, but he's been shot."

Justin could hear the sound of a siren now coming across his phone. "Is that an ambulance?"

"I don't know," she sniffed. "I'll look." There was a short delay. "No it's a police car. I should probably hang up and call for an ambulance, though. Okay?"

"Okay. Call me back, though, at this number." Justin gave Alicia his cell number and closed his phone. He looked up somberly at Rebecca. "It appears that our doctor really is one of the good guys. He just got shot trying to save Alicia Winters."

"Oh no!" a truly shocked expression appeared on Rebecca's face. "Did she say how badly he was hurt?"

"Alicia was crying so it could be pretty bad. She said that a police car has arrived. Out there it's probably the sheriff. Alicia's calling an ambulance."

Rebecca sat down. "Okay. See if you can reach that sheriff and find out what's going on."

"Sure." He took out his PDA to look up a number. He quickly found the number for the Cerro Gordo County Sheriff's office and dialed.

Rebecca shook her head. "Technology," she muttered. She would have had to call the front desk and get someone to look the number up for her. Justin definitely had a handle on how to use it.

Justin was able to be put straight through to the sheriff's cell phone. "Sir, this is Detective Samuelson. I'm involved in the investigation of the two murders recently in eastern Nebraska. Can you tell me what's the situation there?" He had to nearly shout to be heard above the din of background noise, shouts, and rustling noises.

The sheriff's voice boomed so that Rebecca could even hear it.

"Well now, it appears that we have to clean up a little mess out here. We've got two with gunshot wounds and one with a head injury. You know we only have one ambulance in this county."

"Can you tell how serious the injuries are?"

"Well, Detective, let's see. Roy, he lives here. Roy bled a lot, but he's a tough old bird. Missy's already got his arm bandaged up. The pretty woman snake, who tried to kill my niece back at the dress store in town, well- she's out cold. Got a nasty head injury, thanks to your doctor. How come one of you didn't come here with him?"

"It's a long story."

"Well I'd appreciate hearing it sometime. I don't appreciate the paper work you just caused me to have to do."

This was said with a measure of barely controlled anger. "Anyway, I'm not sure about his wound. There's a lot of blood on the floor by him and he's unconscious and barely breathing, but he's alive. This young woman seems to have taken charge of him. It depends on where the bullet went. He's probably first on the ambulance. We may need to take the head injury too. I doubt she'll wake up any time soon. He hit her pretty good. Broke the butt of the shotgun over her head. Now if you don't mind I've got a crime scene to deal with."

"Thank you, sheriff. One of us will be coming out your way as soon as possible."

"That's fine as long as you have answers for me. Just remember whose jurisdiction you're coming to."

"Yes, sir!"

Justin hung up and stared at Rebecca. "It looks like our case is shaping up after all."

The phone buzzed in his hand. He looked down and saw the sheriff's number on the screen. He opened it, "Yes Sheriff?"

But it wasn't the sheriff's voice. He heard a lot of noise and then Alicia's voice. "Detective Samuelson?"

"Yes?"

"I'm still worried. Dr. Sharp said he had to take me somewhere safe because there's is a leak in your office. Are you sure we're safe?"

"We'll do our best to keep anyone from finding out about this right away, but it isn't going to be easy."

"This woman said some things that might be important. She

said there was going to be some big deal. They're selling old diamonds to some Chinese businessmen."

"Is that all she said?"

"Yes. She was just about to shoot Missy after she told us that. Then the phone rang and Dr. Sharp... How did you manage to call right at that second?"

Justin smiled. "Your doctor, there, sent me a text message to make the call. He must have done it to get her attention."

Alicia choked then sniffed. "I think the ambulance is here. I need to go."

"Okay. Try to remember this number."

Justin heard a click then silence.

"We have another lead, but I think we're going to need some help."

48

Kathy lay in her own bed staring through windows streaked with rain. She loved her small house. It was almost fifty years old, but it had been well built and lovingly cared for. Quaint by current housing standards, it had everything she needed within easy reach. To her, this home was the model of efficiency. When her husband had died, the large modern home they had shared had seemed like an empty warehouse where she had felt lost in its expanse. Her children had been alarmed when, only a month after his death, she had sold it, opting for a smaller, one story house in the country. The younger children, still at home, had been afraid they would lose touch with their friends, but she was able to keep them in the same school despite changing districts. They actually didn't have to go farther for church because it was on the same side of town as the acreage. The property had a small fishing pond and lots of trees. Even though it took a lot of work they soon loved the new place almost as much as their mother did.

The house had a basement where two bedrooms were located. There was also a small game room sporting an ancient pool table. Kathy found out that it had been moved in when the house was built and was too large to remove through any doorway. She had remodeled the kitchen with modern appliances and together they had painted the walls. The carpeting needed updating, but the home was well insulated and quiet. Her favorite spot was in the living room in front of the fireplace. She enjoyed evenings sitting there with a good book. Jane Austen was her favorite author.

She was able to get out of bed on her own, now, but was very unsteady. The neurosurgeon had made her promise that she would have someone close by and she had been provided with a walker. It now sat, unused, against the wall of her bedroom.

"I am not an old lady!" she had told her daughter when they had arrived home. "I will get along fine without that thing."

Kathy's last foray to the bathroom had almost changed

her mind. She had felt dizzy and only at the last minute caught the doorknob to keep herself from falling. Now she called her daughter when she wanted to get up, but she staunchly refused to use the walker.

"What's wrong, Mom?" Kathy's reverie was interrupted by Esther's question.

"Nothing's wrong sweetie. I'm just tired." Her gaze swung back to the window.

"Is it that Dr. Jack hasn't been here?"

Kathy looked curiously at her daughter. "Why would you think that?"

"Well you weren't this moody at the hospital. He came around all the time. I saw how you acted when he was around." Esther said, using a mock scolding voice.

Kathy blushed involuntarily then smiled. "I guess I wouldn't mind hearing from him."

"You really like him don't you?" Esther approached and sat gently on the side of the bed. She looked at her mother with her head covered by a colorful cap. A slight stubble of hair was already beginning to grow back where it had been shaved. Kathy made room for her and they snuggled in the bed.

She kissed her daughter's forehead and said, "Yes. I really like him. I don't think I even realized how much until the last week or so, but we have been friends a long time."

"I like him too." Esther's pronouncement came pleasantly much like a stamp of approval. "Are you going to get married?"

"What? Just because two people like each other doesn't mean they will get married."

Esther rolled her eyes and nodded. "Sure, Mom." She said it as if to her it was obvious that her mother didn't have a clue.

Then Kathy whispered, "I don't think I would mind that, though." And they both giggled as they lay next to each other in bed.

The blare of the phone ringing ended their fun and they both stared at it. Esther recovered first and picked up the receiver. "Hello... No, but she's right here. Who is this please?" She put her hand over the mouthpiece and told her mother,

"It's someone called Sam Boniface."

Kathy frowned, not recognizing the name. She took the phone from her daughter.

"Hello?"

The portable phone was a few years old and it often crackled and buzzed. Kathy had intended to replace it. She could just make out the person on the other end of the line.

He said, "Kathy Sanders? Hi, this is Sam Boniface. I'm Jack Sharp's lawyer. He has talked about you a lot the last few days."

"Yes, hello, Sam. What can I do for you?"

"I know he has been visiting you regularly and was planning to see you again tomorrow, but I thought I should let you know. Jack's been... hurt."

The shock was like a lightning bolt, "What?" The forcefulness of her response caused Esther to slip to the edge of the bed. Kathy's hand flew to her head as if in pain. "What do you mean hurt? Was he in an accident?"

Sam expelled some air then continued, "No. I'm afraid he's been ... shot. I don't have all the details, but he is in a hospital in Iowa. The police told me about it just a little while ago."

"Shot! How could that be? How did he get shot? What's going on? He said he had to go away for a few days, but he didn't say he was in any danger."

"I'm sorry, Mrs. Sanders, I don't know much more. It has to do with that case he got involved in. You know, the body he found."

"Yes, I see," was all she could manage. Her mind was racing, trying to process this new information. With tears forming in her throat and spilling from her eyes she managed to ask,

"Do you know how bad it is?"

"No, I don't, but I will find out as soon as possible and let you know more. I'm not even sure what town he was in." He hesitated, "Here is my cell number in case you want to call. Jack isn't answering his."

Kathy fumbled for a piece of paper and a pen. She didn't trust her memory. She carefully laid the phone in its cradle and quietly started weeping. The joy of their laughter had left in an instant.

Esther, sensing this, reached out for her mother and they held each other in silence.

****

Antony paced in his upscale hotel room. This was Des Moines' luxury suite. It was now snowing steadily outside and he had not been able to raise Delia on her phone. He swore repeatedly, angry that he hadn't finished what he had started. He had confidence that she could get the job done, but was even more angry that she was keeping him in the dark.

Sometimes she can be so frustrating.

He found that there was a mini-bar with a selection of individual beverages, but he wasn't satisfied. He picked up the phone, "Room service? I want a bottle of scotch. What brand? I don't care just bring up a single malt. And hurry!"

He normally didn't drink, but he wasn't going anywhere and felt he needed a little 'medicinal support.' He had nothing to do now until Monday. This was only Thursday night. Three days in Des Moines didn't seem like something to anticipate. The weather was keeping his helicopter grounded and he wasn't certain when it would clear.

However, the reward to come on Monday calmed him a little.

He rarely stayed in hotels opting, instead, for rented town houses, if he was away from home. A house allowed for more privacy and security, but he had not been able to make the arrangements at the last minute. A suite in the best hotel in Des Moines was a tolerable option and he finally sat in the cushioned chair facing the forty-eight inch flat screen television.

Used to hundreds of television stations from several satellite networks he was appalled at only half that number of available channels. He looked down the menu and found only a few that came close to interesting him.

There was a knock at the door and he slipped a twenty from his wallet. Opening the door the attendant entered carrying a tray with a large bottle of amber liquid and a crystal tumbler. Antony surreptitiously slipped the bill into the hand of the attendant who, grinning, nodded and stepped back into the hallway.

Antony unscrewed the cap and poured a generous portion into the tumbler. He swirled its contents gently and stared into the liquid as if it would tell him the future. Adding ice, he left the bottle on the tray. Flipping through channels with the remote, he sipped the scotch which was very smooth. He could make out the smoky taste of oaken barrels used in the aging process. He looked again at the bottle, twenty years old.

"I wonder what I just paid for that?" he thought.

Instead of turning to the history channel he decided to see what old movies were on. 'Cassablanca' was the selection and it was just starting. He shrugged his shoulders.

At least its one of my favorites," he said out loud. He raised his glass to the television and sat back down in the easy chair to get comfortable and pass the time.

49

Friday

At first everything was a swirling cloud. Then there was a piercing noise for a while and then, near silence. He then began to hear sounds, but they were muffled, and unintelligible. Feeling like he was suspended, his body was jostled and rolled, but he didn't seem to be able to open his eyes or talk to anyone. He felt like someone had tied a rope around his chest and it was hard to breathe, and then all was blackness.

As the light returned, he was in Zaire sitting in a pew holding hands with Sharon and laughing with Sister Mary Elizabeth. For a nun, she had a great sense of humor. Jack was not Catholic. His own mission station was a fair distance away, but he enjoyed the companionship of these two ladies. He would hop on his little scooter and brave the dirt road with its massive potholes just to see their smiling faces and spend time with Sharon.

The scene changed suddenly. Gunfire erupted in the background and he could see the expression on Sister Mary Elizabeth's face alter. Sharon jumped up and ran out and in the doorway of the church, a large man grabbed her. Jack too slowly jumped up to run after he and then something hard hit his legs. Falling, he could catch a glimpse of a terrified Sharon held in the back of a truck, going away.

The light went away again.

Next, floating above a hospital bed, he could see that there was a body in it. His own face was pale as wax and attached to the body. People were milling around him, but there was no sound.

Then it was dark again.

Time had no meaning. In the darkness he couldn't tell where he was. He gradually became aware of one thing that remained constant was a nagging ache in his side. Soon the pain was so intense that all his whole consciousness was absorbed by it. The pain kept growing, hot, burning in his left side. He coughed and the pain, like a knife, woke him from his deep sleep.

****

Jack's eyes opened and the light was suddenly blinding. Things around him were blurry, but seemed to be developing, like a camera lens coming into focus. Each breath caused a searing pain across his chest. Trying to look to see what was wrong, all he could see were bandages restricting his movement. He had an IV in his right hand and a nasal cannula for oxygen in his nose.

His mind told him that he was alive, and he realized that he was in a hospital, but he sensed somehow that this was not his hospital where he practiced medicine.

Just at the periphery of his vision, an efficient nurse was putting the finishing touches on his swaddling of bed sheets, which were wrapped tightly enough to feel like a strait jacket. He noticed that he could wiggle his toes and that his left arm was free. However, when he tried to move it he found another area of intense pain in his upper arm.

Jack's memory of the previous day was sketchy, but a flash-back of the confrontation began taking shape in his mind as a man in a long white lab coat walked in.

"Good morning," came the deep pleasant voice.

Jack found his voice. "Good? I don't think I like breathing at the moment."

The doctor smiled and leaned over. "Well you're not bleeding through the dressings. It may sound overused, but you were lucky, sir."

"I don't feel lucky. Why do you say I'm lucky and who are you?"

"I'm sorry. I'm Ben Carlson. I'm the thoracic surgeon who stitched you up last night. As for luck, I'll show you." He turned and opened the small closet door near the front of the hospital room. He reached in and brought out an oddly shaped leather strap. Jack recognized it as his shoulder holster. "Now, had you been carrying a weapon maybe things would have happened differently."

"Chalk it up to experience. But why was I lucky?"

"Look here." He leaned forward holding the holster between

two hands. A neat hole appeared directly in the center of the holster. "The bullet that should have killed you entered your arm and struck the holster. It didn't stop it, but two layers of leather slowed it down enough to reduce its penetration. It struck a rib, punctured your lung and stopped just under the rib. You have a chest tube and dressings on your chest and arm. The bullet is now in our pathology department."

"Man, it hurts. And you just make it sound like I cut myself shaving."

Dr. Carlson let out a hearty laugh. "We men don't take pain well, do we?"

"Where am I?" Jack asked, changing the subject.

"Another common question. You are in intensive care at Mercy Hospital in Cedar Rapids. You arrived last night from some farm up north along with a woman. I understand that you are responsible for her injury and that she is responsible for yours." Jack thought a moment and remembered the last few moments before the lights went out. He had swung the gun fairly hard.

"How is she?"

"It is too early to tell. She was badly injured. I know a little about what happened so don't worry, I don't blame you."

Jack was chagrined. He was a physician, sworn to heal wounds not cause them. He knew he had been justified in his actions, but it still didn't feel right. "I guess I'm glad I didn't have my automatic with me after all."

Dr. Carlson's eyebrows went up. "Do you want to tell me about it? I am curious."

Jack closed his eyes feeling suddenly exhausted. "Maybe later. When can I get out of here?"

Dr. Carlson laughed again, "I could have guessed you would say that. A couple of days, no sooner. Just be happy that you'll leave under your own power. In the mean time, use that contraption on the table to keep your lungs open. I'll talk to you later." He swept out of the room having already spent more time than usual with a post-op patient.

Jack stared at the incentive spirometer on his table. It was a device used to encourage patients to suck in enough air to fill up their lungs. With his right hand he brought the mouthpiece to his lips and tried to inhale. The stinging pain brought tears to his eyes and he couldn't raise the gauge more than a few millimeters. He tried again, wincing, with a little better success. Then he laid back and turned his eyes to one side. He had no window and could not tell the time of day. His watch had been taken away and with his glasses off, he couldn't read the clock on the wall. He was beginning to understand how easily a patient could become disoriented in the hospital.

Jack again thought back to the attack from the night before. In his dreams it had been all jumbled up with his experience twenty years earlier, though at that time his injury had been minor. This had often puzzled him because rebels in that part of Africa often liked to make examples of men, especially if they were from another country. They had snatched up Sharon and the diamonds. The murderous band had killed half a dozen bystanders including children but had left him completely alone aside from a hard rap on his shins.

Why had he been spared?

On the previous night during his own attack he had been functioning on adrenaline. It was not the first time he had to take the offensive, but it had been a long time. Nevertheless, his Special Forces training was ingrained in his mind, though his body didn't respond like it once had. If he had been a second quicker he might not have been shot. The violent act for which he had used the shotgun now came back to him and he remembered hearing the skull and gun stock connect with a force that could break bone. Yet, he had been meeting deadly force with deadly force. While he was sorry that she had been severely hurt, he knew he was justified in his actions.

Had he not acted, there would probably be four new corpses today in an Iowa farmhouse.

Who was she? He could not remember seeing her face before his own lights had gone out. He assumed that she was the same person who had done the other killings, and maybe the one who

363

had taken shots at him and Justin. Perhaps there had been some rivalry with the first young woman. That could explain the attack with a knife on Connie. There was vehemence in that attack even after she had already been shot.

Jack shook his head not willing to speculate further. He saw the nurse inject something into the IV and felt a great fatigue descend upon him like a curtain. He did not like the helpless position he was in but, with no choice, his head returned to the pillow automatically and he slept.

****

Justin was focused upon the road ahead as Rebecca sat anxiously in the passenger seat. She preferred to drive at times like this because she didn't have any other way to burn off her nervous energy. She detested reading in the car, but didn't like the inactivity.

"Is my driving bothering you?" Justin asked, noting how Rebecca fidgeted.

"What? Oh, no. I just don't like riding in cars. I prefer to drive."

"I can stop and we can switch."

"If you don't mind. I'd like that."

Justin grinned, "Sure. I can do some work. There's a rest stop ahead. It's too bad we have to go all the way to Cedar Rapids. I wish they had taken them to Des Moines."

"I suppose, but according to the distances Cedar Rapids was closer for them. An ambulance is obligated to go to the closest trauma center. It could have taken the ambulance half and hour longer to go to Des Moines which might mean losing a life."

He nodded, "I guess you're right. If I had been shot I would want the closest place too." He took note as the blue "Rest Area" sign appeared along the roadside and slowed to pull off. The pavement was mostly dry and driving had been uneventful, though patches of snowdrifts remained in sheltered spots. The surrounding landscape was all white, for in this part of Iowa there had been about five inches of new snow. Farther north there were places where they had doubled that amount. Cars littered the ditches where they had gone off the road and Justin hoped that their drivers had all made it to safety somewhere.

After stopping, the two exited their vehicle to stretch their legs. Icy wind whipped swirling clouds of snow between the barren trees of the rest area making a lonely moaning sound. It made Justin wonder if there might be a law enforcement position available in Florida or southern California.

Having exchanged seats, Justin brought out his notebook computer while Rebecca, looking back, began to pull out of the parking place. Before she could move the car, however, she saw that her way was obstructed by a pedestrian. The man merely stood behind her car while she waited growing more impatient. She was about to honk her horn when the man leaned down to peer into the back window. He was wearing dark glasses.

Rebecca groaned, "Where did he come from?"

Justin looked up, "What's going on?"

With disgust in her voice Rebecca shifted back into park and started to open her door, "Just a minute. I've got to see what he wants."

Justin craned his neck around to see, but only caught a glimpse of a man in a black overcoat walking toward a picnic shelter. Rebecca followed him hopping on tip-toe to avoid getting snow in her own shoes. He shrugged and went back to his computer.

"Can't you make an appointment like a normal person or call on the phone?" Rebecca called after him.

"Might be bugged," came the cryptic reply. "Anyway, you called us, remember."

"Have you been following us all this way?" Rebecca asked hands on hips.

"I had to make a trip to Des Moines and just happened upon you at this rest area," said the CIA agent.

"Look, Agent 'Tom'...

"Bob."

"What?"

"It's Agent Bob."

"I thought you said... Is that supposed to be funny? Oh, never mind. Anyway, we could use your help. I just don't understand your tactics. You don't really believe we're being spied upon do you?"

The younger man, the same agent who had previously spoken to Rebecca, pulled his overcoat more tightly around himself, blocking out the bitter wind. "One never knows. And you thought you didn't have a leak in your department. Is that why you secretly sent the doctor to Iowa?"

"How did you know about that?"

"Well you're not being spied upon. Right?" Bob grinned. "We know about your little problem. You actually don't need to worry about the Assistant District Attorney any more. I believe he is sitting on a beach in the Caribbean as we speak."

Rebecca scowled and hit her hand with her fist. "I knew he was dirty. No chance we'll get him back?"

"Uh uh."

"Was he... yours?"

Bob just smiled again. "I didn't say that. Just be assured he is being 'dealt with.' Anyway, you wanted information." He reached into his jacket. Rebecca stepped back and touched her weapon.

Bob's hands went out, "Hey! I'm just getting out another envelope. See? Wasn't I helpful before?"

"Sorry just a reflex," said Rebecca. She relaxed slightly, shivering nonetheless. Taking the folded manila envelope, she glanced around to see if they were being observed. Her eyes returned to her package and she saw that it bore no label, but was sealed with tape. "You know this is hardly a discreet location." She looked up, "What?..." Again there was no one there. She heard a car engine start up and saw a dark sedan pull away from the rest stop. She let out an exasperated breath and shook her head.

"I hate it when he does that!"

Back in the car she tossed the envelope onto Justin's lap.

"Hey. What's that? What were you doing?" he asked.

"Just went to the little girl's room."

"Sure."

"Open it and let me know what's in it." Teeth chattering now she started the car, turned the heat on full blast and backed out. This time there was no one standing behind.

"Where did you get it?"

"Guess."

"Really? Your friendly neighborhood spook?" Justin smiled aware that his boss had once again met with the CIA. "You didn't tell me you had such a good relationship with those guys."

"I didn't know. Maybe Agent Bob likes me."

"Agent Bob? I thought it was Tom?" Justin looked confused.

"Yeah so did I. I guess he went through a name change. What did he give us?" She pulled onto the interstate highway having given up the idea of trying to catch up to the agent's car. He would not appreciate the attempt and probably wasn't really going to Des Moines anyway.

"Let's see. There are dossiers on several Asian men and two women here. The men are business men. Maybe they are the ones who are having this big meeting on Monday. There isn't much about one of the women, another Asian. But the other one is European, I think. It might be an older photo of the woman the doc hit with the shotgun." He held it up so Rebecca could glance over at it. "The caption on document says she may be a hired assassin." He read, "'She has been suspected in several deaths, but nothing could ever be proven. She was never arrested. She has several aliases and may work out of Chicago.' None of these documents is labeled. Probably so we can't prove where they came from. Hey there's a business card here. It says 'BOB's PIZZARIA Deliveries 24 hours' and there's a phone number."

"Funny," she put on a fake grin. "Do you suppose he really expects us to call? He's so paranoid he hasn't wanted to talk on the phone before."

"It's probably just a voicemail."

"Maybe. I wonder if he is really going to Des Moines."

"What are you doing?" Justin asked as their speed exceeded the limit.

"I want to check out a car I saw earlier," she said smiling, as she had changed her mind and hoped she could spot the dark sedan one more time to see if he turned around or actually did go to Des Moines.

****

Antony awoke with a lurch. His head was pounding and his mouth tasted awful. He noticed that his feet were cold and saw that his blanket and sheet were on the floor. The half-empty bottle of scotch swam into his view and he remembered why he should feel so ill. He felt oddly hungry and nauseated at the same time. He contemplated ordering breakfast then thought better of it.

Picking up the phone he said, "Room service? Bring me a pot of strong coffee. Thanks."

They apparently could automatically tell what room he was in because they hadn't asked. Good. He didn't feel like talking much. He picked up his cell phone and checked the "missed calls" and "voicemail" screens. Nothing. *Why haven't you called?*

He tried once again to call Delia. This time he heard a click, but no one spoke. It didn't go to voicemail. "Hello?"

Then panic seized him. If Delia had picked up she would have said something. Someone else had her phone! He tried once again, "Hello?" Then he slammed the phone closed. Something wasn't right. He tried to think what to do, but his mind was muddled by the scotch and the hangover. Delia was no fool. If she had merely lost the phone she would still have tried to contact him. He had heard nothing.

He turned on the news, not sure what to expect. A local Iowa station was filled with the news of the overnight storm and all the stranded motorists to the north. She had been in that area. Had she gotten out before the snow? Had she gotten stuck in the snow?

"Where are you?" he said to the television.

The news had nothing about any deaths or murders as yet. He knew that if she had been as efficient as usual it was likely that the bodies wouldn't be found for a few days anyway. Nevertheless, if she had been successful she should have called him immediately. She always had to crow over her triumphs and she sometimes called him while the blood was still flowing from her victim.

He was angry that he was sitting alone in a hotel in the middle of Iowa and he had no information. He was angry at his own arrogance that he had not left this mess to Delia in the first place and stayed in Chicago. He didn't need to be here until Monday. That was still three days away.

Antony made up his mind. Though he didn't like it he couldn't do anything about Delia at the moment. She could usually take care of herself and would get in touch as soon as possible. He needed to get out of here. He placed a call to the local airport and to his driver. Ripping off his night-clothes he stepped into the bathroom. As Antony turned on the shower he heard a rap on the door.

He opened the door without looking and said over his shoulder, "Just put it on the table," and stepped into bathroom.

****

"Can I get you folks some lunch?" All three looked up at the young deputy in the doorway.

Roy spoke, "Shore. We could use somethin' to perk us up."

Missy and Alicia looked at each other uncertainly. The shock had worn off, but they were uncomfortable staying in this motel room. They felt like prisoners and in a way they were. The sheriff, at first not certain what to do with them, had gotten them all into his car shortly after the ambulance had left. He had driven east toward Cedar Rapids and decided to keep them in "protective custody" in a motel there. He had spoken to his counterpart in Linn County, Matt Franklin, not revealing the names of his passengers. Agreeing to pay for their lodging if Matt could provide couple of deputies to keep an eye on them for a few days seemed like a good idea. He'd figure something out by the next week.

The sheriff determined, from Missy's story, that if they made it to Tuesday they might be all right. He reasoned that once the crooks did their "deal," whatever it was, they would high-tail it out of the area and forget about these people. The sheriff, and his packed car, had made it out of the farmhouse just in time as the storm had closed road behind them within hours of the incident on the previous night. He had taken a room, too, since getting back to his own county would not be possible until later in the day.

They had taken Roy to the hospital, but he had refused to stay. "A little scratch like this can't keep me down. "It ain't near what

I got in Nam." He had showed off burn and shrapnel scars on his back and leg to the interest of the emergency room physician. His upper arm wound had bled significantly, but required only suturing. His face was strained and a little pale, but he had not complained. A sling was wrapped around his neck, nonetheless, to lessen the movement of his injured arm.

Shortly after the deputy left, there was a knock on the door. This was unexpected and the second deputy stood warily. He unsnapped the trigger guard on his nine millimeter automatic and kept his right hand close to his holster as he approached the door of the room. He carefully looked through the peep-hole and let out a sigh of relief. The deputy straightened, re-clipped his weapon and unlocked the door.

"Hi, Sheriff."

The door swung open and Missy recognized the sheriff from her home town, Ron Johnson. Behind him, though, stood a couple unfamiliar to her. The woman was younger than she, and in better shape. Something about her said, "Law Enforcement." The younger man with her was hard for her to read. He looked like a graduate student or college professor with longish hair and a boyish smile. His attention was focused, not upon her, but upon Alicia.

The woman spoke as she entered the room.

"Alicia Winters?" It was a question, but everyone could tell she was speaking directly to Alicia.

"I'm Alicia," she stood from the edge of her bed. Roy, who had been sitting on a roll-away, stepped in front of her.

"Just wait a gall-darned minute. You start by tellin' us who you are. Alicia here's been through a lot and you can't just start bombarding her with questions."

Rebecca put her hands up in a conciliatory manner, "All right. I just wanted to be sure you were safe. We do have a few questions if that's okay. I'm Detective Rebecca Sweate and this is Detective Justin Samuelson. We are from Alicia's hometown in Nebraska."

"Hi." Justin tried to step forward to shake Alicia's hand, but Rebecca scowled at him and he retreated.

"How do we know we can trust you. We heard that you've got

some spy or something back at your department. How do we know we can trust any of you?" Roy was agitated from lack of sleep and the unfamiliarity of the motel. His arm ached and he got dizzy if he stood too quickly.

"You've a right to be upset, sir. We have learned about a leak in our department, but he is being ... dealt with. We just need to find out what we can about this whole business. Two people have been murdered and you were all attacked. We don't really know why or where it will all lead."

"How's Dr. Sharp?" interjected Alicia.

Justin answered first. "We heard he'll be fine. We are going to see him soon. We have questions for him too."

Rebecca looked hard at Justin again then said resignedly, "His wound was not as severe as first suspected. Let's all relax and sit. We just have a few questions and then we'll leave you alone."

Roy, mollified, moved to the side and sat, almost falling, into a chair. Alicia gingerly hugged him and gave him a kiss on the cheek. Turning to Rebecca she said, "I want to see Dr. Sharp. I'll tell you what you want to know in the car. It's okay, Roy, Missy."

Roy began to object, but she put a hand on his arm and glancing at Justin.

"I think this is the young man who helped Dr. Sharp find us to warn us. I think we can trust him. We have to trust somebody." Roy looked over at Missy who hadn't said anything. Tears had sprung up in her eyes. Alicia stepped back and held Missy in her arms. She began weeping softly too. "Thank you so much. Thank you both so much. You saved my life in more ways than you know. I'll come back. I promise."

Missy said, "Are you sure you want to go with them? That ... *woman* is in that hospital too. You stay away from her." She sniffed, "You come back to us. I'm gettin' too old to do all those chores myself."

"I will." Without another word she turned toward the detectives and walked out. There was a dignity in her stride and a look of triumph on her face. She felt stronger inside than ever. That morning before anyone had awakened, she had been up staring at the cold parking lot through the bathroom window. Having found a Gideon Bible in the drawer beside her bed, she had tried to remember what verses to read, but could only remember that the pastor had been teaching from the book of John so she started there. The first few verses stood out for her. Then the pastor's words came back. He had said, face beaming, hand held up,

"Anyone can be saved. God loves you." He had said that the book of John spoke about how much God loves us all. Alicia desperately wanted that love.

She read from the first chapter of John, "The Word was God." Jesus was the Word and he was God. She had never made that connection before. The pastor had said that she needed to believe in God and that Jesus had come to save her from her sins.

Alicia had felt dirty, sinful. She had seen her best friend killed. She had gone with her after she had stolen a diamond. *What had they been thinking?* She had run away and people had been killed because of what they, *what she* had done. She couldn't ask Connie for forgiveness. The only one big enough to forgive her was God. And here it said that Jesus was God. Sitting on the lid of the toilet in the bathroom, tears flowing freely, she had bowed her head and prayed,

"Jesus, I need your forgiveness. I know I have sin deep inside and I want it to be cleaned out. I know you can do it. Please take away that sin. And, God, please help Dr. Sharp to pull through." She didn't know if that was all she needed to do, but she had felt better. There were no fireworks, no voice from heaven, but through her tears she felt she could see a way ahead. There was no longer a black hole waiting in front of her to swallow her up.

She knew she had a future.

As Alicia reached the door of the little motel room she looked back. "Missy, I don't have a Bible. Do you think I can take the one from the drawer?"

Missy smiled. "Hon, that's why it's there."

She opened the drawer and picked it up. She carried it to Alicia and got one more hug in return.

Justin, growing impatient, muttered good-naturedly, "So many hugs!" and walked out into the cold morning air.

50

Kathy was trying to concentrate on the physical therapy, but her mind kept returning to Jack. She had heard nothing more. Sam had patiently answered her several calls to his cell phone, though he had had no new information. Sam told her that he would go to Cedar Rapids himself if he didn't hear something soon. He had called the local police department, but they didn't appear know anything about a shooting in Iowa.

With a cane in one hand she noticed that her right leg seemed less sure than before surgery. It wasn't exactly weak, but she had to focus if she wanted it to move a certain way. She was thankful, however, that her mind was functioning normally. She had no trouble speaking or remembering, in fact, she felt that her mind was clearer now than it had been prior to surgery. Esther echoed that opinion, but Kathy could see the concern on her face every time she tried to walk around in the house.

At fifty she knew her bones weren't as strong as they once had been so a fall could lead to a broken bone. That would slow her down and she didn't want anything to slow her down now. She wanted to get better so she could get on with the radiation and chemotherapy and put this behind her. She wanted to get better so she could spend time with Jack. She wanted to get strong enough that she could walk with him on his "famous" bike path.

Esther walked into the living room munching on an apple.

"How's it going Mom?" Her voice was a little muffled by the presence of the fruit in her mouth.

"I'm getting...stronger...with every step." The physical therapist, Amy, smiled.

"Hello, Esther. Do you want to help your mom?"

"Sure. What do I do?"

The therapist showed her where to put her hand and the two of them walked beside Kathy as she worked her way across the living room. Amy said, "Now, let's work on some stretching exercises.

I'll have you lay down on the carpet for this."

The three of them worked for another twenty minutes after which Kathy felt fatigued. It pleased her to have Esther take an interest. She was confident that they would both grow through the experience.

Once Amy had left and Kathy was seated in the recliner she asked Esther, "Could you get me a glass of ice water, please?"

"Okay Mom." She opened the freezer door to get some ice cubes. "Have you heard anything more about Dr. Jack?"

Eyes closed and head back Kathy sighed, "No. Sam told me he hadn't heard anything yet either. I feel so helpless. I can't go there and he hasn't called."

"I prayed for him this morning." Esther set the water on the coffee table and leaned over to hug her mother. "I don't know anything else to do. I hope he's all right. I love him Mom."

Kathy found fresh tears forming in her own eyes and hugged her back.

"I love him too sweetheart. You're right to pray. That's what I should have been doing. Let's do that right now."

****

James approached the door with trepidation. He felt odd. Though he had been the instigator of two peoples' deaths he had never actually killed anyone in person. Now he could see only one way to end the nightmare that he had been caught up in. He held the large revolver in his right hand. It felt heavy and awkward but he knew he could fire it as he had used it the firing range on several occasions. He held his closed fist up to the door and gave it two quick raps that resounded within the room.

There was no answer and James felt uncertain. He noticed that the door was slightly ajar. *All the better.* He gingerly pushed the door open and took a shooter's stance in the doorway. The room was empty. He entered cautiously and heard a noise coming from the bathroom. At first he approached, gun facing forward, then, carefully he moved his right hand to his side, hiding the weapon. Poking his head around the corner, he peered into the bathroom. His look was met by a shriek. The woman within threw a towel over his face and she shouted incomprehensible Spanish expletives at him.

"It's okay, it's okay." He put up his left hand defensively, continuing to hide his right hand.

"Señor Antony?" he said questioningly in as benign a voice as possible. The cleaning woman scowled and continued to yell at him but he could not tell if she understood. Chagrined, he retreated from the Chicago flat where he had hoped to surprise his "Leader" and put an end to the drama.

Failing in this, he began to believe he had only one other option.

****

Jack's phone rang. He knew it was ringing because he recognized the tune, but was confused about where it was. Eyes closed he reached to his waist, no belt, no phone. Opening his eyes the room light was dim, but reality hit once again. He lay in a hospital bed and the pain seemed to deaden his senses. The phone was distant. Was it in the closet?

He realized the effort to get up would be too great so he let it ring.

He started to relax and let the pain win out again, but the thought came to him that Kathy might be trying to call. Fumbling in the wadded sheets he found the nurse call button and pressed it. "May I help you?" came a pleasant voice over some speaker whose location he couldn't pin down.

"Yes. Please send in my nurse."

"All right Dr. Sharp. I'm calling her now. Have a nice day."

"Thank you."

Jack made a half smile. For all he could tell that could have been a computer generated voice. He was sure that some day it would be. A few moments later a pretty young nurse, reddish blonde hair tied up in a high pony tail, sailed briskly into the room. She walked to the wall to press the "Call Answered" button beneath a small grill indicating the speaker's location.

"Hello, Dr. Sharp. What can I do for you?"

She was young enough to be a young daughter. "I called for a nurse, not a candy-striper," teased Jack.

She laughed, "I'm older than I look."

"I just wanted my cell phone. I heard it ring in the closet."

"Okay. I was about to come in to take you for a walk, though. How about if you check the call, but then we take a few rounds around the hall?"

Jack nodded, "That sounds fine. Do I have to carry all these contraptions with me?"

The young nurse whose nametag read "Mindy" only smiled.

"We can cap the chest tube and the IV is on a rolling pole."

"Ah. How about a shot of pain med before we take off?"

Efficiently Mindy pressed the button on his pain medicine pump. Jack could actually feel a slight warm sensation, first in the arm, then it enveloped his whole body. She helped him gather up his tubes and hung his various items on a rolling IV pole. His pain had lessened, nevertheless, every time she touched the chest tube he felt a jab of pain and taking a deep breath was still a challenge.

"Is that tube just going to stick out like that?"

"I'll walk on that side to protect it. We won't go far." Mindy stepped over to the closet and rummaged through Jack's pants. For some reason that act embarrassed him slightly. He was not accustomed to anyone checking out his clothing. She came away with his small cellular phone and handed it to him.

Jack glanced at the number on the screen, but didn't recognize it. He decided it probably wasn't Kathy and set the phone on the stand next to his bed. "All right, let's go."

Slowly, at first, they walked side by side until they reached the hall. Jack and his young nurse then turned and began their trek through the intensive care unit.

After just one time around Jack felt surprisingly feeble. He was mildly short of breath and his side ached. His left arm burned and walking caused it to rub painfully against the dressings on his chest.

"I didn't realize just how old I was getting."

"Nonsense, Dr. Sharp. You had a serious injury. Don't sell yourself short." Mindy smiled sweetly up at him. She helped him back into bed and reconnected his tubes.

Jack found himself mulling over what she had said. They were words he had spoken to patients many times. Now he was the one who needed encouragement. He picked his phone up intending to call Kathy, but curiosity won out. He instead dialed the number from his missed call.

The phone on the other end of the line rang several times before the answering machine picked up the call. Apparently it was Kathy's home phone, he only knew her cellular number. Jack debated leaving a message and just as he was about to hang up Kathy's voice came through, "Hello? Hello? Don't hang up- I'll turn off the recorder. Who is this?"

Jack hadn't realized how much he was looking forward to hearing Kathy's voice and nearly choked out the words, "Hi, Kathy, it's Jack."

Kathy too gave a little yelp of delight and surprise.

"Oh, Jack. I was so worried. What happened? Can you talk about it? Why did you go to Iowa?"

The last comment came out more as an accusation and scolding than she intended, but her pent up emotion caused some loss of control.

Jack listened to her questions, smiling. "I'm sorry I worried you. I don't think my phone battery will last long enough to tell the whole story. I'm okay, but it hurts and I imagine you know something about pain. What a pair we make. We should have a picture taken with all our bandages."

This received a pleasurable laugh from Kathy. "I'm sorry to go on and on. I was just worried when I heard you were shot. That's awful."

"It was only a 'flesh wound' as they say in the movies."

"Right. For a flesh wound you end up in ICU."

Jack tried to change the subject. "How is your rehab coming?"

"I'm getting stronger. I can get around as long as I have help. One leg is weaker than I expected, but I'll be getting better. You just come back and see for yourself."

The conversation went on to more domestic issues, her children and the house. Kathy told Jack about Sam's call.

"Good old Sam," Jack said, but he was getting a little short of breath and Kathy caught on. "It was nice of him to let you know. I'm sure I'll be out of here soon, but I'm not sure when I'll get back to town."

There was a hissing sound then the connection was severed. He looked at the phone and saw that the power was zero. He had no chargers with him, though there was one in his car.

"I wonder where my car is," he said to the vacant room.

51

Jack was dozing when several people arrived at his doorway. The change in ambient light was enough to rouse him and he opened his eyes. He couldn't see faces as the hallway light was behind them, but he noted something familiar.

Reaching for his glasses he said, "Hello. Come on in."

His voice and breathing had gained strength.

The trio entered his room and one broke away. Alicia moved quickly to his bedside.

"Dr. Sharp." She leaned over and gave him a big kiss on his cheek.

"I could wake up to that any day," he said smiling. He stuck his hand through the bed rail to take Alicia's in his. "I'm glad you're okay. I'm afraid that woman meant business."

Alicia nodded, "I think she would have killed us all. I can't believe you could sneak up on her like that! It was amazing."

Rebecca and Justin looked at each other in mild surprise. They had gotten a mere sketch of what had taken place in the farm house. Alicia had tersely answered their questions, but had not been particularly talkative.

"Can you tell us more about what happened last night?"

"Detective Sweate, how nice to see you. Hi Justin. Sorry you two had to come all this way to see me."

Justin answered, "We actually came for Alicia."

Rebecca glared at him. "We needed to talk to you too sir. It was extremely risky taking this on yourself. Justin should have stopped you."

"I didn't really give him a choice." He tried to readjust his sitting position to see his visitors more clearly. "Have you figured out who your leak is?"

She spoke hesitantly, "We have some information about that. How are you doing?

"I guess it could have been a lot worse but bullets aren't known for being polite." He made another effort to sit higher in the bed, but was defeated by the loose sheets.

"Can you tell us what happened?" came Rebecca's query.

Jack mopped his forehead where his exertions had raised beads of sweat. He gathered his thoughts then related to the pair, in detail, what had transpired in the farm house. Alicia nodded at the salient points. He made note that, had he been in the kitchen and not the bathroom, everything would have ended much differently.

"With the storm we never heard anything until she was in the house. Have you spoken to the woman yet?"

"The doctors say she isn't awake yet. It is a good thing you have stayed in shape. If you had been slower, you would probably have been killed."

"Thanks, but if I had been quicker or if I had bothered keep my own gun with me I might not have gotten shot at all."

Justin changed the subject. "Do either of you know any more about the meeting that is taking place next week, or who is involved?"

Jack and Alicia looked at each other both shaking their heads slowly.

Alicia spoke, "It could be Connie's boss. The diamond was his, I think."

Jack interjected, "I remember, though, that the woman assassin said something about the diamond being hers. If you can get her to talk she'll know the details."

Justin said again, "We haven't talked with her yet. She is still unconscious."

Rebecca nodded, "True. Besides if she is a pro she won't be likely to give up that kind of information willingly, and we don't have much time."

"What do you mean?" Jack had a puzzled look on his face and Alicia looked at Rebecca.

"We have learned that this meeting will take place on Monday, but we don't know yet where or with whom." She wasn't sure why she lied about not knowing who the meeting was slated for, but she didn't want to let too many pieces of information out. Nevertheless, knowing only the general time and not location left them high and dry. The meeting could be anywhere and, at this point, they couldn't do anything about it.

"I should be out of here by Monday," said Jack. "What's going to happen to Alicia?"

Justin looked at the pretty girl. He had found it difficult to speak to her. Despite his attempt at professionalism, what he really wanted to do was flirt with her. He was learning that, at times, it is not easy to remain objective. "We believe it is safe for her to return to her aunt and uncle's home."

"But I don't want to go there." Alicia spoke urgently, "I want to go back to Missy and Roy's place. You can let my aunt and uncle know I'm okay, but I don't want to live with them and I don't want to go back to Chicago either. Let me go with Missy. I'll be all right there."

If the woman assassin was in custody, Rebecca was inclined to believe that she was right. *Was it likely that this group, whoever was in charge, would make a second attempt on her life?* She thought this but instead said, "We'll consider it but, for now, the sheriff wants you to stay in that motel and it's his jurisdiction not ours."

Alicia resignedly nodded, hopeful that she had won points toward her desires.

"We should let you rest, Dr. Sharp. Thank you for your assistance." Rebecca stiffly stepped up to him and attempted to shake his hand, not realizing his left arm was immobilized making it hard to reach with his right. Her hard exterior softened for a second and she gave him a warm smile and gently squeezed his arm. "You showed unusual courage last night."

"I'd rather not do it again," he remarked with a half smile.

****

Antony was now worried as well as angry. She had never been this late in calling in. As his helicopter rose from the pad he felt like yelling. Yet he could do nothing until he reached his office. If Delia had arrived he would have been happy to stay there, but without her he wanted to get back. He needed information and wasn't getting it fast enough.

Antony let out a frustrated sound forgetting that he was wearing a microphone and headset. His yell caused the pilot to grab his own headset and pull it off. He turned in his seat and glared at Antony. Boss or not he had no business yelling in his ear.

The return flight was uneventful and Antony found himself retracing the steps down his stairwell to his office.

"What a colossal waste of time!" he shouted to no one in particular. He was still uncertain what had happened to delay Delia. He tried her cell once more, but went straight through to voicemail. He decided he needed a drink. Remembering the hangover, though, he limited himself to just one.

Standing in his office, drink in hand, he gazed out over the dull gray scenery below him. Cold from the flight and feeling a little numb, his mind slowly began to focus. His deal remained intact, nothing had changed. He didn't have the other diamond but the businessmen would get over that. As soon as he found Delia they could move on to the next phase of their life. But where was *she?* He also realized he didn't want to go alone. He already had money. The thrill of this deal was fading.

Once more he opened his cell. "Cindy? How are things going?"

"Hello, sir. The security set up is complete as you directed."

Antony was impressed. She had been concerned that it would take longer. He was feeling particularly generous. "Excellent. I'll see to it that you have a bonus."

Cindy gasped, "Thank you sir!"

"I have another task I really need done. I need you to track down someone for me."

"James usually does that sort of thing, doesn't he?"

"I want you to do it. You have shown me that you are more than capable. Tell me, have you been thinking of where you will settle when this is over?"

Cindy was puzzled by the whole conversation. This was unlike Antony. *Why the interest in her personal plans?* "I've been thinking, yes, but I haven't had time to plan all of it yet."

"No worries. Anyway, I want you to find out about a woman who may have stayed in a hotel in Mason City, Iowa. You may not be able to find her exactly because she has several aliases.

Try the following names; Delia Peterson, Sharon Jacobsen, Margaret Stauffer, and Francine Bourget. They are aliases of hers. You might try hospitals in the area just in case she was in an accident or something."

"Sir, this will be very hard if she has so many aliases. Couldn't she have just chosen another name?"

Antony had kept his voice calm up to this point, but now let his own agitation surface.

"Just do what I say and get it to me as soon as is humanly possible!" He didn't wait for a reply, but closed his phone. It frustrated him to have to rely on others. Carrying his drink to his desk he pressed a button on its edge. A panel slid open and a keyboard and monitor rose from inside the desk.

With a few keystrokes, Antony opened a file and typed out a short message. He used an encryption program to send the message to three separate places. He didn't want to think it could have happened, but these contacts were police department workers. If Delia had been arrested, he needed to find out. He couldn't allow her to be questioned.

52

Saturday

Saturday arrived and Jack was becoming restless. He felt a strange electricity in the air. Knowing that the situation he was involved in was still unresolved he knew, also, that he should just stay out of it now. He had a good excuse for leaving everything to the police, but there was a nagging feeling in his mind that he should press on. There was something more for him to do. The nurses had said that the woman he had hurt might soon come out of her coma, but was still sedated. He hoped he would be allowed to talk to her. His pain had subsided significantly, though it still hurt to raise his left arm. His doctor had indicated that the chest tube would soon be removed. For Jack it couldn't be soon enough. He had tried reading, but that hurt his elbows. The television seemed to have nothing but reruns and news, and the news seemed inane to him. He didn't have music or books on tape with him. He was frustrated and wanted out. His last walk around the hallway proved successful and he was much less short of breath.

He had asked about his car and was told it would be brought to Cedar Rapids later that day. His phone needed to be charged, but most of all he wanted his freedom. Impatient, he waited to see his doctor whom, he was told, could be in to see him any time from 8:00 AM to 5:00 PM. Jack was beginning to understand some of the angst he and his fellow physicians caused when they were inconsistent in the times that they rounded on their patients. He resolved, from now on, to try to notify his hospitalized patients each day what time he would see them. It would be like making an appointment in reverse.

Jack had tried to call Kathy from the room, but was defeated by the hospital system. He could not make long-distance calls without a calling card. He had settled for watching college football, but was even more vexed to find that all he could find that day were Iowa football games. His beloved Huskers were not even playing.

****

Alicia and Missy were getting tired of playing card games. They had settled into reading books, but even that was getting old. All day Saturday they had sat in their small motel room. Earlier, when he had gotten up to stretch, Roy had complained of chest pain and dizziness and, against his objections, had been taken to the hospital. The deputy had returned alone stating that Roy would be staying there for some tests and antibiotics. This added to Missy's distress. She worried about their farm and had called a few friends to keep an eye on things. The snow was already melting since it was still early in the season. There were no crops to deal with and her garden was already finished, but she fretted, nonetheless.

Alicia had spoken again to her aunt and uncle who were much relieved to hear her voice. Bonnie had found it hard to stop crying. Alicia did not fill them in on the details of the murder or her flight, but reassured them that she was all right. She told them of her plans to stay with Missy for a while and help on the farm, though not revealing anything about where it was located.

Alicia was interested in learning more about the interior design business and was thinking about taking some college classes in that area of study. Missy had told her that there was a community college in Mason City. Alicia didn't mention it, but she also wanted to go back to that church where she her eyes had been opened. Like Missy, Alicia worried about Roy and wanted to see him at the hospital, but the deputies wouldn't let her go there. They were too nervous about having her out of the motel room and wanted to keep her away from her attacker. She was told to stay put until after Monday. She and Missy were assured that they would be kept informed of Roy's condition.

****

Rebecca and Justin, after a heated phone conversation with Chief Barton, had taken rooms at the same motel as Alicia and her new "family." They had left Lincoln without discussing their plans with him, though he was somewhat mollified when Rebecca explained the whole situation and the capture of the suspected killer. Rebecca had taken most of the heat and had painted Justin as more of a "hero" than, perhaps, he really was. She conveniently left out Justin's part in the doctor's trip to Iowa. He was just starting out in his career and a black spot in the record would be a significant detriment. For her, it would be only another bump in the road.

They had heard no more from the CIA and were wondering if waiting was useful. They still didn't know exactly where or when the meeting would take place on Monday. The injured woman was showing signs of waking, but they weren't sure if she would be communicating in time.

Rebecca and Justin had also played cards often, asking a deputy to join them. Justin had an uncanny way of knowing what cards had been played and Rebecca didn't want to be the only loser in their games. She was glad they had not played for money.

Justin was stymied in trying to find out any more information. He had set up a computer hub utilizing a high speed connection in his room. He had found out the name of Connie's boss, but repeated inquiries had been rebuffed. Alicia could not help because she knew little of the upper echelons of either her own or Connie's places of employment. He didn't have enough information to request a search warrant to gain full access to the business or their information and the Chicago police were not being cooperative. He had tried to speak to the man, Mark Antony, who appeared to be one of the top executives, and was told he was "out of town." He explained, "I would be happy to speak to him by phone. Just connect me to his cell."

"Sorry sir, but he cannot be reached at this time."

Justin had left his number, but had little hope that Mark Antony would call back. He had nevertheless, set up his phone with his computer so that he could try to run a trace on any calls that came in.

Waiting appeared to be the word of the day and it was raising their anxiety level. Rebecca had suggested returning to Nebraska so they could at least keep up with other work. Justin had wanted to move to Chicago. In the end they both decided waiting for the woman to wake was more important and she was staying put for the time being. A police officer had been assigned to remain near her bed and would call them as soon as it appeared they could question her.

Dr. Sharp's presence in the same hospital caused a little twinge of concern to Rebecca. The two had nearly killed each other. She wasn't sure they should remain so close to each other. It still bothered her that Dr. Sharp had stayed so close to this investigation. It seemed odd to her that a mere innocent bystander would go to these lengths. When it was over she hoped to have a long talk with him to try to figure him out.

****

Antony did not remain idle. He cleaned out his safe and had its contents neatly stowed in aluminum cases. He had a few books and mementos he wanted to take with him, but he wasn't sure about Delia's things. He had perused her shelves and clothing and had chosen what he thought she might want. The one thing she wanted, her diamond, they had not been able to get. He knew that they could purchase anything else they needed once they were safely away.

Upon his return he had received a report from his cleaning lady of a man who had entered his apartment on Friday. The man had done nothing but ask for him and he could get nothing out of her in the way of a description. Not wanting police presence at this time he decided let the issue drop. He would soon be gone from this city, but he was curious about who it could have been.

Antony's board of directors would receive notice of the sale of their business on Tuesday morning. He smiled as he thought of their faces when they realized they were all out of jobs with no severance. They had been puppets at best and he would be happy to see them squirm.

The best part of all this was that no one would realize what he had done. They wouldn't be chased because no police force would realize they had even broken any laws. The actual theft had occurred years earlier. While this sale was itself illegal, it would be done in secret. He believed that his risk was minimal leaving the country merely prudence.

The murders were regrettable, but only James and Delia could tie him to them. Antony wasn't worried about James who had done what was needed. Antony would have been happy as a lark except for that one thing. He didn't know where Delia had gone. There had been no murders in Iowa as far as he could tell. He had received no calls. She had simply vanished without a trace that he could find.

In the evening, as he was completing the final draft of his letter to the board, the light on his desk flashed. He reached for the desk phone, which was always scrambled, and answered. By the readout he saw that the caller was Cindy.

"I hope you have good news for me."

There was a hesitation then she said, "Sir, I honestly have looked under every rock I can find. I couldn't find anyone with the names you gave me. Our database search came up empty. You told me to focus on Iowa and I did find that there was a significant increase in police and county sheriff activity on the night you indicated. But they have it sealed too tight for my sources so I don't know what that was about. I'm truly sorry sir."

Antony tried to control his rising anger. He still needed Cindy and her expertise. Her security measures would keep him safe in the final moments of his deal.

"Very well, Cindy. You did all you could. I guess I'll see you Monday night to conclude our business together."

"Sir," came her hesitant voice. "Did you hear about James?"

"Hear what about James?" now she had his attention.

"Oh! He was found dead in his office. He shot himself!"

"What! When did this happen?" His voice was soft but carried a venomous pitch.

"I think they found his body Saturday. It was his cleaning service."

Antony was thinking furiously. *Would this derail his plan?* Then a smile slowly crept across his face. This would solve one problem. He no longer had to be concerned about James spilling the beans about the murders. Malcomb and Cindy knew relatively little about them. "You just earned another half share."

Cindy was at first perplexed then her mercenary character surfaced. She realized her own good fortune and had hung up without another word.

Antony had heard nothing from his law enforcement contacts about the girl Alicia. Now, at least, he had something to go on, an increase in police and county sheriff activity in the very area where Delia had been. It was slim. It might have been a drug bust or just a series of accidents. It had been a terrible night of ice and wind. Nevertheless, he placed one more call. When he mentioned what he now knew the response made him smile again.

"Is that what went down? A woman? Which hospital? What is her condition?"

All of his plans now changed.

53

Sunday

Jack had convinced his doctor to remove the chest tube on Saturday night. They had watched him closely overnight and he had done well. His arm still hurt, but he could move it and use his hand. He had walked the halls several times before the change of shift at 7:00 AM. His car had been moved to the parking lot by the law enforcement personnel and now he stood waiting impatiently, dressed in his street clothes, for release.

Jack had tried to get into the room where his assailant was being cared for, but was not even allowed on the floor. The policeman had stopped him as soon as he had gotten off the elevator.

"It's for your own protection sir," had been the overly forceful pronouncement by the uniformed man. Jack saw that arguing would do no good and resignedly got back on the elevator and returned to his room.

By now the hallways were worse than boring. He felt imprisoned and anxious to be free even though he had only been there a few days. He thought about his patients who sometimes remained in bed for weeks.

"No wonder they get irritable," he thought, "One, at least, needs a change of scenery."

At last Dr. Carlson appeared at his door.

"The nurse told me that if I didn't come in early you were going to wear out the tile in the hallway. Ready to leave?"

"You bet!" came Jack enthusiastic reply.

"Doctors make the worst patients. How's your pain?" he asked peering over his glasses.

"Not too bad. I think I can drive."

"Well, I'll give you a prescription of hydrocodone, but you know better that to try to drive after taking that."

Jack nodded, "Of course. I'll wait until I stop somewhere before

I take anything stronger than ibuprofen. I may only go part way today."

The doctor lifted Jack's shirt and listened carefully to the lungs from both sides of his chest. "I still hear plenty of noise in this side," pointing to Jacks injured side. "You take it easy," he changed his finger's aim to the center of Jack's chest. "I mean it. You don't want that lung collapsing on you or you may be worse than before."

Jack was mildly surprised at the intensity of feeling shown by his doctor. He felt all right and hadn't realized there was such risk. "All right. Thank you for everything you've done."

Dr. Carlson laid a hand on his good arm.

"Your insurance company will provide me the thanks I want."

He chuckled at his own joke and waved.

"Take it easy," he threw in for good measure.

The nurse followed with a stack of forms for Dr. Sharp to sign. She gave him a prescription and insisted upon reading all the risks of taking the various medicines. He had to stay on antibiotics for a week and should see a surgeon for a checkup on his wound in a few days.

Jack promised to follow instructions and, when she had finally left, grabbed his packed bag and slipped out the door. He tried once more to check on the woman who had attacked him, but the policeman eyed him all the way down the hall. Jack retreated to the elevator and took it to the lobby.

Jack found his car and took out his cell phone. He decided to plug it in and charge it for a while before trying to use it. The cord on the charger was a little short and it was awkward to try to use the phone while it was plugged in to the accessory outlet.

He had asked if he could see Alicia before leaving town and the detectives had given permission for him to stop by the motel. As he approached the room he noticed that the deputy stepped out into his path.

"Are you Dr. Sharp?"

"Yes."

"Detective Sweate said it was okay for you to visit, but make it short. The ladies want to go to church this morning and they need to finish getting ready."

Jack merely nodded and pushed open the motel door. Alicia was sitting on the end of the bed, apparently already dressed for church. She wore a stylish lavender dress and her hair was perfectly combed. She had on short sparkly earrings and a faux diamond necklace.

"How appropriate," thought Jack to himself. Her make-up was conservative, and complemented her already attractive appearance.

Her head turned as he entered.

Jack smiled warmly and said, "If I were only thirty years younger..."

Alicia gave a little screech of delight, and jumped up.

"Dr. Sharp. Thank you, thank you. How are you?" She started to give him a hug, then, remembering his injuries just took his right hand and leaned close, giving him a kiss on his cheek.

"You look radiant today, Alicia, and may I say, beautiful."

She actually blushed. "Thank you sir."

"Just call me Dr. Jack," he said smiling. "Will you be returning to Nebraska soon?"

Alicia kept hold of his hand and led him to the soft chair in the room. "No. I'm actually going to stay with Missy." She laid out her plans for him as he nodded approval.

"It sounds like you have a good idea. I hear you are going to church. Which church do you attend?"

Alicia didn't know how to answer. "I don't really know. I only went once to the one near Mason City. I don't know what that one is. Today we're going to the Baptist church across the road. Its close and the deputies think it will be all right. Missy said she doesn't care as long as she can worship the Lord." She hesitated a second then said, "I want to too."

Jack looked at her and kept quiet for a moment. "You say you didn't used to go. I think it's wonderful that you want to go now. Did something change your mind?" He wanted to let her speak for herself. He knew that sometimes people go to church out of obligation or guilt, but her comment made him think she was sincerely interested in attending.

"I prayed the other day that God would forgive me. I want to be a better person."

Jack said, "You're not a bad person."

"No, no. But last week the pastor said we all have sin. I want that to be cleaned up. He said all we have to do is pray and God will forgive us. We can ask Jesus to lead us. I don't know everything, but that's what I remember."

Jack smiled again. "I think you understand it very well. I'm a Christian too. You're a better evangelist than a lot of us. Just keep on talking about the Lord and people will hear the message. I guess, maybe, something good has come of this whole thing." He had tears in his eyes as Missy stepped from the bathroom. She had slipped a skirt and blouse on before coming out.

"It's a good thing I got dressed!" she said as she saw Jack sitting with Alicia. "Or you would have been in for a shock." That brought a laugh from both of them. This made Jack wince in pain, however, and Missy apologized for the levity.

"Alicia tells me she is going home with you. That's wonderful. I wish I had time to get to know you both better. Where's Roy?" He looked around the room and found no sign of him.

Missy answered, "He has an infection from his wound so they put him in the hospital. He said he won't stay past tomorrow, no matter what the doctor tells him."

Jack nodded. "I want to get home, too, so I think I should go."

"Won't you go to church with us?" pleaded Alicia.

He started to object then looked at Missy. "Okay, I'll go. I really have a good reason to worship this morning. What about those detectives? Do you think we could get them to come along."

Missy screwed up her face. "Not likely. That lady detective is hard as nails. But, maybe the younger guy will." She put her hand to the side of her mouth as if to make an aside, "I think he kind of likes Alicia. He was over here checking on her four or five times yesterday."

Alicia blushed again, "Missy!"

Jack said, "Leave it to me."

Half an hour later all five of them were pulling into the parking lot of the church just a few blocks from the motel. Rebecca was somewhat irritated. She hadn't been to a church for some time. In fact, she could not remember ever attending a Baptist church. From what she had heard and seen on television, she expected dancing in the aisles, unrestrained singing and speaking in tongues.

Justin maneuvered his position in such a way as to be able to sit next to Alicia. He, likewise, was not a frequent church-goer, but he wasn't actually concentrating on the church. However, both he and Rebecca were surprised and glad to find the service to be very reverent and the music was very good.

Rebecca, though, was uncomfortable that no-one knelt or crossed themselves before the cross in the front of the church, but was not shy about doing so herself. This brought back some pleasant memories from years past. She decided to make it a point to check out her local diocese when she returned. There was no harm in getting a little of God back into her life.

Justin was intrigued by the subject matter of the sermon. The Bible was one book he had not spent time reading. The message from this pastor spoke of how joy doesn't just mean happiness. He also discussed a passage about armor from the book of Galatians. He resolved to purchase a Bible, but knowing that there were many versions, decided to talk to Dr. Sharp sometime about which one he should get.

At the end of the service Jack made his good-byes and at last was on the road again. Headed south to interstate 80 and then west, his mind began to move on to what he would do yet this week. He had to rest, but he was sure that there was paperwork he could catch up on in his office.

He hoped everything would work out for the police and the young lady. It seemed like an ending, but he was aware that the real criminals had yet to be caught. He knew, too, that he would probably end up being a witness at a future trial for the woman who had attempted to kill them and had killed the two other people. But right now he only wanted to put this behind him and focus on the future. He thought of Kathy and once again checked to see if his phone was charged. It was close to one hundred percent so he decided at the next rest stop he would give her a call.

****

Antony could mobilize a small army if necessary. He had his business contacts and his spies, but all that was needed for manpower was cold hard cash, of which he had plenty. Now he had a new operation to quickly plan and execute so his mind was clicking at high gear. He had always relied on Delia, or Sharon, her real name, for many things, but the plain truth was that he loved her. He didn't want her to die and he would do everything in his power to get her back and to get her out of the hands of the police. He smiled to himself. If he could both save Sharon and complete the big deal, life would be sweet indeed.

He had already put James' suicide out of his mind. It would not affect his plans. He needed a few specialists who would keep their mouths shut and he would lead them himself. His time was short, but he had a plan and he was confident it could be done. He was sure he had the element of surprise on his side.

First he confirmed with Malcomb about the pick-up point for his share from the deal to be finalized the next day. He had no reason to back out of his agreements and he wasn't generally stingy. Someday in the future Cindy and Malcomb could again be useful to him. Next he made the necessary arrangements for drivers, pilots, muscle, and medical assistance that he would need to get Sharon out of the hospital and safely out of the country.

Antony's primary repository of wealth languished in off-shore accounts which he believed were safe from the prying eyes of the various governments, in nations where these had been in the past. He also had accounts in Switzerland.

Sharon had once asked why he had to keep making money and he had countered, "Why do you need to keep killing people?" She had said it was for the thrill, but he knew that she had just as much of a compulsion to kill as he did for acquiring wealth.

He had learned, from his police sources, a thin sketch of what had happened in the Iowa farmhouse, but wasn't sure how Sharon had been hurt. He did know which hospital she was being treated in and was certain he could get her away from there. The latest physician's report was that she was waking up and that they hoped to remove her endotracheal tube later that day. Antony hoped that this would be the case as it would make her extraction simpler. His plan was set and most of the players were getting ready. He congratulated himself at having set up such an intricate plan in a short time.

****

Kathy had ditched the cane. She now was able to walk around her house without stumbling and only occasionally leaning against a wall. She had begun writing friends and family detailing her recent experiences and asking them for prayer explaining that she trusted God to take care of her, but she was also aware that He hadn't promised to spare her from illness.

Kathy's faith was based upon knowing that God had promised to keep her "in the palm of His hand." This meant to her that she didn't need to be worried about dying, as she knew she would be in heaven. Yet she hoped to go on living and, despite her grim diagnosis, she was happy that Jack's initial concern about dementia had been wrong. Though a tumor could mean a more imminent death the thought of slowly losing her memory seemed scarier to her. She had seen members of her family go through the long agonizing journey of losing their ability to think. First they had forgotten names and places, but ultimately they could not even care for themselves.

Kathy had good insurance and her savings would be adequate so she didn't have financial worries. Her older children were living on their own. However, she grieved for Esther, the light of her heart. As the last child, Esther was very close to her mother. Unlike many young people Esther loved to be with her and "hang out" with her. She had many friends and they rolled their eyes when she said things like, "... but Mom wouldn't want me to do that." However, she was never embarrassed to be seen holding her mother's hand.

Kathy wasn't sure what would become of Esther if she died. Her oldest son, Frank, had already told her not to worry as he and his wife would gladly finish raising her and care for her. Nevertheless, she wanted to continue to be there for her. She only wished that Esther still had a father in her life.

The last thought brought Jack to her mind. Why hadn't he called back? As if by the mere thought of him, the phone rang and Jack was on the other end.

"Hi," was his simple greeting.

"Hi, yourself." He could hear the smile in her voice.

"Did I catch you at a good time?" he said.

"You can catch me anytime. Well, almost anytime. Midnight might not be the best."

He laughed, "All right no midnight calls. I'm on the road and heading west."

"That's great. How do you feel? When will you be back?" Kathy was having a hard time restraining her delight.

"I'm still sore, but I can drive. I'm about six hours away if I keep up a steady pace. It's a little hard to hold the steering wheel with my bum arm. I guess the doctor was right that I should take it easy."

"'Physician heal thyself?' I've heard that doctors make the worst patients, but I'm not one to speak. I have been a patient too recently. With our wounds we'll look like quite the pair."

"You have been a wonderful patient. I'll see you soon."

"Bye."

Jack closed his phone and was about to get back into his car when he noticed the little voicemail symbol on the phone's screen. He hadn't seen it before and wasn't sure how long it had been present. He opened it up, curious to see who had called, and speed-dialed the voicemail box.

After the introduction the message he heard sent shocks down his spine,

"Dr. Sharp. This is James Rizzo. I'm the one who told you where the girl was. I hope you helped her. I'm sorry I couldn't speak to you personally, but I have one more piece of information you might need. I wasn't going to do this, but the burden is too great to bear. I need to share it with you before the end. The Leader, Mark Antony, plans to sell diamonds to a group of Chinese businessmen. It's to take place Monday in Des Moines at Adventureland. The park is closed on weekdays this time of year so it is private and they will have security. I'm afraid I don't know exactly where or when. I couldn't find out. I'm sorry. Please tell them all. I'm sorry..."

The connection went dead at that point, whether from too much time or just a lost signal he couldn't tell. Jack couldn't believe his ears. He had thought he was finished with this whole affair. Now one more piece of the puzzle had fallen into place. He tried to call the number back, but there was no answer. He listened to the message two more times to be sure he understood correctly. It was now Sunday afternoon. There was just enough time to let the police know.

Jack knew he should let the police take care of everything, but he had been involved from the beginning. This Mark Antony was responsible for at least two deaths and attempts on his life. Jack knew now that he could trust Rebecca and Justin and he realized one more thing, he wanted to see this through. He would also be there.

Next, he called Kathy to let her know he would be delayed. He didn't tell her the whole truth, but let her think he was stopping in Des Moines, in order to rest.

His last call was to Justin. He decided to take a chance, "Hello Justin?"

"Yes Dr. Sharp?"

"Justin, I have a proposition for you."

****

"You did what?" Rebecca was furious. Justin had never seen her in such a state. "Do you realize what you've done? It could mean your badge, buddy. Again!"

Justin was now less certain about his course of action than he had been, but stood his ground. "Wait a minute. Hear me out."

"I can't believe it. You'd probably want to negotiate with terrorists if that made sense to you too!" She was stomping around the room paying little attention to Justin's plea.

Justin took the offensive, "Stop! I know you are in charge, but if I hadn't been here we wouldn't have found out half of what we *do* know. You still treat me like a kid!"

Rebecca did stop, as Justin stood eye to eye with her. Her face red, she exhaled, stared for a moment and then turned away. She was silent for a few more seconds. After regaining her composure she turned back, and said, with a challenge in her expression, "Okay, detective, explain your actions."

"Dr. Sharp said he had a voicemail that explains where we need to go. He said he didn't want to say anything over the phone, but to meet him in Des Moines as soon as possible. He just wants to be with us when we go in."

"But he wouldn't tell you where or when?"

"Like I said, he was worried about telling us over the phone."

"Justin we can't take a civilian into an arrest."

"But we need this information."

"If he withholds it we will have to arrest him."

Justin laughed, "Oh that would look good in the papers. 'Hero from Iowa farmhouse attack arrested for keeping his mouth shut.' He's no stranger to risk. We just get the information and give him Kevlar. We can have him sign all kinds of release papers if he wants to come along. We keep him behind us out of the way."

Exasperated, Rebecca sat down. Unfortunately Justin's argument made some sense but the doctor's lack of trust was maddening. They desperately needed the information if they were going to try to get to the bottom of this whole mess. It was too bad the doctor could not be more forthcoming. At last, giving in, she said, "Who'll interview the woman when she is more awake?"

"If we already know about the deal we won't need to talk to her. Leave it to the local guys."

She thought a minute searching for yet another argument. Picking up her purse she found the business card given to her by Agent Bob.

Glancing at the number she said, "You want some pizza?"

54

To Jack's surprise there were people in the parking lot and crowds going in and out of Adventureland. He had expected the amusement park to be completely shut down. Then he read above the gate in large lettering, "LAST DAY HALF PRICE."

This was a break he could not pass up, deciding, despite his injury, to walk around inside the park. He had not frequented amusement parks as the parks usually held little interest to him. He imagined, though, how much fun they might be with young children along, an experience he regretted missing since he had never been a parent. Perhaps if things worked out with Kathy he could come back with her and her grandchildren. Esther probably would have fun at a place like this too.

As he sauntered up to the gate he could see the giant rollercoaster rails towering over the park to the right. It had been years since he had ridden on anything like this and he was certain it had not been so big back then. There were no cars running and he assumed it was due to the cold weather and recent snow. What would draw people to an amusement park at the beginning of winter, especially if some of the rides weren't working?

Large posters with bright red lettering announced an afternoon concert by a fairly well known country music artist of whom even he had heard. There was a craft fair and a quilt showing. To Jack it seemed much like a county fair. The midway was open so he assumed people wanted one more chance for a little fun before the really cold winter set in.

He paid the entrance charge and passed through the gate. Directly ahead he saw a vertical tower, which did appear to be functioning. People sat in seats on a car that shot straight up the tower. According to his map it was called the "Space Shot." He considered it, but decided his arm might not like the "g" forces.

A miniature train passed in front of him and he heard squeals of delight from small children riding the carousel with its brightly painted horses. There were excited and terrified screams to his left and looked up in time to see a platform going through an arc with people strapped into their seats upside-down. It was called "The Inverter."

No, thanks!

Walking around he tried to imagine the park empty of people. The constant noise made it hard to do, but tomorrow the place would be deserted except for maintenance people and clean-up crews. He tried to decide where the most likely spot for a meeting would be. He figured that because of the potential for bad weather it was probably indoors. There were many buildings in the park, but he supposed that they would be locked up, though a lock would probably not deter a criminal who had already shown a willingness to kill.

As he turned to his right he had a vague sense of déjà vu. There stood a small white chapel complete with a small steeple. His mind fled to Africa and the village church where Sister Mary Elizabeth, Sharon and he had stood as men ransacked the village. It was from there that they had taken Sharon away. That African church had been made of mud brick, but white-washed and styled after just such a building as this. To him it had always seemed so out of place in that dusty Zairian village.

For some reason he felt certain that this was the place where the deal would take place. As if to thumb his nose at God, this monster, whoever he was, would carry out his act of defiance right here. It was only a guess, but Jack felt that it was as good as any other. He found the door unlocked, in fact; there was no bolt or lock on the door. He went in. Wooden pews marched up to a slightly raised choir area. A small, square, honey oak lectern stood in the center of the choir flanked by double rows of solid oak pews facing each other in the choir. A wooden board hung along the side wall depicting the assigned hymn numbers and the number of parishioners who last attended. Jack wondered if they actually had held a service there in the morning.

Exploring the choir area he found one panel on the right that was slightly out of proportion to the others. Looking more closely he noted a small catch, painted to match the wood. It was difficult to see from more than a few feet away. Lifting the catch he gave a slight push. The panel budged. Pushing again, harder this time, the panel opened. Musty air greeted him, but he ducked his head and stepped forward finding himself in a small room. Along one wall was an old broom, its frayed and broken bristles littering the floor. A small pine bench sat along the wall corresponding to the outside of the building. There was no outside entrance. A light switch worked, but the bulb had long ago given out. He found scattered papers on the floor. Picking one up, he saw that it was a church bulletin.

Hand-typed, it was dated May 15, 1966. The congregation had sung hymns 462, 133, and 17 from some hymnal on that Sunday and title of the sermon had been, "What do we do with SIN?"

He stood thinking. If he was right about the church being the location of the meeting, this would make an ideal hiding place. He could be here ahead of the deal-makers. But what if they chose the train station or midway? It seemed far-fetched and foolish. What made him think he could figure out the mind of a criminal of this caliber? Stepping back out of the small room he carefully closed the door and checked to see that he had left no trace of his explorations Satisfied, he exited the chapel.

****

Justin finished checking them into the Des Moines motel. Staying in small motels was fast becoming his least favorite pastime. He wanted to get back to his own apartment and his own bed. Young as he was, the poor mattresses he had been sleeping on had left him with an ache in his low back. Likewise, the last bed had been so short that his feet had gotten cold sticking out from under the covers.

He and Rebecca were given adjoining rooms which they quickly found and then parked nearby. As they left their vehicle Rebecca said,

"I wonder where our good friend the doctor has gotten to?"

"Maybe he changed his mind and decided to go home."

"Fat chance of that!" Rebecca lifted her bag from the trunk. It was twice the size and weight of Justin's overnight case.

"What did you put in there?" he asked.

"Just a few things I find necessary. Justin, that's just one thing you'll need to learn about women."

He merely shook his head. His electronic key took three swipes to work in the lock, but he was pleasantly surprised at the up-dated facilities in his room. The exterior of the motel looked well-worn, but they had remodeled earlier that year and he, for one, appreciated the result.

And the bed was queen-sized.

Rebecca came through the door which connected their two rooms. "Maybe you should try calling him. See if he is willing to talk."

"All right, but don't count on it." He slipped his phone from its belt case.

****

The guard had watched, mildly interested, as the small group of doctors, nurses and respiratory therapists had entered the room. He recognized several of them and had been told to expect the entourage. They seemed to mill about the patient he was guarding then he heard a sound that made him cringe. It sounded like some-one coughing, choking, and swallowing at the same time. Next, he heard the suction machine and a woman's cough. He didn't like to hear "bodily" noises and the sound of this woman's endotracheal tube being removed nearly caused him to lose his last meal.

Between the healthcare workers, he could see the woman in bed put her hand to her mouth and heard her cough, though he didn't hear her say anything. A few minutes later as most of them were leaving he asked the doctor,

"Sir, will the prisoner be able to answer questions now?"

The doctor looked disgusted. "Can't you let her rest? We just extubated her." At the puzzled look he received, he said in explanation, a little more kindly, "I removed her "breathing" tube. She can barely whisper. It would be best to wait."

"Thank you doctor." Despite the warnings of the doctor the

policeman was on the radio a few minutes later. "Yes sir, they removed the tube... Yes I think she is awake. Okay, an hour. Yes sir." It looked like they would finally get some answers.

The guard was about to turn around when a shadow passed to his left. Next he saw sparkling lights, a sudden pain, and then nothing. Antony had koshed him from behind. As he entered Delia's room, a nurse let out a yelp and tried to push past him. He struck her down with the same billy club he had used on the guard and dealt her a savage blow to the back of her head. She dropped, unconscious, without another sound. One of the nurses from his own entourage, pulled the limp body of the nurse to one side and Antony moved to Delia's bed.

There was surprise on her face when she saw him and she tried to speak to him, but no sound came from her lips. Antony's team followed closely behind with all the equipment they would need. Right now was the most delicate time because another nurse or doctor could stumble onto them and raise an alarm.

Delia reached out her hand and said groggily, "Antony?"

It came out as a hoarse croak. "You didn't leave me. You fool!" The last was said as she gave in to being lifted onto a moving gurney. She sounded upset, but had a faint smile on her lips and tears in her swollen eyes. "Use a wheelchair," she said. They complied, pleased that it would seem less out of place.

Antony stood near her. With real tenderness on his face he reached out and touched hers. "Sharon, I was so worried about you. I didn't know for a long time what had happened."

"I can't remember," she whispered.

Antony nodded and motioned to the others. She was quickly wheeled into the hallway. They had shielded her face and were able to make it to the staff elevator without raising suspicion. Most of the house personnel didn't know that she was off the ventilator and able to travel in a wheel chair.

Once on the ground level Antony's team quickly loaded Delia into an ambulance and drove away. The entire successful operation had taken less than fifteen minutes. Antony shook his head in amazement at their efficiency. He had not believed it would be so easy.

"How do you feel?" he said.

"My head hurts and I can't use my right arm."

He now noticed the soft plastic brace holding Delia's slightly bent elbow.

"Have you been out of bed?"

"I've only been awake a few hours. I was still on that horrible machine until a few minutes ago. The drugs are just starting to wear off and I feel like I've been floating in clouds. How long have I been here? Where are we?"

"You went to the farm house on Thursday. This is Sunday evening. They brought you to Cedar Rapids for hospital care. The care notes said you have a fractured skull and a small blood clot under the skull so I brought a couple of nurses to take care of you if needed. It's a good thing you're breathing on your own." He held her face in both hands, "We'll get clear of this country in just a few days."

"Sunday?" She tried to rise, but felt too much pain and lay back again. "I don't remember any farm house or even how I got hurt."

"That's not important. Do you remember what we're doing tomorrow?"

"Tomorrow? Monday? Let me think. It has to do with money and a big sale. Des Moines?"

"Good! What do you think, Jocelyn?" He turned to a middle-aged woman wearing a nurse's uniform.

"It sounds to me like she only has amnesia for the immediate injury period. Delia, I'm a neurosurgical nurse. What's the last thing you do remember about the day you were hurt?"

Antony looked at his woman, anxiously hoping she wouldn't go into detail about her plans. He needn't have worried, however.

"I remember driving into some little town. I was in a dress shop. It all gets blurry there."

Jocelyn looked at Antony, "Do you know when that was?"

Antony answered, "Yes, that was the day of her injury. Thank you, Jocelyn."

"Sir, I think she should rest now. She will not be able to travel far unless she gets significantly stronger."

Antony, with a rare show of emotion, leaned over and kissed Sharon on the lips.

"I'm so glad we found you."

She was already asleep.

****

Jack had wandered around the amusement park trying to decide upon the wisest course of action. He knew that the wisest action of course, would be to go home and leave the whole thing to the police. But his stubbornness was keeping him in the game. He was growing hungry, cold and tired and would have loved some good dinner, a warm bed and a good night's rest. His pain was still significant, but he was happy that his breathing seemed little affected and he was sure that this meant his wound was still healing well.

His mind kept coming back to the idea of staying at the park. While the "bad guys" might have a way to get in on Monday he would have to wait with the police. He thought about what James' message had said. "There will be security." How could the police get in unnoticed? Once they showed up anyone in the park would be able to get away through dozens of potential exits. It would take a small army to thwart this business. He had a unique opportunity to forestall the plan.

Making up his mind against all reason, he headed for the main gate. On his cell phone he dialed a now familiar number. "Hello, Justin? This is Dr. Sharp. I have the information you needed."

Jack told him about the plan for the deal at the amusement park. "But I don't know how you are going to be able to get in unnoticed."

Justin answered, "Doc. You need to leave that to us. We'll figure it out."

"Okay, Justin. You go ahead and figure it out. I'll make my own plans. I'll let you know in the morning how things are going."

"But ... "

Jack folded up the phone. He didn't know why he felt so strongly that he needed to take care of things. He was a doctor, not a maverick. Even in the Special Forces he was expected to stay in the rear and follow the shooters, though there wasn't always a "rear" and he had taken part in plenty of firefights. Nevertheless, this time, he pressed forward with his own course of action expecting that he would face the consequences when the time came.

As he headed out he let the gate attendant stamp his hand with a symbol that would allow reentry. He also noticed the metal detectors which had not caught his eye at his first approach. This would pose an obstacle he had not counted on, though he understood the worry any large park might have of gun-toting criminals wandering about their facility.

Jack found his car and drove to the nearest shopping mall. He found the stores he needed and purchased a few food items. He bought thermal underwear at a department store and a small backpack in which to carry his items. Glancing at his watch he noticed, too, that his time was growing short. The final closing of the entrance to the park was scheduled for less than an hour away.

The sun was below the horizon as Jack pulled along the road paralleling the amusement park. There was a magenta glow along the western skyline. The chapel spire could be seen above the wall on the North side of the park. He opened his glove compartment and took out his nine millimeter semi-automatic. This part was going to be tricky, but necessary. He would not be caught unarmed this time.

Jack left his car parked on the roadside and, as quickly as possible, moved along the perimeter of the park. Pain in his side occasionally shook him and he found that his pace was slowed by a new tightness in his chest. His arm ached and he was very fatigued. Yet he relied upon his old training and put the pain aside in his mind. As he reached the point opposite the church he took out the bag in which he had stowed his pistol, ammunition, and foodstuffs. He had prepared it for this plan. He swung the sack high into the air clearing to top of the wall and over. He had given some forethought at the mall and purchased a blanket, which he had wrapped around the bag to cushion it as it was tossed. He could use the cover against the cold this night when he returned to the amusement park. The effort made him wince, and he hoped that he would be able to find the parcel again in the dark.

He got back in his car and drove to the parking lot. There were significantly fewer cars and he hoped he would not look too conspicuous as he entered again. He had the foresight though to park away from the entrance and he even tied a white cloth he kept in the glovebox, on the door handle.

Jack needn't have worried. There was still a large presence in the amusement park and a crowd was forming near the train station. Cars filled with new arrivals were letting people off for the official closing ceremonies as well. There was still a guard and Jack could see a green light glowing on a panel to the side of the metal detector. He was glad he had not tried to enter with his weapon.

Jack skirted the crowd, anxious now for a place to sit down. He found his way to the chapel. Lights flickered over the paths, but there were few people in this section of the park. Glancing from side to side, he approached the wall next to the chapel. With a small LED flashlight he searched the brush at the base of the wall. Spotting the blanket wrapped bag, he scooped it up, quickly entered the chapel and closed the door behind him. His plan was to stay ahead of everyone no matter what time the deal was to take place.

Jack took out some water and dosed himself with two of the hydrocodone tablets he had been given for pain. It was intense in several areas now and he could no longer ignore it. He chose crackers, some food from the bag and he thought he would try to eat a little bit once the pain improved. Jack figured that if he didn't use his light no one would notice his presence in the chapel, but he could duck into the small storage area if necessary. Only then did he remember that his car would sit alone in the parking lot, all night long. Sighing, he laid down on a pew to rest. It was locked and marked as if there was car trouble; perhaps that would would help it go unnoticed until tomorrow when he could move it.

55

Monday

Antony had made a final check on the arrangements. Everything was in order. He was assured that his clients had entered the country inconspicuously and were, even now, getting ready to meet him at the park. The security crews were taking up their positions and would be in contact with him via headset communication devices. Cindy was in town, but was not to go to the meeting. Malcomb was waiting in Chicago as planned. James' body rested, finally, safe in a Chicago morgue.

Sharon was stronger this morning, but still unable to walk very far on her own. She had a racking cough, but had not run a fever, and Jocelyn had started her on antibiotics, just to be safe. Her memory was still fuzzy and she still had difficulty getting her right arm to do what she wanted it to. Part of her difficulty walking was due to weakness in her right leg as well. Jocelyn had told Antony that this was like having a stroke, indicating that there was some brain damage. Antony refused to let Sharon out of his sight. She could sit up now and they would use a wheelchair for her, but he intended for her to accompany him to the deal. This would change things with the Chinese a little, but he believed they would be able to adapt. They had little to fear from him and a great deal of wealth to gain.

Everything was ready to go. Despite their setbacks, he was basically pleased with the arrangements. Laughing to himself that he had, once again, hoodwinked law enforcement, he believed he had planned for any eventuality.

With confidence he stepped out into the bright sunlight of a calm brisk fall morning. There had been a few bumps in the road, but they were near the end of this journey.

****

Rebecca finished the last Velcro strap of her Kevlar body armor. Justin, chafing in his, was buckling on his holster. All around them policemen were going through the same routine, checking weapons, adjusting helmets. Their uniforms bristled with extra magazines and flash-bang grenades. They didn't know if this assault would end in bloodshed, but they would make every effort to see that it was not theirs.

The Des Moines police chief stood before them like a general. "All right people. Get ready to mount up."

Justin said in an aside to Rebecca, "He thinks he's in the Marines."

Rebecca shot a look back at him, "He was, and you know what they say, 'once a Marine, always a marine.'"

Everyone in business-like fashion moved toward their vehicles. The past two hours had been spent in rapid-fire briefings outlining the plan of action. Under no circumstances were they to fire weapons unless they received explicit orders. With a group of prominent Chinese businessmen involved, the potential for an international incident loomed dangerously before them.

The Chinese had been identified upon their arrival in Los Angeles, but they had managed to avoid attempts at surveillance since then. This bothered Rebecca. Shouldn't the Department of Homeland Security (DHS) be interested? Nevertheless, these men were not considered to be terrorists, and she assumed DHS had to follow certain rules as well.

The big problem was in approaching the amusement park. They could not drive vehicles right up to the gate without being noticed and they could not surround so large a facility. They had infiltrated a spotter near by who was keeping an eye on the main entrance, but it was too big to see the entire area. Their best option was to watch for the men to gain entrance then to converge on the park entrance in rapid sequence once they thought the deal was going down. Helicopter assault teams were prepared to enter the fray if needed.

Rebecca said, "I hope that doctor knows how much trouble he is in."

"Hey look," Justin replied, "If it were not for him we wouldn't have a clue about this. I tried to call him this morning, but I only got his voicemail."

"Yeah, but he should have given us the location sooner."

"Agreed. I don't know what he is up to. I don't know where he is, maybe he slept in, but at least he's out of the way." They had given a copy of a photo of Dr. Sharp to each of the other policemen with instructions to treat him as "friendly." They didn't want him to be shot if he showed up in the area.

****

Rebecca approached the Des Moines police chief.

"Spotter working?"

"Yes. She can see into the front of the park, but buildings limit her perspective. I wish we had someone inside that place. She spotted three vehicles in the parking lot. You'll be interested to know that one of them belongs to your doctor friend. Otherwise no activity."

"The doctor's car is there? Do you suppose he is in there? I'm going to wring his neck!" came Rebecca's heated response.

The police chief, mildly surprised, raised his eyebrows, and shrugged. "He could be a hostage, but we have no way of knowing what is going on deep inside that place."

Rebecca, mollified, said, "I suppose I shouldn't be so angry with him. We would still be waiting to speak to the woman if he hadn't called."

This last comment brought color to the cheeks of the chief. "I'm afraid I have a little news about that too."

"What now!" Rebecca showed surprise.

"She was 'broken out' of the hospital yesterday. No one even saw her leave, but the guard and a nurse have concussions."

"How could that happen? She was still on life support when we left."

The chief straightened his frame, "They weren't expecting any-thing, but apparently she had been taken off the machines and a group of medical people somehow spirited her out of the facility."

"Great! What next?" She shook her head looking at the floor.

"Well, we can't worry about that now. I wish I knew where this guy gets his help. He seems one step ahead of us all the time. I hope he hasn't been warned about our assault."

The chief said shortly, "Our department is clean. Besides we didn't let anyone make calls or leave since we assembled the group last night. I believe you said that your department had a leak."

Rebecca put up a hand, "No offense meant, Chief. You're right. Let's see where we are with this plan." They moved to a table with a large map of the park and began going over the assault plan one more time.

****

Jack woke with a start. He found himself shivering despite his long underwear, blanket, coat and gloves. He felt congested and had a sore throat.

"Great! A cold is all I need." he muttered.

He had no way to warm up the little room in which he had slept and he could see his breath as he exhaled. He tried wrapping his arms around himself and he moved around the room, but his shivering wouldn't stop. He had a plastic thermos of hot chocolate which he had left for this morning. He opened the stopper and poured it into the lid. It was still warm enough to give off steam so he greedily drank the warm, sweet liquid. It wasn't too hot, but it helped him start to thaw out.

Seeing light coming through chinks in the wall he figured that the sun was up. He chided himself for sleeping too long and hoped they hadn't planned the meeting for dawn.

Jack sat on the low bench and checked his weapon. He also inventoried his wounds. He was not bleeding and his breathing came easily enough. But every movement he made felt like he was trying to move rusty hinges. His ordeal and hospital stay had left him stiff and out of shape.

The pistol was in excellent working condition and the parts moved freely despite the cold. It was a little awkward with gloves, but he released the magazine, checked the slide and the safety. Quietly pressing the magazine home he chambered a round and slipped the icy cold metal into his coat pocket. He no longer had a functional holster and needed easy access.

Poking his head out of the concealed door he found the chapel empty. He slipped into the worship area of the little church and eased open the front door. He could discern voices somewhere to the right. They were speaking in hushed tones and appeared to be approaching. Jack quickly re-closed the door and sidled up to the front window. Careful to keep his head down, he kept one eye over the sill so that he could spot the men as they passed.

In a moment two men emerged from trees along the path. They did not stop at the chapel, but one gave it a quick glance. Both were fit, athletic men and they carried submachine guns. They wore earpieces indicating communication devices. Jack still needed to know where the main event was going to occur. It didn't look like the chapel would be the location after all. He debated only a second before easing out the front of the church to attempt to follow the two men.

He paralleled them, staying behind trees. The bushes still provided cover as their leaves had not all fallen to the ground. The moist grass kept his footfalls quiet and he did not raise any alarms. Soon he had an unobstructed view of the picnic area and the carousel beyond. The men joined two others approaching from the opposite direction. They, too, carried automatic weapons. Appearing relaxed these men obviously did not expect trouble and they had brought cups of steaming coffee which the men began to drink.

Soon the four men were pointing in his direction, though he knew they weren't looking at him. They spoke on their microphones and in a moment two more large men arrived. As they all began looking toward him he became uncomfortable and wary. He had a feeling they would head in his direction very soon.

When he deemed it was safe he worked his way back toward the chapel and once again entered his "safe room."

"Time for the cavalry," he said out loud. He flipped open his phone and turned it on. Leaving the phone turned off had conserved battery power. This was not a time to be out of communication with the good guys. He saw the flashing voicemail symbol, but ignored it this time. He pressed the "3" key speed dialing Justin. Keeping his voice low Jack spoke into the phone, "Hello, Justin?"

Justin's voice came back strongly. He adjusted the volume.

"Justin, just listen. The security men are here. So far I've seen six in pairs armed with submachine guns. They didn't appear to be wearing body armor. No helmets. The meeting is either at the chapel or the picnic ground, I'm almost certain."

Justin relayed the information to Rebecca. "Where are you?" he asked Jack.

"I'm holed up in the chapel at the amusement park. I have a safe spot and can signal to you when things happen. I'll send a text because I doubt I'll be able to speak to you. You'd better get ready because it's looking imminent."

Justin was incredulous. "You're where? Do you have a death wish? You stay put!"

Jack smiled, "Justin, you need me. Admit it. I can be your eyes in here."

He heard Justin swear and thought he heard Rebecca repeat the same thing in the background. "Jack. I can't tell you or ask you to do this. Do you understand? You're doing this on your own. Jack you could get killed in there!"

Jack understood that with this last statement he was trying to absolve the police from any liability. "I have no intention of getting killed, but I understand that we need to take this guy down. I'll stay out of the way as much as possible. I am armed and wearing a red winter coat and I'll strap a reflector belt over my shoulder. Don't let your men shoot me in the back if they see me with a weapon. I'll be in touch." Without waiting for an answer he closed his phone. He made sure the ringer was turned off and placed the phone in his left coat pocket.

****

A long black limousine pulled up to the entrance of the park. The police spotter, stationed outside the park, made her report. Four men and a woman, who appeared to be Asian, emerged from the sleek vehicle. A Chevy Suburban pulled up behind and four large men, all visibly armed, stepped out to flank the first group. Together they approached the entrance gate.

Their approach was steady and confident. They were certain that they had special status, here in the United States. Prominent and well known, they were in the upper echelon business circles. Though they had not been to America before, their financial interests within the country were substantial. As guests here they could say that their business was legitimate, at least until the deal went down.

They had not broken any laws ... yet.

The security leader of the group found the gate to be open and all of them entered the park unopposed. The area ahead appeared deserted, but they knew that eyes were watching them as they turned to their right. Such precautions were expected.

At the picnic ground two armed men stepped out from the underbrush. They did not aim their weapons, but motioned with their chins. One of the Chinese men spoke to their guards who took up stations near the armed men. The key players continued on.

As the little group was led on through the park they found Mark Antony in front of the chapel, standing with arms held before him. Beside him sat a woman in a wheel chair. While this was unexpected they did not hesitate. They made their greetings to Antony.

Each of the five carried a small case handcuffed to their wrists. The tallest of the Chinese stopped, however, and said a few words to his compatriots. The second man spoke, "Antony. Where are the diamonds? We have played this game your way and are here in good faith." His voice was somewhat urgent, but there was no anger in his tone.

Antony smiled his most endearing smile. "Sirs and madam, first a greeting. Then business." He bowed low. "Welcome to the United States. I hope our business here will be most rewarding."

The head of the small delegation bowed in return and spoke several words in Chinese. His second translated, "We are most gratified in making your acquaintance and wish you well."

"Gentlemen, let me introduce my fiancé, Sharon." He placed

his hand upon her shoulder, but she only nodded.

"Sir you said nothing about her being present." It was nearly a rebuke.

Antony's voice turned steely. "You must be Yo Wang. You gave me no other names and didn't let me see you before hand. Besides you didn't say I needed to be alone. Sharon is privy to everything I do. If you are in a hurry perhaps we should continue our business. Shall we?"

He motioned toward the chapel. "I prefer to do the exchange indoors. It isn't any warmer, but it is private."

Jack, who had been keeping watch, had seen a man pushing a wheelchair coming up the path toward the chapel. *He had guessed right after all.* Being careful to make no sound, he had ensconced himself in the safe room. He hoped that the walls were thin enough for him to hear what was going on. It was too risky to remain exposed in the open area of the chapel. In fact, he could just make out their voices and tensed as they approached the inside of the chapel.

Without another word Antony turned and pushed Sharon's wheelchair before him. With only a slight struggle he was able to get the chair over the threshold of the doorway and into the interior. The early morning sunlight bathed the pews with a golden glow, but the choir remained in shadow. The floorboards creaked as the small group entered.

Jack held his breath as if they could hear his breathing. He now wished he had been wrong. He saw no way to get into the main area of the church quickly or quietly. Typing out his signal on the phone he hoped the police would be stealthy, not coming in with guns blazing. The thin wooden walls of this little church provided little protection from bullets.

He had dared to open his panel door just enough to allow one eye a field of view and he could see the man, whose back was facing him, leaning down to open a wooden case, the size of a foot locker, on the floor. A woman was next to him in a wheelchair. From behind he couldn't be sure who she was, but the bandage on her head made him suspect that they had met before. He was incredulous. Just yesterday she had been in the hospital under armed guard. *How did she get loose?* He made it a point to ask Justin what had happened to allow her to be free.

Jack sent another text describing what he was now seeing. He replaced his phone and waited. To be ready he slipped his weapon from his pocket, though he left the safety on.

He watched as the Chinese men and the woman removed the handcuffs, unlocked their cases, and opened them for inspection by the man whose face he still had not yet seen. When he opened his own wooden cases all four of the Chinese stood straighter and gaped in surprise. They began murmuring among themselves in their native language. He next opened a small box which the woman took lovingly in her hands. She showed the large uncut diamonds to her companions, hardly noticing that one was still missing.

The man who had provided translation spoke.

"Mr. Antony. From your original proposal we were expecting good things, but what you have brought is much greater than we anticipated. We are amazed at your gems. These are a wonder to behold."

Antony smiled broadly. "You can't get diamonds like these any more. They were found many years ago. I have been waiting for the right time. You, gentlemen and lady," he nodded to the woman who had, as yet, remained silent, "have made the deal of a lifetime. And I am well satisfied with the payment. Gaining these shares and bonds is well worth parting with my little diamonds."

Antony had bargained for some money, but had desired shares in some of China's fastest growing companies. He would not have a controlling share in any one company, but at the current growth his net worth would double in less than two years with this acquisition. In fact, there was nothing inherently illegal about purchasing the shares, except that he had smuggled the diamonds into the country illegally. Just possessing "blood diamonds" was a crime punishable by a long prison sentence.

Antony was aware that each of the literally thousands of diamonds in his cases could represent a life. Men and women had risked their lives to steal them from the mines in which they were found. Often the money used to purchase them, albeit twenty years in the past, had been used to buy guns and bullets and other weapons which ultimately had killed thousands. Some of those bullets were used in the genocidal attacks in the early nineties in Rwanda and Zaire. Some had been used against the dictator Mobutu Sese Seko. He didn't care. Antony wanted to believe that these diamonds were a mere means to an end. He wanted to believe these were just a commodity.

But the truth was that he was constantly haunted by faces and bodies he had seen. He wanted to be rid of them. By so doing he would also gain what he most desired, an even more comfortable life. Nevertheless, he secretly hoped that the dead faces would leave him in peace once the diamonds were no longer in his possession.

As they stood, about to finish the transaction the first shot rang out. Antony cursed and felt panic rising in his chest.

"No!" He looked with suspicion at the Chinese, but saw that they, too, were fearful and confused.

"What have you done?" came the reproach from Yo Wang. He apparently spoke excellent English after all.

"It's not me," he looked at them uncertainly.

Suddenly a rattling noise drowned them out and a line of holes was stitched in the sunny side of the church. Splinters flew from pews and a cry was heard. Antony looked around, but could not tell from which direction the cry had come. He ducked low, but feared for Sharon. She was holding her right arm in front of her face as if to ward off a blow as splinters flew in all directions. While Antony and the others were able to hit the floor she could not lay flat or even get out of her wheel chair.

As silence followed the first spurt of gunfire, the Chinese men bent low and grabbed the boxes of gems. Their female companion drew a weapon and crept toward the door. She peered out then spoke a few clipped words to her companions. The weight of the cases slowed them down, but the men chose not to leave their prizes. They stopped at the door then, hunched low, emerged from the front of the church moving quickly around to the rear. Not sure what else to do they huddled low and waited for calm to return.

The thump thump thump of a helicopter reverberated in the air. Gunfire erupted once again and seemed to be everywhere. Antony pushed Sharon and her chair out and passed the Chinese cowering behind the church. He had piled the cases of bonds and money on Sharon's lap and she was attempting to hold them. So far she had not spoken a word.

Cindy had set up the security arrangements to be prepared for a rapid escape if things went sour. Antony and his party had an alternative exit plan, though he had hoped it would not be necessary. He had memorized the details intimately, and now made for a designated area near the rear of the park. He pulled out his cell phone and made a quick call. The gunfire was still behind him, nearer the entrance, and so far no one pursued him. The footbridge was right where it was supposed to be, and crossing it with Delia ahead of him, he felt relief. He was puffing hard when he heard a shout behind him.

"Stop!"

Antony was steps away from the opposite side of the bridge. There were explosive charges set to blow it up as a method of slowing any pursuit, but he couldn't risk setting them off until he was well past the bridge. He let the wheel chair glide down the bridge to the other side and he stood facing forward. He did not raise his hands or turn around.

"Turn around! Hands up!" came the next command.

Slowly with his hands only slightly raised he began turning. He glimpsed the man in his peripheral vision. He also knew that most men wouldn't shoot someone in the back. Taking advantage of this he dropped suddenly and attempted to roll to the end of the footbridge. The man fired once, missing Antony.

Antony had not been idly moving. He also carried a weapon and had it out firing soon after his dive forward. Though his shots were wild they, nevertheless, had their desired effect of sending his attacker searching for cover. In another second he was back on his feet. He grabbed the wheelchair and shoved it forward. The slight rise in the bridge gave them a moment's worth of protection. He noticed a definite slackening of gunfire in the distance and heard a few reports nearer at hand. Antony dashed into the building on the other side of the bridge. It was designed to be used for an entrance to the large roller coaster. In his pocket he had a small device similar in appearance to a cell phone. There was a red LED already lit up on the face. He pressed a button and an explosion ripped the air.

The foot bridge disintegrated in a cloud of smoke and dust. This action would merely slow his attacker, as the water in the small man-made stream was not deep, but had Jack been crossing the bridge when it exploded he would most likely have been killed. Antony pressed another button and heard a dozen or so popping noises. These were smaller explosives designed to snap the flags which lined the top of the building in which he had taken refuge.

"Sharon, I need you to try to walk." For the first time he noticed that she was slightly hunched over and didn't respond to his speech. He bent down and spoke to her face. He was struck by the pale visage that met him. Her eyes were closed and she was barely breathing. He touched her face and found blood along her shoulder. Pulling her toward him she gave a groan, but did not resist. There were two neat holes in the back of her jersey and it was soaked with blood. He had no idea when this had occurred, but looked again into her face. "Sharon! Sharon!" He was now truly panicked. Tears began to form in his eyes. He looked up the stairs to the roof and back at her.

"Mark Antony!" came a shout from outside. "Come out now!"

He remained silent but, panic rising in his brain, attempted to lift Sharon from the chair. He could hear a helicopter approaching. Sharon's limp body was nearly impossible for him to manage alone. He tried desperately to drag her, but saw he would not be able to quickly get her to the top of the building that way. He looked at the cases of bonds, then back at Sharon. He knew he had to make a choice.

"I'm sorry," he said and grabbed the cases leaving his love, Sharon, sprawled on the floor.

****

Two of the Chinese body guards ran up to their employers as quickly as they could. One was limping and, with a grimace, was sweating profusely and breathing hard. Nevertheless, the guards knew their job and had been prepared to die to protect their masters. They found the well-dressed, though now disheveled group debating what to do about the diamonds. The guards settled the issue by herding the five business men and women toward the front of the park. The lead guard, in clipped unemotional speech told them that they would have to leave the weighty boxes. They could not move quickly, provide armed protection, and carry the load at the same time. They pushed and prodded the five who reluctantly left their treasure behind. Moving away from the gunfire by staying along the perimeter of the park they hoped to find an exit that was not covered. By crossing under the railings of the main roller coaster they still had hopes of finding a way out of the situation.

They found no resistance as they moved along the perimeter fence, but could find no way over it. The front gate of the park was rapidly approaching and they knew that there, they were trapped. Suddenly, out of the bushes, came half a dozen men all wearing black jump suits and masks. All, likewise, carried automatic weapons aimed at the entourage of Chinese. They made no sound, but quickly disarmed the body guards and motioned them all through a gap, they had just made, in the fence.

An ominous black helicopter sat, rotors slowly revolving, just outside the park. All of the Chinese were quickly moved into the helicopter as the men in the unmarked uniforms formed a perimeter protecting their exit. At first the helicopter seemed to rise only slowly then, just as quickly as they had been caught and corralled, they were whisked away.

These men were not the assault troops Rebecca and Justin had been told to expect.

The police forces had swept in and were moving forward against the crumbling armed opposition. Rebecca and Justin had fought their way through the gunfire and had been in a position to glimpse some of the drama with the masked men at the fence. However, by the time they reached the gap all they could see was the helicopter already lifting off. The masked men, in their black uniforms, were still on the ground, but they were moving away toward the perimeter road. A large blue van replaced the helicopter before them and the men began clambering into it. As they did so they removed their masks. The last one glanced back over his shoulder and caught sight of Rebecca. He smiled and threw her a mock salute.

"Agent Bob!" she exclaimed beginning to see the light. She stamped her foot and swore. "He knew about this all along."

Justin was puzzled. "What just happened?"

"Looks like my call for a pizza backfired. That, Justin, was the CIA. I hope that didn't just blow our whole case!"

****

Jack was still slightly stunned from the explosions which had ripped apart the foot bridge. His side ached and his arm was on fire as he had taken cover at the last second. He was glad he hadn't attempted to cross the bridge. The water in the man-made stream before him wasn't deep, but it would slow him and there was no cover so he dashed, as quickly as he was able, back behind one of the rides. As he did so he saw another bridge off to his left. There were no gunmen firing in this area so he did his best to hurry over to the bridge. He felt a severe fatigue, but his breathing was even. By keeping his arm stiffly by his side he was able to lessen the pain somewhat. He dodged around trash containers and crossed the new bridge which had been left intact. He then headed back toward the building into which his quarry had disappeared.

Jack's brain had taken in the scene mechanically and he had not had time to process what he had seen. As he made his way toward the building, it dawned on him that he recognized Antony. The face actually belonged to Jacques Levant. It was the diamond dealer from Africa, twenty years older! He mentally kicked himself.

"You should have figured that out!" he yelled out loud, to himself. Nevertheless, he found the coincidence hard to believe.

Moving ahead, now, he tried to shut out the past. So far no police had arrived in his location. He appeared to be the only one who knew this was happening. As he reached the corner of the building he heard the sound of a helicopter. Not the deep drone of an assault craft, but a higher pitched whine. *I'm too late.* His thoughts were involuntary.

First he heard someone call "Mark Antony! Come out!" Then, directed at him, "Halt!" came a shout from across the water. "Put you weapon on the ground. Hands in the air! Do it!"

Jack ground his teeth. He knew that if he proceeded ahead he risked immediate action and possibly being shot again. This sounded like police. *Don't they know I'm with them?*

"I'm Jack Sharp. We have to stop Levant!" He shouted his words, but complied reluctantly. He set his nine millimeter on the pavement and knelt. He lifted his right hand, but was unable to raise his left successfully.

"He's in this building! That helicopter is going to take him away." He stole a glance at the man confronting him. He had his own weapon trained on Jack and the distance was too close for a trained professional to miss.

Jack looked directly at him. "I'm Jack Sharp, the doctor." He saw hesitation in the man's face as he was joined by others. "There is another bridge off to your left. You need to get over here fast."

One police officer decided the detour was too far and started to wade out into the moat. He immediately was thrown backward as a marksman in the helicopter found his target. This sent the other officers scurrying for cover. Seeing his chance to continue, Jack picked up his weapon and did his best to hurry into the building. He was out of the line of sight of the helicopter.

The outer door was ajar and he quickly slipped in. There, Jack saw the woman lying on the floor face away from him. She was unmoving and silent. Jack saw the blood-soaked jacket and tested her carotid pulse. Nothing.

The building shook as the helicopter touched down on the roof and the noise was deafening. Grunting with effort, now breathing hard, he found the stairs and, keeping his face upward and gun in front ascended them one at a time.

The door at the top was swinging freely and Jack stepped into sunlight just as he heard the helicopter engine whine increase in intensity. A man's legs were disappearing into its fuselage. Jack aimed and fired. He was a good shot, but at fifty feet with a target moving he couldn't be sure of his aim. He spotted the muzzle of a rifle sweeping toward him and he hit the deck.

A blast of air hit him as the chopper rose and wood splintered near his face as the sharpshooter made one last effort to silence him. Jack heard the engine noise quickly lessen and swiveled his head to see the helicopter banking away. It was already well out of his range. He heard the rapid popping of automatic gunfire from below as the police attempted to bring down the craft, but it had no apparent effect.

Soon all around him was silent. There were no more gunshots. Jack felt exhausted and was beginning to shiver. He had slept poorly and had been cold throughout the night. His meals of granola bars had not satisfied him and the carbs were burning away quickly in his system leaving him hungry and a little light headed. He sat, defeated. The man, Levant, had gotten away.

When no one joined him on the roof of the building he glanced around. Broken flags lay all across the roof snapped off cleanly at the level of the corrugated metal. Feeling a little better, he rose and meandered to the spot where he had seen the man enter the helicopter. He found a pool of blood just there. It was enough to make him realize his shot had found flesh, though he doubted that it would be a mortal wound.

He tucked his weapon into his belt and heavily descended the steps.

****

There was, indeed, no more gunfire. The "all clear" signal had been transmitted over their radios and police were leading prisoners away. There were a few unmoving bodies and some being assisted. Rebecca and Justin were jostled as a medical team rushed past them. Following their direction of travel Rebecca could see a policeman lying just ahead near a pool of water. The pillars of the ruined bridge remained like shortened totems, scarred by the blast which had leveled it.

Several other officers knelt next to the prostrate figure, but he appeared to be moving his arms. They walked more quickly and found the policeman to be alive. He had taken a high-powered round in the chest, but his Kevlar vest had dissipated its force. The bullet had, nevertheless, penetrated the vest and he was pale and showing significant effort to breathe. He already had an oxygen mask in place and was rapidly being prepared for transport.

"Base one-two we are ready for medevac. ETA two minutes at the entrance," one of the medics voiced into his shoulder microphone.

A crackling sound was followed by "Rrroger that. ETA two minutes copy. We'll see you at the gate."

Despite herself Rebecca asked, "Will he be all right?"

"We don't know ma'am, but he hasn't bled too much. We'll get him right to the hospital by medevac helicopter."

She nodded in response and backed away. As she did so Justin tugged at her sleeve.

"There's the doc!" He was pointing at the building situated across the water.

Dr. Sharp knelt inside the doorway. He was hunched before another figure lying inside on the concrete. In the shadow Rebecca could not see who it might be. The body was covered and lying with a deathly stillness. She wondered how many victims there had been that day.

The police chief with his assistant and a small gaggle of policemen and policewomen appeared to one side.

"Well young lady how did we do?" He asked as if they were talking about a football game. She had not seen him during the shooting and assumed that he had remained in the command vehicle until the battle was all, but over. He wore full riot gear, though his assistant carried his helmet. She smiled to herself as she saw the pearl-gripped revolver strapped to his side. Glancing at Justin, she noted that he had spotted it and he gave her a sheepish grin.

"Sir, it appears that we have taken the gunmen prisoner,

but I don't know the status of the primary suspect. Our Chinese businessmen were ferreted away by some "unknown" agency.

"Really?" He made an exaggerated frown. "Hmmm. I wonder who that could have been?" His lack of real interest made Rebecca suspect that he *was* aware of exactly who had liberated the Chinese. "Well we didn't want an international incident now did we?"

"Of course not, sir."

"What about the money or diamonds?"

"I don't know yet sir. The doctor who alerted us about this deal is over there. I was just about to question him."

"By all means go right ahead. I'll just check on the troops." He moved away his little group maneuvering around him to let him lead.

The chief approached the wounded man's gurney and was about to ask questions when the medic, without looking up, roughly pushed past him and deliberately began wheeling him toward the gate. The police chief, a little perturbed, nevertheless smiled and moved on to one of the other officers.

"Where are you from, son?"

Rebecca shook her head and quietly said so only Justin could hear, "He thinks he's Patton."

****

The Bell helicopter was flying smoothly now. Low over the rooftops of the city they had detected no pursuit. However, the interior was bedlam as Antony writhed in agony on the blood-soaked floor of the main cabin. The shooter, who had provided covering fire for him, had bandaged his wound but, despite pressure dressing, blood continued to soak through. "Put a tourniquet on you idiot. I'm bleeding to death! Ahhhh."

The nine millimeter round had struck him just above the knee as his leg was swinging into the helicopter. He had almost gotten away cleanly except for one final shot. "I can't believe it," he gasped. "How did that doctor get into the park? How did he even know about it?" He had recognized Dr. Sharp in the brief encounter on the bridge. He was older now than he had been at their last meeting, but there was no mistaking him. That his shot had been the one to ruin his day angered him enough to almost forget his pain. Nevertheless, his groaning was uncontrollable. The pain was greater than anything he had ever experienced, but he kept his thoughts upon the doctor.

"I should have taken care of him twenty years ago," he bellowed. As the gunner tightened the tourniquet Antony desperately tried to take a deep breath, but lost consciousness as the pain finally became too much to bear.

****

Jack had seen the blood from the wounds on the woman's back. He considered his first shot at Levant on the bridge. He thought it had missed him completely, but now he was afraid it had, somehow, been the bullet that had struck the poor woman in the wheelchair. *Had he been responsible for killing this woman?* He hadn't stopped to look at her face but feeling fearful and ashamed, walked away.

Why had he stayed here? Why had he decided to bring his gun? This wasn't his life anymore; he was a doctor, for heaven's sake. He wasn't supposed to take life, but to do his best to preserve it.

Jack found himself instinctively back at the chapel. This time he entered slowly and solemnly. He made his way to the altar and knelt on the bare wooden floor. Tears came of their own accord and Jack buried his face in his hands.

"Dear God, forgive me." He stayed like that and quietly prayed for all those involved. "I can't bring back the dead, but Lord help me to do my best to heal the living."

Jack felt like he had been beaten up. His arm ached. His chest stung and there was a slight stain of blood on his shirt. He was hungry and cold and not sure he was even thinking straight. After a time shivering he rose and stepped back into the light.

The detectives were approaching the little church.

Justin spoke first, "Is that where you stayed last night? Aren't you cold?"

Too weary to answer he merely nodded. Each step felt like he was walking in mud. "There were Chinese men and a woman in the party who came to buy the diamonds. They took them and I don't know where they went. I think they ran around to the back of this church, but I didn't see where they escaped to."

Rebecca answered him, "We have a good idea what happened, but they weren't carrying anything."

He and the pair walked around the small wooden structure. There, at the rear corner of the church, sat the two wooden cases, lids ajar. Jack stared at the boxes. They hadn't changed in twenty years. They were the same ones he had used to tempt Jaques Levant in the sting operation back in Zaire. He leaned over and opened the first one.

"My goodness!" he exclaimed. While the boxes were the same, their contents had multiplied greatly.

Rebecca gasped and Justin said, "Wow! What a haul." He picked up a handful of the stones and let them sift through his fingers. "I don't suppose they can use any of this to supplement our budget next year?"

Rebecca gave a short laugh, "Sure. It will probably get snatched up by the FBI. But aren't they pretty?"

Jack was pensive. He said, "I've seen these before." Tiredly he leaned down and closed the box's lid. The writing on the cover was in French and he was able to make it out.

He said, "This crate once held assault rifles. Levant used it to carry un-cut diamonds." The second case was slightly different. There was a top shelf which contained a hinged box. Jack opened this as well. The inside was covered with a scarlet felt. There was a foam insert with four huge uncut diamonds resting in their own custom-fitted space. A fifth space was empty. Above each one was a label with a number similar to the one etched on the stone from Connie's stomach.

All Rebecca could do was shake her head in awe.

More policemen began to arrive at the church and Rebecca could see the chief moving toward them. His entourage had grown to a small crowd of people. There appeared to be civilians with him now, probably reporters. They shielded the cases from view and let the group pass without comment.

"Shouldn't you tell him about the diamonds?" Jack asked benignly.

"We don't want the press involved. I'll make sure he is informed, but I'm not certain that we should let the full extent of this deal become public knowledge. There are enough diamonds there to destabilize a small country."

"At least some of these diamonds were stolen twenty years ago. They are the ones I told you about, Justin. These are 'blood diamonds' and they're still claiming victims."

Justin was nodding. "Man! There must be thousands of stones here."

"We need to post a guard here until we can move them to a secure location." Rebecca spoke into her microphone to the head of the assault force. They closed the second lid and latched the cases. "... and I would recommend an armored vehicle to transport the evidence," she said in conclusion.

There was a hesitation at the other end then, "Okay, you got it."

In a few minutes the police captain arrived. He was all business. To Rebecca he said, "Where is the 'evidence?'" She pointed to the cases.

"I recommend keeping them closed and out of sight until the guard is set," she said.

He glanced toward the front of the amusement park where he supposed the chief to have gone and smiled, "Okay detective. I think I agree."

Jack caught sight of a body being solemnly wheeled down the sidewalk in their direction. He moved out onto the path and held up the bearers. They wore jumpsuits with the word "CORONER" stenciled on the back. The body was in a bag and Jack stepped up to the gurney. An unexplained curiosity spurred him to desire to see who this woman had been. Earlier he hadn't taken time to view her face. He zipped open the head of the bag as Justin reached his shoulder.

As they looked down Justin heard a shocked Jack whisper,

"Oh, my dear, Lord. Sharon! How could it be?" Twenty years had made its changes but Jack saw before him the woman he had loved and had thought was long dead. Jack found he couldn't stand and sank to his knees beside the gurney, tears already falling from his eyes.

56

Wednesday

Alicia woke once again with the bright fall sunlight dancing on her eyelids. She felt comfortable and warm. Gone was the nagging sense of impending doom she had felt for what had seemed like weeks. Her life was taking a new turn, but she knew it was a good one.

A voice from downstairs rang out,

"Alicia, are you dressed yet? We got chores, girl."

There were footsteps on the stairs and a knock on the door.

"Come in," she said, curious about her visitor.

Roy's balding head poked through and his eyes peeked around the edge of the door.

He hesitated for a moment and then said,

"Pardon me, Alicia, but I just wanted to come and say good mornin' before I took off for the day. I'm right glad you decided to stay with us."

Alicia smiled at him and swept the sheets from her legs. She wore a flannel gown and worked her feet into a pair of slippers waiting at her bedside. She moved over to Roy and gave him a hug, careful to avoid his still sore arm.

"I'm glad I can stay here too."

He whispered, "You know Missy got another decoratin' job today. She's just foolin' about the chores. I already done em." He crinkled up his nose and grinned. "You have fun." He patted her shoulder and left her room, padding down the steps once again.

Alicia quietly followed and moved into the kitchen, just as Missy called,

"Alicia! Breakfast is ready." Missy didn't know she was right behind her and she yelled loudly enough to be heard upstairs.

"I heard," she said giggling at the start she gave Missy.

"Oh! Child, you scared me! Well the coffee's ready. We've got

431

to get moving."

"We do? Where are we going?"

Missy gave her a look of curiosity. "Hm, Roy told you didn't he?"

Alicia laughed again she poured coffee and sat. "What are we going to do today?"

"Today you get to begin learning about interior design. Later, maybe you can get some formal schooling on the subject."

Alicia pursed her lips, "I suppose so. I had hoped to be done with school, but you have made it sound interesting. Where are we going?"

"We get to visit the pastor to re-do the kitchen and dining area."

"In his tiny house? That won't be much."

"Small isn't always easy. Besides his wife's a good cook and ... they have a son about your age. He works their farm."

"Oh no. You can't be boss and match-maker!" Alicia said laughing.

"Just watch me." They hugged and Alicia, tears in her eyes, found contentment.

****

"Rebecca! Well done!" Lincoln Police Chief Max Barton actually stood up and offered his hand. "I must admit I had my doubts about you trusting a civilian like that, but you pulled it off."

Rebecca stood a little embarrassed especially since Chief Barton appeared to completely ignore Justin. "Uh, thank you sir. But it wasn't just me ..."

"Yes, yes I know," he smiled briefly at Justin, "Detective Samuelson used his computer skills and brains. Nice job, son."

Justin was about to retort that he wasn't his son, but Rebecca cut him off.

"Yes sir. Justin played a key role in staying in touch with Dr. Sharp and in tracking down the identity of the leader of the group."

The police chief's eyebrows went up a little higher, "I see. Well I guess we have a little more to thank you for too." He turned and took Justin's hand. "But, please, don't try to explain it to me. I am a simple man." He laughed at himself.

"Sir did we find out who else was involved in the whole affair?"

"Oh, sit down. Sit," he said more as a command than a request. "That *is* interesting. We probably still wouldn't have had a clue, but a suicide victim in Chicago was apparently one of the ringleaders. He left a packet with his lawyer that names names and places. It might not hold up in court, but I think it will open the door for some warrants. The Chicago PD sent us copies. This man also appears to be the one who actually ordered the deaths of the young woman and your male suspect."

He put on his reading glasses and picked up a single sheet of paper. He sat reading for a few seconds as if he were alone in the room then looked up.

"There is one thing though. It's too bad the 'bad guy' got away with all the loot. "

"He got money but we believe he was wounded sir."

"Yes, yes. Hm. Well, it couldn't be helped. The Des Moines policeman is doing well. The bullet didn't hit anything too vital. By the way, we have made an extradition request for Assistant District Attorney Sears. He apparently didn't realize that we could get him in the Bahamas. Is the doctor healing up?"

"We believe so sir. He returned to town yesterday and hasn't called either of us."

The police chief stood again, followed by Rebecca and Justin.

"Well, good work."

"Sir," Justin said a little hesitantly.

"Yes Detective?"

"What happens to the diamonds?" Rebecca had been curious too but had not dared ask.

"Interesting question, Justin. I believe we will not see them here, though we still have the one in evidence. I believe their existence is being kept secret for obvious reasons."

Rebecca nodded.

Chief Barton changed the subject. "I think a day or two off is deserved, but since you've been gone things have kind of piled up. Can you take those days off at the end of the month?"

The pair looked at each other. "Yes sir," they chimed in together.

"Good. Why don't you check on the Rivers case and give me a report later? Okay?"

"Sir, does that mean you want Justin to remain in my department?"

"Well, he seems to work well with you, doesn't he? Is that okay? Good." He answered his own question without waiting for a response.

"Thanks again. Oh, and ... your mother wanted me to tell you that she would like you to call her." He then looked down and began shuffling papers on his desk.

The last comment took Rebecca by surprise, but she answered, "Yes, sir," then, seeing that they were dismissed, sidled out the door and stepped into the hall a smile slowly forming on her lips.

Mom and Chief Barton!!

"Well, Justin, I guess we'll have to find you a desk."

"Oh, the cubicle I've been using is fine. But..."

"Yeah?"

"I had made some arrangements for an evening out. Do you suppose I could take off in a little while?"

"You heard Chief Barton. 'Things have piled up.'" She grinned as they stepped back onto their floor. Then she spotted the young forensic technician standing near Justin's corner cubicle. "But I see you have a little work over at your own cubicle." She patted him on the arm, "Just don't let the chief see you leave."

Justin smiled back and glanced over his shoulder. Wordlessly he walked away and waved at the smiling Cindy.

Rebecca gazed after them. She longed to take the rest of the afternoon off too, but realized she had nothing special to do. Work was her release. She walked up to one of the clerks.

"Can you please bring me the file on Rivers?"

Then she walked toward her desk. One more case completed and thanks to the use of Justin's laptop she had already written the after-action report on their activities in Des Moines and Cedar Rapids. The Iowa police would have to deal with the majority of the paperwork, leaving her relatively free to start a new case.

The light was blinking on her phone. Someone had left her a message. It was a phone number to call with no explanation. She dialed the number.

"Hello, Fred here," came the voice on the other end.

"Fred?"

"Hello. Detective Sweate?"

"Yes. Do I know you?"

"I think so. How about dinner?"

Rebecca was instantly confused and pleased at the same time. A sneaking suspicion was working in her mind. "Is this Bob or Tom?"

"No I'm Fred."

"I see. Okay I'll bite. Dinner where?"

"Frianti's Italian. I'll pick you up at 6:00. Okay?"

"Sure. See ya."

"Bye."

Rebecca was again amused. She was fairly certain that Fred was her intrepid CIA agent. Was this going to be just another information drop? She didn't think so. What had looked to be a lonely evening at home now just might turn out to be fun and maybe she would get answers to some of her remaining questions.

****

At the door, Jack stood with his finger hovering over the doorbell. He debated if he should have come so late. Maybe she was too tired. There was only one light on in the house that he could see from outside. He put his hand down and was about to turn away when the door opened.

"Well are you going to knock, or do I have to drag you in?"

Through the screen door he could make out Kathy's face. She wore a scarf over her head but, even in the dim light of the front porch, her smile was heavenly. Her eyes shone with a warmth that he had never seen in any woman's face before. She really did want to see him, despite the lateness of the hour.

He opened the screen and Kathy swung the inner door wide. Esther stood to one side also smiling.

"Isn't it past your bedtime young lady?" he asked.

Esther rolled her eyes, "Get real, Dr. Jack. I don't have a 'bedtime' anymore. I go to bed when I'm ready."

Jack's eyebrows arched as he looked questioningly toward Kathy. She merely shrugged her shoulders. Then to Esther she said, "Why don't you just say goodnight to Dr. Sharp and let us have some time together?"

Esther, seeing the futility of arguing, reluctantly acceded to this request.

"Goodnight Dr. Jack." She moved toward him slowly at first then she ran up to him and gripped him tightly. "I'm glad you're back." She hugged him fiercely until he groaned with a slight pain. She gave her mother a peck on the cheek and turned toward the bedroom. Then, with one last wave she disappeared down the hall.

The look in Kathy's eyes now changed slightly. They seemed to have a slight greenish tint that made her look more like a cat on the prowl as she languidly walked toward him.

"Now, sir, you need to fill me in on what has been going on for the last week."

Jack backed up slowly as she approached. As his legs struck the edge of the sofa he sat down abruptly. Kathy quickly joined him on the couch.

"First I want to give you a more pleasant greeting." She carefully wrapped her arms around his neck, avoiding his painful chest and arm. Pulling him close she kissed him and said, 'But why don't you tell me later?"

CPSIA information can be obtained at www.ICGtesting.com
Printed in the USA
268314BV00006B/1/P